Kingdoms in Peril

The publisher and the University of California Press Foundation gratefully acknowledge the generous support of the Simpson Imprint in Humanities.

Kingdoms in Peril

*A Novel of the Ancient Chinese
World at War*

Feng Menglong

Translated by Olivia Milburn

UNIVERSITY OF CALIFORNIA PRESS

University of California Press
Oakland, California

© 2022 by Olivia Milburn

Library of Congress Cataloging-in-Publication Data
Names: Feng, Menglong, 1574–1646, author. | Milburn, Olivia, translator.
Title: Kingdoms in peril : a novel of the ancient Chinese world at war /
    Feng Menglong ; translated by Olivia Milburn.
Other titles: Xin lie guo zhi. Selections. English (Milburn)
Description: Oakland, California : University of California Press, [2022] |
    Includes bibliographical references.
Identifiers: LCCN 2021026170 (print) | LCCN 2021026171 (ebook) |
    ISBN 9780520380516 (paperback) | ISBN 9780520380523 (ebook)
Subjects: LCSH: China—History—Zhou dynasty, 1122–221 B.C.—Fiction.
Classification: LCC PL2698.F4 H813 2022 (print) | LCC PL2698.F4 (ebook) |
    DDC 895.13/46—dc23
LC record available at https://lccn.loc.gov/2021026170
LC ebook record available at https://lccn.loc.gov/2021026171

Manufactured in the United States of America

31 30 29 28 27 26 25 24 23 22
10 9 8 7 6 5 4 3 2 1

CONTENTS

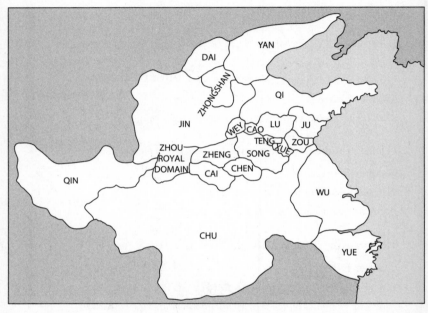

MAP 1. The Zhou Confederacy circa 500 B.C.E. Adapted from *Map of the Five Hegemons* by SY, CC-BY-SA 4.0.

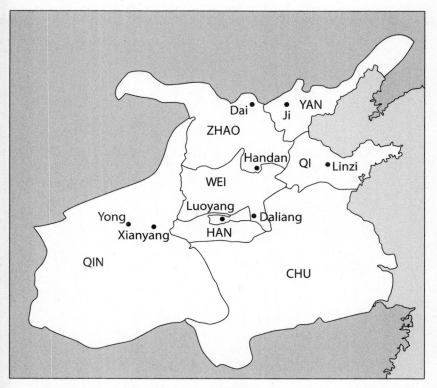

MAP 2. The Kingdoms of the Warring States Period in circa 260 B.C.E. Adapted from *The Warring States of China c. 260 BCE* by Philg88, CC-BY-SA 3.0.

Introduction

Kingdoms in Peril is an epic historical novel covering the five hundred and fifty years of the Eastern Zhou dynasty, from the civil wars and invasions that marked the birth of a new regime in 771 B.C.E. to the unification of China in 221 B.C.E. This period saw the numerous states that made up the Zhou confederacy riven by intense and intractable conflict as they lurched from one crisis to the next. Every concept of what constituted a civilized society was tested again and again through centuries of political instability, and any momentary peace was soon threatened by the relentless intriguing of ministers, eunuchs, and harem favorites. It was a time when political life was punctuated with poisonings, assassinations, and sinister conspiracies, and those who escaped other murderous attacks might still fall victim to warfare or the rioting populace. As old certainties crumbled and hierarchies collapsed, it was no longer possible to maintain traditional social norms, and new opportunities opened up for the intelligent and able. Men and women were quick to take advantage of this, testing the boundaries and seeking self-advancement in ways that would have been impossible in a more stable environment. As an international market opened up for talented individuals, clever men increasingly sought to build careers abroad, secure in the knowledge that their social and ethnic background would not be held against them in a foreign country. Women too resisted traditional assumptions that their sphere should be confined to childrearing at home, and found that they were now expected—at least at an elite level—to be able to provide sagacious advice, arrange murders, defuse political conspiracies, and, in the event of a crisis, potentially even to take over the running of the country.

Kingdoms in Peril was written in the 1640s, at the very end of the Ming dynasty, by the great novelist Feng Menglong (1574–1646). An expert in the history of the Eastern Zhou dynasty, he was inspired to write this novel by reading an earlier work on the same subject: *Tales of the States* (*Lieguo zhi*) by Yu Shaoyu (active 1522–73). Horrified by the many mistakes and anachronisms this book contained, Feng Menglong decided to produce a new and improved account of the same historical events, which would explore the careers and personalities of the many remarkable individuals who lived through and defined this crucial era of Chinese history. In the course of the one hundred and eight chapters of the complete novel, he documents the collapse of the Zhou confederacy during the Spring and Autumn period (771–475 B.C.E.) and the slow rebuilding of civil society during the Warring States era (475–221 B.C.E.), which culminated in the unification of China under the First Emperor of the Qin dynasty (r. 246–221 B.C.E. as king; r. 221–210 B.C.E. as emperor). Thus, overall, this novel describes a grand arc, from stability to chaos and back again. As a novel about politics, much of the narrative in *Kingdoms in Peril* concentrates on the exercise of power. During the Eastern Zhou dynasty, there were two words in use to cover different aspects of the concept of power. *Quan* was used for the power that comes from quantifiable resources: the size of the army, the financial reserves in the treasury, the extent of the tax base, stockpiles of weapons, armor, and so on. *Shi,* on the other hand, refers to power that comes from taking advantage of the opportunities provided by a developing situation. It is the interplay between *quan* and *shi* that provides many of the most dramatic incidents in the history of this period, and therefore of this novel. Power that comes from circumstantial advantage could be utilized in all sorts of different contexts: whether it is a silver-tongued diplomat persuading a king to accept a disadvantageous treaty; a cunning general tricking the enemy commander into an unfavorable situation by playing to his prejudices; or a rival convincing a neglected wife to spy on her husband to set him up for assassination—these chinks in the armor allowed for stunning reversals of fortune.

Whether they were making history or being crushed by it, the characters of *Kingdoms in Peril* are presented in a way that reminds us of their human qualities. There are no heroes and villains here, just flawed individuals trying their best to survive in often impossible circumstances, all too often discovering that the choices available to them ranged from bad to worse. One of the key features of this novel is the emphasis on the terrible conflicts many of its characters faced—raised in an ethical system that valued loyalty, justice, benevolence, and filial duty and yet placed in circumstances in which they were torn between their duty to the ruler or the country, and their love for family and friends. Regardless of whether they were monarchs, aristocrats, hereditary ministers, or clan leaders, members of the Eastern Zhou ruling elite almost always had complicated private lives, surrounded as they were by wives, concubines, mistresses, cronies, bodyguards, hangers-on, and hordes of servants, male and female. The ties of affection created within these households did not necessarily run neatly according to rank and status, where sons of the main wife held priority in the inheritance, followed by the children of concubines, while illegitimate offspring were generally treated little better than slaves. Although this social hierarchy might appear rigid, it could always be overturned by the intelligent, while ruthless ambition and violence occasionally found themselves tempered by loving relationships strong enough to withstand the brutality of the age. *Kingdoms in Peril* has long been recognized as a masterpiece for its exploration of the personalities of individuals caught up in momentous historical events.

KINGDOMS IN PERIL: HISTORICAL BACKGROUND

Kingdoms in Peril opens with a brief account of the political problems at the end of the Western Zhou dynasty, which were allayed with the accession of the highly competent King Xuan of Zhou (r. 827–782 B.C.E.). However, though the reign of King Xuan offered a temporary respite, the dynasty would collapse in a civil war during the reign of his son, King You (r. 781–771 B.C.E.). The fall of the Western Zhou dynasty is today understood as the result of multiple factors: natural disasters created enormous social disruption and forced many people to become refugees; attacks by powerful northern nomadic peoples increased; and the ensuing humanitarian crisis was exacerbated by an incompetent government riven with internal dissension. However, this is not how ancient Chinese people regarded these events. For them, the key figure in the fall of the Western Zhou was an accursed woman, Bao Si, the favorite slave-girl of the last king. She was believed to be the living embodiment of an ancient malediction, imposed upon the people of Zhou by the Bao lords, and hence predestined to bring about the fall of the dynasty. As a result, Bao Si came to represent a counterpart and antithesis to Hou Ji, the mythical founder of the Zhou royal house. Just as Hou Ji was born after his mother stepped in the footprint of a giant, and survived thanks to the protection of various birds and animals when his mother attempted to abandon her baby, Bao Si was born after her mother stepped in the footprint of a magical turtle, and survived an attempt to drown her as a baby through the intervention of the local wildlife. To an ancient Chinese audience, Heaven created Hou Ji to bring civilization to the world as the ancestor of the Zhou ruling house, and Bao Si was sent down to destroy everything that they had worked so hard to create.

In the year 771 B.C.E., Crown Prince Yijiu of Zhou, furious at having been dispossessed by his father, launched a rebellion against him. In the ensuing carnage King You and Bao Si were killed, together with vast numbers of government officials. The ordinary inhabitants of the capital were massacred, women were raped, and the city was pillaged by the crown prince's self-declared supporters. Faced with a burned palace and a ruined city, the newly enthroned Yijiu, now King Ping of Zhou (r. 770–720 B.C.E.), decided to move the seat of government permanently to the secondary capital at Luoyang. The immediate consequences of this decision were not necessarily apparent; however, it would gradually become clear that these events had completely destroyed the authority of the Zhou kings. With the center crumbling, violence began to spiral out of control. Over the course of the next few centuries, the states of the Zhou confederacy suffered social collapse and political cataclysm, from which no one would emerge unscathed. The violence spread outwards from each epicenter like the ripples when a stone is dropped into water. An assassination in one state would lead to further revenge killings, sucking more and more people into the maelstrom. The resulting political vacuum would result in popular uprisings, innocent people were slain, and foreign enemies invaded. Occasionally, an individual ruler and his ministers would try to make a stand and preserve the peace, but all too soon, that regime would pass away and the fighting would break out again. At the same time, centrifugal forces ripped the Central States apart, as power increasingly came to be vested in regimes more and more remote from the old center: the Zhou Royal Domain. This was a function of the way in which territory had been allocated since the founding of the Western Zhou in 1045 B.C.E. The political center consisted mainly of city-states, with limited opportunities for expansion. Over time it proved to be the peripheral regimes—sometimes even foreign kingdoms— that showed they had the capacity to expand rapidly, conquering their neighbors and recruiting ever vaster armies. The precise number of states within the Zhou confederacy at the beginning of the Eastern Zhou dynasty is not known, since not all are mentioned in surviving historical records and some appear only in inscriptions on ceremonial bronze vessels that have been excavated in modern times. However, there are thought to have been at least twelve hundred states in 771 B.C.E., at the beginning of the dynasty. By the end of the Spring and Autumn period in 475 B.C.E., these had been consolidated into seven vast countries, whose rulers were powerful enough to declare themselves kings. During the Warring States era, it became increasingly obvious to everyone that unification was necessary in order to bring the violence to an end. In the process, the seven kings of the Warring States would fight each other until there was only one left—Qin— which proceeded to unify China.

This abridged edition of *Kingdoms in Peril* consists of nine key storylines taken from the novel. The first story, titled "The Curse of the Bao Lords," contains the opening three chapters of Feng Menglong's tale, and describes the fall of the Western Zhou dynasty and the murder of the last king and his family. This story closely follows the standard histories of this period, but in recent years the events surrounding the death of King You and the installation of King Ping have been thoroughly reevaluated in the light of archaeologically excavated material dating to this period and ancient bamboo texts discovered through tomb robbery. These new sources suggest that the conflict after the death of King You was much worse than previously believed, and it took approximately two decades after the murder of the last king of the Western Zhou before his son and heir was able to take the throne as King Ping. Indeed, if the *Annalistic History* (*Xinian*), a text donated in 2008 to Qinghua University, is correct, the crown prince's claim to the throne was disputed by one of King You's younger brothers, Prince Yuchen, and it was only after a prolonged civil war that the Eastern Zhou dynasty was finally established.

The second story is titled "An Incestuous Affair at the Court of Qi" and documents the troubled lives of Lord Xiang of Qi (r. 697–686 B.C.E.), his sister Lady Wen Jiang (d. 673 B.C.E.), and the affair between the two which brought about the murder of her husband, Lord Huan of Lu (r. 711–694 B.C.E.). Lu and Qi were the two most important states on the Shandong peninsula, and political marriages were frequently arranged between members of these ruling houses in order to ensure peace within the region. When Lord Xiang of Qi ordered the killing of Lord Huan of Lu, this seriously destabilized the governments of both states and entailed terrible consequences: Lord Xiang was murdered in his turn, plunging Qi into civil war as his heirs fought among themselves, while Lord Huan of Lu's son, Lord Zhuang (r. 693–662 B.C.E.), would find himself deeply troubled by being forced to marry the daughter of the man who murdered his father in order to maintain good relations between the two countries. The removal of Lord Xiang from the scene would have particularly significant political repercussions, because the conflict following his demise would allow an unexpected candidate to seize power: the Honorable Xiaobai, Lord Huan of Qi (r. 685–643 B.C.E.). A highly intelligent, ambitious ruler, Lord Huan of Qi would proceed to dominate the political life of the Central States for a generation and was widely admired for his personal generosity and strong principles, the enlightened government he instituted at home, and the commitment he showed to keeping the peace abroad. Lord Huan of Qi would be honored for his achievements by being appointed as hegemon (ba), an extraordinary title that recognized the most powerful nobles of the Spring and Autumn period.

The third story, "The Wicked Stepmother, Lady Li Ji," turns to the political troubles of the state of Jin (based in what is today Shanxi Province in northern China) in the time of Lord Xian of Jin (r. 676–651 B.C.E.). The court of Jin seems to have been an unusually louche one, with Lord Xian producing children with one of his father's wives, as well as with a series of junior wives and concubines who bore the same clan name as himself—relationships which would have been considered incestuous in the Eastern Zhou dynasty. Some of his many children would prove every bit as tiresome as their father, but others were to become famous for their moral values and the loving affection that they showed to each other, regardless of parentage. This particular tale focuses on the terrible malevolence directed by Lord Xian and his favorite wife, Lady Li Ji (d. 651 B.C.E.), towards his son Shensheng (d. 655 B.C.E.), who had earlier been appointed as the heir to the marquisate of Jin. The way Shensheng was tormented by his father and stepmother until finally he committed suicide has traditionally been cited as the classic argument against taking filial piety and obedience to parents too far. Although filial reverence and respect for senior family members was always strongly promoted by Confucian thinkers, and has frequently been presented as a quintessential value within Chinese society, discussion of what happened in Jin offers a way of balancing this dominant cultural narrative. A good son and a good brother, Shensheng suffered a dreadful death in order to spare his father from pain. His fate was undeserved and resulted in two decades of serious political upheavals in Jin, during which countless people were killed. It was not until his half-brother, the Honorable Chonger, was finally installed as Lord Wen of Jin (r. 636–628 B.C.E.) that the situation gradually began to stabilize.

In "The Fight for Lady Xia Ji," the action moves to the minor state of Chen, located in what is now Henan Province. This is where the famously beautiful Lady Xia Ji, the daughter of Lord Mu of Zheng (r. 628–606 B.C.E.), lived as a widow following the death of her first husband, Xia Zhengshu. The lovely Lady Xia Ji is here portrayed both as a licentious woman, engaged in affairs with a couple of different grandees in Chen, and as a victim of sexual harassment, since she is forced into a relationship with Lord Ling of Chen (r. 613–599 B.C.E.) against her will, because she and her son are entirely in his power. When her son grew up and discovered what had been going on, he murdered Lord Ling. This killing provided King Zhuang of Chu (r. 613–591 B.C.E.) with an excuse to invade the state of Chen. Prevented from installing Lady Xia Ji in his own harem by the impassioned remonstrance of one of his government ministers, Wu Chen, King Zhuang ordered that she be married off to a minor official. This second husband, however, did not last long, and in the end Lady Xia Ji eloped with the very minister who complained about her being taken into the Chu king's harem. The fate of Lady Xia Ji is indicative of the way in which elite women during the Spring and Autumn period were increasingly being treated as trophies: her beauty was used to justify and excuse sexual exploitation. Passed from one man to another, married off on a whim, she appears to have had no control over her own destiny. However, the portrayal of Lady Xi Ji in *Kingdoms in Peril* is taken straight from the *Scandalous History of Zhulin* (*Zhulin yeshi*), a late Ming dynasty erotic novel, and so this account also incorporates some of the themes frequently found in such writings. Although on one level she is subjected to horrific exploitation, Lady Xia Ji, like other Chinese femmes fatales, is able to turn the tables on the men who abuse her: she has learned the techniques of sexual vampirism and is therefore able to drain them of life-force and use this to restore her own remarkable beauty. In this way, Feng Menglong is able to move the portrayal of Lady Xia Ji away from being just a victim suffering in silence, since by mistreating her a series of powerful and important men destroy themselves.

"The Orphan of the Zhao Clan" is included in this abridged edition because of its importance within Western culture, above and beyond its significance in China. This short tale describes how Tu'an Gu (d. 473 B.C.E.), a senior minister in the government of the state of Jin, persuaded Lord Jing of Jin (r. 599–581 B.C.E.) to agree to execute the Zhao clan as punishment for the role of an earlier generation of the family in the murder of the sadistic Lord Ling of Jin (r. 620–607 B.C.E.). Such mass executions were unheard of in other states of the Zhou confederacy, but in Jin, the ruling elite seem to have been exceptionally violent in this regard, and rivalries between different hereditary ministerial clans commonly ended in the deaths of an entire lineage. In this case, in spite of every effort by Tu'an Gu to ensure that nobody escaped, there was one survivor: Zhao Wu (598–541 B.C.E.), then a newborn baby, was successfully smuggled to safety. When he grew up, Zhao Wu appealed to Lord Dao of Jin (r. 573–558 B.C.E.) for justice, and the Tu'an clan were butchered in their turn. This famous tale of revenge would subsequently prove immensely popular and has been retold in countless forms, in fiction, poetry, drama, opera, film, and television. The Yuan dynasty play *The Orphan of Zhao* (*Zhaoshi guer*) was the first Chinese drama to be translated and performed across Europe, and it would have an enormous impact on Western theater in the eighteenth century with numerous adaptations being produced, including Voltaire's *L'Orphelin de la Chine*. However, where these later retellings focus on the orphan's personal revenge, *Kingdoms in Peril* makes it clear that it was Lord Dao of Jin who avenged the Zhao clan. This point is stressed to alert the reader to the importance of the theme of loyalty, which runs through this story. Unpleasant as he was in many ways, Tu'an Gu was utterly loyal to the marquises of Jin, and his belief that the Zhao family had become too powerful was undoubtedly correct. Zhao Wu would consolidate his authority, and his descendants, along with those of Han Jue and others, would eventually destroy Jin. This denouement was entirely made possible by Lord Dao's misplaced benevolence.

"The Downfall of the Kingdom of Wu" is concerned with events beyond the borders of the Zhou confederacy in the ancient kingdoms of Wu in what is now southern Jiangsu Province, and Yue in northern Zhejiang Province. The rise and fall of Wu is given particular prominence in *Kingdoms in Peril* as a whole, which was at least partly due to the fact that the capital city of this ancient kingdom was Feng Menglong's hometown. This story begins with King Fuchai of Wu (r. 495–473 B.C.E.) being determined to take revenge for the death of his grandfather, King Helü (r. 514–496 B.C.E.), who had been killed in battle against Yue. Seeking vengeance for this, King Fuchai defeated King Goujian of Yue (r. 494–465 B.C.E.), who in turn retreated to the mountain fastness at Kuaiji, from which he negotiated a humiliating surrender. After years of being held captive in Wu, the king of Yue finally succeeded in convincing King Fuchai to release him and allow him to return home to his own country. From this vantage point, King Goujian of Yue would spend years secretly building up his forces while ceaselessly conspiring to disrupt and destabilize the government of Wu, before finally accomplishing his revenge—conquering Wu and forcing King Fuchai to commit suicide. In this account, King Goujian is a truly nightmarish figure. The king of Yue proves to be a consummate actor: while held prisoner, he is able to convince King Fuchai that he is utterly harmless and a completely loyal subject; on his return to Yue, his endless machinations cause terrible disruption and loss of life in Wu as the government of this kingdom is hollowed out from the inside. Yet the violence does not stop just because King Goujian has achieved the vengeance against his enemies that he had so long desired, since after the conquest of Wu his paranoid suspicions become more and more focused on the men who helped him achieve his victory.

"Rival Students of the Master of Ghost Valley" turns the tale to events in the kingdom of Wei during the reign of King Hui (r. 369–319 B.C.E.). This kingdom was created when the vast ancient state of Jin was partitioned at the beginning of the Warring States era, forming the kingdoms of Wei, Zhao, and Han. King Hui of Wei recruited Pang Juan (d. 342 B.C.E.) into his service and gave him command of the army, but subsequently also hired one of his former fellow students, Sun Bin (d. 316 B.C.E.)—a descendant of the famous Sun Wu, the author of *The Art of War* (*Sunzi bingfa*). As these two men were supposed to be close friends, King Hui of Wei imagined that they would work well together, but he was unaware that Pang Juan was bitterly jealous of Sun Bin. Determined to destroy his rival, Pang Juan trapped Sun Bin into admissions that he could twist into an appearance of treason, for which the latter suffered the appalling mutilation punishment of having his kneecaps cut out. By various stratagems, however, the crippled Sun Bin was able to escape and find sanctuary in the kingdom of Qi. During the reign of King Wei of Qi (r. 356–320 B.C.E.) he commanded a number of successful campaigns against his enemies—his revenge was complete when Pang Juan was shot to pieces in the Battle of Maling. Although Sun Wu's *The Art of War* has been translated many times into every Western language, rendering its author familiar to anyone interested in the history of military strategy, the career of Sun Bin is much less well-known. Although Sun Bin's own writings, also titled *The Art of War* (*Sun Bin bingfa*), were lost in antiquity, this text was rediscovered in 1972 when a copy was excavated from a Han dynasty tomb at Yinqueshan. This means that today the development of the Sun family school of military thinking can be properly appreciated for the first time in two thousand years.

The last two stories in this collection are concerned with the First Emperor of Qin. "The Family Troubles of the King of Qin" focuses on his family background. At the time of the First Emperor's birth, his father was being held hostage in the kingdom of Zhao: a minor princeling of the Qin ruling house, neglected by his grandfather, King Zhaoxiang of Qin (r. 306–251 B.C.E.), and ignored by his father the crown prince, also known as the Lord of Anguo (later to rule as king of Qin for three days, d. 250 B.C.E.). An intelligent and ambitious man, the Royal Grandson Yiren (later King Zhuangxiang of Qin, r. 250–247 B.C.E.) survived thanks to the generosity of a wealthy friend, Lü Buwei (d. 235 B.C.E.), who was to mastermind and fund his rise to power in Qin—he arranged that Yiren be adopted by the Lord of Anguo's childless favorite, who in turn ensured his accession to the throne. According to this account (and here Feng Menglong follows Han dynasty propaganda on the subject), Lü Buwei's actions were far from being altruistic; he had presented his pregnant concubine Zhao Ji (d. 228 B.C.E.) to Yiren, and therefore the baby born in captivity in Zhao—the future First Emperor of China—was his own son. On becoming the king of Qin, the future First Emperor found his position assailed by rival half-brothers on both sides of the family. His paternal half-brother, the Lord of Chang'an, would attempt to rise in rebellion against him, claiming to be the true heir to the Qin throne. Meanwhile his mother, who had produced two more children with a new lover, became involved in a plot to murder her oldest son to allow one of these infants to become king. Dealing with these stupid and badly executed conspiracies would leave the First Emperor with virtually no living family members and a reputation for harshness that is perhaps not entirely deserved.

The final story, "The Assassins Strike," is the conclusion of *Kingdoms in Peril*. As children, the future First Emperor of Qin and Crown Prince Dan of Yan (d. 226 B.C.E.) were close friends when they were both held hostage in Zhao. As adults, they turned against each other, and Crown Prince Dan was determined to assassinate his former friend. At this time, the unification of China was imminent; Crown Prince Dan had convinced himself that the only way to prevent the kingdom of Yan from being incorporated into the nascent empire was by disrupting the government of Qin through the targeted assassination of the young king. To this end, he recruited a number of swordsmen, and two of them—Jing Ke (d. 227 B.C.E.) and Qin Wuyang—were entrusted with the task of traveling to Qin to kill the future First Emperor. All too often these events are presented in highly romantic terms, with Crown Prince Dan and Jing Ke in particular being described as a tragically doomed figures. Feng Menglong eschews any such interpretation, preferring to stress the ill-conceived and over-hasty nature of the assignment, with the crown prince repeatedly warned by many different people that he was putting everyone's lives at risk by engaging in such a poorly planned conspiracy. The assassins still set out on their mission, knowing that they were not properly prepared. This realistic note does not detract in the slightest from the true horror and brutality of the final confrontation between the First Emperor and Jing Ke in the royal palace in Xianyang.

THE AUTHOR: FENG MENGLONG

Feng Menglong was born into a gentry family in Suzhou in 1574, as the second of three sons. As with other young men of this kind of privileged background, he was destined for a career in the civil service. However, in spite of numerous attempts to pass the necessary examinations, he consistently failed, as a result of which the stellar career in government which he and his family had hoped for never materialized. In 1630, at the age of fifty-six, his scholarly achievements were finally recognized with appointment as a tribute scholar (*gongsheng*), which opened the way for him to receive a minor official appointment in Dantu County, Jiangsu Province. Having successfully completed this tour of duty, he served for four years as the magistrate of Shouning County in Fujian Province, from 1634 to 1638. On completing this second term of office, he retired and returned to live in Suzhou. That his ambitions to serve as a government official misfired so badly would have one important connection to Feng Menglong's career as an author: each candidate for the civil service examinations was required to study one classical Chinese text. In his case, Feng Menglong chose to specialize in the *Spring and Autumn Annals* (*Chunqiu*), a historical text that covers the events of the early Eastern Zhou dynasty. The fact that he never succeeded in passing the examinations should not be seen as a reflection of any lack of diligence, intelligence, or expertise on the subject: he would go on to produce three textbooks that would be regarded as standard works in the field for centuries to come. This academic training and specialism would prove crucial when writing *Kingdoms in Peril*. The language of the primary sources on which he based his novel is extremely difficult and requires many years of study to be able to read. A rigorous scholarly background can also be discerned in the structuring of *Kingdoms in Peril*. Feng Menglong was determined to produce a novel that was as historically accurate as possible, paying close attention to chronology (an issue of particular importance at a time when many states were using their own calendars), nomenclature, precise geographical locations, and so on. This attention to detail does not add to the literary qualities of the novel per se, but certainly serves to give readers the confidence that they are in the hands of a highly competent author.

Feng Menglong's place of birth was to have a very strong influence on his life and career. During the course of the Ming dynasty, Suzhou had emerged as the commercial capital of China. This ancient city, founded in 514 B.C.E., was originally constructed as the capital of the kingdom of Wu by its penultimate monarch, King Helü. Throughout the imperial era, it continued to be an important regional administrative center, and its location—dominating trade routes along the Yangtze River, the Grand Canal, and through the Lake Tai region—would make it the preeminent commercial hub where goods from every province of the empire were bought and sold. One of the many industries based in Suzhou was that of publishing, with numerous printing presses in operation producing everything from the cheap single-sheet texts handed out as amusing novelty fast-food wrappers to deluxe illustrated editions of the classics printed on the finest paper and elegantly bound for discriminating and wealthy customers. For an educated gentleman needing to make a living, becoming involved in the publishing industry was an obvious step. The majority of Feng Menglong's writings seem to have appeared before he was appointed to a government post in 1630, with the remainder dating to after his retirement in 1638. The dates of first publication of a number of his works are not known, and so the precise chronology of his development as an author remains unclear. However, it is evident that Feng Menglong was an extraordinarily prolific writer who was far from confining himself to a single genre. His popularity was such that a number of works by inferior authors were published with his name on the title page; a great deal of research has been done by modern scholars to identify and remove these spurious works from his oeuvre, and hence they are not included in the list below. However, in addition to writings that were published in his own name, he also appears to have produced some anonymous or pseudonymous works, where an attribution to Feng Menglong remains highly controversial.

The reception of Feng Menglong's writings has varied enormously. While his short story collections have consistently been very much admired and widely read, other writings that he produced have much more patchy histories. In general, the fall of the Ming dynasty can be said to have brought a significantly more conservative regime to power, and during the Qing dynasty (1645–1911) the government would ban many of Feng Menglong's writings—and indeed a great deal of late Ming literature—as indecent. This would particularly affect the reception of his two collections of folk songs, many of which are sexually explicit and describe pre- or extramarital relationships in positive (and sometimes humorous) terms. These song collections were rendered even more unacceptable by the fact that many pieces were produced in the female voice, and in some cases have explicitly female authorship. Both the *Mountain Songs* and the *Hanging Branches* collections have been virtually unobtainable until very recently. The *Anatomy of Love* was also banned because of the supposedly pornographic nature of the contents—this collection too has suffered neglect until modern times, when reprints have appeared to at last allow people to read these tales of love and lust again. While these writings survive, the impact of bans on Feng Menglong's anonymous and pseudonymous works is much harder to gauge, since by their very nature, their attribution to his authorship is controversial and uncertain. During the early part of his career as a writer, Feng Menglong appears to have authored at least one short erotic novel (and most likely more). This kind of text was subject to extremely strict legal prohibitions during the Qing dynasty and beyond, and hence their role within his development as a writer has not been properly appreciated. However, this part of his oeuvre is particularly important given that one text that has survived, the *Scandalous History of Zhulin,* forms the basis of the tale of Lady Xia Ji in *Kingdoms in Peril.*

During the course of the Qing dynasty, an abridged version of *Kingdoms in Peril* was produced by Cai Yuanfang, an otherwise completely obscure eighteenth-century writer. His revised text, titled *Tales of the States of the Eastern Zhou* (*Dongzhou lieguo zhi*), proved to be enormously popular, to the point where Feng Menglong's original novel ceased to be reprinted. The difficultly of laying hands on a copy of the original text has served to confuse many readers as to the nature and extent of the abridgement. Most of Cai Yuanfang's changes are extremely minor, cutting a sentence here and a poem there. The most significant changes lie in the removal of much of the more sexually explicit material, which would fit with the conservative agenda of the government of the time and with changing tastes among readers. This English-language abridged edition is based upon Feng Menglong's original text, with the only cuts introduced being those necessary to remove extraneous story lines and some of the longer strings of poetry from the chapters selected for inclusion. The present translation is based upon the critical edition of the text produced by Hu Wanchuan for the Lianjing Publishing Company as part of the *New Printings of Classic Chinese Novels* (*Zhongguo gudian xiaoshuo xinkan*) series. The text reproduces the only surviving copy of the first edition, produced by Ye Jingchi—who also published many of Feng Menglong's other writings—which is preserved in the Naikaku Bunko in Japan. The Naikaku Bunko collection of Chinese literature comprises many important Ming and Qing editions purchased for the library maintained by the Tokugawa shoguns, which have not survived elsewhere.

It is not known when exactly *Kingdoms in Peril* was written, and there is no date of publication given on the only surviving copy of the first edition. However, there is a reference in the writings of Qi Biaojia (1603–45) to reading a copy in 1644 on a boat journey back to his hometown. Some scholars have suggested that this novel was published as early as the 1620s, but this would seem to be extremely unlikely for several reasons. First, as a very popular author with a large and devoted readership, it is hard to imagine that a major novel by Feng Menglong could exist for twenty years without anyone mentioning it. The second reason is practical: between 1620 and 1630, Feng Menglong appears to have been fully occupied with other writing projects. He produced a vast body of work during this decade, and the dates of publication of these writings are known. It would seem unlikely that with such a packed schedule it would have been possible to make room for the production of an additional one-hundred-and-eight-chapter novel, particularly one that required very extensive background research. Finally, throughout the novel, Feng Menglong refers to himself as "the old man" or "bearded old man" (*ranweng* or *ranxian*). This term of self-address is also found in other writings dating to the end of his life, and it would seem reasonable that he adopted it in his seventies, rather than in his late forties to early fifties. However, it is certainly true that Feng Menglong was an extraordinarily productive author, and considerable work remains to be done to elucidate the full scope of his literary legacy.

The dating of *Kingdoms in Peril* is significant, because it suggests that at some level the writing of this novel should be understood in the context of contemporary political events. During the reigns of the last Ming emperors, the regime lurched from one crisis to another: the Great Jiajing earthquake of 1556 killed nearly a million people and reduced vast areas of the northwest to ruins; Wokou pirate attacks of 1522–66 made life along the southern coast of China miserable for one and all (including repeated attacks on Suzhou and the surrounding area); and the Imjin War of 1592–98 obliged the bankrupt Ming state to go to the aid of its allies in Korea when under attack by the Japanese, thus worsening the political and economic situation at home. These events all took place during an era of global cooling, which saw crop failures, widespread famine, increased banditry, and significant social upheaval as hordes of refugees moved from one place to another struggling to find a way to survive. It was against this background of ever-intensifying misery that a rebel commander in the northwest, Li Zicheng (1606–45), came to power. In 1641, he would capture Luoyang, once the capital of the kings of the Eastern Zhou dynasty, and execute Zhu Changxun, king of Fu (1601–41), the uncle of the last Ming emperor. In 1643, the last of the Ming kings of Qin would surrender the city of Xi'an, and Li Zicheng would crown himself emperor of the Shun dynasty there on New Year's Day, 1644. From these lands, formerly the site of the Western Zhou capital, Li Zicheng would march on the city of Beijing, to bring the Ming dynasty to an end. The Chongzhen emperor (r. 1627–44), trapped within the Forbidden City, realized his peril too late: the city was under siege. On April 24, 1644, having ordered his wife and concubines to commit suicide and after murdering several of his children personally, the last Ming emperor hanged himself.

At the time that Feng Menglong wrote *Kingdoms in Peril*, the dreadful end of the Ming dynasty had not yet played out. The imperial family died, and Beijing fell to the forces of Li Zicheng only in late April 1644. The power vacuum that this created allowed the Manchu people to invade China from the northeast—the first wave of troops crossed the border in May, and was followed by further massive incursions over the next few weeks and months. The Manchu conquest would take decades and cost many millions of lives; indeed, it was not until 1683 that the last remnants of Ming loyalist resistance were mopped up on the island of Taiwan. However, the imminent collapse of the Ming dynasty would have been much on everybody's minds in the early 1640s, and this experience must have affected Feng Menglong's personal understanding of the historical events described in *Kingdoms in Peril*. Although no explicit parallel is drawn at any stage, and the author never mentions any contemporary relevance, it is because he does not have to. *Kingdoms in Peril* is a political novel, and it describes the exercise of power and the rise and fall of dynasties. When Li Zicheng was crowned as emperor in 1644, it was not by accident that he chose the city of Xi'an for this ceremony: this region was the location of the Western Zhou dynasty capital, and subsequently served as the capital for first the kingdom and then the empire of Qin, not to mention the Han and Tang dynasties. The legitimation of power by calling on the vestiges of past glory was a process that everyone understood—just as the rulers described in *Kingdoms in Peril* laid claim to the legacy of the founders of the Zhou dynasty, Li Zicheng wanted to see himself walking in the footsteps of the First Emperor of Qin.

The narrative of *Kingdoms in Peril* consists of three elements. There is the main story, which forms the bulk of the text. When writing *Kingdoms in Peril*, Feng Menglong made use of every single surviving ancient Chinese text relevant to this period in Chinese history, and the narrative is constructed using two techniques: translation and amplification. On the principle that nothing he could invent for his characters to say could possibly be as striking and characteristic as what they thought of for themselves, Feng Menglong relies heavily upon conversations reported in ancient texts, which he has translated from the classical Chinese of two thousand years earlier into the vernacular language of the early seventeenth century. Sometimes, however, his sources do not provide enough material to work with, and there the author resorts to amplification. Thus, for example, in the earliest account of the confrontation between Lord Huan of Lu and his wife over her incestuous adultery with her brother, *Zuo's Tradition* (*Zuozhuan*) simply says, "The lord upbraided her." This is amplified in *Kingdoms in Peril* into a dramatic interrogation sequence in which the angry Lord of Lu presses his ever-more humiliated wife with a series of searching questions. In addition to the main narrative, Feng Menglong periodically incorporates quotations of poetry and prose into his novel. The presence of these literary works serves a couple of different purposes. Sometimes they act as a kind of punctuation, marking the end of a particular story sequence or the final appearance of an important character. In other instances, these writings highlight some aspect of the narrative that the author wished to emphasize, or provide a contrasting reading of the events described. Alternatively, they are there to remind the reader of the ongoing cultural significance of these events in China: these people and their actions have a legacy in Chinese literature that should not be ignored, and they have inspired some of the most important writers and poets of the past two thousand years. Finally, there are Feng Menglong's own comments, which are indicated in this translation by italics. These serve to clarify unusual terms that he expected to be unfamiliar to his readers, to explain things that occurred outside the time frame covered by his book, or to note the precise location at which a particular event took place. This geographical information was included to remind his Chinese readership that these dramatic and often horrifying events occurred right there where they were living in the late Ming dynasty.

Feng Menglong and Late Ming Literature

Feng Menglong was a major figure in the late Ming Romantic movement. This would have personal implications as well as giving a particular flavor to his literary works. As a young man, he is known to have engaged in a series of intensely passionate relationships with courtesans in Suzhou, most notably with a woman named Hou Huiqing. Their relationship ended abruptly when Hou Huiqing was purchased from the brothel in which she was indentured by a wealthy salt merchant. The sudden end to their love affair seems to have been a devastating shock to Feng Menglong, and one from which he took long to recover. Society in the Ming dynasty was heavily segregated, and respectable women did not appear in public, so their opportunities to meet and mingle with men who were not close relatives were very limited. This meant that men seeking female companionship had little choice but to seek the company of courtesans, who not only provided sexual services but were also trained as entertainers—singing, dancing, and playing music for the enjoyment of their clients. However, these courtesans were slaves, often sold into brothels as children, with virtually no control over their own lives. No matter how beautiful, charming, highly educated, and talented, there was little chance for them of leaving slavery. Even if they were bought out, the stigma remained: their engagement in sex work made them part of a legally circumscribed underclass. It is for this reason that courtesans were the focus of much late Ming Romantic sensibility, for these women embodied the tragic side of the commercialism and commodification of the age. Feng Menglong's writings are interesting not only for the great sympathy he expresses concerning the fate of these women, but also because he clearly spent time discussing their lives with them, and records their thoughts and opinions. The respect he accords these women by allowing them an opportunity to speak for themselves is unusual and admirable.

One key feature of the late Ming Romantic movement in China was the tolerance that was expressed towards more unconventional relationships. As love came to be seen as an adequate justification for pretty much any attachment, no matter how frowned upon in society as a whole, it became possible to present a wide range of unconventional lifestyles in a positive light. Chinese society was traditionally monogamous, but polygynous—in other words, a man might only marry one wife, but he could have numerous concubines and junior consorts. Some individuals would take the Romantic ideal to extremes, expressing contempt for any social restraints and adopting a completely hedonistic way of life. For example, Zhang Dai (1597–1684) would write in his "Epitaph to Myself" (*Ziwei muzhiming*) that he "loved extravagance, loved luxurious houses, loved beautiful maidservants, loved pretty boys, loved colorful clothes, loved fine foods, loved pedigree horses, loved bright lights, loved red-light districts, loved the theater, loved loud music, loved antiques, and loved flower and bird paintings."Here, the maidservants and pretty boys should be understood as the focus of his sexual attentions, in the same way as the female denizens of the red-light districts and the male actors that he met at the theater.

As can be seen from the portrayal of unusual sexual relationships in *Kingdoms in Peril,* the author felt confident enough in his readers' engagement with these Romantic ideas to be able to describe brother-sister incest as an expression of true love. Although this abridged edition does not contain any stories about homosexual relationships, they too find a place in the novel, as they did in real life. However, in *Kingdoms in Peril,* Feng Menglong does not shy away from documenting the appalling consequences of unrestrained lust—sexual obsession can lead to exploitation and abuse for the unfortunate victim, but worse than that, when these emotions afflict members of the ruling elite, there can be serious political consequences. In this novel, all too often, "love" leads to assassination, rioting, civil war, invasions, and the deaths of many innocent individuals as the situation gets completely out of control. As a result, *Kingdoms in Peril* can sometimes seem like an extended paean to the virtue of self-control and thinking through the consequences of one's actions.

In Feng Menglong's writings, women characters play an unusually prominent part, and they are accorded a deeper and more complex characterization than is often seen in premodern Chinese literature. The role of women in the history of the Eastern Zhou dynasty is not well recorded, but wherever a female character does appear, the author makes every attempt to include her in the narrative in a substantive way. Hence, rather than portraying women as purely the ciphers—the unhappy victims of male lust—they appear in this novel in much more complicated guises: ambitious and intelligent participants in the government of the country, masterminds of cunning stratagems to turn events to their advantage, and persons of high moral values determined to preserve these qualities in the teeth of the dubious activities of their male relatives, as well as bewildered personalities who have blundered into situations far more complicated and serious than they can even begin to grasp. Some women are shown as every bit as unrestrained and promiscuous as their male counterparts, while others strongly resent or suffer through the degradation of unwanted sexual attentions. The intelligent and strong female characters in this novel are every bit a match for their male peers. At the same time, the stupid and ignorant women are as just as dull as the worst of the men, and prove equally incapable of extracting themselves from the dangerous situations in which they find themselves.

THE WORLD OF *KINGDOMS IN PERIL*

Places

The majority of the action in *Kingdoms in Peril* focuses around the states of the Zhou confederacy, also known as the Central States, a civilization based around the Yellow River valley. This was a highly urban culture, found within vast walled cities, connected together by great highways. The people of the Central States lived either safe inside an array of moats, earthworks, fortifications, and huge pounded earth walls or immediately outside the walls in suburban areas. The inhabitants of walled cities were "the people of the country" or "the people of the capital" (*guoren*), who formed the background audience for every public appearance on the part of the ruling elite. Although there was no mechanism for consulting the people of the capital about political decisions, monarchs and ministers were very conscious of the importance of their approval and support. Although far from being wealthy or socially advantaged, living cheek by jowl with the lords and clan chiefs inside the great walls of the city, the people of the capital could play a major role in historical events, providing enthusiastic support—even rioting—to ensure that a favored candidate took power or that unpopular legislation should be repealed. They had to be constantly propitiated with favorable treatment, and in times of famine or unrest, they required further generous gifts, because if mobilized against the government they could easily overthrow it.

In addition to the city residents, there were also those who lived immediately outside the walls in suburbs. In return for paying less tax towards the maintenance of these defensive structures, suburban dwellers risked losing their property and their lives in the event of a sudden attack. Politically, these people were also significantly less relevant than the inhabitants of the city, and their historical role was accordingly more restricted. The suburbs were, however, the location of the official guesthouses in which much diplomatic activity was centered. Ambassadors or distinguished visitors from foreign countries tended to arrive with heavily armed guards, even military units, and were therefore not allowed to stay within the confines of the city walls in case they were intending to cause trouble. Quite apart from these city and suburban residents, there were other people who had not assumed an urban lifestyle. A significant proportion of the population would have been agricultural workers, based on small farms or on the great manorial estates owned by grand aristocratic houses. In addition, within the confines of each state, it was possible to find *yeren* or "people of the wilds," who wished to live free of any government control, as well as bandits who had retreated to the margins of society and nomadic or aboriginal peoples of one kind or another—such persons, individually or collectively, could occasionally play a major role in historical events. At the beginning of the Spring and Autumn period, many of the states within the Zhou confederacy were city-states, but over time increasingly such regimes were subject to conquest by more aggressive, powerful neighbors, creating the enormous kingdoms of the Warring States era.

The vast majority of the characters in *Kingdoms in Peril* are members of the ruling elite, and therefore they are to be found living in palaces, emerging periodically in order to attend ceremonies at the ancestral temple, to visit their hunting parks, or to go on campaign against their enemies. Other travel involved attendance at international meetings or blood covenants, designed to keep the peace between warring factions. When travel took place outside the confines of one's own country, the most important associated architecture was the sacrificial altar, erected upon a pounded earth platform, where agreements could be made and oaths sworn. Building such structures was an opportunity to show off one's wealth and ability to mobilize the resources of the population not only of one's own country, but also of one's neighbors. Meanwhile, within each state, ruling families in the Eastern Zhou dynasty took particular pride in constructing towers, and a great many significant historical events took place in or around these structures. Since constructing high-rise buildings was beyond the capability of architects at this period, towers were multilevel structures constructed on top of massive, stepped, pounded earth platforms. From the outside, the tower might appear to be as much as ten or twelve stories high, but in fact, each part of the structure was only a couple of stories, with the impression of height achieved by building up the core on which it was erected. These towers quickly became an essential feature of elite life for the aristocracy of the Central States and their neighbors: they were a form of conspicuous consumption, which could be used to impress both subjects and foreign visitors; they allowed the aristocracy the privilege of quite literally looking down on everyone else; and they provided a luxurious space for elite socialization in a slightly freer form than the highly ritualized formal events held in palace halls or ancestral temples.

The action of *Kingdoms in Peril* is not confined exclusively to the Central States. Three foreign regimes are treated in some detail in this novel, in accordance with their historical significance. All three were located along the Yangtze River: the kingdom of Chu was based inland, while Wu and Yue occupied the delta region. To the inhabitants of the states of the Zhou confederacy, Chu was an exotic kingdom of fabulous wealth and apparently limitless resources, whose lands stretched in a vast swath southwards from the Yangtze, ending somewhere in the jungles of Southeast Asia. Chu often appears in *Kingdoms in Peril* as a counterbalancing regime to the Central States; although the two regimes were frequently in conflict, both sides are accorded a more-or-less legitimate position in their disagreements. Meanwhile the kingdoms of Wu and Yue are given particular prominence in this novel thanks to the fact that an exceptionally fine body of early literature survives about the rivalry between these two kingdoms, which would eventually coalesce during the early Eastern Han dynasty into a truly remarkable epic retelling of these events—*The Spring and Autumn Annals of Wu and Yue* (*Wu Yue chunqiu*), which is also the first historical novel to be written in the Chinese language. The dramatic incidents attendant on the rise and fall of the kingdom of Wu, culminating in the suicide of their last king, form a well-known and much-studied story cycle that remains popular right up to the present day. However, Feng Menglong was himself a native of the city of Suzhou, once the capital of the kings of Wu, and hence the setting of these famous events would have been familiar to him from his birth, so highlighting them in his novel was an expression of pride in his own hometown. Unlike some other accounts of the history of these ancient kingdoms, Feng Menglong accepts the foreign and alien characteristics of the Wu and Yue people: they are described here sailing about on boats around their riverine homeland, armed with the finest of swords, and dressed in magnificent feather regalia.

People

People in ancient China used a very extensive nomenclature. Each person was affiliated with a clan, and individual branches within a clan were distinguished by a separate surname. Surnames were often derived from job titles or geographical locations, which meant that two people might have the same surname but belong to different clans, thus indicating that they were unrelated. This was of considerable importance to marriage practice in ancient China, since any sexual relationship between persons of the same clan was regarded as incest. Within each family, brothers and sisters were also allocated a one-character name to indicate birth order: *bo* for eldest son, *meng* for eldest daughter, and so on. For day-to-day use, individuals were designated by their style-names, which provided a respectful form of address for use by friends and strangers. Personal names tended to only be used by very close family members, and for anyone else to address one by one's personal name was considered extremely offensive. Because of this consideration, women's personal names never appear in historical texts (though many such names are documented in archaeologically excavated bronze vessel inscriptions), and in the case of men, even for some very famous individuals their personal names are simply not recorded. In addition to these names, persons might also be designated according to the job they performed or the title that they held. Furthermore, persons of aristocratic rank would normally receive a posthumous title, a one- or two-word summary of their career. These ranged from the highly positive and desirable Wen (cultured) and Wu (martial)—these were also the posthumous titles of the first two kings of Zhou—to pejorative terms such as Ling (numinous), which was normally reserved for rulers who had proved dangerously insane. These titles provide an immediate alert as to what to expect of the reigns of the kings and lords who bore them, and Chinese readers would have been strongly aware of these meanings, even if not familiar with the precise details of the careers of the individuals concerned.

For this translation of *Kingdoms in Peril,* in order to minimize confusion, men are commonly designated by only one name, and mostly I have chosen to use their personal name where this is known. In order to keep persons with identical or very similar names separate in readers' minds, I have sometimes used unusual readings of the Chinese characters. In the case of rulers, they are given two names in this translation: princes and aristocrats are called by their personal names prior to their accession, and afterwards, they are always designated by their posthumous titles. Women are generally named either according to their clan and posthumous title, or clan and birth-order designation. In the case of foreign individuals, particularly those living in nomadic or tribal groups, the nomenclature is very confusing for this early stage in Chinese history. Many of the names accorded to characters of this kind in *Kingdoms in Peril* seem to have been invented by Feng Menglong. So far as is known, these peoples did not have surnames, and hence their multicharacter names have been translated as a single word. The kingdom of Chu, which originally seems to have been culturally indistinguishable from the states of the Zhou confederacy during the Western Zhou dynasty, increasingly absorbed foreign influences as it expanded through the conquest of numerous aboriginal peoples, achieving independence during the early Eastern Zhou. As a result, their language took on new vocabulary from the different peoples absorbed into this polity, and they came to develop a unique nomenclature for their government officials that would have appeared profoundly alien and exotic to the people of the Central States. In order to preserve this linguistic feature, Chu titles have been translated using comparable Persian terms, which for an English-language readership carry many of the same connotations.

It is one of the striking features of *Kingdoms in Peril* that there are virtually no descriptions of what any of the hundreds of characters looked like. Instead, their individual personalities are rendered distinct through their words and deeds, and there is virtually no mention of their physical features or manner of dress. In part, this reflects the fact that early Chinese literature contains very few descriptions of what even the most important historical individuals looked like (except perhaps in the event of one person possessing an obvious physical peculiarity or disability), and there are merely a handful of known portrait sculptures that date from the classical era. Most early artistic representations of human beings in the Chinese tradition are generic types: servants, warriors, captives, entertainers, and so on, rather than being portraits of individuals. There seems to have been no widespread tradition of representing famous historical figures in art until the Eastern Han dynasty (25–220 C.E.); when such depictions became popular, they appeared in a wide variety of mediums including stone sculpture, low relief bronzes, and wall paintings. However, these are entirely imaginary re-creations of the appearance of individuals who lived and died many hundreds of years earlier. Rather than attempt to ascribe particular physical features to the men and women of the Eastern Zhou dynasty, Feng Menglong leaves the reader free to imagine the beautiful women and battle-scarred men who people the pages of his epic novel.

Much of the action within *Kingdoms in Peril* is concerned with politics at a national or international level. However, in some instances, arguments arose within the family, as disputes emerged over the inheritance of titles and land. Status within each family was determined by a number of factors. Of primary importance was position within the clan, since the most senior branch had priority over all the others in issues of inheritance and would decide the distribution of clan property. Seniority among siblings was also important, since an oldest child would have priority over younger brothers and sisters. However, among the aristocratic houses of the Central States, concubinage was standard, and some elite men established extensive harems. Therefore a distinction was also supposed to be maintained between the offspring of the main wife—known as *dizi* or "legitimate" children—and the *shuzi* (commoner) children born to concubines. This gave rise to some perfectly predictable problems. First, affection did not follow legal prioritization, and many fathers much preferred the intelligent, charismatic, and lovable offspring of junior consorts to the children of their main wife. Secondly, although not the main wife, lesser consorts might nevertheless be women associated with powerful factions at court, or taken from other aristocratic houses to confirm an alliance— unlike later eras, Eastern Zhou dynasty concubines might be vastly wealthy and powerful in their own right. Such women were not necessarily prepared to see their own children's interests set aside in favor of the offspring of the main wife. Finally, it might be that an aristocrat did not have children at all by his main wife but produced a plethora of potential heirs by junior consorts, in which case maternal seniority and child birth order would potentially make selecting an heir immensely controversial. Concubinage provided an important mechanism for tying the interests of other powerful families to those of the ruling house, bringing stability to the regime. However, if badly managed, it could equally create appalling internal crises, in which rival heirs fought endless bloody battles with one another over the right of succession.

Ideas

The states of the Zhou confederacy lacked any kind of organized religion, with a hierarchy and textual tradition, but both religious and ethical considerations were crucial for how their people understood the world around them. Ever since the founding of the Zhou dynasty, the kings had claimed to be the representatives on earth of the supreme deity Heaven (*Tian*), and hence assumed the title of Son of Heaven. In a related claim, the Zhou kings declared that they possessed the

Mandate of Heaven (*Tianming*), which legitimated their right to rule. Even as the Zhou kings lapsed into political irrelevance, they retained a very important religious function and performed a series of ceremonies throughout the year that were believed to be crucial for the ongoing functioning of the entire realm. In a more limited way, the lords of the Central States also had a religious function, performing annual sacrifices at the altars of soil and grain. Any failure to perform these agricultural ceremonies was regarded as an existential threat to the entire country; lords thought to be unable to carry out the sacrifices were routinely dispossessed, and a cessation of rituals at the altars was synonymous with the fall of the state itself.

The people of ancient China believed themselves to be surrounded by a vast array of spirits and ghosts, who could be supportive or malevolent. In an attempt to safely navigate these forces, individuals called upon a wide range of mantic skills, including oracle bone cracking, casting hexagrams (milfoil divination), and the interpretation of dreams, as well as seeking the advice of shamans who could communicate with the spirits in a trance. It is one of the striking features of *Kingdoms in Peril* (and indeed its source texts) that these divinations are always correct, and the personages who receive them are in extreme danger if they decide to ignore a warning divination. Obtaining benevolent interest from a ghost or spirit could come about by pure chance, though there are a number of instances in *Kingdoms in Peril* where a living person is rewarded for some act of kindness in the past. At the same time, deceased ancestors were always believed to take a kindly interest in their descendants, and this concept undoubtedly served to strengthen bonds of clan and family solidarity. This would have been reinforced at regular ancestral sacrifices and gatherings, at which elders could become acquainted with and offer patronage and support to promising younger members, creating a strongly corporate identity within the clan. As a result, loyalty to the clan head would often trump any consideration of duty towards the king or lord, or to the country as a whole. It is therefore not surprising that the social reforms that made the Qin unification possible were aimed at strengthening the position of the central government and nuclear families at the expense of the power of individual aristocratic clans.

Numerous ancient texts stress the moral qualities that were s upposed to underpin Eastern Zhou dynasty society: benevolence, justice, respect, loyalty, and so on. These attributes seem to have been hymned because they were in very short supply. However, the concept of ritual propriety (*li*) does seem to have formed an important tool for promoting social cohesion. In the Eastern Zhou dynasty, everyone seems to have been armed more or less constantly. Men were supposed to remove their weapons in the presence of the ruler but otherwise would always have a sword strapped to their belts, while women had at least a hairpin to hand with which they could stab anyone who offended them. In a society which was at one and the same time very hierarchical and very unstable, a situation in which one individual appeared to disrespect another could easily end in bloodshed. Throughout the Eastern Zhou dynasty a mastery of ritual continued to be highly admired because this offered a mechanism for interacting with other people that minimized the chance of conflict. Ritual, here understood in a social and not a religious sense, was a key part of the education of members of the ruling elite, since it continued to provide an essential technique for negotiating relationships with others in a highly formalized and nonconfrontational way.

FURTHER READING

Works by Feng Menglong

The following novels, short story collections, literary anthologies, essays, poems, and writings in other genres are of undisputed authenticity.

Historical Novels:
Quelling the Demons' Revolt (*Pingyao zhuan*), 1620.
Kingdoms in Peril (*Xin lieguo zhi*), c. 1643?

Short Story Collections:
The best-known of Feng Menglong's works today are collectively called the *Sanyan* or *Three Story Compilations*:

Stories to Instruct the World (*Yushi mingyan*), 1620 (also known as *Stories Old and New* [*Gujin xiaoshuo*]).
Stories to Caution the World (*Jingshi tongyan*), 1624.
Stories to Awaken the World (*Xingshi hengyan*), 1627.

Feng Menglong's other major collection of short stories is a compilation of eight hundred and fifty tales of romance, infatuation, and sexual obsession:

Anatomy of Love (*Qingshi*), 1628.

Anthologies of Fiction:
Feng Menglong produced an abridged version of an important collection of early Chinese fiction, compiled in 978.

Excerpts from the Extensive Records of the Taiping Reign-Era, 976–984 (*Taiping guangji chao*), 1626.

In addition, he edited a compilation of three short religious novels, where he was also the author of the first novel:

Random Gleanings from the Three Faiths (*Sanjiao ounian*), date unknown.

Textbooks:
Examples Drawn from the Unicorn Classic [*Spring and Autumn Annals*] (*Linjing zhiyue*), 1620.
New Light on the Central Ideas of the Spring and Autumn Annals (*Chunqiu dingzhi canxin*), ca. 1623.
Thesaurus to the Spring and Autumn Annals (*Chunqiu hengku*), 1625.

Folk Song Compilations:
Mountain Songs (*Shan'ge*), date unknown.
Hanging Branches (*Guazhi'er*), before 1619.

Song Compilations:
Celestial Airs Played Anew (*Taixia xinzou*), c. 1627.

Plays:
An Authoritative Edition of Chuanqi Dramas from the Studio of the Inky Simpleton (*Mohan zhai dingben chuanqi*), 1620s.

Joke Collections:
Treasury of Laughter (*Xiaofu*), after 1610.
The Book of Wit and Wisdom (*Zhinang*), 1625.

A History of Humor Old and New (*Gujin xiaoshi*), date unknown (also known
as *A Survey of Stories Old and New* [*Gujin tan'gai*]).

History and Local History:
Expectant Gazetteer for Shouning County (*Shouning daizhi*), 1637.
An Account of Events of Shenjia Year [1644] (*Shenjia jishi*), 1645.
Grand Proposals for National Rejuvenation (*Zhongxing weilüe*), 1645.

Translations of Feng Menglong's Writings:

The three volumes of the *Sanyan* compilation have been translated
into English in their entirety:

Shuhui Yang and Yunqin Yang, *Stories Old and New: A Ming Dynasty Collection* (Seattle: University of Washington Press, 2000).
————, *Stories to Caution the World* (Seattle: University of Washington Press,
2005).
————, *Stories to Awaken the World* (Seattle: University of Washington Press,
2014).

There have been many translations of individual short stories by
Feng Menglong, and these can often be found in anthologies of Chinese literature, including the following examples:

Cyril Birch, *Stories from a Ming Collection: The Art of the Chinese Storyteller*
(Bloomington: Indiana University Press, 1958).
Yang Xianyi and Gladys Yang, *The Courtesan's Jewel Box: Chinese Stories of the
Xth–XVIIth Centuries* (Beijing: Foreign Languages Press, 1981).
Ted Wang and Chen Chen, *The Oil Vendor and the Courtesan: Tales from the
Ming Dynasty* (New York: Welcome Rain Publishers, 2007).
Shuhui Yang and Yunqin Yang, *Sanyan Stories: Favorites from a Ming Dynasty
Collection* (Seattle: University of Washington Press, 2014).

In addition, there are three different English-language translations
of Feng Menglong's other major novel:

Nathan Sturman, *The Sorcerer's Revolt* (Rockville: Silk Pagoda, 2008).
Lois Fusek, *The Three Sui Quash the Demons' Revolt: A Comic Novel Attributed
to Luo Guanzhong* (Honolulu: University of Hawai'i Press, 2010).
Patrick Hanan, *Quelling the Demons' Revolt: A Novel from Ming China* (New
York: Columbia University Press, 2017).

Other works of Feng Menglong translated into English include:

Hua-yuan Li Mowry, *Chinese Love Stories from "Ch'ing-shih"* (Hamden: Archon Books, 1983).

Ōki Yasushi and Paolo Santangelo, *Shan'ge, the 'Mountain Songs:' Love Songs in Ming China* (Leiden: Brill, 2011).

Hsu, Pi-ching, *Feng Menglong's Treasury of Laughs: A Seventeenth-Century Anthology of Traditional Chinese Humour* (Leiden: Brill, 2015).

Translations of Key Source Texts:

Kingdoms in Peril makes use of a very wide range of early Chinese texts, not all of which have been translated into English. Feng Menglong occasionally quotes the most important classical works, in particular the *Book of Songs* (*Shijing*):

Arthur Waley, *The Book of Songs* (London: George Allen and Unwin, 1937).

Bernhard Karlgren, *The Book of Odes* (Stockholm: Museum of Far Eastern Antiquities, 1950).

The historical texts used as a basis for this novel include *Spring and Autumn Annals* (a text on which Feng Menglong was a specialist), as well as *Zuo's Tradition, Stratagems of the Warring States* (*Zhanguo ce*), and compilations focusing on specific locales such as *Lost Histories of Yue* (*Yuejue shu*). *Kingdoms in Peril* also makes extensive use of the first of the official dynastic histories, *Records of the Grand Historian* (*Shiji*), which covers the history of China up until the reign of Emperor Wu of the Han dynasty (r. 141–87 B.C.E.):

William H. Nienhauser, ed., *The Grand Scribe's Records* (Bloomington: Indiana University Press, 1994–).

James Crump, *Chan-kuo Ts'e* (Ann Arbor: University of Michigan Center for Chinese Studies, 1996).

Olivia Milburn, *The Glory of Yue: An Annotated Translation of the Yuejue shu* (Leiden: Brill, 2010).

Stephen Durrant, Wai-yee Li, and David Schaberg, *Zuo Tradition/Zuozhuan: Commentary on the "Spring and Autumn Annals"* (Seattle: University of Washington Press, 2016).

A number of the source texts used by Feng Menglong are yet to be translated, or the translations were produced so long ago that they are unavailable outside specialized academic libraries. However, since the writings of Sun Bin were rediscovered in the 1970s, they have been translated a number of times:

Ralph Sawyer, *Sun Pin: Military Methods* (Boulder: Westview Press, 1995).

D. C. Lau and Roger Ames, *Sun Bin: The Art of Warfare: A Translation of the Classic Chinese Work of Philosophy and Strategy* (New York: State University of New York Press, 2003).

There is also a full translation into English of the key work of statecraft to survive from the court of the First Emperor of Qin:

John Knoblock and Jeffrey Riegel, *The Annals of Lü Buwei* (Stanford: Stanford University Press, 2000).

Careful study of these source texts indicates just how faithful Feng Menglong was to the chronology they provide and attests to the accuracy with which he tried to convey the key events of this historical period. However, unlike the text that inspired the production of this novel, *Kingdoms in Peril* does not generally include later overtly fictional material, and so the myths, legends, prophetic dreams, encounters with ghosts, and so on that scatter the pages are in fact taken from the ancient sources.

The Curse of the Bao Lords

Chapter One

King Xuan of Zhou hears a children's song and kills a woman for no good reason.

Grandee Du becomes formidable as he protests his innocence.

When Heaven and Earth emerged from primordial confusion,
The Three August Ones and the Five Gods held power in turn.
After this era of enlightened rule, yielding to the better man ceased,
As the Xia, the Shang, and Zhou dynasties succeeded each other.
The Xia lasted for four hundred years, the Shang for six hundred,
But the Zhou kept on flourishing, longer than any other.
When a worthless king moved to the east to escape the Dog Rong,
He destroyed the fabric of the state and placed his kingdom in peril.
Factions were formed in a fight for supremacy.
In Linzi, the first of the hegemons was shot to power.
Jin and Chu, Song and Qi each took it in turn to lock horns;
When storms blow through the forest, not a single branch is safe.
When the Five Hegemons failed, Wu and Yue took over,
As King Goujian rose to power by the shores of the Eastern Sea.
When the Six Ministers partitioned Jin, the Tian family usurped Qi;
The Seven Kingdoms divided into the Horizontal and Vertical Alliances.
Su Qin and Zhang Yi sent these Seven Kingdoms to their doom,
And twelve bronze statues were set up in Xianyang.
The Zhou capital at Luoyang was overgrown with weeds, its treasures lost,
The last survivors of its ruling house exposed to killing frosts.
Who could stop the killing? Who could restore peace?
Even the clearest streams ran turbid, as endless fighting boiled.
When will we see the golden age of Kings Cheng and Kang again?
These mountains and rivers hold fast to a legacy of greatness.

You will have heard how the Zhou dynasty held the position of the Son of Heaven after the attack of King Wu on the evil last king of the Shang dynasty, and how Kings Cheng and Kang inherited the throne, both of them stamping their authority on the regime and building on the accomplishments of their predecessors. There were also the Duke of Zhou, the Duke of Shao, the Duke of Bi, the Grand Historian Yi, and so on—a group of wise ministers who supported the government and who were so skilled in the demands of civil administration that they had no need for the arts of war, whereby wealth was abundant and the people were at peace. After King Wu of Zhou, the throne was handed down through eight generations until it reached King Yi, a man who was neither sober nor correct, and the feudal lords gradually became strong. In the ninth generation, the throne passed to King Li, a violent and unrestrained man, who in the end was murdered by the people of the capital. This was the beginning of a great change, which would affect the people of China for a thousand years and more. Once again it was thanks to the sympathy and backing of the Duke of Zhou and the Duke of Shao that Crown Prince Jing was established as the monarch, taking the title of King Xuan. He was a true Son of Heaven, both enlightened and principled. He employed wise ministers such as Fang Shu, Shao Hu, Yi Jifu, Shen Bo, and Zhongshan Fu. They reinvigorated the righteous government that had existed under Kings Wen, Wu, Cheng, and Kang, and the Zhou house flourished brightly.

There is a poem that attests to this:

As Kings Yi and Li succeeded each other, the kingdom lost direction.
Any plans to employ wise men and reform the government had to
    wait for King Xuan.
If the Gonghe regency had destroyed the rule of the flourishing
    Central States,
How could the Zhou dynasty have survived for eight hundred years?

Although it is said that under the rule of King Xuan righteous government prevailed, in fact he did not write out prohibitions in royal red ink, nor were the wise words of sage-kings written on the lintels and posts of every door as during the reign of King Wu. Although it is said that the Central States flourished, they did not reach the great heights achieved during the time of King Cheng and King Kang, when barbarian peoples from the far south presented pheasants as tribute to the

Zhou king. In the thirty-ninth year of his reign, the Jiang and the Rong peoples rebelled against his rule. King Xuan rode on a chariot and personally led the campaign against them, only to be defeated in engagement after engagement at Qianmu, suffering a terrible loss of war chariots and soldiers. He planned to raise another army for a second campaign but was alarmed to discover that the number of soldiers was insufficient, and so he personally conducted a census of the population at Taiyuan.

This Taiyuan is the place now called Guyuanzhou, and it bordered upon the territory of the Rong and the Di peoples. Taking a census means that the population registers of a particular place were checked to see how many people there actually were, and how many chariots and horses, how much grain and fodder, in order to make proper preparations before going on campaign.

The prime minister, Zhongshan Fu, came to court to remonstrate with him, but the king paid no attention. Later on, someone wrote a poem about this:

> Why were these dogs and pigs able to humiliate us with their sharp
>   blades?
> When you use a pearl to shoot a sparrow, both suffer severe injuries.
> The authority of the august one was flouted but he could not be
>   avenged;
> He decided to personally count his people, but it was all in vain.

When King Xuan returned from conducting his census of the population at Taiyuan, when he was not far from the capital at Hao, he hurried on by chariot and thus by traveling day and night he soon reached the city. Suddenly he saw a group of a couple of dozen little children in the marketplace, clapping their hands and singing, and they all harmonized. King Xuan then stopped his royal chariot and listened to them. Their song ran:

> The moon will rise,
> The sun will set.
> A rush quiver and a wild-mulberry bow
> Will bring destruction on the kingdom of Zhou.

King Xuan was appalled by these words, and so he ordered the charioteer to arrest and interrogate the children. At that time the children were terrified and ran away, so he was only able to grab hold of one very young and one slightly older child, who were made to kneel below the royal chariot. King Xuan asked them, "Who composed these words?"

The younger of the two children was too frightened to speak, so it was the older child who replied: "They were not composed by any of us. Three days ago there was a child in a red dress who came to the marketplace and taught us to recite these four lines. I do not know why. Afterwards it spread, and all the children in the city came together to sing it, not just here."

"So where is the child in the red dress now?" King Xuan asked.

"I do not know where the child has gone since teaching us the song," he replied.

King Xuan was silent for a long time, and then he yelled at the two children to go away. Immediately he summoned the official in charge of the marketplace to promulgate the command: "From this point on, if a child sings this song, the parents and older siblings are also guilty of treason." That night he went back to his palace without a word.

The following day at the early morning court, the Three Dukes and the Six Ministers met below the main audience hall of the palace, where they bowed and made obeisance. King Xuan recited to the assembled ministers the children's song that he had heard the day before. "How do you explain these words?"

Shao Hu, the minister of rites, replied, "Wild mulberry is the name of a type of tree, a variety of mulberry that grows in the mountains. It can be used to make archery bows; that is why the song mentions a wild-mulberry bow. Rush is the name of a plant, and it can be woven to make quivers, therefore the song speaks of a rush quiver. In my humble opinion, I am afraid that the country is destined to suffer warfare."

The prime minister, Zhongshan Fu, then offered his opinion to the monarch. He said: "Bows and arrows are weapons used by the country in times of war. Your Majesty has recently been conducting a census in Taiyuan in the hope of taking revenge upon the Dog Rong. If you do not demobilize your troops, I am afraid that you will suffer the calamity of losing your crown."

Although King Xuan did not say anything, he nodded his head in agreement. Then he asked, "These words come from a child in a red dress. Who can this child be?"

The Grand Astrologer, Bo Yangfu, offered his advice to the monarch. "The baseless rumors generated on the streets and in the marketplace are what is known as gossip. Heaven has warned Your Majesty of the oncoming disaster by ordering Mars to take the form of a child and compose these words, teaching them to all the other little children and creating a children's song. At best this song reflects the fate of Your Majesty alone, at worst it is linked to the rise and fall of the dynasty. Mars is a fiery planet, and so it is colored red. Today we have gossip concerning the destiny of our kingdom; this is the way in which Heaven is warning Your Majesty of the danger you are in."

"If I now pardon the Jiang and Rong for their crimes," King Xuan asked, "and demobilize the troops in Taiyuan, as well as ordering that all the bows and arrows stored in the armories should be burnt, and then command that no one should be allowed to make or sell them in the whole country, will disaster be averted?"

"I have observed the movements of the heavens, and the signs are already there," Bo Yangfu replied. "It seems as if the problem derives from Your Majesty's harem, for bows and arrows do not threaten you from the lands beyond the passes. It is certain that in a later generation there will be a queen who brings the calamity of civil war to this country. Besides which, the children's song said: 'The moon will rise, the sun will set.' The sun represents the king, while the moon is womankind. For the sun to set and the moon to rise, this means that *yin* will advance and *yang* will retreat, and thus it is clear that a woman will interfere in the government of the country."

King Xuan then asked: "I have placed my wife, Queen Jiang, in charge of the Six Palaces, and she has behaved with the utmost wisdom and circumspection. The concubines and junior wives that she presents to me have all passed through stringent selection procedures. So where will this dangerous woman come from?"

"The words of the song said 'will rise' and 'will set,' so nothing is going to happen for the foreseeable future," Bo Yangfu replied. "Furthermore, 'will' is a word that expresses future potential, rather than something that will definitely happen. If Your Majesty now averts disaster by instituting reform, this will naturally turn bad luck into good, in which case you will not need to go to the extreme of burning your bows and arrows."

King Xuan listened to his advice, but was not sure what to think. He then stopped the audience and drove back to the palace in a foul mood.

Queen Jiang welcomed him, brought him into her chambers, and seated him carefully. Afterwards, King Xuan told her what the ministers had said, reporting everything verbatim to his wife. Queen Jiang said, "Something very strange has happened in the harem; I was just about to report it to you."

"What strange thing?" the king asked.

"There is an old palace maid now in her mid-fifties, who served His Late Majesty," Queen Jiang replied. "Having been pregnant for more than forty years, last night she gave birth to a baby girl."

King Xuan was astounded and asked her for details: "Where is the baby?"

"I thought this was an evil omen," Queen Jiang said, "and so I ordered the servants to wrap the baby in a straw mat and throw her into the Qing River twenty *li* away from the city."

King Xuan immediately had the old palace maid summoned and asked her about the pregnancy. The old palace maid knelt and said: "I have heard that in the final years of King Jie of the Xia dynasty the guardian spirits of the city of Bao transformed themselves into two dragons that came to His Majesty's audience hall, their mouths dripping with drool and foam. Suddenly they spoke in the words of men and said to King Jie, 'We are the two lords of the city of Bao.' King Jie was terrified and wanted to kill the two dragons. He ordered the Grand Astrologer to perform a divination about it, but it was not auspicious. Then he wanted to expel them and ordered a second divination, but this too was not auspicious. The Grand Astrologer spoke. 'A guardian spirit has come to earth which is definitely a wonderful omen for Your Majesty. Why not ask their permission to collect their spit and store it? Spit is the pure essence of a dragon, and if you keep it safe it will bring good luck to you in the future.' King Jie ordered the Grand Astrologer to perform yet another divination, and this time it was extremely auspicious. Then he laid out silk cloths and presented a sacrifice in front of the dragons, collecting their drool in a golden basin, which he placed inside a cinnabar casket. Suddenly a great storm blew up, and the two dragons flew away. King Jie ordered that this casket should be stored in the treasury. From the time of the Shang dynasty to the present day has been six hundred and forty-four years, and the throne has passed to twenty-eight kings in succession.

"For the last three hundred years of our Zhou dynasty, no one ever opened the casket to look at it. In the last year of His Late Majesty's reign, the casket emitted a bright light, and the official in charge of the treasury reported this to your father. His Late Majesty asked, 'What is inside the casket?' The official in charge of the treasury took out the little docket that recorded the whole story of how the dragon's spit came to be collected and presented it to the king. Your father ordered him to bring it for inspection. A servant broke open the golden casket, and with his hands he lifted up the golden bowl to present it to the king. Your father stretched out his hand to take the bowl, but in a moment of clumsiness he dropped it on the floor, and the dragon's spit that it held spilled out across the audience chamber. Suddenly it metamorphosed into a tiny little turtle, while the bowl went spinning across the floor of the hall. The servants chased the turtle, which headed straight to the harem, where in an instant it disappeared. At that time I was just twelve years old, and purely by chance I stepped on the turtle's footprint, which caused an unusual sensation within my body. After that my belly gradually swelled, as if I were pregnant. His Late Majesty thought it was most strange that I became pregnant without a man, and so he imprisoned me in the Cold Palace, where I have spent the last forty years. Last night my belly became painful, and then suddenly I gave birth to a baby girl. The palace guards did not dare to cover this up, and so they reported it to the queen. The queen said that this was an evil omen, which could not be kept within the confines of the palace. She ordered the servants to take the baby away and abandon her by the riverbank. My crime merits death!"

"This is a matter pertaining to a previous dynasty; it has nothing to do with you," King Xuan said. Then he told the old palace maid to withdraw. Afterwards, he ordered the palace servants to go to the Qing River to discover what had happened to the baby girl. Not long afterwards, the servants returned and reported, "She has already been carried away by the river waters." King Xuan saw nothing to be concerned about in this.

At court early the following morning, he summoned the Grand Astrologer, Bo Yangfu, and told him the story about the dragon's spit.

Then he said, "The baby girl has already died in the river, so would you mind performing a divination about this, to see if the evil omens have dispersed or not?"

When Bo Yangfu had finished performing a milfoil divination, he presented the following oracle to His Majesty: "Where there are tears there is also laughter; where there is laughter there are also tears. A sheep is swallowed by a ghost; a horse is chased down by a dog. Beware! Beware! The wild-mulberry bow and the rush quiver."

King Xuan could not understand what this meant. Bo Yangfu explained his opinion to the king: "If we extrapolate from the twelve animals of the zodiac, Sheep is the zodiac sign Wei, and Horse is the zodiac sign Wu. Tears and laughter are indications of sadness and happiness, and they must refer to the events of the years Wu and Wei. According to my reading of events, although the evil omen has been expelled from the palace for now, it has not yet been eliminated completely."

King Xuan listened to his explanation and was obviously unhappy. Then he issued a command: "Search every house inside and outside the city for the baby girl and find her, dead or alive. Anyone who assists with her capture or who hands her over to the authorities will be rewarded with three hundred lengths each of cloth and silk. If someone has taken her in and looked after her without coming forward, and if one of the neighbors turns them in, that person will be rewarded accordingly, and the offender and his whole family will be executed."

He ordered Grandee Du Bo to take sole command of overseeing the implementation of this edict. Given that the words of the oracle had also mentioned the wild-mulberry bow and the rush quiver, he also commanded Junior Grandee Zuo Ru to keep an eye on the officials who toured the marketplace, to prevent anyone from either making or selling bows made from the wood of mountain mulberries or quivers woven from rushes. Anyone who disobeyed would be put to death. The head of the market officials did not dare to relax his vigilance, so he led a company of guards around to explain everything clearly and make sure everyone was obeying the regulations. At that time the people in the city respected the prohibition, but the people from the surrounding countryside were not yet aware of it.

When they made their rounds on the following day, they found a woman carrying several basket-work quivers, which she had woven out of rushes. There was a man with a dozen or more mountain mulberry-wood bows on his back, walking just behind her. This couple lived in a distant village, and they had hurried to get to the market by midday to trade, since they had to come to the city to sell their wares. Before they had even entered the gates to the city, they came face to face with the official in charge of the marketplace. He shouted, "Arrest them!" His subordinates first laid hands on the woman. The man saw that something was terribly wrong, so he threw his mulberry bows to the ground and ran away as fast as he could. The official put the woman in chains and, gathering up both the mulberry bows and the rush quivers, presented all of them to Grandee Zuo Ru.

Zuo Ru pondered the situation and said to himself, "The bows and quivers correspond exactly to the words of the children's song. Furthermore, according to the Grand Astrologer, the woman is the danger; so, having arrested her, I can go back and get further directions from His Majesty."

Keeping quiet about the man, he simply informed the king about the woman disobeying the prohibition on making or selling wild-mulberry bows and rush quivers, for which the punishment was death. King Xuan ordered the woman to be beheaded. The bows and quivers were burned in the marketplace, as a warning to anyone else thinking of either making or selling them. That was the end of the matter.

Later on, someone wrote a poem about this:

> Without good government you cannot prevent dynastic change.
> Who interpreted this children's song to justify the death of an
>   innocent woman?
> In going wrong, there are many opportunities to put right your
>   mistakes,
> But in such circumstances, what minister would dare to speak out?

Let us now turn to another part of the story. The man who had been selling mulberry-wood bows and who ran away as fast as he could at the first sign of trouble had absolutely no idea why the authorities would want to arrest him and his wife. He was desperate to discover what had happened to her, and so that night he stayed just ten *li* from the city walls. The following morning, someone told him: "Yesterday a woman was arrested by the North Gate for contravening the ban on the manufacture and sale of mulberry bows and rush quivers, and she was killed immediately after her arrest." This was how he found out that his wife was already dead.

Wandering through a desolate and uninhabited wasteland, he cried a few bitter tears. However, he was pleased to have escaped with his own life, and so he walked away as quickly as he could. Having traveled for about a further ten *li*, he arrived at the banks of the Qing River. Far in the distance he could see a flock of birds flapping around and cawing. As he got closer and looked more carefully, he could see that there was a bundle wrapped in a straw mat floating in the middle of the river. The birds were all pecking at it with their beaks, nudging it along and cawing, and it seemed as if they were moving it closer to the bank.

"How strange!" the man said to himself.

He waved away the flock of birds and waded out into the river to pick up the bundle. When he got to the grass-covered bank, he opened it up to have a look. The first thing that greeted him was a cry, for there was a baby girl inside. He thought to himself, "I have no idea who could have abandoned this baby, but given that a flock of birds were trying to get her out of the water, she must be a very important person. If I take her home and raise her, there will certainly be something in it for me when she grows up." Then he took off his shirt and wrapped up the baby, holding her in his arms as he thought about where he could go to hide. He headed for the city of Bao, where he hoped he could find sanctuary with a friend.

An old man wrote a poem about the strangeness of this baby girl's birth:

> A pregnancy delayed for forty years,
> Plucked safely from the waters after three days' immersion.
> Born to be a scourge for the kingdom,
> Royal laws have never overcome the will of Heaven!

After King Xuan had executed the woman selling mulberry bows and rush quivers, he thought that he had responded to the words of the children's song, and he felt entirely secure. As a result, he never spoke again about sending troops out from Taiyuan. No one even mentioned these events for many years. However, in the forty-third year of his reign, the time had come for a great sacrifice. King Xuan was spending the night in the Purification Palace, and after the second watch the sound of people's voices gradually faded into silence. Suddenly he saw a beautiful young girl walking slowly from the west, and she went straight into the main hall of the palace. King Xuan was worried that her presence would contravene the rituals of purification and fasting, and so he yelled loudly. He bellowed at his entourage to arrest her, but not a single person responded. The girl seemed completely unafraid. She walked into the main ancestral temple, where she laughed heartily three times and cried loudly three times. Then, without haste and without alarm, she tied up in a bundle the tablets dedicated to the seven main ancestral spirits commemorated in the shrine before walking away to the east. The king got up and was just about to go in pursuit himself, when suddenly he woke up with a start; the whole thing had been nothing but a dream! His heart was thumping erratically, but nevertheless he forced himself to go to the ancestral temple and perform the proper rituals. When the nine rounds of offerings had been presented, he went back to the Purification Palace and changed his clothes. He ordered his entourage to secretly summon the Grand Astrologer, Bo Yangfu, and informed him of what he had seen in his dream.

"Surely Your Majesty cannot have forgotten the words of the children's song three years ago?" Bo Yangfu asked the king. "I stick to my original opinion: the king will suffer because of a woman; the signs of evil have not been eradicated. There was a reference in the riddle to laughter and to tears, and now Your Majesty has had this dream, which corresponds exactly."

"We have already executed the woman," King Xuan said. "Is that not enough to extirpate the prophecy concerning the mulberry bow and rush quiver?"

"The Way of Heaven is mysterious indeed; it is only after the event that you realize the significance of what has gone before," Bo Yangfu said. "How can a peasant woman affect the destiny of nations?"

King Xuan sighed deeply and said nothing.

Suddenly he remembered that three years before he had ordered Grandee Du Bo to keep an eye on the situation in the marketplace and investigate the ill-omened girl, but nothing had been reported to the authorities. After the sacrificial meats had been distributed, King Xuan returned to court, and all his officials gave formal thanks for the gift of food that they had received.

"Why have you not reported all this time about the baby girl?" King Xuan asked Du Bo.

"When I searched, I found no trace of her," Du Bo informed His Majesty. "It was my belief that, since the woman we arrested had answered for her crimes, the children's song had already been fully borne out. I was deeply worried about the prospect that further investigations would merely result in a reign of terror for the people of the capital, and so I called a halt."

King Xuan was absolutely furious. "If this is indeed the case," he demanded, "then why did you not report it to me? Clearly you have been disregarding my orders, doing just what you feel like. I do not need disloyal ministers like you!" He then shouted at his guards: "Drag this man out of the Chao Gate and behead him, as a warning to the populace!"

All the officials present were so terrified that their faces went chalk-white. Suddenly, one of their number burst out from the midst of the serried ranks. Running forward, he grabbed hold of Du Bo, shouting: "No! No!"

King Xuan recognized him; it was Junior Grandee Zuo Ru, a good friend of Du Bo, who had come to serve at court with him. Zuo Ru kowtowed and said, "I have heard that under the sage-king Yao, the world suffered nine years of floods, but that this did not prevent him from becoming a god; in the reign of Tang, there were seven years of drought, which did not harm his rule as king. Given that the natural cycles of Heaven cannot be interrupted, how can you believe that human beings can be evil omens? If Your Majesty kills Du Bo, I am afraid that the whole country will be given over to rumors of witchcraft, and when foreigners hear about this, they are going to despise us. I beg that you will show him mercy."

"You have disobeyed my orders for the sake of your friend; this means that you value your friend more than your king!" King Xuan exclaimed.

"If my king is right and my friend is wrong, then it is proper that I should turn my back on my friend and obey my king," Zuo Ru proclaimed. "If my king is wrong and my friend is right, then it is correct that I offend against my king and agree with my friend. Du Bo has committed no crime that can possibly merit the death penalty, so if Your Majesty kills him, everyone will think that you are completely stupid. If I do not remonstrate and try and stop you, then everyone will believe that I am not loyal. If Your Majesty is determined to kill Du Bo, then I ask your permission to die with him!"

King Xuan's rage was unabated, and he said, "For me to kill Du Bo is a matter of as little moment as digging out a weed; do not waste your time and energy!" Then he gave his instructions: "Behead him now!" The guards dragged Du Bo out of the Chao Gate, and a short time later his head was displayed at the foot of the steps. Zuo Ru beat his breast and wept, but before King Xuan could order his execution, he drew his sword and committed suicide by cutting his throat.

A bearded old man wrote a lament:

> Wise Zuo Ru!
> In this direct remonstrance, his argument was faultless.
> At once he agreed with his friend,
> And offended against his king.
> He resigned his job for the sake of principle,
> He cut his throat out of true friendship.
> His name has been esteemed for a thousand years;
> He has become a model for later generations.

The following day, when King Xuan heard that Zuo Ru had cut his own throat, he began to regret his hastiness in having Du Bo killed. It was thus in a somber and depressed mood that he returned to the palace. That night, he could not sleep, and his mind was confused; subsequently, he had great difficulty in putting his words in the right order, and there were many things that he had forgotten, to the point where he was no longer capable of holding court. Queen Jiang realized that he was seriously sick, and so she never said a word of criticism again. In the autumn, in the seventh lunar month of the forty-sixth year of King Xuan's reign, he gradually recovered and felt sufficiently well that he wanted to go out of the city for some hunting to cheer himself up. His attendants promulgated his command: "The minister of works must prepare the chariots; the minister of war must arrange for a military escort; and the Grand Astrologer must conduct a divination to select an auspicious day."

When the time came, the king rode out on his fine chariot drawn by six stallions, with Yi Jifu on his right hand and Shao Hu on his left hand. The flags and standards fluttered and the arms and armor appeared in serried ranks, as all were gathered in the eastern suburbs before they set out. Near the eastern suburbs there was a flat plain, overgrown with wild plants, which had frequently been used for hunting before. It had been a long time since King Xuan had last set foot outside the palace, and so he felt in a very good mood. He issued commands to build a stockade and told the guards: "One, you are not allowed to trample the crops. Two, you are not allowed to burn the trees for firewood. Three, you are not allowed to disturb the people who live here. It does not matter whether you capture a great deal of game or very little, it should all be handed in and then everyone can have their fair share. Any selfish behavior will be investigated and punished."

Once these commands had been given, they all set out to do their best, each competing to be the finest hunter. Advancing and retreating, the men moved in a great circle. The charioteers exerted all their skill in driving left and right; in front and behind, the bowmen displayed their abilities. Eagles and dogs took advantage of every opportunity to bring down their prey, while the rabbits and foxes scuttled this way and that in terror. The bows resounded, and thus flesh and blood were torn apart; the arrows arched towards their targets, and fur and feathers flew into the air. The battue progressed, building pace. King Xuan was absolutely delighted. The sun had already begun to set in the west when he gave the order to call off the hunt. The officers and men picked up the animals and birds of every variety that they had captured and went home singing songs of triumph.

Before they had gone more than three or four *li*, King Xuan felt rather dizzy, perched high up on the royal chariot. Suddenly he caught sight of a little chariot far away in the distance, driving straight towards him. There were two people standing on the chariot, and they each held a vermilion bow in one hand and a scarlet arrow in the other. They shouted at King Xuan, "Your Majesty, it has been a long time since last we met!"

King Xuan stared at them fixedly: one was Senior Grandee Du Bo, and the other was Junior Grandee Zuo Ru. King Xuan was terribly alarmed, but when he rubbed his eyes, they and their chariot simply disappeared. He questioned the men standing to his right and left, but they both said that they had seen nothing. King Xuan was at once frightened and alarmed. Just at that moment Du Bo and Zuo Ru reappeared, driving the little chariot just in front of the king's horses. King Xuan was absolutely furious and shouted, "Insolent ghosts, how dare you come and interfere with my travels!"

He drew his precious sword Tai-e and brandished it into space. However, Du Bo and Zuo Ru both shouted back, "Deluded, unjust king! You have failed to institute good government and compounded your errors by executing innocent men! Today your time is up! We have come specially to avenge those you have unjustly put to death! Prepare to die!"

Before they had even finished speaking, they flexed their vermilion bows and drew back their scarlet arrows, sighting their shots straight at King Xuan's heart. King Xuan screamed and fainted on the royal chariot. Yi Jifu was so alarmed that his legs gave way beneath him, while Shao Hu's eyes were practically starting from their sockets. The king's attendants fussed around, making a ginger soup in the hope of bringing him round. Given that he never stopped crying with pain, they drove back as quickly as they could to the city, whereupon they carried King Xuan into the palace. The soldiers did not wait to receive their rewards but went home. Truly, this was a case of the rats leaving the sinking ship.

An old man wrote a poem, which reads:

Vermilion bows and scarlet arrows gave them the appearance of gods;
Amid a great army they galloped with spinning wheels.
Even a king who kills an innocent man should expect to be punished,
Not to mention an ordinary man in a village!

If you do not know what happened next in the life of King Xuan, READ ON.

Chapter Two

*The people of Bao atone for their crimes
by handing over a beautiful woman.*

*King You lights the beacon fires to tease
the feudal lords.*

When King Xuan went hunting in the eastern suburbs, he met the
ghosts of Du Bo and Zuo Ru, who demanded his life. He consequently
got sick, forcing his return to the palace. Every time he closed his eyes,
all he could see was the pair of them. Knowing that he would not
recover from this, he refused all medication. Three days later, his illness
had become critical. By that time, the Duke of Zhou had long since
retired from office on account of old age, and Zhongshan Fu was dead.
Therefore, all King Xuan could do was to summon his old advisors Yi
Jifu and Shao Hu to ask them to look after his son. The two ministers
went straight in to stand in front of the king's bed, whereupon they
bowed their heads and asked after his health. King Xuan ordered his
attendants to help him up, and, leaning against the embroidered cush-
ions, he spoke to his two advisors. "Thanks to the abilities of my ministers, I have ruled now for forty-six years. I have campaigned in the
south and done battle in the north, and I have brought peace to the
lands within the four seas. I never expected to be laid low by disease!
Even though Crown Prince Gongni is now no longer young, his character is still unformed. I hope that you, as my ministers, will do your
utmost to support him; please do not allow the dynasty to decline!"

His two advisors bowed their heads and accepted his commands.

Just as they left the palace gates, they met the Grand Astrologer, Bo
Yangfu. Shao Hu spoke privately to him. "After hearing the words of

the children's song, I said that I was afraid that in the future there would be some disastrous change brought about by a bow and arrow. Now the king has met a powerful ghost that grabbed a vermilion bow and scarlet arrow and shot him. That is why his illness has become critical. The signs all correspond: His Majesty will die!"

"At night I observe the patterns of the Heavens, and an evil planet is currently lying in ambush beyond the starry wall of the Purple Palace constellation," Bo Yangfu declared. "The state will suffer further disasters, for the king's death alone is not sufficient to warrant such portents."

"Heaven determines the lives of men, but men can also change what happens in the heavens," Yi Jifu remarked. "Lords just say that Heaven determines what happens and ignore the importance of men, but where does that leave us?"

When these words had been spoken, each went his own way. Not long afterwards, all the government officials gathered by the gates of the palace to ask after His Majesty's health. When they heard that the king was sinking, they did not dare to go home. That night, His Majesty died. Queen Jiang issued an edict summoning the old ministers Yi Jifu and Shao Hu to take control of officialdom, and they brought Crown Prince Gongni into the palace to begin the funeral ceremonies; thus he was crowned King You in front of his father's coffin. The following year was declared the first year of his reign. He appointed his wife, the daughter of the Earl of Shen, as queen, and their son Yijiu became the crown prince. He granted his father-in-law, the Earl of Shen, the new title of Marquis of Shen.

A historian wrote a poem praising the revival in the fortunes of the Central States effected during the reign of King Xuan:

Good King Xuan!
His virtue encompassed the entire age.
He struck awe into the inhabitants of the wilderness,
He reformed the regime in response to an evil omen.
With ministers like Zhongshan Fu outside and Queen Jiang inside the
    palace,
He instituted an era of prosperity and good government.
He dealt with the poisonous relics of his father's regime,
Thus the flourishing Central States set out their pennants.

Queen Jiang was overwhelmed with grief, and not long afterwards she too died.

King You was a violent and vicious man, and his temper was unstable. Although he was supposed to be in mourning, he carried on partying with his unsuitable friends; he drank wine and ate meat, seemingly lacking any feeling of sadness over the death of his father. After Queen Jiang passed away, he became even more shameless and lost himself in the pleasures of music and sex, never paying the least attention to the affairs of government. The Marquis of Shen remonstrated repeatedly, but he never listened, and so in the end he went back to his home. This is when the Western Zhou dynasty finally came to an end, as the last old ministers Yi Jifu and Shao Hu died one after the other. King You appointed the Duke of Guo and the Duke of Zhai in their stead, and Yi Jifu's son, Yi Qiu, took the final position as the third of the Three Dukes: the most senior officials serving in the government of the country. These men flattered the king while being greedy for titles and coveting ever-greater wealth. Everything that the king wanted, they would do without delay. At that time the only worthwhile senior member of the government was You, Earl of Zheng, who held the position of minister of education, but King You did not trust him.

One day King You did decide to hold court, and the prefect of Mount Qi reported: "The three rivers—the Jing, the Yellow River, and the Luo—have all suffered earthquakes on the same day."

King You laughed and said, "For mountains to crumble and lands to suffer earthquakes is all perfectly normal. Why bother to report it to me?" Then he dismissed the court and went back to the palace.

The Grand Astrologer, Bo Yangfu, took Grandee Zhao Shudai by the hand. He sighed and said, "Those three rivers all have their source at Mount Qi. How can they have suffered an earthquake? In the past, the Yi and the Luo Rivers ran dry and the Xia dynasty fell; later on, the Yellow River ran dry and the Shang dynasty collapsed. If these three rivers have all suffered an earthquake, then their source will be blocked. The pressure of these blocked waters will cause the mountain to crumble. Mount Qi is where the founder of the house of Zhou was born. If this mountain crumbles, can the destruction of Zhou be far behind?"

"If there is going to be a change of dynasty, when will it happen?" Zhao Shudai asked.

Bo Yangfu counted on his fingers and said, "Within the next ten years."

"How can you be so sure?" Shudai questioned him.

"Doing many good deeds creates good luck, accumulated evil causes disaster," Bo Yangfu said. "Besides which, ten is a 'full' number."

"The Son of Heaven is uninterested in government and he employs wicked men," Zhao Shudai said. "However, I have a job that allows me to speak to His Majesty, so I must do my very best to warn him of the dangers."

"I am afraid that there is no point," Bo Yangfu said.

The two men spoke in private for a long time, and someone immediately reported their conversation to Shifu, Duke of Guo. Shifu was afraid that Shudai would go into the palace and remonstrate, revealing all his evil deeds, so he went straight into the harem and related everything to King You concerning the secret discussions between Bo Yangfu and Zhao Shudai. He claimed that they were plotting to bring down the dynasty and misleading the populace with their wicked words.

"Silly men often speak wildly about the government," King You said. "This is just the same as a marsh releasing its vapors into the air. I really can't be bothered to listen to this!"

Zhao Shudai possessed a deep sense of loyalty and justice, and he repeatedly tried to get into the palace and remonstrate with the king, but he was never able to do so. A few days later, the prefect of Mount Qi again sent a letter to report to the king: "The three rivers have all run dry, Mount Qi has collapsed, and the homes of countless people have been buried by the landslides." King You was completely unconcerned. Instead, he ordered his attendants to find beautiful women with whom he could fill his harem.

Zhao Shudai then came forward and said, "A mountain has collapsed and rivers have run dry. This is a sign that something has gone very wrong deep within the system. The heights have collapsed into the valleys, which is an ill omen for the country. In addition to that, Mount Qi is where the Zhou dynasty began, and now this place has been destroyed overnight and become bare. Such a thing cannot have come about for a minor cause! Now is the time to improve the government, give succor to the people, and seek out wise men to assist in your administration, for there is still time to avert disaster. Surely it is not right that you pay no attention to gathering clever and talented men, but instead are seeking out beautiful women."

"The dynasty established its capitals at Feng and Hao many, many years ago," Shifu, Duke of Guo, said to the king. "Mount Qi is like a cast-off shoe; what has it to do with us? Shudai has long behaved with extreme arrogance, seizing every opportunity to slander and defame others. I hope that Your Majesty will investigate this situation with dispatch."

"Shifu is indeed correct," King You proclaimed. Then he ordered that Shudai be stripped of his offices and sent into exile in the wilds.

Zhao Shudai sighed and said, "You should not go into a city that is torn apart by violence; you should not try to live in a place suffering a civil war. I cannot bear to just sit and watch the Western Zhou dynasty go the way of the Shang."

Someone wrote a poem bewailing this:

A loyal minister fleeing civil war set out for the north.
As generations passed, they were assimilated, gradually fixing their
    ambitions on the east.
Since antiquity old servants have been an important resource;
Once the trustworthy and wise have gone, the kingdom is bereft.

Grandee Bao Xiang, visiting from the city of Bao, heard that Zhao Shudai had been forced into exile, and he quickly rushed to court to remonstrate with the king. "Your Majesty does not seem to be worried about the coming disaster, but instead you devote your energies to alienating your wisest advisors. I fear that the country will be left at the mercy of others and the state altars are in danger."

King You was absolutely furious and ordered that Bao Xiang should be thrown into prison. From that point onwards, there was no way to remonstrate with the king, and his cleverest advisors left his service.

· · ·

It has already been described how the man who sold mulberry-wood bows and quivers of woven rushes picked up the ill-omened baby girl and took her to the lands of Bao, where he tried to raise her. She needed milk to drink, and by a fortunate coincidence he encountered the wife of Si Da, whose own baby girl had just died, so he gave her some cloth and begged her to take in the infant he had found. She grew up there and took the name Bao Si. The years passed until she was fourteen, at which point she was grown up, looking just like a girl of sixteen or seventeen who has reached the age of pinning up her hair. Her beautiful eyes were framed by elegantly arched eyebrows; her lips were carmine and her teeth were white, her hair like a raven cloud and her hands as pale as jade. She had a face as beautiful as flowers and as lovely as the moon; she was a woman for whom men would sack cities and overthrow kingdoms. Given that Si Da lived in a poor and isolated hamlet and that Bao Si herself was still very young, even though she was so outstandingly good-looking, she had still not been betrothed.

Bao Xiang had a son named Hongde, who by chance was placed in charge of collecting taxes—a circumstance that took him to this humble village. Purely by coincidence, Bao Si left the house to draw water, and not even her rustic clothes and unkempt appearance could conceal the fact that she was incredibly beautiful. Amazed, Hongde wondered, "How can such a poor village produce such a lovely lady?" Then he made a secret plan: "My father is imprisoned in the fortress at Hao, and even though three years have passed he still has not been released. If I present this woman to the Son of Heaven, perhaps it will atone for my father's crime."

First he made inquiries of a neighbor about her name and surname; then, he went home to discuss the matter with his mother: "My father annoyed the king by his direct criticisms, but this is not a crime that cannot be pardoned. The Son of Heaven is a vicious and debauched man who has brought beautiful women from every corner of the realm in order to fill his harem. Si Da's daughter is exceptionally lovely, and if I buy her with silks and gold, we can request that Father be released from prison. This is the same plan as that used by San Yisheng to get King Wen out of prison."

"If this plan has a chance of working, I would not begrudge any amount of gold and silk," his mother said. "You must go as soon as you can!"

Hongde went in person to the Si house and struck a deal with Si Da to buy Bao Si for three hundred lengths of cloth, after which he took her home. Having bathed her in perfume, fed her the finest delicacies, clothed her in embroidered silks, and instructed her in proper behavior, Hongde took her to Hao. There he began by bribing the Duke of

Guo with gold and silver, begging him to transmit the following message to the king: "Your humble servant, Bao Xiang, knows that his crime merits death ten thousand times. Xiang's son, Hongde, understanding that once his father is dead he can never return to life, has specially sought out a beautiful woman whose name is Bao Si, to be presented to Your Majesty in atonement for his father's crimes. I hope that Your Majesty will pardon him."

When King You heard this message, he ordered that Bao Si should be brought to the audience chamber. When she had made her obeisance, King You looked at her carefully. She was indeed of exceptional beauty, such as he had never seen before. She was so lovely that she was the cynosure of all eyes. The king was very pleased. Even though women had been presented from every corner of the kingdom, none could hold a candle to Bao Si. Without even letting Queen Shen know, he established Bao Si in her own separate palace and issued a royal edict pardoning Bao Xiang and releasing him from prison. He even restored his official position and titles. That night with great delight, King You slept with Bao Si for the very first time, an event that does not need to be described here. From that point on they were never apart; they drank from the same cup and ate from the same plate. For ten days in a row, the king did not hold court, leaving his ministers to wait at the gates of the palace, none of them even catching a glimpse of His Majesty. They all sighed and left. This happened in the fourth year of King You's reign.

There is a poem that attests to this:

He found a great beauty and made her famous throughout the realm;
From poverty and hardship overnight she was promoted to share the royal bed.
A playboy king overwhelmed with lust
Was unaware of the disaster long-concealed in the dragon's saliva.

From the moment that King You first laid hands on Bao Si, he was bewitched by her beauty. They lived together in the Agate Tower, and for three months at a stretch the king did not even enter Queen Shen's palace. Naturally, people were quick to tell Queen Shen exactly what was going on, and she could not restrain her anger. One morning she decided to take all the palace ladies in a delegation to the Agate Tower, where she found King You and Bao Si sitting curled up together. Neither of them even got up to acknowledge her arrival. Queen Shen could not keep quiet at this insult, and so she cursed Bao Si, saying, "Who is this diseased whore who dares to ignore palace regulations!"

King You, afraid that Queen Shen might actually physically attack the girl, shielded Bao Si with his own body, speaking up for her: "This is my new beauty, and I have not yet decided what rank to give her. That is the reason why you have not seen her before. You should not be so angry."

Queen Shen carried on cursing her for a while and then left, still in a towering rage.

"Who was that who just came in?" Bao Si asked.

"That was the queen," King You explained. "Tomorrow you should go and pay your respects to her."

Bao Si said nothing to this, but the following day she did not go to pay court to Her Majesty.

Meanwhile Queen Shen, living in her palace, became deeply depressed. Crown Prince Yijiu knelt before her and said, "Mother, you hold the rank of the head of the Six Palaces, so why are you so unhappy?"

"Your father favors Bao Si, completely disregarding the distinctions between wife and concubine," Queen Shen said. "If in the future that little whore gets her way, neither you nor I will know a moment's peace!"

Then she explained all the details to the crown prince of Bao Si's failure to come to pay court and her refusal to get up and welcome her. Without being aware of what she was doing, she began to cry. The crown prince said, "There is no problem. Tomorrow is the first day of the month, and so my father will have to hold court. You, Mother, can then take some of the palace servants to the Agate Tower to pick flowers, which will certainly lure that nasty little bitch out of the building so that she can look at you. I will then give her a real beating to teach her to know her place. If Father is upset about it, he can blame me; it is nothing to do with you."

"My son, do nothing precipitate," Queen Shen exclaimed. "Let this pass and we will discuss what to do another time."

The crown prince left the palace in a rage. Thus they passed a night.

The next morning, sure enough, King You held court, and all his ministers were present to congratulate him on the occasion of the first day of the month. The crown prince intentionally sent a couple of dozen palace servants to the Agate Tower, ordering them to go round picking any flower that they fancied and not to ask anyone for permission. Some servants came out of the Agate Tower to stop them, saying, "These flowers are grown for His Majesty, and Consort Bao enjoys them, so stop wrecking the place before you are severely punished."

"We have been ordered to do this by the crown prince, for he wants to present these flowers to Her Majesty the queen," the other palace servants said. "How dare you try to prevent us?"

At this point the two sides started shouting at each other, which alarmed Bao Si so much that she came out to discover for herself what on earth was going on. She was absolutely furious and wanted to show them who was in charge. Just at that moment, the crown prince suddenly emerged from hiding. Bao Si had no means to protect herself, so when the crown prince came upon his enemy, he glared at her. Then he took a step forward and grabbed her by the hair, shouting curses at her. "Nasty little bitch, who the hell do you think you are? A nameless piece of scum flaunting yourself shamelessly and wanting to be a royal! Today I am going to teach you your proper place!"

He balled up his fist and started punching her. After he had hit her a few times, a number of the palace ladies started to get frightened, for they were worried that King You might blame them. They all knelt down and kowtowed, imploring: "Please forgive her, your highness! Please think of the effect that this will have on your father!"

The crown prince began to be afraid lest he had caused her life-threatening injuries, and so finally he stopped. Bao Si swallowed her humiliation and crept back to the Agate Tower in terrible pain. She was perfectly well aware of the fact that the crown prince was doing this for his mother's sake, and the tears coursed down her cheeks. Her attendants tried to cheer her up by saying, "Don't be so sad, my lady, His Majesty will deal with this himself."

Just as they were speaking, King You dismissed the court and went back to the Agate Tower. When he caught sight of Bao Si's disheveled hair and the tears sparkling in her eyes, he asked, "My darling, why have you not combed your hair today?"

Bao Si took hold of King You's sleeve and began to cry. She said, "The crown prince brought some palace servants to the tower to pick flowers. I did nothing to annoy him, but the moment the crown prince caught sight of me he started hitting and cursing me. If it were not for the intervention of some of the palace ladies, I really think he would have killed me. I hope that Your Majesty will see justice done!"

When she had finished speaking, she burst into tears and wept bitterly. King You now understood exactly what had happened. He told Bao Si, "You did not pay court to his mother; that is why things have been brought to this pass. This is an expression of Her Majesty's enmity; it is not the crown prince's own idea. Don't blame the wrong person."

"The crown prince is taking revenge for his mother and he wants me dead," Bao Si said. "Naturally it does not matter at all if I die, but having been favored by you, I find that I am now two months pregnant. This is not about me; it is about my baby's life! Please let me leave the palace, to save both my life and the baby's!"

"My darling, please look after yourself," King You said. "I know how to deal with this situation."

That very day, he issued a royal edict saying: "Crown Prince Yijiu is a brave but unprincipled man who has behaved with conspicuous lack of filial piety. I therefore exile him to the state of Shen, in the hope that his grandfather, the Marquis of Shen, can teach him to mind his manners! The crown prince's senior tutor, his junior tutor, and the other officials in his train have proved completely useless in instructing him, and so henceforth they are dismissed from their offices."

The crown prince wished to go to the palace to plead his innocence, but King You told the guards at the gates not to announce his arrival. Therefore, he could only get on his chariot and go to the state of Shen for good.

Queen Shen, wondering why she had not seen the crown prince come to the palace for such a long time, asked around among the palace servants. In the end, she discovered that he had already been exiled to Shen. Friendless and alone, she missed her son terribly and hated her husband, but she had no choice other than to pass her days concealing her tears.

. . .

After nine months of pregnancy, Bao Si gave birth to a baby boy that King You loved deeply. He gave him the name Bofu, meaning "Senior," to signal his intention of disinheriting his son by the queen in favor of this child by a woman of humble birth. However, without some adequate excuse it would be difficult to do so. Shifu, Duke of Guo had guessed the king's wishes in this matter, and so he discussed the situation with Yi Qiu before secretly getting in touch with Bao Si.

"The crown prince has been exiled to his mother's people," he explained, "so the moment has come for Bofu to be proclaimed the heir to the throne. With Your Ladyship speaking to His Majesty across the pillow on the one hand and the two of us supporting your son's candidature on the other, there is no reason to worry that we might fail."

Delighted, Bao Si replied, "I rely on the support from the two of you. If Bofu is proclaimed crown prince and does indeed come to the throne, then he will share the kingdom with you."

From this point on, Bao Si secretly promoted her faction among the king's entourage and spoke day and night of the shortcomings of Queen Shen. She had her ears and eyes inside and outside the palace gates. If the wind so much as blew and the grasses moved, she knew all about it.

Queen Shen at this time lived alone and spent her waking hours in tears. There was, however, one old palace servant who knew her troubles. She knelt before the queen and said: "Since Your Majesty misses the crown prince so much, why do you not write a letter and send it secretly to the state of Shen asking him to apologize to the king for his mistakes? If he is reconciled with the lord of ten thousand years, then he will be summoned back to the East Palace, and you will be reunited with him. Would that not be wonderful?"

"It is a lovely idea," Queen Shen said, "but I have no one to take my letter."

"My mother, Old Woman Wen, knows a little about medicine," the palace servant said. "If Your Majesty were to pretend to be ill, then you could summon her to the palace to examine you and ask her to take your letter out. My older brother could then get it to Shen. This is a plan with no flaws."

Queen Shen agreed with this and wrote her letter. It read:

The Son of Heaven is an unprincipled man and he trusts an evil bitch, with the result that we have been forced apart. Now the wicked slut has given birth to a son, so she is even more firmly in favor. You must send a letter to the king in which you pretend to be sorry for your mistakes:

"I realize what I have done wrong and I have turned over a new leaf, so I hope that Father will forgive me." If Heaven ordains that you return to court, we will be reunited and can make other plans.

When she had finished writing her letter, she pretended that she was ill and took to her bed, summoning Old Woman Wen for a consultation. Naturally, someone immediately reported this to Bao Si. Bao Si said, "This must be about sending information out. Prevent Old Woman Wen from leaving the palace and conduct a body search. Then we will know the long and the short of it."

When Old Woman Wen came to the Queen's Palace, her daughter, the palace servant, had already told her exactly what was required. Queen Shen pretended to stretch her wrist out to allow her pulse to be taken, but in fact she was taking the letter out from her pillow. She told the old woman, "This must go to Shen under cover of darkness, for any mistake will be fatal."

She ordered one of the maids to give her a length of brocade and a length of silk gauze. Old Woman Wen put the letter in her bodice and picked up the silks; thus she left the palace with a flourish. The eunuchs guarding the palace gate stopped her to inquire, "Where did you get this silk?"

"I gave Her Majesty the queen a medical examination, and they are a present from her," the old woman explained.

One of the eunuchs demanded: "Are you taking anything else out?"

"No," she said.

She clearly wanted to leave, but one of the other eunuchs said, "If we don't search her, how will we know if she is smuggling something else out or not?"

He then grabbed the old woman by the hand and spun her round. The old woman did everything she could to get away and appeared in a complete panic. The eunuchs were suspicious, and became more and more determined to search her. They came forward together and ripped open the bodice of her dress. The corner of the letter was then revealed. The woman and the letter that the eunuchs had found were then taken to the Agate Tower and brought before Bao Si. Bao Si opened the letter and read it, which made her absolutely furious. She ordered that Old Woman Wen should be locked up in an empty chamber, so that no news of this could leak out. She then took the two lengths of silk and ripped them into shreds.

When King You came to the palace, the first thing he saw was the pieces of gauze and the remnants of the brocade, and he asked where they had come from. Bao Si choked back her tears and said: "Ever since I was so unfortunate as to be brought to your harem and receive your favor, the queen has hated and been jealous of me. Things are even worse now that I have given birth to your son, for her enmity is even greater. The queen has just sent a letter to the crown prince, and the last line says that they 'can make other plans'; this must mean some kind of plot against my life and that of my son. I hope that Your Majesty will see justice done for me!"

When she had finished speaking, she gave King You the letter to read. The king recognized the queen's handwriting and asked about the messenger.

"Old Woman Wen is here right now," Bao Si explained.

King You then ordered that she be brought before him. Without a word, he drew his sword and cut her down.

An old man wrote the following poem:

Before the letter had even left the palace harem,
The frosty blade was already spotted with the blood of an innocent
    victim.
In other circumstances, had he asked what was going on,
Old Woman Wen would have been recognized as a loyal subject.

That night Bao Si made a great play of her charms and affection for King You. Then she complained, "My fate and that of my son is in the hands of the crown prince."

"I am still in charge here, so what can the crown prince do?" King You asked.

"Sooner or later the crown prince will succeed to the throne," Bao Si pointed out. "The queen is holed up in her palace right now, eaten up with hatred and cursing me day and night, so if she and her son come to power, Bofu and I will die and our bodies will be left to rot without even a decent burial!" When she had finished speaking, she burst into tears.

"I would like to divorce the queen and demote the crown prince, sending you to live in the Queen's Palace and Bofu to live in the East

Palace, but I am afraid that my ministers will not stand for it," King You said. "What can I do?"

"For a minister to listen to the king is a sign of his devotion, but for a king to listen to his ministers is just stupid," Bao Si pointed out. "Why don't you clearly express your intention to your most senior advisors and discuss the whole matter with the Three Dukes?"

"How right you are, my darling," the king said.

That very night Bao Si communicated her intentions to the Duke of Guo and Yi Qiu, so that they would be ready to say the right things at court.

The following day, when the ceremonies for the early morning court had been performed, King You summoned the Three Dukes and the senior ministers to the great hall of audience. He began by asking them, "Her Majesty the queen is jealous and eaten up with hatred, going so far as to curse me, which makes it inappropriate for her to keep the honor of being the wife of the Son of Heaven. Would it be legal for me to have her arrested and put to the question?"

Shifu, Duke of Guo, then advised the king: "The queen is the head of the Six Palaces. Even if she has committed a crime, you cannot have her arrested or interrogated in any way. If she really cannot maintain the dignity of the position that she holds, you ought to promulgate an edict of divorce and select another more suitable wife to fulfill the role of queen. This would indeed be a blessing for ten thousand generations!"

Yi Qiu also advised the king: "In my opinion, Bao Si would be a very suitable candidate. Given her virtue and purity, she would be able to take charge of the palace."

"The crown prince is in Shen," King You said. "If I divorce Queen Shen, how will the crown prince react?"

"I have heard it said that a mother derives her status from her son and her son likewise receives titles of nobility thanks to his mother," Shifu, Duke of Guo, explained to the king. "The crown prince has gone to live in Shen to avoid the consequences of his crimes, so the rituals which express the tender regard between a father and a son have long been discontinued. Besides which, if you divorce his mother, how can anyone expect you to keep him in place? We all support the investiture of Bofu as crown prince, and the whole country will rejoice at this resolution of the issue."

Delighted, King You immediately issued an edict sending Queen Shen to the Cold Palace and demoting Crown Prince Yijiu to the status of a commoner. He established Bao Si as queen and Bofu as crown prince. Anyone who tried to reason with the king was said to be part of Yijiu's faction and punished severely. This all happened in the ninth year of King You's reign. The civil and the military officials were all deeply disturbed by these events, but they knew that King You's mind was already made up and they would only get themselves killed to no purpose if they tried to do anything about it, so they simply kept their mouths shut.

The Grand Astrologer, Bo Yangfu, sighed and said, "Three warp threads have now been cut; the Zhou dynasty is doomed!" That very day he retired on the grounds of old age. There were many officials at this time who gave up their jobs and went home to till the fields. At court, only Yi Qiu, Duke Shifu of Guo, and Duke Yi of Zhai remained, together with a whole host of toadies and flatterers. King You spent day and night in the palace, enjoying himself with Bao Si.

Although Bao Si had been elevated to living in the Queen's Palace and monopolized the king sexually, she never ever laughed. King You wanted her to be happy, and so he summoned musicians to sound the bells and bang the drums, play the flutes, and pluck the strings, and the palace servants sang and danced as they came forward to present cups of wine. From start to finish, Bao Si maintained a countenance of stone. King You asked her, "If you don't enjoy music, my love, what do you like?"

"I don't like anything," Bao Si said. "However, I do remember that the other day when I ripped up the silk gauze and brocade, I found the sounds of rending very enjoyable."

"If you enjoy listening to the sound of silks being ripped to shreds, why on earth did you not mention it before?" King You responded. He ordered the official stores to send one hundred bolts of silk a day and ordered the strongest of the palace maids to rip them to pieces, just to entertain Bao Si. Strange to say, even though Bao Si clearly enjoyed the shredding of the silk gauze, she still never smiled.

"Why don't you laugh, darling?" King You asked.

"But I never laugh," Bao Si replied.

"I am determined to make you laugh, my love, even if only once," King You proclaimed. He then issued a command: "Anyone who can make Queen Bao laugh just once, regardless of whether they are part of the palace personnel or not, will be rewarded with one thousand pieces of gold."

Shifu, Duke of Guo, explained his plan: "Some years ago your father, His Late Majesty, was worried by the growing strength of the Dog Rong and became afraid that they would invade one day. Therefore, he had more than twenty beacon stations built below Mount Li. He also set up several dozen war drums. If there is ever an invasion by the barbarians, we should light the wolf beacons and send the smoke straight up into the sky; then the nearby lords will send their armies to come to our aid. If the great war drums are sounded at the same time, they will hurry to our side. The kingdom has been at peace now for many years, so the beacon fires have never been lit. If Your Majesty wants the queen to show her teeth in a smile, then you must take her to Mount Li. Light the beacons at night, and the relief armies of the feudal lords are sure to come. Seeing them rush to your assistance when there is no invasion will certainly make the queen laugh."

"That's a wonderful idea!" King You exclaimed.

He then traveled to Mount Li with Queen Bao. When it got dark, he had a banquet served at the Li Palace and issued a command for the beacons to be lit. It so happened that at that time You, Earl of Zheng, was at court, since as minister for education he was then the most senior official present. When he heard the command, he was very alarmed and rushed to the Li Palace to talk to the king.

"The beacons were built by His Late Majesty in preparation for some dire emergency—that is why the signal is trusted by the feudal lords," he said. "Now you want to light the fires for no good reason, to trick the feudal lords. If at some point in the future something goes wrong and you really need the beacons, the lords will not trust in them again. How will you then call troops to your side in a crisis?"

"The kingdom is at peace, so why should we need troops by our side?" King You demanded angrily. "The queen and I have come here to the Li Palace for this very purpose, and I am not going to call it all off. I want to have a joke at the expense of the feudal lords, and if at some point in the future there is an emergency, any problems will be my fault and not yours!"

Therefore, he paid no attention to the Earl of Zheng's remonstrance but lit all the beacon fires and banged the great drums. The sound of the drums was like thunder, and the flames from the fires lit up the sky. The lords of the Royal Domain believed that the capital city of Hao was under attack, so each of them appointed their generals and mobilized their troops, hastening that very night to Mount Li. When they got there, all they heard was the sound of flutes and pipes coming from the tower where King You and Bao Si were drinking wine and enjoying themselves. The pair sent someone out to apologize to the feudal lords, saying, "Thankfully we are not under attack; I hope you don't mind trekking all this way."

The lords just looked at each other, struck their flags, and went home. Bao Si was up in the tower. Leaning over the railing, she could see the feudal lords rushing forward and then hurrying back home, all for nothing. Without even realizing what she was doing, she clapped her hands and burst into peals of laughter.

"The smile of my beloved wife is the most beautiful thing in the world," King You remarked. "Shifu, Duke of Guo, has done well." Then he rewarded him with one thousand pieces of gold.

The expression still in use today, "buying a laugh with one thousand pieces of gold," is derived from this story.

There is a poem by an old man which describes how the beacon fires were lit to play a joke on the feudal lords:

> One night at the Li Palace music was played on the flutes and the pipes.
> The blaze of countless beacons lit the skies.
> Pity the troops rushing through the darkness,
> Only to earn a laugh from Bao Si.

When the Marquis of Shen heard that King You had divorced his queen and put Bao Si in her place, he wrote a letter of complaint to the king:

> In former times King Jie favored Mo Xi and brought about the fall of the Xia dynasty, while King Zhou favored Da Ji, which caused the decline of the Shang dynasty. Your Majesty now favors and trusts Bao Si, which has led you to demote your legitimate heir and establish a lesser princeling in his place. This strikes at the heart of the relationship between a husband and wife and ruins the affection that should exist between a father and son. The horrors perpetrated under King Jie and King Zhou will be seen again in our own times; the kind of disaster that overtook the Xia dynasty and the Shang cannot be far away. I hope that

Your Majesty will revoke this appalling edict, for perhaps that way the country will survive.

King You read this letter and then hit the table with his fist in a towering rage: "How dare this bastard speak such traitorous words!"

"The Marquis of Shen has seen the crown prince sent into exile, and he has been filled with resentment ever since," Shifu, Duke of Guo, said. "Now he has found out that the queen has been divorced and the crown prince has been demoted, so he is planning to rebel. That is the reason why he dares to criticize what you have done."

"In that case, what should I do?" King You asked.

"The Marquis of Shen actually never did anything for the crown; he received his title because his daughter was the queen," Shifu explained. "Now that she has been divorced and her son demoted from the position of crown prince, it would be entirely appropriate to strip the Marquis of Shen of his title, reducing him to his old rank of earl. You should also send troops to punish him for his crime, for that way you can avoid storing up trouble for yourself in the future."

King You followed his advice and issued an order stripping the Marquis of Shen of his title. He appointed Shifu as general with responsibility for gathering weapons and mustering chariots, for he wanted to raise an army to attack Shen.

If you want to know who won and who lost, READ ON.

Chapter Three

*The chief of the Dog Rong invades
the capital at Hao.*

King Ping of Zhou moves east to Luoyang.

After the Marquis of Shen sent his letter to the king, someone at the capital city of Hao was appointed to keep him informed of developments. This spy discovered that King You had invested the Duke of Guo as commander-in-chief and that he would be leading his troops to attack Shen any day now. He fled under cover of darkness to report to the Marquis of Shen. The Marquis of Shen was deeply alarmed, and said, "This is only a little country with a few soldiers; how can we possibly resist the might of the royal army?"

Grandee Lü Zhang came forward and said, "The Son of Heaven is an unprincipled man, and so he has divorced his wife and demoted his legitimate heir. Good and loyal ministers have lost their jobs, and everyone is furious about it. This is a situation in which His Majesty has become isolated. Now, the Dog Rong are a very powerful nomadic people, whose lands border with Shen. If you, my lord, were to send a letter to the chief of the Rong, asking to borrow troops to attack Hao, we can save the queen and force the Son of Heaven to pass his title to the former crown prince. This is the kind of thing that great ministers like Yi Yin or the Duke of Zhou would have done. There is a saying that goes, 'The one who acts first controls the situation'; so this opportunity cannot be lost."

"What you say is absolutely correct!" the Marquis of Shen replied.

He then prepared a cart full of gold and silk and sent an ambassador to deliver them, together with his letter about borrowing troops from the Dog Rong. They agreed that on a certain day they would attack Hao, promising that the Rong would be allowed to take all the gold in the royal treasuries and the silks in the storehouses.

The chief of the Rong declared, "The Zhou Son of Heaven has lost control of the government and his father-in-law, the Marquis of Shen, now summons me to kill this wicked man and support the establishment of the crown prince. This I am only too happy to do!" He then ordered the mobilization of fifteen thousand Rong soldiers, divided into three columns. A man named Bo Ding commanded the vanguard for the right-hand column, Man Yesu commanded the vanguard on the left-hand column, and the Rong chief himself commanded the central column. Their spears and sabers blocked the roads; their banners and pennons filled the sky. The Marquis of Shen mobilized his own army to assist. Like a great wave, they rolled towards Hao, killing everyone in their way. Before its inhabitants were even aware of the danger they were in, the royal city was under siege by three concentric circles of troops, and the water supply to the city had been cut.

When King You heard about this development, he cried out in great alarm: "Our plans are known and disaster has already overtaken us! The Rong army has moved before my troops have mobilized! What can I do?"

Shifu, Duke of Guo, presented his opinion to the king: "Your Majesty, you should send a man to Mount Li to light the beacons as soon as possible, for then troops from the lords are sure to come to your aid. If an attack is coordinated between those inside the city and those outside, we are sure to be victorious!"

King You did exactly what the duke suggested and sent a man to light the beacons. Not a single soldier came from any of the feudal lords' armies. The beacons having been lit once for fun, this time they assumed it was a joke as well, and so none of them mobilized their men. King You now realized that the relief troops were not coming. The Dog Rong attacked the city walls day and night.

"We do not yet know how strong these barbarians really are, so why don't you go and find out?" the king said to Shifu. "I ought to review our soldiers, and they can then follow in your wake."

The Duke of Guo was not a good general, but he had no choice but to follow orders. In command of a force of two hundred chariots, he opened the city gates and fought his way out. The Marquis of Shen had made camp on a hill, and when he looked out into the distance and saw Shifu coming out of the city, he pointed this out to the chief of the Rong, saying, "That bastard led the king astray and ruined the country; don't let him get away!"

The chief of the Rong heard this and shouted, "Who will capture him for me?"

"Let me go!" Bo Ding bellowed.

He brandished his sword, whipped up his horse, and rode straight ahead to take on Shifu, Duke of Guo. Before they had even crossed swords ten times, Shifu was beheaded in front of his chariot by a single sweeping stroke of Bo Ding's weapon. The chief of the Rong and Man Yesu then advanced together, killing everyone in the way. With screaming and shouting, they fought their way into the city. If they came across a house, they set fire to it; if they came across a person, they raised their swords. Even the Marquis of Shen was not able to prevent them; he could only look on helplessly.

The city was in complete chaos. Before King You had even had time to carry out his inspection of troops, he saw that things were going really badly. He found a small chariot that would carry Bao Si and Bofu, and they left together by the Servant's Gate to the palace. You, Earl of Zheng, the minister of education, caught up with them and yelled, "Do not be afraid, Your Majesty, I will protect you!"

They departed the capital by the north gate and hurried in the direction of Mount Li. On the way, they came across Yi Qiu, who said, "The Dog Rong have set fire to the palace, and they are looting the treasury and storehouses. The Duke of Zhai has already been killed by the rebel army!"

King You was both heartbroken and desperate. You, Earl of Zheng, again ordered that the beacons be lit. The smoke from these fires pierced the heavens, but relief troops still did not come. The Dog Rong army pursued them to the foot of Mount Li, where they surrounded the Li palace, shouting, "Don't think you are getting out of this, you bastard!"

King You and Bao Si were so frightened they collapsed into a heap together, crying in each other's arms. You, Earl of Zheng, entered and said: "Things are in a desperate state! I will do my very best to protect you, Your Majesty, as we fight our way out of this encirclement, even if it costs me my life. We should go to my country first and then make plans to retake the capital."

"It is because I ignored your advice, my cousin, that things have come to this pass," King You said. "Today the lives of my family are in your hands."

The Earl of Zheng instructed some people to start a fire in front of the Li palace, in order to confuse the Rong soldiers. He himself led King You out of the back of the palace to try and break through the siege. The Earl of Zheng held a long spear with which he opened a route in front. Yi Qiu, who was responsible for protecting Bao Si and her son, pressed close behind King You. Shortly after they set out, they found their path blocked by Dog Rong soldiers led by the junior general, Gu Lichi. The Earl of Zheng gritted his teeth in rage, and they started to fight. After they had crossed swords a few times, with one spear-thrust the Earl of Zheng forced Gu Lichi off his horse. When the Rong soldiers saw how valiant the Earl of Zheng was, they all ran away.

When the royal party had gone on for about half a *li*, they again heard shouting behind them. The commander of the vanguard for the right-hand column, Bo Ding, was leading a great host in pursuit. The Earl of Zheng ordered Yi Qiu to protect them in front, while he himself guarded the rear. They fought on every step of the way, only to have to sustain a charge by the Dog Rong armored cavalry, which split them into two groups. The Earl of Zheng was isolated at the center of a phalanx of enemy troops, but he was completely unafraid. His spear flashed in and out, and none of the enemy frontline was able to resist. The chief of the Dog Rong ordered archers to shoot from every direction. The arrows fell like rain, making no distinction between friend and foe. How sad that such a fine aristocrat should die that day under a hail of arrows!

The commander of the vanguard of the left-hand column, Man Yesu, quickly brought King You's chariot to a halt. The chief of the Dog Rong spotted his royal robes and jade belt and realized that this was King You. He cut him down as he stood on his chariot with a single blow from his sword. In the same way, he killed Bofu. Bao Si was so beautiful that he could not bear to slay her, hence he ordered up a light chariot to take her back to his yurt, where he could enjoy her himself. Yi Qiu was hiding among the baggage on the chariot, from whence he was dragged out by the Rong soldiers and beheaded.

In all, King You was on the throne for eleven years. The man who sold mulberry-wood bows and rush quivers plucked a cursed baby out of the Qing River and fled with her to the state of Bao: that baby was Bao Si. She bewitched her ruler with her wicked wiles, causing him to bully and maltreat his true wife, and that is what brought about King You's death and his country's collapse. It was just as the children's song of earlier days had said:

> The moon will rise,
> The sun will set.
> A rush quiver and a wild-mulberry bow
> Will bring destruction on the kingdom of Zhou.

Everything corresponds to this prophecy. The plans of Heaven were already fixed in the time of King Xuan.

Master Dong Ping wrote a poem which speaks of this:

> Every means was used to extract a smile from the woman in the palace,
> The flickering light from the beacon fires is now red, now black.
> Having alienated himself from the lords, the king has no choice,
> But to allow the state altars to suffer at the hands of barbarians!

The Recluse from Longxi wrote a poem titled "An Evaluation of History":

> One laugh from Bao Si at Mount Li resulted in the battle cry of the Dog Rong;
> The bows and arrows of the children's song have already proved to be true.
> After eighteen years this karmic debt has been paid;
> Who can be said to be responsible for this?

There is also a poem that describes how neither Yi Qiu nor any of his cohort died a good death, which is a warning to treacherous ministers. The poem reads:

> Cunning words and slanderous speeches deluded your ruler;
> All you thought of was wealth and honors to last your lifetime.
> The whole court was butchered and killed together,
> Causing you to be cursed as a wicked minister for a thousand years.

There is also a poem praising the loyalty of You, Earl of Zheng. This poem runs:

Shifu passed away and Yi Qiu died;
The brave Earl of Zheng was killed the same day, protecting his king.
Though all three can be said to have suffered for the Zhou royal house,
Which one of them left an honorable reputation?

When the Marquis of Shen arrived inside the city walls, he saw that the palace had gone up in flames. He quickly led the troops from his own country into the palace, where everything in his path had been ruined and destroyed. First he went to release Queen Shen from the Cold Palace. Then he went to the Agate Tower, but there was no sign there of King You or Bao Si. Someone pointed and said, "They have already left by the north gate." He guessed that they were heading for Mount Li, so he quickly set off in pursuit. On the way it just happened that he bumped into the chief of the Rong. As their chariots ran abreast, each asked after the other's labors that day. When the chief of the Rong said that the deluded monarch was already dead, the Marquis of Shen was deeply shocked; he said, "The only thing I ever wanted was to arouse His Majesty to a sense of his wrongdoing, I never thought that things would come to this pass! In later generations, those who are disloyal to their lords are sure to take me as a precedent!"

He immediately ordered his followers to collect the body and prepare to bury it with all proper ritual. The chief of the Rong laughed and said, "In spite of your high honors, you really are as silly as a woman!"

The Marquis of Shen then returned to the capital, where he prepared a banquet to be held in honor of the chief of the Rong. The treasures and jades in the treasuries had all been taken, but he still managed to gather together ten carts of silk and gold as a bribe, in the hope that this would satisfy the chief and he would go home. Who could have imagined that he thought that killing King You made him a matchless hero! His soldiers and horses occupied the capital and they ate and drank and made merry day and night, so it was clear that he had no intention of dismissing his troops and returning home to his own country. The populace all blamed the Marquis of Shen for this situation. There was nothing that the Marquis of Shen could do about it, so he secretly wrote three letters and sent his messengers to the three marchemont lords to arrange a meeting at which they would crown the new king.

*The three marchemont lords were Ji Chou, the Marquis of Jin, to the
north; Ji He, the Marquis of Wey to the east; and Ying Kai, the Lord of
Qin, to the West.*

He also sent someone to the state of Zheng to report the terrible
death of the Earl of Zheng to his son, Scion Juetu, instructing him to
raise an army to take revenge. Of this no more.

. . .

At that time, Scion Juetu was twenty-three years old, some six feet tall,
and of exceptionally handsome appearance. When he heard that his
father had been killed in battle, he was extremely upset and angry. He
put on a mourning robe with a plain white silk sash, and, in command
of an army of three hundred chariots, he sped overnight in the direction of the capital. Spies soon reported his movements to the chief of
the Dog Rong, who made his preparations. When Juetu arrived, he
wanted to advance his troops. The Honorable Cheng remonstrated:
"Our troops have advanced by forced marches, so they are exhausted
and have not yet had time to recover. We should build a fortified camp
and wait for the troops from the other lords to arrive. After that we can
join battle. This would be by far the best plan."

"Avenging my father is the most important thing," Juetu proclaimed. "Besides, the Dog Rong are arrogant and their ambitions
have recently been satisfied, so we can attack them while they are off
guard—thus we are sure to be victorious. If we have to wait until the
forces of the other lords arrive, surely this will cool our own troops'
ardor."

He commanded the chariots to drive straight towards the city
walls. No banners showed on top of the walls, and the war drums were
still; in fact, the place was completely silent. Juetu shouted loudly:
"You barbarians are like dogs or sheep! Why don't you come out of the
city and fight?"

There was no response from anyone on top of the walls. Juetu
ordered the left and right columns to get ready to attack the city. Suddenly they heard a loud noise from deep within the forest as the great
gongs resounded and a military column came forward to attack. This
was the chief of the Dog Rong's plan, for he had prepared an ambush
outside the city. Terrified, Juetu rushed to pick up his spear to do battle. Then the sound of massive gongs also arose from the top of the city

walls, and the gates were thrown open to allow a military column to attack from that side. In front of Juetu was the army commanded by Bo Ding, behind him was that of Man Yesu, and the two held him in a pincer movement. He could not withstand such an onslaught and ran away after suffering a terrible defeat. The Rong troops chased Juetu's forces for more than thirty *li*.

Juetu collected the scattered remnants of his army and told the Honorable Cheng, "I did not listen to your advice, and that has been extremely bad for us. Do you have any plan to offer now?"

"We are not far from Puyang now, and the Marquis of Wey is a trustworthy and competent man, so why not throw ourselves on his mercy?" the Honorable Cheng suggested. "If we can join forces with Wey, then we can achieve our object."

Juetu did as he said and ordered everyone to march towards Puyang.

After traveling for two days, they saw a great cloud of dust, and in the distance they observed countless soldiers and chariots advancing in an unbroken wall. In their very midst was an aristocrat wearing a brocade robe and jade belt—due to his age his hair was white, but his movements were still elegant and graceful. This lord was in fact Ji He, Lord Wu of Wey, and at that time he was already more than eighty years old.

Juetu stopped his chariot and called out loud: "I am Juetu, the Scion of Zheng. When the Dog Rong troops attacked the capital, my father was killed in battle. Now my army has also been defeated, so I have come specially to ask for your assistance."

Lord Wu made obeisance and replied, "Do not worry, we will do our very best to assist His Majesty. I have heard that the troops of Qin and Jin will soon arrive. There is no need to worry about those barbarians!"

Juetu yielded precedence to the Marquis of Wey, allowing him to go in front. Then he turned his chariot around and began the journey back to Hao.

When they were twenty *li* away from the city, they divided into two groups to make camp. He sent someone to find out news of the Qin and Jin armies, and the spy reported back: "To the west a bronze war drum is sounding loudly and the rumble of chariots can be heard, while high overhead there is an embroidered banner reading 'Qin.'"

"Although Qin is only an obscure minor state," Lord Wu remarked, "they are familiar with Rong customs and their soldiers are exceptionally fierce and good at fighting: the Dog Rong fear them greatly."

Before he had finished speaking, the spy who had gone north also reported back: "The Jin army has also arrived, and they have already made camp by the northern gate."

Lord Wu was very pleased, and said, "Now that troops have come from those two countries, everything is ready!"

Then he sent someone to greet the rulers of Qin and Jin. A short time later the two lords both arrived at Lord Wu's camp, and they asked after each other. The two lords saw that Juetu was wearing mourning, and asked, "Who is this?"

"This is the Scion of Zheng," Lord Wu said. He then explained how the Earl of Zheng had died and King You had been killed. The two lords sighed without cease.

"I am old now," Lord Wu continued, "but I am still a loyal subject, and so I have not refused to do my duty. I have forced myself to come here at some cost. I am relying on your assistance to get rid of these stinking barbarians. What plan do you propose?"

"The only thing the Dog Rong care about is stealing silk and gold and raping women," Lord Xiang of Qin said. "Now, although they know we have arrived, they are sure not to have taken proper precautions. Tonight at midnight we should attack in three directions at once—north, south, and east—but we will leave a gap at the west gate, so they can escape that way. However, the Scion of Zheng will have his troops waiting in ambush there, so that when they run away he can attack them. That way our victory will be complete."

"What an excellent plan!" Lord Wu exclaimed.

. . .

Inside the city, the Marquis of Shen heard that the armies of four states had arrived, and he was very pleased. Then he and Xuan, one of the sons of the Duke of Zhou, secretly discussed the situation: "We will wait for them to attack the city, and then we will open the gates for them."

They further encouraged the chief of the Rong to send home some of his booty of treasure, gold, and silk. He ordered Bo Ding, the commander of the left-hand vanguard, to divide up his soldiers to escort the train; this served to reduce the Rong chief's military strength. They suggested that the commander of the right-hand vanguard, Man Yesu, should immediately take his troops out of the city walls to meet the enemy. The chief of the Dog Rong thought that this was sensible advice, and so he followed it to the letter. He told Man Yesu to make camp just outside the eastern gate to the city, opposite the fortifications of the Wey army. They agreed to do battle the following day, but unexpectedly in the middle of the night, the Wey army entered their camp. Man Yesu immediately drew his sword and leapt onto his horse, advancing to tackle the enemy. But what could he do with the Rong soldiers running around in confusion everywhere? Though he waved his arms, he could not stop the rout, and so he had to run away with his men. The three marchemont lords then gave their battlecries and launched their attack upon the city. Suddenly the city gates opened. The chariots and horses of the three lords advanced together, and no one offered the slightest resistance. This was the Marquis of Shen's plan.

The chief of the Rong woke in alarm from his dreams. Leaping onto a bareback horse, he made his way to the western part of the city, followed by just a few hundred of his men. There he came across the Scion of Zheng, Juetu, who barred his way, forcing him to do battle. Just as things were at this critical pass, it so happened that Man Yesu arrived with the remnants of his defeated army; in the chaos and confusion of the fighting, the chief of the Rong was able to escape unharmed. Juetu did not dare to pursue him, so he entered the city and met up with the other lords. By then it was broad daylight, which meant that Bao Si was not able to follow the Dog Rong chief, so she hanged herself.

Master Hu Zeng wrote a poem on this:

First in her brocade silk bower she was called the mother of the
    nation,
Then in a stinking yurt she became a traitorous slut.
In the end she could not escape the pain of the tightening noose;
Would it not have been better to accept being a mere concubine?

The Marquis of Shen arranged a great banquet to pay tribute to the marchemont lords. However, the guest of honor, Lord Wu of Wey, put down his chopsticks, got up from his seat, and addressed the company as follows: "Today our king is dead and his capital is in ruins, so surely this is not the moment for his subjects to be feasting."

The assembled multitudes all stood, and said, "Please tell us what we should do!"

"The country cannot be left without a monarch even for one day," Lord Wu proclaimed. "Now the former crown prince is in Shen, and we should crown him as king. What do you think, my lords?"

"Your words, Marquis, bring solace to the spirits of our former kings: Wen, Wu, Cheng, and Kang," Lord Xiang said.

"I have done nothing in this great enterprise, but escorting His Majesty to the capital is something that I am happy to undertake, in the knowledge that it would meet with the full approval of my father, the late minister of education," Scion Juetu announced.

Lord Wu was very pleased and lifted his beaker in a toast. Then, using straw from the mat on which he was sitting as an official tally, he went to prepare his chariots. Every state wanted its soldiers to assist.

"We are not going to launch a punitive expedition against the enemy, so why do I need so many soldiers?" Juetu pointed out. "My own forces are enough."

The Marquis of Shen, "My state has three hundred chariots. I hope that you will allow them to lead the way."

The following day Juetu set off for the state of Shen, where he met Crown Prince Yijiu and told him that he had become king. Yijiu had stayed in Shen while all this was going on, and he had become deeply depressed, not knowing whether his grandfather had been successful or not in his mission. When suddenly he heard that the Scion of Zheng had been bestowed with a tally bearing the names of his grandfather, the Marquis of Shen, and the other lords, which commanded him to return to the capital, he was absolutely astounded. When he opened up the accompanying letter, he learned for the first time that King You had been killed by the Dog Rong. Since he still loved his father, he burst into loud sobs.

"As crown prince," Juetu said, "the security of the state altars should be your first concern. We hope that you will soon assume kingship and thus bring peace to your people."

"Everyone in the world now thinks that I am not a filial son!" Yijiu sobbed. "However, since the situation has come to this, I will just have to carry on alone."

Within a day, he arrived in the capital city of Hao. The Duke of Zhou was the first to enter the city walls, to clear out the palace. The king's grandfather, the Marquis of Shen, led the lords of Wey, Jin, and Qin, together with the Scion of Zheng and the civil and military officials, to go thirty *li* beyond the city boundaries to meet the new king. A diviner determined an auspicious day for him to enter the city. When Yiqiu saw the palace reduced to ashes and cinders, he cried bitterly. He first gave audience to the Marquis of Shen, to whom he issued his commands; then he changed into formal royal robes and reported his accession at the ancestral shrines, thus assuming the position of monarch. Yijiu took the title of King Ping of Zhou: the Bringer of Peace.

King Ping ascended to the main audience hall, and the assembled lords and officials completed their ceremonial congratulations. His Majesty summoned the Earl of Shen to come to the audience hall, where he said, "I was demoted and degraded: that I have been able to come to the throne is all thanks to the efforts of my grandfather. I therefore promote you to the rank of Duke of Shen."

The Earl of Shen declined, saying: "When rewards and punishments are not issued for good reasons, the government is not respected. That the city of Hao was destroyed and has been restored is thanks to the merit of all these lords in coming forward to help Your Majesty in a time of national crisis. I could not control the Dog Rong, and thus I have offended against our former kings, a crime that merits death! How could I dare to accept any reward?" He resolutely refused to accept the promotion three times. King Ping then ordered that he be restored to the rank of marquis.

Lord Wu of Wey reported to His Majesty: "Bao Si and her son received favors which exceeded all bounds, while Shifu, Duke of Guo, Yi Qiu, and the others led their ruler astray and brought disaster on the country. Even though they are dead, the nature of their crimes demands an exemplary punishment."

King Ping agreed with every point of this submission. Ji He, the Marquis of Wey, was promoted to become a duke. Ji Chou, the Marquis of Jin, was granted the lands of Henei as dependent territories. You, Earl of Zheng, died in the king's service, so His Majesty bestowed upon him the posthumous title of Huan, "The Brave." Scion Juetu succeeded to the title and became an earl; in addition to that, he was granted one thousand *qing* of land. The Lord of Qin originally just ruled a dependent territory, but now he was granted the title of Earl of Qin and numbered among the lords of the Zhou confederacy. Ji Xuan, the son of the Duke of Zhou, was granted the office of prime minister. Queen Shen was given the rank and honors of a dowager queen. Bao Si and her son Bofu were both posthumously demoted to become commoners. As for Shifu, Duke of Guo, Yi Qiu, and the Duke of Zhai, in remembrance of the merits of their ancestors in earlier generations and given that they had died in the king's service, though they were themselves stripped of all titles and honors, His Majesty agreed that these could then be inherited by their sons and grandsons. Placards were erected encouraging people to report crimes committed against them, and this consoled the suffering inhabitants of the capital. A great banquet was held for all the ministers and officials, at which everyone enjoyed themselves to the full, and then they went home.

There is a poem that testifies to this:

On this day the officials met their generous master.
Now everyone is overjoyed at the prospect of peace.
From this time on the court will be meritorious, virtuous, and
    magnanimous;
Our mountains and rivers can look forward to an era of florescence.

The following day the lords thanked the king for his munificence. King Ping issued further appointments, whereby the Marquis of Wey became minister of education, and Juetu, Earl of Zheng, became minister of personnel, and thus they stayed at court working in the government, assisting Prime Minister Ji Xuan. Only the lords of Shen and Jin said goodbye and left, on the grounds that their countries were too close to the Rong and the Di peoples. The Marquis of Shen saw that Juetu was of exceptionally fine appearance, and so he married his daughter to him: she was Lady Wu Jiang. Of this no more.

. . .

After the Dog Rong caused all this trouble in the capital of Hao, they came to know the routes into the Central States well. Even though they were forced out of the city by the marchemont lords, their rapacity was undaunted. They muttered among themselves about how hard they had worked for so little gain, and they were deeply angry. Therefore the chief of the Rong again raised an army and invaded the borders of Zhou, taking control of half the lands of Qi and Feng. Gradually they pressed closer upon the capital at Hao, so that the beacon fires were lit month after month. After the conflagration at the palace, barely half of it remained standing. These smoke-stained walls and broken columns formed a very bleak and miserable vista. King Ping found his treasuries and storehouses empty, so he could not rebuild the palace. Furthermore, he was afraid that sooner or later the Dog Rong would be back, and thus he formulated a plan to move the capital to Luoyang in the east.

One day, when the early morning court was over, he spoke to his assembled ministers. "In the past, my ancestor King Cheng fixed the capital here at Hao, but he also built the city of Luoyang. Why was that?"

With one voice, his ministers replied: "Luoyang is the center of the world; when tribute is brought from the four directions, all roads lead there. That is the reason why King Cheng ordered the Duke of Shao to build houses there and the Duke of Zhou to raise fortifications: he gave it the title of the Eastern Capital. The architecture of that city is exactly the same as that of Hao. Every year that there is a great interstate meeting, the Son of Heaven must travel to the Eastern Capital to meet the lords there. This makes governing the people much easier."

"Now the Dog Rong are pressing ever closer upon the city of Hao, threatening us with a terrible disaster," King Ping said. "I want to move the capital to Luoyang, how would that be?"

Prime Minster Ji Xuan offered his opinion: "Now the palace and gatehouses have been destroyed, and it is not going to be easy to rebuild them. It will put the people to great trouble and waste our money, which the populace is sure to resent bitterly. If the Dog Rong barbarians take advantage of this anger to attack, how will we defend the city? Moving the capital to Luoyang is indeed the best idea."

Both the civil and the military officials were worried about the Dog Rong. They all said, "The prime minister is right in what he says!"

Only the minister of education, Lord Wu of Wey, lowered his head and sighed deeply.

"My dear old minister of education, why are you the only one to say nothing?" King Ping asked.

Lord Wu then made his opinion known to the king: "I am nearly ninety years of age now, and thanks to the fact that Your Majesty still appreciates me, I have been ranked among the six most senior ministers. If I do not speak out about what I know, then I am disloyal to my king. If I go against the opinion of the majority in what I say, then I am not in harmony with my friends. However, though I can accept annoying my friends, I would never dare to be disloyal to my king. To one side of Hao are the lands of Xiao and Han, while to the other you have Long and Shu. It is enfolded by mountains and girdled by the river, with one thousand *li* of rich lands. Of all the auspicious sites in the world, none are better than this. Luoyang is indeed the center of the world, but it is sited on a flat plain with enemy territory on all four sides. The reason why our former rulers established two capitals was so that they could live in the Western Capital where they could satisfy the demands of governing the country, going to stay in the Eastern Capital only when they needed to prepare for royal progresses. If Your Majesty abandons Hao and moves to Luoyang, then I am afraid that this will fatally weaken the royal house."

"The Dog Rong have already seized control of Qi and Feng, and their power grows ever greater," King Ping pointed out. "My palace is in ruins; I have no means to make a majestic impression. The reason I propose a move to the east is because in fact I have no choice."

Lord Wu submitted his opinion: "The Dog Rong indeed have a wolfish nature; you cannot allow them into your home in any safety. When the Marquis of Shen borrowed troops from them, his plan failed, for in fact he was opening the door and inviting in robbers. He allowed them to burn the palace and murder the king. This is a crime that must be avenged. Your Majesty must now fix your ambition upon making the country strong, economizing on your own expenditure and demonstrating your love for your people, training your soldiers and developing their martial powers, for then you can invade to the north and campaign to the south just as our former kings did. You can then take the chief of the Rong prisoner and offer him in sacrifice at the shrines to your seven ancestors to wipe away our shame. If you decide to put up with this situation and swallow your anger, abandoning this place to the enemy, then they will take every foot of territory that we leave. I am afraid that they will gradually assert their authority, and their depredations will not stop at Qi and Feng. In the past, when these lands were ruled by the sage-kings Yao and Shun, they lived in thatched cottages with earthen floors. Likewise later, the sage-king Yu lived in a simple residence and did not believe himself to be humiliated thereby. Surely, for a majestic impression, the capital does not depend solely on the appearance of the royal palace, does it? I hope that Your Majesty will think this matter over carefully."

Prime Minister Ji Xuan then spoke again. "I think that what the old minister of education has said is correct in times of peace, but not in such a troubled age. Our former king neglected the government and destroyed the principles by which we have all lived, bringing wicked bandits down upon himself, but we are already in a position where we can draw a line under this matter and move on. Now Your Majesty has cleared away the ashes and debris of the invasion, and you have been formally invested as the monarch, but your storehouses and treasuries are empty, while your soldiers are weak and their morale is low. The populace is as terrified of the Dog Rong as they would be of wolves or tigers. If one day the Rong cavalry were to launch a lightning strike on us, the people's morale would simply collapse. Who here is willing to be responsible for that kind of national disaster?"

Lord Wu then spoke again. "The Marquis of Shen was able to summon the Rong, so he ought to be able to send them away again. Your Majesty should send someone to ask him, for he is sure to have a good plan."

While they were in the midst of this discussion, the king's grandfather, the Marquis of Shen, sent someone with an urgent message. King Ping opened the letter and looked at it. It read:

> The Dog Rong are making constant incursions and my country is on the verge of collapse. I beg Your Majesty to send troops to rescue us, for after all we are family.

"My grandfather cannot even take care of himself, so how can he help me?" King Ping exclaimed. "I have now made up my mind, we are moving east!"

He ordered the Grand Astrologer to select a day to move eastwards. Lord Wu of Wey said, "It is my job to act as minister of education, so I must point out that if you leave right away, the populace will simply panic. That would be an unforgiveable dereliction of duty on my part."

Then they set a date for the move and issued placards that informed the people: "If you wish to follow His Majesty on the move to the east, make your preparations quickly and we will all leave together." One of the court scribes prepared a text explaining all the reasons for the move, and His Majesty performed a sacrifice at the ancestral temple at which it was proclaimed. On the appointed day, the minister of rites carried the spirit tablets of the seven ancestral temples and rode in a chariot in advance of the rest. When Ying Kai, the Earl of Qin, heard that King Ping was moving east, he personally led his troops to protect the royal convoy. Too many ordinary people followed to be counted, helping the old along and carrying the babies.

Many years before, on the night when King Xuan was holding the great sacrifice, he dreamed that he saw a beautiful girl who laughed loudly three times and cried three times and then, without haste and without alarm, walked up to the spirit tablets of the seven ancestral shrines, gathered them up in a bundle, and walked away to the east. The three loud laughs represented Bao Si at Mount Li when she made fun of the lords rushing to the king's side in response to the beacons. The three cries were for the deaths of King You, Bao Si, and their son Bofu. The spirit tablets being gathered into a bundle and her walking east represented the move to the east that happened that day. Everything in the dream was borne out by subsequent events.

As the Grand Astrologer Bo Yangfu said, "Where there are tears, there is also laughter; where there is laughter, there are also tears. A sheep is swallowed by a ghost; a horse is chased by a dog. Beware! Beware! The mulberry bow and the rush quiver!"

The sheep being swallowed by a ghost referred to the fact that, in the forty-sixth year of his reign, King Xuan died after meeting a ghost; this happened in the year of the Sheep. The horse being chased by a dog referred to the invasion by the Dog Rong, which happened in the year of the Horse, which was the eleventh year of the reign of King You. This marks the end of the Western Zhou. That the calculations of Heaven had been settled in advance can be seen from the miraculously accurate prognostications of Bo Yangfu!

If you want to know what happened after the capital moved to the east, THE STORY CONTINUES . . .

An Incestuous Love Affair at
the Court of Qi

Chapter Four

The Marquis of Qi gives Lady Wen Jiang in marriage to Lu.

Lord Huan of Lu and his wife travel to Qi.

Let us now turn to another part of the story. Lord Xi of Qi had two daughters, both of whom were exceptionally beautiful. The older daughter, Lady Xuan Jiang, married into the ruling house of Wey, a story that will be told elsewhere. His younger daughter was Lady Wen Jiang, who was born with an elegant appearance and an exceptionally beautiful face; she was as pretty as a flower with lovely pale fragrant skin—a remarkable, kingdom-toppling beauty. In addition to that, she was both well-informed about contemporary issues and learned in history, and her speaking voice was very charming and persuasive: this earned her the epithet Wen, meaning "cultured." Meanwhile, Scion Zhuer of Qi was an alcoholic lecher. Even though he was called Lady Wen Jiang's older brother, they were actually born to different mothers. Zhuer was only two years older than Lady Wen Jiang, and they grew up together in the palace, playing with each other. When Lady Wen Jiang gradually grew up and revealed her full beauty, Zhuer was already caught up in affairs with other women, but seeing how lovely and clever Lady Wen Jiang was and how close the two of them had always been, he started to flirt with her. Lady Wen Jiang was not only innately vicious but also completely unrestrained by any sense of decency, so she would talk and joke with him, not avoiding even the most disgusting and degenerate gossip of the day. Zhuer was tall and strong, with a handsome face; a very good-looking young man. He and Lady Wen Jiang would have made a wonderful couple. Unfortunately, the two of them were born into the same family as brother and sister, so it was impossible for them to get married. However, whenever they found themselves together in the same place, they did not observe proper segregation between the sexes, but instead leaned against each other and held each other's hands: in fact, they touched each other all over. It was only because they were prevented by the presence of their entourage and the palace servants that they did not actually share the same bed. The Marquis of Qi and his wife spoiled their children and did nothing to control them, as a result of which their sons and daughters behaved like animals. They created the situation that led eventually to the assassination of Zhuer and civil war in Qi.

. . .

Lord Xi of Qi always praised Scion Zihu of Zheng as a great hero in front of Lady Wen Jiang, and when it came to discussions about a marriage alliance between the two of them, she was deeply pleased by the suggestion. However, afterwards she was informed that Scion Zihu had resolutely refused the match. This caused her to become depressed to the point where she became ill, running a temperature in the evening and shivering in the morning. Her mind was confused, and she just lay there in a daze. She did not really either sleep or eat.

There is a poem which testifies to this:

A sixteen-year-old, hidden deep in the harem, overwhelmed by
    emotion,
A love affair carves lines in her brow.
Only phoenixes escape the silken snare of love;
Wild birds and domestic fowl feel its pain.

Scion Zhuer, on the pretext of asking after her health, would from time to time burst into her chambers in the harem and sit by the head of the bed. He massaged and rubbed her body all over, asking where it hurt. However, since there were other people present, he went no further. One day, it happened that Lord Xi of Qi decided on the spur of the moment to go and see Lady Wen Jiang. When he saw that Zhuer was right there in her room, he upbraided him: "Even though you are brother and sister, the dictates of ritual propriety demand that you keep a proper distance from each other. In future you can send one of your palace servants to ask after her; you should not come yourself."

Zhuer agreed and withdrew. From this time onwards, the pair only saw each other rarely.

Not long afterwards, Lord Xi married Zhuer off to a daughter of the ruling house of Song, with junior wives taken from the states of Lu and Ju. Zhuer fell deeply in love with his new wife, so he became even further separated from his younger sister. Lady Wen Jiang was profoundly bored, living in seclusion within the harem, and she missed Zhuer a great deal, so her illness worsened. In fact, it was her emotions that were troubled, but she would have been hard put to explain this. As the saying has it: when a dumb man swallows his medicine, only he knows how bitter it is.

There is a poem that testifies to this:

> Spring flowers are drenched in spring rain,
> Deep in the harem a woman sleeps alone.
> Resentment has aged her,
> Her thoughts burn her breast.
> Often on bright moonlit nights,
> In her dreams she flies to meet her lover.

When Lord Huan of Lu came to power, he was already grown up but still not yet married. Grandee Zangsun Da came forward and said, "Since ancient times the rulers of states have become fathers by the age of fifteen. Now the position of Your Lordship's principal wife is still vacant, so in the future where will the heir to your title come from? This is not the proper way to show respect for the ancestral temples."

"I have heard that the Marquis of Qi has a favorite daughter named Lady Wen Jiang," the Honorable Hui said. "He wanted to marry her off to Scion Zihu of Zheng, but the match was broken off. Perhaps Your Lordship might like to ask for her hand in marriage?"

"I suppose so," Lord Huan said. That very day he sent the Honorable Hui to propose a marriage alliance with Qi.

Lord Xi of Qi requested permission to delay setting a date on the grounds that Lady Wen Jiang was unwell. However, the palace maids informed Her Ladyship that the Marquis of Lu had requested her hand in marriage. Lady Wen Jiang's depression resulted from having too much time to fret, but when she heard this news she gradually cheered up and her illness disappeared. When Qi and Lu met at Ji to deal with the problems with the Duke of Song, the Marquis of Lu requested the marriage alliance in person, and the Marquis of Qi then set a date to meet the following year. In the third year of the reign of Lord Huan of Lu, he went in person to the lands of Ying in order to meet the Marquis of Qi. Lord Xi of Qi was moved by his obvious sincerity and agreed to the alliance. The Marquis of Lu paid the bride-price right then and there, and the ceremony was performed with much greater pomp and circumstance than would usually have been the case. Lord Xi was delighted and agreed that the wedding would take place in the autumn, in the ninth month, and he would personally escort Lady Wen Jiang to Lu for the occasion. The Marquis of Lu then sent the Honorable Hui to Qi to collect the bride.

When Scion Zhuer of Qi heard that Lady Wen Jiang was going to be married abroad, all his old feelings for her revived. He sent one of the palace servants ostensibly to take a bunch of flowers to his younger sister, but in fact to deliver the following poem to her:

> The peach tree is covered in flowers, a beautiful red cloud.
> If the owner does not pluck them, the flowers float away to wither
>   and die.
> Alas! How sad!

Lady Wen Jiang got the poem and understood exactly what he meant by it. She replied with her own piece:

> The peach tree is covered in blooms, how lovely they are.
> If you do not pluck them now, how can it flower again next spring?
> Go ahead! Hurry up!

When Zhuer read her poem in response, he realized that Lady Wen Jiang reciprocated his feelings, and she was constantly in his thoughts.

A short time later the Lu ambassador, the Honorable Hui, arrived in Qi to collect Lady Wen Jiang. Since Lord Xi of Qi loved his daughter so much, he was going to escort her personally to her new home. When Zhuer heard this, he said to his father: "I have heard that my younger sister is going to be married to the Marquis of Lu. This is a good thing, given that Qi and Lu have been on friendly terms for many generations. Since the Marquis of Lu does not come in person to collect her, she must have a close relative to escort her. You, my father, have many matters of state to attend to, and it really is not easy for you to get away. Since I have nothing important to do, I am happy to represent you on this journey."

"I have already told him that I agree to escort the bride myself," Lord Xi replied. "How can I go back on my word?" Before he had even finished speaking, someone came in to report: "The Marquis of Lu has halted his cortege at the city of Xuan. He is waiting there specially to meet his bride."

"Lu is a state in which propriety and decorum reign, and they have come to the midpoint to meet the bride, so I don't have to go to the trouble of leaving the country," Lord Xi said. "I really have to go." Zhuer withdrew in silence, and Lady Jiang was also disappointed.

At that time, it was already the first week of the ninth month of autumn, and the date of the wedding was almost upon them. Lady Wen Jiang went to say goodbye to the denizens of her father's six palaces, and then she went to the East Palace to bid farewell to her older brother. Zhuer poured wine and served her himself, and they looked deep into each other's eyes, unwilling to let each other go. Given that his principal wife was present at this banquet, and that his father, Lord Xi, had sent some of his palace maids to attend them, they could not talk openly, but they sighed bitterly in secret. When the time came for them to part, Zhuer stood in front of the chariot and said, "Be careful, little sister, and do not forget your 'go ahead.'"

Lady Wen Jiang replied: "Look after yourself, brother. We are sure to meet again in the future."

Lord Xi of Qi ordered Zhuer to guard the capital while he personally escorted Lady Wen Jiang to Xuan to meet the Marquis of Lu. The Marquis of Lu performed all the proper ceremonies to greet his father-in-law, held a banquet for him, and gave lavish gifts to all the people in his train. Afterwards, Lord Xi said goodbye and returned home. Meanwhile, the Marquis of Lu took Lady Wen Jiang back to his capital where the wedding ceremonies would be performed. There were two reasons for such extensive ceremonies; one was that the state of Qi was a great country, the other that Lady Wen Jiang was of such exceptional beauty that the Marquis of Lu had fallen deeply in love with her. On New Year's Day they held an audience at the ancestral temple, and the wives of the grandees of Lu all came to pay court to the lord's principal wife. Lord Xi sent his younger brother, Yi Zhongnian, on a formal embassy to Lu to ask after Lady Wen Jiang. From this point on, the relations between Qi and Lu became very close.

An anonymous author wrote a poem that speaks of Lady Wen Jiang's marriage. This poem runs:

> People have always been suspicious of the relations between men and
>   women.
> How can brothers and sisters not be kept apart?
> Before leaving she told him to look after himself,
> Just encouraging him to ruin her reputation later on.

When Lord Xi of Qi died, Scion Zhuer was installed as Lord Xiang of Qi. At this time he requested a marriage alliance with Zhou. The Zhou king had agreed to this and sent the Marquis of Lu to preside over the marriage, for he could not attend in person when a royal princess was marrying a mere aristocrat. Lord Huan of Lu wanted to go to Qi in person to discuss the arrangements. Lord Xiang remembered his younger sister, Lady Wen Jiang, whom he had not seen for a long time, and he decided to invite her too. He sent an envoy to Lu to request that Lady Wen Jiang come in person. When Lady Wen Jiang saw the Qi ambassador come to meet them, she remembered how much she missed her older brother and decided to make the journey to Qi with Lord Huan, on the pretext of visiting her natal family. Lord Huan was besotted with his wife and did not dare to refuse her request.

Grandee Shen Xu remonstrated: "It has been a rule since antiquity that men and women should live separately. The rituals cannot be confused, for if they become unclear there will be social disorder. When a woman has married, if her father and mother are still alive, she is allowed to go home once a year to visit them. However, Her Ladyship's parents are both dead; there is no reason for a younger sister to pay a visit to her older brother. Lu is a state founded on the proper ritual principles—surely you are not proposing to do something that flies in the face of all our norms?"

Lord Huan had already made his promise to Lady Wen Jiang, so he did not listen to Shen Xu's remonstrance. The husband and wife set off together, and when their carriage arrived at the Luo River, Lord Xiang of Qi was already there. They greeted each other respectfully and made polite inquires, then rode on to the capital city, Linzi. The Marquis of Lu, in accordance with the instructions he had received from the Zhou king, discussed the marriage alliance between their two houses. The Marquis of Qi was absolutely thrilled, and he immediately held a great banquet in honor of the Marquis of Lu and his wife. Later on, Lady Wen Jiang went to the palace, saying that she wanted to meet her old friends in the harem. No one knew that Lord Xiang had already arranged for another private banquet to be set out in a secret room to show his love for Lady Wen Jiang. Over the wine cups, their eyes met in love and lust, without any thought for the proper principles of behavior. Thus this terrible thing happened. The two were so deeply in love that they could not bear to be parted, so she stayed overnight in the palace, and even when the sun was high in the sky, they lay in each other's arms and did not get up.

> There is an anonymous poem about this:
> A modest lady should preserve her delicate reputation,
> But having experienced these illicit pleasures, how could she live
>   without them?
> A moment of passion brought a thousand ages of shame,
> All because a younger sister fell in love with her older brother.

The pair were deeply in love and forgot all other considerations, sparing no thought for Lord Huan of Lu, all on his own outside the palace. The Marquis of Lu, deeply concerned at his wife's disappearance, sent someone to the palace gate to make a detailed inquiry. The report came back: "The Marquis of Qi has not yet married a principal wife, but he has a junior wife, Lady Lian, who is the cousin of Grandee Lian Cheng. She has already lost favor and has nothing to do with the Marquis of Qi. The reason that Lady Wen Jiang went to the Qi palace was because of her love for her older brother. She has not met with any of the harem ladies."

The Marquis of Lu knew that his wife was up to no good, and he wished that he could leap into the Qi palace and see for himself what was actually going on. Just then, someone came to report: "Her Ladyship has left the palace and is on her way back."

With difficulty, the Marquis of Lu settled himself for the wait. When she arrived, as if it were quite an ordinary question, he asked Lady Jiang, "Who were you drinking with last night in the palace?"

"With Lady Lian," she told him.

"At what time did you get up from your seats?"

"We had a lot to talk about after such a long separation and chatted until the moon shone high over the palace walls, so it must have been about midnight."

"Was your older brother present when you were drinking?"

"My older brother did not join us."

The Marquis of Lu laughed mirthlessly and continued his questions. "Doesn't he care about you? Why didn't he come and drink with you?"

"While we were drinking he did come and have one cup, but then he went away again."

"Why didn't you leave the palace when the party broke up?" the Marquis of Lu demanded.

"It was too late at night."

"Where did you sleep?"

"What on earth is the matter, that you feel it necessary to question me like this?" Lady Wen Jiang asked. "The palace has many empty rooms, and certainly there is plenty of space to put down a bed. As a matter of fact I spent the night in the Western Palace, in the rooms that I had when I was a little girl."

"Why did you get up so late today?"

"I had a hangover from last night, and so today when I got up and did my hair and makeup, it took much longer than usual."

"Who was present where you spent the night?"

"The palace maids."

"Where did your brother sleep?" the Marquis of Lu demanded.

Lady Jiang went quite pink, and said, "It really isn't the place of a younger sister to speculate on where her brother sleeps."

"But I am afraid that your brother is very interested in whereabouts you sleep!" the Marquis of Lu retorted.

"Why do you say that?"

"Since ancient times men and women have been segregated," her husband said. "I know that last night when you stayed in the palace you slept with your older brother. You can't fool me."

Lady Wen Jiang tried to excuse herself and then burst into tears, feeling deeply ashamed and humiliated. Lord Huan of Lu was at this time within the borders of Qi state, so there was nothing that he could do. Even though he was filled with anger and resentment, he had no way to express it. This really was a situation where anger had to be bottled up for his own safety. He sent a messenger to say farewell to the Marquis of Qi and then set off home, where he would deal with what had happened.

Lord Xiang of Qi was well aware that what he had done was very wrong, so when Lady Wen Jiang left the palace, he was worried about her and secretly ordered one of his trusted bodyguards, Shi Zhi Fenru, to follow her and find out what the Marquis of Lu said when he met his wife. Shi Zhi Fenru came back and reported: "The Marquis of Lu and his wife have quarreled with each other."

Lord Xiang was quite taken aback. "I knew that the Marquis of Lu would be sure to find out eventually, but I had no idea that it would happen so quickly!"

After a short time, he had the ambassador from Lu coming to say farewell, and he was sure that the truth had been discovered. Therefore the Marquis of Qi insisted that they all make a journey to Mount Niu together, where a farewell banquet would be held. He sent someone several times to insist upon this point, and in the end the Marquis of Lu had to give orders to drive his chariot out to the suburbs. Lady Wen Jiang was left behind at the guesthouse, in a deep depression.

Lord Xiang of Qi was very upset to think that Lady Wen Jiang was going home, and he was also afraid that henceforth the Marquis of Lu would treat him as a personal enemy, so he was determined to deal with this situation. When the party broke up, he ordered the Honorable Pengsheng to escort the Marquis of Lu back to the guesthouse, and instructed him that while they were riding on the chariot he should put an end to the Marquis of Lu's life. Pengsheng happily accepted this command.

. . .

That day a lavish spread was served at the banquet at Mount Niu, with singing and dancing for their entertainment. Lord Xiang was extremely respectful, while the Marquis of Lu hung his head and said nothing. Lord Xiang told his grandees to keep the wine circulating, and he ordered the palace maids and serving women to present the cups to the guests on their knees. The Marquis of Lu was torn with anger and depression, so he decided to drown his sorrows in drink. He became so sodden with wine that when the time came to say goodbye, he could not perform even this simple ceremony, so Lord Xiang ordered the Honorable Pengsheng to lift him onto the chariot. Pengsheng then rode off with the Marquis of Lu. When they were about two *li* from the city gates, seeing that the Marquis of Lu was fast asleep, he grabbed hold of him and crushed his chest. Pengsheng was a strong man with arms like iron, and he used their full force on the Marquis of Lu until his ribs cracked. Lord Huan screamed once and died, his blood pouring out into the chariot. Pengsheng told the others present: "The Marquis of Lu has become dangerously ill from drinking too much. We must go at full speed back to the city to report this to His Lordship."

Even though they knew that they had just witnessed a murder, nobody dared to say a thing.

A historian wrote a poem that reads:

No ambiguous relationship should ever be allowed between a man
    and a woman,
It was too dangerous to allow both a husband and wife to leave the
    borders.
If he had originally listened to Shen Xu's remonstrance,
Would Lord Huan's body have lain stretched out in the chariot?

When Lord Xiang of Qi heard that the Marquis of Lu had died suddenly, he pretended to be upset and cry, and gave orders that the body should be placed in the most expensive coffin. He also sent someone to report this sad news to Lu. However, when the Marquis of Lu's escort returned to that state, they told the truth about the assassination on the chariot.

"The country cannot be without a ruler for as much as a single day!" Grandee Shen Xu proclaimed. "We must support Scion Tong through the funeral ceremony. Once the chariot carrying His Lordship's body has arrived back, we can hold the ceremony of accession."

The Honorable Qingfu, whose style-name was Meng, was Lord Huan's oldest son by a concubine. He waved his hands, shouting: "The Marquis of Qi has contravened every standard of proper behavior, and now he has also murdered my lord and father. Please give me three hundred chariots that I may attack Qi and make his crimes known to the world."

Grandee Shen Xu was impressed by his words and privately went to ask one of his advisors, Shi Bo, "Can we feasibly attack Qi?"

"You must not let your neighbors know about this unfortunate incident," Shi Bo told him. "Lu is weak and Qi is strong, so if we attack them, not only are we unlikely to win, but this disgusting scandal will also become widely known. It would be better to endure the situation. However, you must insist upon an investigation of what happened in the chariot, which will force the Marquis of Qi to execute the Honorable Pengsheng. That way we have an explanation to give the other states. At the very least, Qi will have to grant us that."

Shen Xu reported this to the Honorable Qingfu. Afterwards, he asked Shi Bo to draft an official letter on behalf of the government. Since Scion Tong was in mourning for his father, he could not be involved, so the grandees of Lu sent this document to Qi in their own names. When Lord Xiang of Qi opened the letter and read it, the text said:

> Grandee Shen Xu and his fellows bow respectfully to His Lordship, the Marquis of Qi. Our lord received an order from the Son of Heaven to discuss a marriage alliance with you, so he did not dare to delay. He has gone but has not come back, and everywhere we hear rumors that he has been murdered on his chariot. If this killing goes unpunished, we will be humiliated before all the other aristocrats. We therefore request that you execute Pengsheng.

When Lord Xiang had finished reading this, he sent someone to summon Pengsheng to court. The Honorable Pengsheng thought that he had done a great deed, so he went off quite happily. Lord Xiang cursed him in front of the Lu ambassador: "I ordered you to help the Marquis of Lu into his chariot and see him home when he had too much to drink, but you did not attend to him carefully, and so he died. You are guilty of an unpardonable crime!" He shouted at his entourage to tie him up and behead him in the marketplace.

"The affair with your younger sister and the murder of her husband are your wicked deeds, yet now you put the blame on me," Pengsheng screamed. "If the dead have consciousness, then I will become a vengeful ghost! I will come back to claim your life!" Lord Xiang put his hands over his ears and his entourage all laughed.

Afterwards, His Lordship sent someone to go to the king of Zhou to thank him for the proposed marriage alliance and set a date for the wedding. He also sent someone to escort the Marquis of Lu's body back to his home country. Lady Wen Jiang, however, stayed in Qi and did not go home. Later on, Grandee Zhuan Sunsheng arrived in Qi, as part of the escort of the Zhou princess there. In accordance with the orders he had received from the newly established Lord Zhuang of Lu, he went to collect Lady Wen Jiang and take her back. Lord Xiang of Qi was extremely unwilling to be parted from her, but he was constrained by public opinion—he had to send her home. As they were about to be parted, they clung to each other and kept repeating: "We will meet again!" They both said goodbye with tears in their eyes.

Lady Wen Jiang was deeply in love and did not want to leave the Marquis of Qi. Furthermore, she had done so many dreadful things that she was embarrassed to go home. Every step she took was reluctant. When her carriage arrived in Zhuo and she saw how neat and clean the guesthouse there was, she sighed and said, "This place is neither in Qi nor in Lu, so I will stay here!" She instructed her entourage to this effect and ordered them to report to the Marquis of Lu: "Your father's widow needs her own space—I would not be happy returning to the palace. I will come back when I am dead!"

The Marquis of Lu realized that his mother had no intention of returning home, and so he built a residence for her at Zhuqiu and invited Lady Wen Jiang to live there. Afterwards, she would travel between these two places, and the Marquis of Lu kept in regular contact, sending her frequent presents.

When later historians discuss this matter, they point out that on the one hand Lord Zhuang of Lu was Lady Wen Jiang's son, and on the other hand, she murdered his father. If Lady Wen Jiang had returned to Lu, it would have been very difficult to know how to deal with her, so letting her move between these two places allowed the Marquis of Lu to behave as a filial son.

A bearded old man wrote a poem which reads:

Having murdered her husband, she could not face going home.
Living in Zhuo, she placed herself between Qi and Lu.
If she had steeled herself to return to her old home,
How could the demands of love and punishment have been reconciled?

Do you want to know what happened next? READ ON.

Chapter Five

The Honorable Wuzhi loses his privileges and joins a conspiracy.

Lord Xiang of Qi goes out hunting and meets a ghost.

When the Zhou princess arrived in Qi, she got married to Lord Xiang. The princess was a very refined and quiet young woman, always careful of her words and actions. Lord Xiang, on the other hand, was an unrestrained and debauched man, so the two of them did not get along well together at all. After the princess had been several months in the palace, she discovered that Lord Xiang had committed incest with his younger sister. After being silent for some time, she sighed and said to herself, "What a disgusting thing to do! He is worse than an animal! What terrible bad luck for me to have to marry such a wicked man! But such has been my fate!"

Her depression resulted in her becoming sick, and before the year was out she was dead.

. . .

After the death of the princess, Lord Xiang became even more uncontrolled. He missed Lady Wen Jiang intensely, so he would go quite regularly to Zhuo, with the excuse that he was going hunting. He would send someone to Zhuqiu to escort Lady Wen Jiang to Zhuo in secret, and then they would pursue their incestuous pleasures day and night. He was afraid that Lord Zhuang of Lu would object to this and he wanted to threaten him with the might of the forces under his command, so he personally led his army to make a surprise attack on Ji, capturing the three cities of Ping, Zi, and Wu. His troops then moved to the city of Xi, and he sent a messenger to tell the Marquis of Ji, "Write a letter of surrender now, before we destroy you!"

The Marquis of Ji sighed and said, "Qi has been opposed to us for many generations. I will not bend my knee at the court of my enemies and beg to be allowed to live!"

He asked his wife, Lady Bo Ji, to write a letter and sent someone to Lu to ask for assistance.

Lord Xiang of Qi issued orders: "I will attack anyone who comes to the aid of Ji!"

Lord Zhuang of Lu sent an envoy to Zheng suggesting that the two of them should band together to rescue Ji. The Honorable Yi had only just been installed as the new Earl of Zheng, and so he did not dare to send out his army—therefore, he sent a messenger to refuse. This left the Marquis of Lu without any support. Having advanced as far as the lands of Hua, he became more and more frightened of the strength of the Qi army, so having spent three days there he set off home. When the Marquis of Ji heard that the Lu army was retreating, he realized that he would not be able to hold out. He entrusted the capital city, together with his wife and children, to the protection of his younger brother, Ying Ji, and, having said farewell to his ancestral temples, he wept bitterly. That night he ordered that the gates to the city be opened to allow him to leave. He was never seen alive again.

Ying Ji discussed the situation with his senior ministers: "Which is more important, the survival of the state or the preservation of our family sacrifices?"

The ministers all said, "The preservation of your family sacrifices is the most important!"

"If I can preserve the ancestral temples of Ji, any humiliation that I myself may suffer is worth it!" Ying Ji proclaimed.

Accordingly, he wrote a letter of surrender, expressing his wish to become a vassal of Qi, on the condition that he could preserve the ancestral temples in the city of Xi. The Marquis of Qi agreed to this. Ying Ji then presented the records of the lands of Ji and the census of their population to Qi, kowtowed, and begged for mercy. Lord Xiang of Qi took these documents and declared that thirty households living around the ancestral shrine should be responsible for continuing the sacrifices to Ji, and he appointed Ying Ji as Master of the Temple. Lady

Bo Ji had been so terribly shocked by these events that she had died, so Lord Xiang of Qi ordered that she be buried with all the ceremony due to the principal wife of a lord, in the hope that this would please Lu. Lady Bo Ji's younger sister, Lady Shu Ji, had come with her to Ji when she got married and joined her as a junior wife. Lord Xiang wanted to send her back to Lu.

"It is proper for a married woman to follow her husband," Lady Shu Ji said. "In this life I have been a wife of the Ying family; when I am dead I will become a Ying ghost! If I leave here, where could I go?"

The Marquis of Qi agreed to let her spend her widowhood in Xi, and Lady Shu Ji died there a few years later. So it happened that Lord Xiang of Qi destroyed Ji in the seventh year of the reign of King Zhuang of Zhou.

. . .

When Lord Xiang of Qi returned in triumph from having destroyed Ji, Lady Wen Jiang met her brother on the way. They then traveled to Zhuqiu, where she had prepared a magnificent banquet for him. She greeted him with the same ceremonies as would be used when two lords met, and they toasted each other again and again, as she gave a feast for the entire Qi army. Afterwards they went to Zhuo together, where they spent many happy nights in each other's company. Lord Xiang had Lady Wen Jiang write a letter summoning Lord Zhuang of Lu to Zhuo for a meeting. Lord Zhuang was afraid of disobeying his mother's orders, so he journeyed to Zhuo to have audience with Lady Wen Jiang. Her Ladyship forced Lord Zhuang to treat Lord Xiang of Qi with the ceremonies due to an uncle from his nephew, and he had to express thanks for the way in which he had buried Lady Bo Ji. Lord Zhuang was not able to refuse: he had no choice but to obey. Lord Xiang was very pleased, and he treated Lord Zhuang with the utmost ceremony.

At that time, Lord Xiang had recently had a daughter born to him, so Lady Wen Jiang proposed a marriage alliance, since at that time Lord Zhuang still had not married a principal wife.

"She is just a baby," Lord Zhuang said. "She isn't a suitable match for me!"

Lady Wen Jiang was annoyed. "Do you want to create a breach with your mother's family?"

Lord Xiang was also concerned about the difference in their ages, but Lady Wen Jiang said, "We will wait another twenty years and then they can be married. That is not too late."

Lord Xiang was afraid that he might alienate Lady Wen Jiang; Lord Zhuang did not dare to disobey his mother's orders, and so the two of them could only agree. As uncle and nephew, they would now become father-in-law and son-in-law, making their relationship even closer.

The two lords went hunting together in the wilds of Zhuo. Lord Zhuang turned out to be a very fine shot, hitting his target with every arrow. Lord Xiang could not praise him enough. The local people made fun of Lord Zhuang of Lu, saying, "That is our lord's 'son.'" Lord Zhuang was furious and ordered his entourage to hunt those people down and kill them. Lord Xiang did not make the slightest protest.

A historian wrote a poem criticizing Lord Zhuang, since his concern for his mother and disregard of his father's memory meant that he did not take revenge:

> Having bottled up your anger over the murder of your father for so
>   many years,
> How could you be happy to share a sky with such an enemy?
> How can you blame the people who called you his "son,"
> When you agreed to a marriage alliance with his daughter?

After the lords of Qi and Lu had gone hunting together, Lady Wen Jiang behaved with less and less restraint, spending all her time with Lord Xiang of Qi. Sometimes they were in Fang, sometimes they were in Gu, and the rest of the time they were in the capital of Qi, where they would openly live together in the palace, just as if they were husband and wife. The people of the capital composed the song "Galloping Horses" to criticize Lady Wen Jiang. This song runs:

> The galloping horses move quickly,
> The chariot is canopied and the door is hung with vermilion trap-
>   pings,
> The road to Lu is clear,
> The lady from Qi sets out in the evening.
> The waters from the Wen sweep on,
> The travelers are in crowds.
> The road to Lu is clear,
> The lady from Qi travels at her ease.

'*Quickly*' *refers to the appearance of the horses galloping at speed. The canopy would cover the chariot, while the door is the entrance at the back of the chariot. The vermilion trappings would be the red-dyed leather that was used to ornament the chariot. The crowds mentioned means that she was attended by many servants and followers.*

They also composed the song "The Broken Trap" to criticize Lord Zhuang. This song runs:

> The broken trap lies in the pond, its fish are the bream and the *guan*.
> The lady from Qi goes to her home, her retinue like clouds.
> The broken trap lies in the pond, its fish are the bream and the tench.
> The lady from Qi goes to her home, her retinue like water.

A trap is used for catching fish. This song describes how a broken trap or net cannot control these large fish, which is an allegory for Lord Zhuang of Lu being unable to restrain Lady Wen Jiang, as a result of which her servants came and went without let or hindrance.

· · ·

In the wake of his campaign against Ji, Lord Xiang of Qi appointed Grandee Lian Cheng as commander-in-chief, and Guan Zhifu as his deputy, and sent them to camp at Kuiqiu to guard the southeastern border. As the two generals were about to set out, they told Lord Xiang, "This kind of duty is very tough. We would not dare to disobey your orders, but when will our tour be completed?"

At that time Lord Xiang happened to be munching on a melon, and he said, "This is melon season, so next year when melon season comes round again, I will send people to take over from you."

The two generals then went to make camp at Kuiqiu. Their year-long tour of duty slipped by, and suddenly one day the soldiers in the camp were all eating fresh melons. The two generals thought of the terms of their agreement: "This is the time when we should be relieved. Why has His Lordship not sent anyone to replace us?"

They sent a trusted servant back to the capital to find out what was going on. He reported that the Marquis of Qi was enjoying himself at Gu with Lady Wen Jiang and would not be back for another month.

Lian Cheng, absolutely furious, said: "After the princess died, my sister should by rights have become Marchioness of Qi. Instead that bastard of a marquis pays no attention whatsoever to the proper standards of behavior, but spends all his time outside the state involved in this disgusting affair with his own sister, leaving us to rot in this hellhole. I am going to kill him . . . and you are going to help me do it!"

"His Lordship told us himself that he would send replacements in the melon season," Guan Zhifu said. "I am afraid that he has forgotten his promise, so we should remind him about it. If he still refuses to relieve us, the army will be mutinous. We can make use of that!"

"Good idea," Lian Cheng said. Then he sent someone to present a melon to Lord Xiang and beg to be relieved.

"It is up to me whether replacements are sent out or not," Lord Xiang said crossly. "How dare you come and ask for them? You will simply have to wait until the next melon season."

When the messenger came back and reported this, Lian Cheng was rendered speechless with rage. He said to Guan Zhifu, "Now is the time to strike! Do you have a plan to suggest?"

"To achieve this, we are going to need help in order to be successful," Guan Zhifu told him. "Noble Grandson Wuzhi is the son of the Honorable Yi Zhongnian. He was the younger brother of our deceased ruler, Lord Xi, by the same mother. The late Lord Xi was very fond of both Zhongnian and Wuzhi. From a very young age he was brought up in the palace, and his clothes and emoluments were no different from those of the scion. After His Present Lordship was established, there was a time when Wuzhi went to the palace and His Lordship challenged him to a wrestling bout in which Wuzhi hooked Lord Xiang's feet out from under him and he fell to the ground. That displeased His Lordship very much. On another occasion Wuzhi was arguing with Grandee Yong Bing and His Lordship was very angry that he would not give way, so he dismissed him from office and reduced his titles and honors by more than half. Wuzhi has been bottling up his resentment for a long time now! He would be happy to rebel, but he needs help. If we get in contact with Wuzhi secretly, then he can support us from inside the capital and everything will go well."

"When will we attack?" Lian Cheng asked.

"His Lordship likes going to war and he also enjoys hunting," Guan Zhifu reminded him. "When a tiger leaves its lair, it is much easier to deal with. We will have to wait until we hear that he is leaving the capital, then we will have our opportunity."

"My younger sister is in the palace, and she deeply resents having lost His Lordship's favor," Lian Cheng said. "If we tell Wuzhi to get in touch with my sister secretly, she can keep an eye out for any opportunity and inform us immediately. That way there will be no mistake."

He sent the following letter to Noble Grandson Wuzhi by means of a trusted servant:

> You, sir, were loved by His Late Lordship as if you had been his own son, and now all of a sudden you have been stripped of all your privileges, which has caused much unease among the people. In addition to that, His Lordship behaves more unacceptably every day and the government is in chaos. We have been encamped at Kuiqiu for a long time and yet even though melon season has come round again, we have not been relieved. The officers of all three armies are in mutinous mood. If there is any opportunity to do so, we plan to let slip the dogs of war and do our utmost to put you in power. My younger sister is immured in the palace, eaten up with resentment at having lost favor with His Lordship. She too is willing to help you by providing inside information. This opportunity should not be missed.

Noble Grandson Wuzhi was very pleased to get such a letter. He wrote back immediately:

> Heaven abhors wicked men. Having received this expression of your innermost thoughts, I can only say that I honor your words. Please send further information as soon as possible.

Wuzhi secretly sent a maidservant to take the original message to Lady Lian. He wrote an extra line of the top of Lian Cheng's letter: "The day that this matter is accomplished, I will make you my marchioness." Lady Lian agreed to help him.

. . .

In the tenth month of winter, in the eleventh year of the reign of King Zhuang of Zhou, Lord Xiang of Qi heard that in the wilds of Gufen there was a mountain called Beiqiu that was stuffed with game, so he wanted to go hunting there. He instructed Fei and his other cronies to prepare chariots and muster an entourage, for the following month they would go there to hunt. Lady Lian sent one of her palace maids to take a message to this effect to Noble Grandson Wuzhi, and he immediately passed this information on to Kuiqiu. He set a date in the first week of the eleventh month for himself, General Lian, and General Guan to strike.

"When His Lordship leaves to go hunting, the capital will be empty," Lian Cheng said. "We can lead our soldiers straight in through the city gates and install Noble Grandson Wuzhi. How would that be?"

"His Lordship is on good terms with all his neighbors, so if he asks them to send their armies to punish us, how will we resist them?" Guan Zhifu reminded him. "It would be better to set an ambush at Gufen and assassinate that bastard, then have Noble Grandson Wuzhi succeed to the title formally. That is how this matter should be done."

At this time the soldiers stationed at Kuiqiu had been away from home for a long time, and they all missed their families. When Lian Cheng issued secret orders that they were to prepare food and get ready to march on Beiqiu, everyone was happy to oblige.

. . .

On the first day of the eleventh month, Lord Xiang of Qi set out in his chariot, accompanied only by the knight Shi Zhi Fenru and his favorite servant, Meng Yang. They had hawks on their wrists and dogs on leashes, for they were getting ready to go hunting. They did not have even one senior minister accompanying them. When they arrived at Gufen, a traveling palace had been built there to receive them, and they spent a day wandering around the neighborhood. The local people had presented wine and meat, so Lord Xiang held a party that lasted late into the night. He slept there that evening. The following day, he set out on his chariot for Beiqiu. The whole way, the road ran through a dense forest overhung with lush creepers. Lord Xiang halted his chariot on a high promontory and gave orders to burn the forest. Then he commanded his entourage to work a battue, and he let his hawks and dogs go. As the fire burned fiercely, foxes and rabbits ran around wildly. Suddenly an absolutely enormous wild boar leapt through the flames and charged straight for the high promontory, coming to a halt just in front of His Lordship's chariot. At that time everyone else was off shooting, and only Meng Yang stood by Lord Xiang's side.

Lord Xiang of Qi glanced at Meng Yang and said, "Shoot that boar for me."

Meng Yang stared at it wide-eyed and then cried out in alarm: "That is no wild boar! That is the Honorable Pengsheng!"

"How dare Pengsheng come and bother me!" Lord Xiang bellowed angrily. He grabbed hold of Meng Yang's bow and shot at the boar himself, but he did not hit it, even though he shot three arrows in a row. The boar got up on its hind legs, its two front trotters placed together and walked forward like a human being. It then uttered a chilling, painful scream, which scared Lord Xiang so badly that every hair stood on end. As he fell from his chariot, his left foot buckled under him and his embroidered silk shoe fell off. The boar picked this up in its mouth and walked away. Suddenly it disappeared.

A bearded old man wrote a poem about this:

> Back then it was Lord Huan of Lu who died on top of a chariot,
> Today it is you who meet a ghost while riding on your own vehicle.
> By killing Pengsheng you made him yet more formidable,
> There was no point in Zhuer bending the painted bow.

Fei and the other servants lifted up Lord Xiang and laid him flat on the bottom of the chariot, giving orders that the hunt should be called off and that everyone should go back to the traveling palace at Gufen for the night. Lord Xiang was still petrified, and his mind was exceedingly disturbed. The soldiers had already struck the second watch when Lord Xiang, tossing and turning and unable to sleep because of the pain in his left foot, said to Meng Yang, "Could you lift me up and help me to walk for a few steps?"

When he had fallen from his chariot earlier that day, he had been in such a state that he did not notice that he had lost a shoe, but now he discovered that one was missing. He asked Fei to go and get it.

"Your shoe was carried off in the mouth of the wild boar," Fei informed him.

Lord Xiang felt curiously disgusted by this and, flying into a rage, he screamed: "It is your job to look after me! Surely you can keep an eye on my shoes! If it was carried off by the boar, why didn't you say so earlier?"

He grabbed hold of a leather whip and started belaboring Fei's back. He did not stop until blood had spattered all over the ground. After his whipping, Fei went out of the door holding back his tears, only to walk straight into Lian Cheng, who had come in with a small group of soldiers to investigate what was going on. They immediately took Fei prisoner.

"Where is that bastard, our ruler?" they demanded.

"In his bedroom," Fei said.

"Is he asleep?"

"Not yet."

Lian Cheng raised his sword and was just about to behead him when Fei said, "Don't kill me! I will go on ahead and act as your eyes and ears." Lian Cheng did not believe him, but Fei continued: "I have just been severely beaten. I would be happy to kill that bastard myself!" He then stripped off his shirt to show them his back. When Lian Cheng saw how it was raw and dripping with blood, he trusted every word he had said and released Fei from his bonds. He told him that he should keep an eye on the situation for them and then went back to summon Guan Zhifu and the bulk of his soldiers, who would actually carry out the attack on the traveling palace.

Fei went back, and when he ran across Shi Zhi Fenru, he told him that Lian Cheng was planning a revolt. Afterwards he went to Lord Xiang's bedchamber and reported this to him. Lord Xiang was so appalled he did not know what to do.

"It is too late to run away," Fei told him. "If someone dresses up as Your Lordship and lies down in your bed, you can hide behind the door. If we are lucky and the soldiers don't look too closely, you may yet escape!"

"Your Lordship has always been kinder to me than I deserve, so I am happy to act as your proxy," Meng Yang told him. "If I die, I will have no regrets!" He lay down on the bed, keeping his face turned towards the wall. Lord Xiang took off his brocade robe and covered him with it, then went to hide behind the door.

"What are you going to do?" he asked Fei.

"I will be helping Shi Zhi Fenru to hold off the rebels."

"Do you not mind the injuries that I inflicted upon you?"

"Even if you killed me, I would not mind. These injuries are nothing!"

Lord Xiang sighed and said, "You are indeed a loyal subject!"

Fei ordered Shi Zhi Fenru to take his men and defend the main gate, while he himself went the other way, holding a sword. He would pretend to welcome the rebels, but in fact he was hoping for an opportunity to kill Lian Cheng.

By this time the main force had already fought their way through the main gate: Lian Cheng, with a sword in his hand, was cutting a path through the defenders while Guan Zhifu and his troops were waiting outside the gate, to prevent anyone from escaping. When Fei saw the violence of Lian Cheng's attack, without a moment's hesitation he took a step forward and stabbed him. How could he have anticipated that Lian Cheng was wearing double-thickness armor so the blade did not penetrate? The first sweep of Lian Cheng's sword cut off two of his fingers; the second blow took off half of his head. He died in the middle of the gate. Shi Zhi Fenru then picked up a spear and came forward to fight. They crossed swords a dozen times, Lian Cheng advancing all the way. Shi Zhi Fenru was retreating gradually when he lost his footing, stumbling over a stone step, and he too was beheaded by a single blow from Lian Cheng's sword.

When they entered His Lordship's bedchamber, his bodyguards had already fled in panic. There was only one person lying in bed amid the flowered curtains, and he was covered by a silk brocade gown. Lian Cheng raised his arm and let his sword fall. The head bounced down from the pillows. He lifted up a torch to light the scene, but seeing that the head was that of a young and beardless man, Lian Cheng shouted, "That is not His Lordship!"

He ordered his followers to search the room, but there was no sign of anyone else. Lian Cheng was searching with a torch in his hand to light the way when suddenly he caught sight of one embroidered silk shoe sitting on the doorstep. He realized that someone was hiding behind the door. Who could that be if not Zhuer himself? When he pulled back the door to see, the wicked marquis collapsed in a heap from the pain in his foot; the other embroidered silk shoe was safe and sound on his right foot. The shoe that Lian Cheng had spotted was the one that had been carried off in the mouth of the wild boar. No one could imagine how it had come to be on the doorstep. It must have been the work of ghosts—how terrifying!

Lian Cheng recognized Zhuer, who was now as helpless as a baby bird, and with one arm he dragged him out from behind the door and hurled him to the ground. He cursed him: "You wicked bastard! You send your armies out year after year, getting your people killed for no reason other than that you enjoy fighting—that is not benevolent! You disobeyed your father's orders and dismissed the Noble Grandson Wuzhi from office—that is not filial! You have had an incestuous relationship with your own younger sister and paid no attention to the proper standards of behavior—that is immoral! You have spared no thought for your soldiers stationed far away, and even when melon season came round again, you did not send replacements—that means that you have broken your word! If you fail in the four great virtues of benevolence, filial piety, morality, and trustworthiness, can you really be considered human? Today I will take revenge on behalf of Lord Huan of Lu!"

He hacked Lord Xiang to pieces and wrapped up the remains in the blanket on the bed. He and Meng Yang were buried together, their bodies covered by the door. In all, Lord Xiang of Qi ruled for only five years.

When historians discuss this matter, they point out that Lord Xiang paid no attention to his senior ministers but was very partial to some of his juniors. Shi Zhi Fenru, Meng Yang, Fei, and so on all benefited from his favoritism and encouraged him in his wickedness. Even though in the end they died for him, they cannot be considered in the same light as virtuous ministers who die out of loyalty. Lian Cheng and Guan Zhifu plotted this assassination because they had been on duty for a long time without relief; if Lord Xiang had kept his promises, they would not have done this. Before he was executed, Pengsheng shouted: "When I die I will become a vengeful ghost, then I will come back to claim your life!" The appearance of the wild boar was no coincidence.

A bearded old man wrote a poem commemorating the deaths of Fei and Shi Zhi Fenru. This poem reads:

> To die for your ruler is a loyal and virtuous act,
> But Fei and Shi Zhi Fenru are not remembered in this way.
> If obeying a wicked ruler to the end earned you an honorable reputation,
> Then would not Fei Lian and Chong Hu be of glorious memory?

There is also a poem bemoaning Lord Xiang of Qi's career:

> Your evil actions caused the death of another lord,
> And in turn your life was snuffed out by a wild boar.
> Having done such wicked things, of course you had to die,
> There is no doubt that this encourages people to do good!

Lian Cheng and Guan Zhifu collected their forces and set off at all speed for the Qi capital. The Noble Grandson Wuzhi had recruited his own private army, and when he got the news that Lord Xiang was dead, he led his soldiers to open the city gates and allow Lian Cheng and Guan Zhifu into the city. The two generals issued a statement: "In accordance with the dying wishes of our late ruler, Lord Xi, we will install the Noble Grandson Wuzhi as the new marquis." At the same time, Lady Lian was appointed as marchioness, while Lian Cheng became a senior minister and received the honorific title "Leader of the Nation." Guan Zhifu became a middle-ranking minister. Although the other grandees were forced to take office, none of them obeyed willingly. It was only Yong Bing who kept kowtowing and apologizing for having argued with him in the past in a very demeaning manner. However, Wuzhi pardoned him, and he kept his post as a grandee.

Do you want to know what happened after that? THE STORY CONTINUES . . .

The Wicked Stepmother,
Lady Li Ji

Chapter Six

Lord Xian of Jin ignores a divination against establishing a principal wife.

Lady Li Ji plots the murder of Shensheng.

Let us now turn to another part of the story. The ruling family of the state of Jin were members of the Ji clan, and they held the title of marquis. When Lord Xian of Jin was still just the scion, he married Lady Jia Ji as his principal wife, but they did not have any children together. His junior wives included a niece of the chief of the Dog Rong, Lady Hu Ji, who gave birth to a son named Chonger, and a daughter of the Yun clan of the Lesser Rong, who gave birth to a son named Yiwu. Lord Xian's father, Lord Wu, in the last years of his reign, had requested a marriage alliance with Qi, and thus Lord Huan of Qi sent him one of his own daughters as a bride: she was Lady Qi Jiang. At this time Lord Wu was already elderly and could no longer control his womenfolk, while Lady Qi Jiang was young and very pretty. Lord Xian fell in love with her and they began an incestuous relationship, which resulted in the birth of a son. He was sent away to be brought up secretly in the Shen family, and therefore he was given the name Shensheng.

When Lord Xian succeeded to the title, Lady Jia Ji was already dead, and he wanted to establish Lady Qi Jiang as his marchioness. At that time Chonger was already twenty-one years of age, and Yiwu too was older than Shensheng, but because Shensheng was the son of the marchioness, he took precedence over them in seniority, if not in age. Shensheng was thus appointed as the scion. Grandee Du Yuankuan was made his senior tutor, and Grandee Li Ke was his junior tutor, with the aim that both should support and guide the scion. Lady Qi

Jiang died shortly afterwards, giving birth to a daughter. Afterwards Lord Xian appointed Lady Jia Ji's younger sister, Lady Jia Jun, as his marchioness. They had no children together, but Lady Jia Jun brought up Lady Qi Jiang's daughter.

In the fifteenth year of Lord Xian's reign, he raised an army and attacked the Li Rong people. The Li Rong requested a peace treaty and gave two women from their ruling house to Lord Xian: the older was called Lady Li Ji, and the younger was called Lady Shao Ji. Lady Li Ji was the most beautiful woman in the world, but as wicked as the temptress Da Ji. She was also extremely intelligent, but this concealed a vicious cunning. Whenever Lord Xian was present, she made a play of her affection for him and her loyalty, all the while making sure that she looked as attractive as possible. As a result, he let her participate in the government, and she gave very good advice. Lord Xian came to love and favor her above all others. They ate and drank together and were never to be found apart.

The following year, Lady Li Ji gave birth to a son called Xiqi. The year after that, Lady Shao Ji gave birth to a son named Zhuozi. Lord Xian was bewitched by Lady Li Ji and he was thrilled about their baby, so he forgot all about his earlier love for Lady Qi Jiang. He wanted to appoint Lady Li Ji as his marchioness, so he ordered the Grand Astrologer Guo Yan to perform a divination about it using a turtle shell. Guo Yan inspected the cracks in the shell and reported the following reading: "The change made by inordinate devotion will steal away the lord's good qualities. One is fragrant, one is disgusting, and after ten years it will still stink."

"What does that mean?" Lord Xian demanded.

"Change refers to some sort of problem," Guo Yan explained. "This means that if you are overly devoted to something or other, it will have a detrimental effect on your mind. That is why it says, 'The change made by inordinate devotion.' Stealing away refers to something being lost, and your good qualities are at present admired by one and all. If something has a detrimental effect on your mind, then you can no longer distinguish properly between good and bad. That is why it says, 'will steal away the lord's good qualities.' Pleasantly scented herbs are said to be fragrant, while those that smell unpleasant are said to be disgusting. If the fragrant cannot overcome the disgusting, corruption will endure for a long time. That is why it says, 'after ten years it will still stink.'"

Lord Xian was besotted by Lady Li Ji and did not believe a word that Guo Yan said, so he ordered another diviner, Astrologer Su, to perform a milfoil divination about it, in which he obtained the hexagram "Observing" and the words "Observing briefly: favorable for an unmarried woman."

"For a woman to live in the harem and observe what is going on outside from that vantage point is very proper," Lord Xian said. "What could be more auspicious than that?"

"Ever since the dawn of time, omens came first and numerology came second," the diviner Guo Yan reminded him. "A divination performed with a turtle-shell qualifies as an omen, while one performed with milfoil is simply numerology. You should pay attention to the turtle-shell divination and not to that obtained from milfoil."

"According to the strict rules of ritual propriety, a feudal lord cannot marry for a second time," Astrologer Su said. "That is the point made by the 'Observation' hexagram. How can marrying a second wife be called proper? If it is not proper, then how could it be beneficial? The wording found in the *Book of Changes* should not necessarily be interpreted as auspicious."

"If divinations actually worked, everything would be decided by the ghosts and spirits," Lord Xian said crossly. In the end he decided to ignore what both Astrologer Su and the diviner Guo Yan had told him. He selected an auspicious day to go to the ancestral temples, and then he established Lady Li Ji as his marchioness and Lady Shao Ji as his secondary wife.

Astrologer Su spoke in private to Grandee Li Ke: "What are you going to do when the state of Jin collapses?"

Li Ke was very shocked. "Who will be responsible for the destruction of Jin?" he demanded.

"Who other than Lady Li Ji!" Astrologer Su retorted. Li Ke did not understand what he meant, and so the astrologer explained: "In antiquity King Jie of the Xia dynasty attacked the state of Shi, and they gave him a woman named Mo Xi as wife; King Jie's favoritism brought about the destruction of the dynasty. King Zhou of the Shang dynasty attacked the state of Su, and they gave him a woman named Da Ji as wife; King Zhou's favoritism brought about the destruction of the dynasty. King You of Zhou attacked Bao, and the people of that state gave him Bao Si as wife; King You's favoritism brought about the destruction of the Western Zhou dynasty. Now Jin has attacked the Li Rong people and captured one of their women, whom he favors above all others—how can this not cause disaster?"

Just at that moment, the Grand Astrologer Guo Yan arrived, and Li Ke told him what Astrologer Su had said. Guo Yan responded: "Jin will certainly have to endure a civil war, but it is not clear whether or not the state will be destroyed. When our founding lord was enfeoffed with these lands, he performed a divination, which said, 'Your descendants will govern the lords well and reestablish the royal house.' With such an important task yet to be accomplished, how can Jin be destroyed?"

"When will this civil war occur?" Li Ke asked.

"Whether you do good deeds or bad, you will be repaid within ten years, because ten is a 'full' number," Guo Yan told him. Li Ke recorded his words on a bamboo scroll.

Lord Xian loved Lady Li Ji so much that he wanted to establish her son Xiqi as his heir. One day, he discussed this with Lady Li Ji. She was very willing, but Shensheng had already been appointed as the scion, and she was afraid that the ministers would not accept a change in the succession made for no good reason. She was sure they would remonstrate and try to prevent this. In addition to that, Chonger and Yiwu were both very close to Shensheng and loved him very much. The three of them would definitely stand together. In such a situation, her faction could only fail. Therefore, she knelt down before Lord Xian and said, "All the aristocrats know that you have already appointed an heir. He is a clever young man and has done nothing wrong. I would rather commit suicide than see Your Lordship depose the rightful heir for the sake of my son!"

Lord Xian thought that she was in earnest and did not say anything more about it.

. . .

His Lordship particularly favored two of the grandees working in his administration. One was named Liang Wu and the other Dongguan Wu. They kept an eye on things outside the palace for Lord Xian and took advantage of the favor he showed them to bully other people. The inhabitants of the Jin capital called them the "Two Wus." There was also a young and handsome actor named Shi, who was much favored by the Marquis of Jin for his sharp intelligence and witty speech, to the point where he was allowed in and out of the palace without any hindrance. Lady Li Ji was having an affair with Shi, and they became closer as their relationship deepened. She told him that her dearest wish was to remove her husband's three older children to facilitate her plan to seize the succession for her own son.

The actor came up with a stratagem to help her: "You must send His Lordship's three sons far away from the capital on the pretext that they are needed to guard the borders. Then you will be left at the heart of things to carry out the next stage of your plans. However, in order to bring this about you will need the support of at least some of the senior ministers, who can present this suggestion to His Lordship as 'loyal advice.' Your Ladyship should buy the 'Two Wus' into your service with presents of gold and silk. When we all tell His Lordship the same thing, he will have to listen to us."

Accordingly, Lady Li Ji gave silk and gold to Shi and told him to give half to each of the "Two Wus."

The actor Shi went first to see Liang Wu, and said, "Her Ladyship would like to become friends with you, so she has sent me to give you some humble gifts."

Amazed, Liang Wu said, "What does Her Ladyship expect me to do for her? She must have given you some instructions! If you do not tell me exactly what is going on, I cannot possibly accept your presents!"

The actor then told Liang Wu of Lady Li Ji's plans, to which he responded, "This is impossible without Grandee Dongguan's assistance."

"Her Ladyship has prepared further gifts for him, just like yours," Shi assured him. They went to visit Dongguan Wu together, and the three of them discussed what they would do.

The following day, Liang Wu presented advice to Lord Xian. "Quwo was your original fief, and it is the site of the ancestral temples of our former lords. The cities of Pu and Qu are located close to the barbarian Di and Rong peoples, and these border territories are vital for our security. We need someone responsible in charge in all three places. If the home of your ancestors is left unattended, the people will despise you. If crucial border territories are left undefended, the Rong and the Di will take advantage of this. If you send the scion to Quwo and the Honorable Chonger and Yiwu to Pu and Qu, respectively, Your Lordship can keep control in the capital and everything will go well."

"Do you think it is a good idea to send the scion away from the capital?" Lord Xian asked.

"The scion is Your Lordship's deputy, and Quwo is your secondary capital," Dongguan Wu assured him. "Who could be more suitable than the scion to take charge there?"

"Quwo is perfectly comfortable," Lord Xian said, "but Pu and Qu are right out in the wilds. How will my sons endure it?"

"If the houses are not enclosed within a wall, then they are indeed right out in the wilds," Dongguan Wu replied. "Once there is a wall, they become a city."

The two men praised this plan with one voice: "If you gain two cities in a single day, they can protect your present borders and assist in opening up new territory. Jin will soon become a great state!"

Trusting their advice, Lord Xian sent Scion Shensheng to live at Quwo and take control of the government of the city where his ancestors had lived. The scion was assisted in this task by his tutor, Du Yuankuan. Lord Xian sent the Honorable Chonger to live in Pu and the Honorable Yiwu to live in Qu, with a view to keeping control of these border regions. Hu Mao followed the Honorable Chonger to Pu, while Lü Yisheng escorted Yiwu to Qu. Lord Xian ordered Zhao Xi to build a wall around the city of Quwo, which was much higher and wider than the old one; henceforward, this was known as the New City. He also ordered Shi Wei to supervise the walling of the two cities of Pu and Qu. Shi Wei collected a bit of brushwood and piled up some earth, completing the work in a very lackadaisical manner. Someone said to him, "I am afraid that these walls will not hold."

Shi Wei just laughed: "In a few years' time when these cities become enemy strongholds, we won't want them to hold." He then composed a song:

> Fox-fur cloaks have become confused,
> In this one state there are three lords,
> Who should I follow?

A fox-fur cloak was a garment worn only by members of the nobility. Confused refers to a chaotic situation. This song describes a situation where there are so many members of the nobility that distinctions between the children of noble mothers and the sons of concubines and the divisions between older and younger siblings have become blurred.

Shi Wei was aware of Lady Li Ji's plan to get rid of her husband's heir. That is why he spoke as he did. When Shensheng and his two brothers were sent away to live on the borders of the state of Jin, Xiqi and Zhuozi were left by His Lordship's side. Lady Li Ji did her best to ingratiate herself with her husband and monopolize his favors, in the hope of bewitching Lord Xian.

A bearded old man wrote a poem about this:

> Women's beauty has always been a cause of trouble,
> Thus Lord Xian was seduced into favoring Lady Li Ji.
> It was pointless to build these walled cities at the distant borders,
> When real danger lurked within the palace gates!

At this time Lord Xian created two new armies, and he took personal command of the Upper Army. He appointed Scion Shensheng to command the Lower Army, and Shensheng then directed Grandees Zhao Xi and Bi Wan in attacks on the three states of Geng, Huo, and Wei, in which they were destroyed. The lands of Geng were given to Zhao Xi, and the lands of Wei were bestowed upon Bi Wan as his fief. The scion had played a major role in these successful campaigns, but Lady Li Ji was jealous of any achievements he might make, so her plans to get rid of him were even more vicious.

Subsequently, Lord Xian of Jin conquered the two states of Yu and Guo, whereupon his ministers all congratulated him. Lady Li Ji was the only one left unhappy. She had originally wanted to see Scion Shensheng sent on the mission to attack Guo, but he had been replaced by Li Ke, who achieved an enormous success with very minimal effort. However, right at that moment there was nothing that she could do about the situation. She discussed the matter with her lover, the actor Shi: "Li Ke is part of Shensheng's faction and now he has achieved a great victory, making his position even more secure. I cannot possibly take him on. What should I do?"

"It was actually Xun Xi who masterminded the destruction of Yu and Guo," Shi said. "He is far cleverer than Li Ke. His Lordship knows well that he was quite as important in achieving this victory as Li Ke himself. If we beg Xun Xi to act as tutor to the Honorable Xiqi and Zhuozi, we will be more than able to deal with Li Ke when the time comes."

Lady Li Ji requested permission for this from Lord Xian, and he appointed Xun Xi as Xiqi and Zhuozi's tutor. Then she spoke again to

Shi: "Xun Xi has now joined our faction. However, as long as Li Ke is at court, he is sure to bring our plans to naught. Do you have some means to get rid of him? If Li Ke is removed, we can deal with Shensheng!"

"Li Ke may appear tough on the outside, but in fact he is a very indecisive man," the actor said. "If we can sway him by pointing out the advantages and risks he faces, he will respond by refusing to take sides—we can make use of that fact. Li Ke enjoys a drink, so if Your Ladyship will arrange for a banquet of lamb and beef in his honor, I will get him drunk and test out his attitudes. If he falls for it, that is all to the good. If he does not fall for it, then I am just an actor who forgot my place and teased him a bit. He won't hold it against us."

"Good!" exclaimed Lady Li Ji. She prepared the banquet on the actor's behalf.

Shi had carefully prepared the words that he would use to invite Li Ke: "You, sir, have been rushing between Yu and Guo, so you must be absolutely exhausted. I would like to hold a party for you in the hope that you may enjoy at least a moment's leisure. What do you think?" Li Ke agreed.

The wine cups were set out at Li Ke's house, and he and his wife, Lady Meng, sat on the western side to show that they were the guests on this occasion. Shi bowed twice and handed him a beaker of wine, then stood respectfully to one side ready to top it up. They chatted and joked together very happily. When they had drunk so much that they became tipsy, Shi got up and started dancing. He said to Lady Meng, "If you would give me something to eat, I will sing a new song for you."

Lady Meng poured wine into a rhinoceros-horn goblet and handed it to Shi, after which she fed him a morsel of lamb. Then she asked, "What is the name of this new song?"

"It is called 'The Pleasures of Idleness,'" the actor replied. "If you would serve His Lordship according to these words, I can guarantee that you will remain rich and noble." He then cleared his throat and sang:

> "The pleasures of idleness have palled on me;
> I cannot be as free as a bird.
> All the others have gone to the thickets,
> You alone have stayed by the single tree.
> Why are the thickets so dense and so lush?
> The tree invites the blows of the axe.
> When these blows start to bite,
> What can you do to change the fate of the tree?"

When the song was over, Li Ke laughed and said, "What do you mean by the thicket? What do you mean by the single tree?"

"Well, you might compare it to a person whose mother was the principal wife of a lord who was originally destined to become the next ruler," Shi said. "In that case, his roots would run deep, his branches would be closely packed, and a whole host of birds would come to roost there—you could then call that a thicket. But then if his mother died and people slandered him, disaster would threaten. In that case his roots would become shallow and his leaves drop, giving the birds nowhere to settle, just like the lone tree of my song." When he had finished speaking, he left.

Li Ke felt extremely uncomfortable and gave orders for the banquet to be cleared away. He got up and walked to his library where he could be alone, where he paced up and down the room for a long time. That evening he did not eat dinner, but put out the lights and went to bed. He tossed and turned, unable to get to sleep. He thought to himself: "That actor, Shi, has been acclaimed both inside and outside the court, and he comes and goes from the palace without any restraint. There must be a reason why he sang that particular song today. He must have something to tell me. I will go tomorrow and pay a call on him."

It got later and later and he was still on tenterhooks. He told his servants, "Go in secret to fetch Shi and bring him here. I want to talk to him."

Shi knew exactly what the problem was, so he quickly put on a hat and robe and went with the servants back to Li Ke's bedroom. Li Ke summoned Shi and told him to sit on the bed. With his arms wrapped round his knees, he asked him: "When you talked about the thicket and the lone tree, I have already worked it out—you meant the situation in Quwo, didn't you? You must know something . . . please tell me! Do not keep it a secret."

"I have wanted to tell you what I know for a long time," Shi replied, "but you are the tutor of the man at Quwo, so I did not dare to speak. I was afraid that you would punish me."

"If you tell me what is going on far enough in advance to allow me to make my plans and avoid getting caught up in a disaster, I will be deeply grateful," Li Ke told him. "Why should I punish you for that?"

Shi then leaned his head down towards the pillow and whispered, "His Lordship has already promised Her Ladyship to kill the scion and establish Xiqi in his place. Their plan is just about to come to fruition."

"Is it yet possible to stop them?" Li Ke asked.

"Her Ladyship has His Lordship wrapped around her little finger," Shi replied. "You know that perfectly well! The two grandees, Liang Wu and Dongguan Wu, are much trusted by His Lordship—you know that too. Her Ladyship is in charge of the palace and the two grandees are in charge of the court. You might want to stop them, but how can you?"

"Even if it is His Lordship's wish," Li Ke exclaimed, "I cannot just stand by and watch the scion being murdered. On the other hand, I also cannot possibly support the scion in a fight with his father. If I just sit on the fence and do nothing, do you think I will be able to get through this crisis?"

"You will," Shi told him.

After the actor had left, Li Ke sat and waited until dawn, at which point he got out the bamboo strips that he had written all those years earlier. Counting up, he realized that it was now indeed ten years later. He sighed and said, "Divinations are really amazing things!" Then he walked round to the home of Grandee Pi Zhengfu and ordered his servants and attendants to leave them alone. He said, "Astrologer Su and Diviner Guo Yan's predictions have been entirely borne out!"

"What has happened?" Pi Zhengfu asked.

"Last night the actor Shi came to my house," Li Ke explained, "and told me: 'His Lordship is going to murder the scion and put Xiqi in his place.'"

"What did you say to that?" Pi Zhengfu inquired.

"I said that I will do nothing," Li Ke said.

"That is like noticing that a fire has broken out and deciding to fan the flames," Pi Zhengfu wailed. "This particular plot is aimed at you—you should have pretended to go along with it and found out what they are up to. You have been a mainstay of the scion's faction and crucial for him maintaining his position thus far. You could have taken advantage of this situation to change His Lordship's mind—who knows but it might have worked! Now that you have announced that you are going to do nothing, disaster will overtake the scion any moment now."

Li Ke stamped his foot and said, "What a shame! I should have come to discuss the matter with you much earlier." He said goodbye and got onto his chariot. Then he pretended to stumble and fall. For the next few days he did not go to court, claiming that he had injured his foot.

A historian wrote a poem which reads:

An actor danced in front of tables groaning with beef and lamb.
The scion was ruined by a single song.
Is it not laughable that such a senior minister had no idea what was
    going on,
And his neutrality led to the outbreak of war?

Shi reported back to Lady Li Ji, and she was very pleased by these developments. That night she spoke to Lord Xian as follows: "The scion has been living for a long time in Quwo. Why don't you call him back to court? You can say that I would like to see him. If I show him some generosity, perhaps we can avoid all these constant conflicts. What do you think?" Lord Xian did exactly as she asked and summoned Shensheng back to court.

. . .

When the Scion Shensheng received the summons, he set off at once and went first to have an audience with Lord Xian, bowing twice and asking after his health. When this ceremony had been completed, he went into the palace to see Lady Li Ji. She had prepared a banquet for him, and they spoke very happily together. The following day Shensheng went back to the palace to thank her for the banquet, and Lady Li Ji again kept him for a meal.

That evening, Lady Li Ji went to Lord Xian in tears and said, "I wanted to establish good relations with the scion, so I asked you to summon him. I have treated him with all proper ceremony, and I really was not expecting him to behave so badly towards me."

"What has he done?" the horrified Lord Xian asked.

"I invited the scion to stay for lunch," Lady Li Ji sobbed. "He kept on drinking until he was half-drunk, and then he started teasing me, saying, 'When my grandfather got old, my mother, Lady Jiang, started an affair with my father. Now my father is getting old, so sooner or later you will be looking for someone new; who could be better than myself?' He then tried to grab hold of my hand, but I fought him off. If you don't believe me, then I will go for a walk with the scion in the park. You can watch from the tower, and you will see the truth of what I am saying with your own eyes."

"I will!" Lord Xian exclaimed.

The following day, Lady Li Ji summoned Scion Shensheng to walk with her in the park, and she prepared for this by smearing a tiny bit of honey into her hair. Bees and butterflies clustered around her tresses.

"Do you mind trying to get rid of these insects for me?" Lady Li Ji said.

Shensheng, who was walking respectfully behind her, used his sleeve to flick them away. Lord Xian, who was watching from some distance away, genuinely thought he was molesting her. He was furious and wanted to give immediate orders to have Shensheng arrested and executed. However, Lady Li Ji knelt on the ground before him and begged: "It was I who summoned him here, so if you kill him, it will all be my fault. No one other than yourself knows how badly he has behaved here in the palace. You will have to endure the situation a little longer."

Lord Xian ordered Shensheng to go back to Quwo, and he sent people to go there secretly to inquire if he had committed any crimes.

A couple of days later, when Lord Xian had gone out hunting at Dihuan, Lady Li Ji came up with a new scheme with her lover. They sent someone to tell the scion: "His Lordship dreamed that your mother appeared to him and said, 'I am suffering starvation and have nothing to eat.' You must perform a sacrifice to her memory as soon as possible."

A separate shrine had been established at Quwo to the memory of Lady Jiang of Qi, so Shensheng held a sacrifice there for his mother and sent a messenger to take the sacrificial meats to Lord Xian. Lord Xian had not yet returned from his expedition, so the meats were kept in the palace. Six days later, Lord Xian came home.

Lady Li Ji had poisoned the sacrificial wine and meat and she now presented them with the words: "I dreamed that Lady Jiang of Qi was suffering terrible torments from starvation. Since you had gone off hunting, I instructed the scion to perform a sacrifice for her. The sacrificial meats have now been sent here and we have kept them for you."

Lord Xian picked up the beaker and was just about to taste the wine when Lady Li Ji sank to her knees and stopped him, saying, "This wine and meat have come from outside, so we have to test them."

"You are quite right!" exclaimed Lord Xian.

He poured the wine on the ground, only to see it bubble and split. Then he had a dog brought in and gave it a lump of meat to eat. It died the moment it bit down. Lady Li Ji pretended she was unable to believe her own eyes. She summoned a young eunuch and had him taste the wine and meat. The eunuch refused, but they forced him, and the moment he had swallowed them, blood poured from every orifice and he died. Lady Li Ji pretended to be horror-struck and ran around the hall, screaming: "Heavens! Heavens! Whatever happens, the scion will inherit everything sooner or later. His Lordship is old—surely he can wait a little longer? Why does he want to assassinate his own father?"

As she spoke, the tears streamed down her cheeks. Again she fell to her knees in front of Lord Xian, and said in a voice choked with emotion: "The scion launched this conspiracy because he hates me. Let me take this meat and wine and die in your place, my lord. That way the scion will have achieved all that he wants!" She picked up the goblet as if she were really going to drink from it.

Lord Xian wrenched it from her grasp and dashed it to the ground, so overcome that he could not speak. Lady Li Ji collapsed in a tearful heap on the ground and said angrily, "How can the scion be so wicked? He is prepared to murder even his own father, so Heaven only knows what he will do to other people! Originally when you wanted to strip him of his titles, I was against it. Then when he assaulted me in the park and you wanted to kill him, I prevented it. Now he has almost murdered you! It is my fault that he got the opportunity!"

Lord Xian stammered out a few words as he lifted Lady Li Ji in his arms: "Get up! I will explain the situation to my ministers and then execute my wicked son."

He announced that court would be held immediately and summoned his grandees to discuss what had happened. Everyone came and filled the palace audience hall, with the exception of Hu Tu, who was living in reclusion; Li Ke, who was claiming that his foot had been injured; and Pi Zhengfu, who was off on a diplomatic mission. Lord Xian informed his officials that Shensheng had made an attempt on his life. The ministers knew perfectly well that Lord Xian had been plotting to strip his son of his title for ages, so they looked at each other but did not dare to argue.

Dongguan Wu stepped forward and said, "The scion has behaved very badly. I ask Your Lordship's permission to punish him."

Lord Xian immediately appointed Dongguan Wu as a general and ordered Liang Wu to assist him. They led a force of two hundred chariots to attack Quwo. He instructed them as follows: "The scion has had charge of the army on a number of occasions, and he is a brilliant strategist. You must be very careful!"

Although Hu Tu was living in reclusion, he sent people out to investigate what was going on at court. When he heard that the "Two Wus" were getting their chariots ready, he knew that they would be heading for Quwo. He ordered someone to go to report this to Scion Shensheng as quickly as possible. Shensheng discussed what to do with his Grand Tutor, Du Yuankuan.

"The sacrificial meats were kept in the palace for six days, so it is quite clear that the poison must have been introduced by someone there," Du Yuankuan said. "You must appeal! Make sure that the ministers know the truth rather than sitting here waiting for them to come and kill you."

"If my father had to do without Lady Li Ji, he would not be happy," Shensheng said. "If I were to make an appeal and it were unsuccessful, this would simply compound my offense. But if my appeal were successful, my father would simply protect Lady Li Ji from the consequences of her actions. I would not necessarily escape punishment, but I would certainly make my father deeply unhappy. The best thing that could happen now would be for me to die!"

"You could go into exile abroad and wait to see how the situation develops," Du Yuankaun suggested. "Would that not be a good idea?"

"My father has sent these people to punish me without investigating whether I am guilty or not," Shensheng said sadly. "If I were to run away, I would take my reputation as an attempted parricide with me— people would treat me like a bird of ill omen! If I were to leave and succeeded in convincing people that it was my father who was in the wrong, he would go down in history as a wicked ruler. To declare how badly my father has behaved would be to humiliate him in front of all the feudal lords. I am in an impossible situation whether I stay or go. If I expose what my father has done in order to excuse myself of the crimes of which I have been accused, then I am simply escaping punishment. I have heard it said that 'a benevolent man does not hate his ruler, a wise man does not place himself in impossible situations, and a brave man does not escape punishment.'"

In the end, he sent a letter back to Hu Tu, which said:

> I have committed a crime for which I will atone with my death. However, my father is old, and Xiqi is still very young, and there are many dangers facing the country. I hope that you will do your best to guide the country through them. That way, even though I am dead, I will still be greatly helped by you.

When he had finished writing this letter, Shensheng turned towards the north and bowed twice, and then he hanged himself. The day after his death, Dongguan Wu arrived with his army. When he discovered that Shensheng was dead, he arrested Du Yuankuan and put him in prison. Afterwards, he reported to Lord Xian, "The scion realized that having committed such a crime there was nowhere to go, so he killed himself."

Lord Xian ordered Du Yuankuan to testify as to the crimes that the scion had committed.

"He was innocent!" Du Yuankuan screamed. "The reason that I let myself be taken prisoner rather than committing suicide was so that I could prove that the scion was innocent! The sacrificial meats that he sent were kept for six days in the palace! Surely, if they were poisoned, should someone not have noticed something odd about them?"

Lady Li Ji, who was present but sitting behind a screen, shouted out, "Du Yuankuan led his student astray. Why don't you just kill him?"

Lord Xian ordered a guard to crush his skull with blows from a bronze hammer. The other ministers all mourned him, but they did so in secret. The Honorable Chonger and Yiwu of Jin both fled into exile, seeking safety from assassins sent by their father and Lady Li Ji.

If you want to know what happened when Lord Xian died, READ ON.

Chapter Seven

Li Ke murders two infant rulers in succession.

*Lord Mu pacifies a civil war in Jin
for the first time.*

When Lord Xian of Jin died, Xun Xi presided over the establishment of
the Honorable Xiqi as the new lord in front of his father's coffin. All the
officials attended the funeral and wailed ceremonially. Hu Tu was the
only one who refused to go, with the excuse that he was seriously ill.

Li Ke spoke privately with Pi Zhengfu: "Even though this child has
now become the new lord, what will happen about his brothers in
exile?"

"Xun Xi seems to be in complete control of the situation," Pi Zhengfu
said, "so you had better go and find out what he intends to do."

Accordingly, the two men got onto a chariot and went to Xun Xi's
mansion together. Xun Xi invited them in, and Li Ke made his repre-
sentation to him: "His Lordship has just passed away and the Honorable Chonger and Yiwu are both in exile abroad. You are one of the
most senior ministers in the country, so why did you not invite the
oldest son to succeed to his father's position, instead of establishing
the son of a base-born favorite? How will you persuade anyone to submit to his authority? They may have been prevented from expressing
their opinions to His Late Lordship, but the faction behind his three
older brothers hate Xiqi and his mother right down to the marrow of
their bones. Now that Lord Xian is dead, they will be planning a rebellion. Xiqi's brothers will have the support of our neighboring states, as
well as that of the residents of the capital. What plans have you come
up with to deal with this?"

"I have supported Xiqi purely because that was His Lordship's deathbed wish," Xun Xi explained, "so he has now become my ruler. I do not care about his exiled brothers! If there is anyone who does not agree with what I have done, they can kill me. In that way at least I will be able to requite our former lord's kindness to me."

"Your death will avail nothing," Pi Zhengfu retorted. "Do you really not have any better ideas?"

"I have always repaid His Late Lordship with absolute loyalty," Xun Xi said proudly. "Even if dying is indeed completely pointless, at least I will have kept my word!" The two men kept trying to persuade him, but Xun Xi's mind was made up. From start to finish he just repeated the same thing, so in the end they just had to say goodbye and leave him.

"We have been good colleagues," Li Ke remarked to Pi Zhengfu, "but even though I have explained the delicacy of the situation so clearly, he simply will not listen. What should I do now?"

"He is working for Xiqi," Pi Zhengfu said, "and we are working for Chonger. Each of us is serving our own master. What is wrong with that?"

The two men made a secret agreement to send a trusted knight, dressed up as one of His Lordship's guards, to mix in with all the others. His mission was to stab Xiqi to death while he was attending to his father's coffin in the mourning hut. When the assassin struck, the actor Shi was by the young boy's side, and he drew his sword to defend him. Although he succeeded in slaying the assassin, both he and Xiqi were killed in this attack. In an instant, the whole party was in an uproar. Xun Xi was some way away, wailing over the late Lord Xian's coffin. When he heard the news, he was deeply alarmed and immediately rushed over. He patted the boy's body and said sadly, "It was His Lordship's dying wish that I should support your accession, and I have been guilty of a terrible crime in not protecting you."

He attempted suicide by dashing his head against one of the pillars of the hut, but Lady Li Ji quickly ordered someone to prevent him. "His Lordship's body is still lying there unburied," she said. "Are you the only person who is not aware of that fact? Even if Xiqi is dead, the Honorable Zhuozi is still alive. You should support his accession."

Xun Xi ordered the execution of the couple of dozen men who had been guarding the party. That very same day he convened a meeting of all the officials, at which they discussed installing Zhuozi as the new ruler. At that time, he was just nine years old. Li Ke and Pi Zhengfu pretended to know nothing at all about what was going on, and they did not attend this meeting.

"The murder of this child was the result of Li Ke and Pi Zhengfu taking revenge for the death of the late scion," Liang Wu said. "Now they have not come to this meeting, so the truth could not be clearer. I request your permission to take the army to punish them."

"Those two men are long-serving ministers of the state of Jin," Xun Xi reminded him, "and they are both well-connected and widely supported. Most of the seven senior grandees of our state are related to one or another of them. If you fail in your attempt to punish them, things will only get worse. It would be better to ignore the whole situation, letting them imagine that they have got away with it, so that they proceed with their plan. Once the funeral is out of the way, we can formally establish a new ruler, and then, with support from our allies, we can get rid of their faction. Once that is done, we can deal with the pair of them."

As Liang Wu walked away, he said to Dongguan Wu, "Xun Xi is a very loyal minister, but he is not a good conspirator. He seems to want to let things drag on, but we cannot wait! Li Ke and Pi Zhengfu may be on the same side, but of the two of them, Li Ke suffered the most with what happened to the scion, and so his hatred is correspondingly deep. If we get rid of Li Ke, Pi Zhengfu will not fight us."

"How do you plan to get rid of him?" Dongguan Wu inquired.

"The funeral cortege is now approaching the city," Liang Wu said, "so if you were to arrange an ambush by the East Gate, all we would need is one soldier to attack him out of the blue."

"That's fine!" Dongguan Wu exclaimed. "I have a client named Tu'an Yi who can run at full speed while carrying a three-thousand-*jun* weight. If I hold out the prospect of a title and money to spend, he will do this for us."

He summoned Tu'an Yi and explained what they had in mind. However, Tu'an Yi had always been on good terms with the Grandee Zhui Chuan, and so he secretly leaked the details of the plot to him. "Should I do this or not?" he asked.

"Everyone in the country was devastated by the terrible death of the innocent scion," Zhui Chuan reminded him, "and that was all the fault of Lady Li Ji. Now the two grandees, Li Ke and Pi Zhengfu, want to extirpate her faction at court and establish the Honorable Chonger as the new ruler, which is an entirely virtuous action. I will not let you help the wicked to punish the loyal by carrying out such a heinous crime. You cannot do something that will see you cursed by ten thousand generations, you cannot!"

"Ordinary people like me don't know anything about the bigger picture," Tu'an Yi said. "How would it be if I simply refused?"

"If you refuse," Zhui Chuan told him, "they will just find someone else. It would be better if you pretended to agree and then, when the time comes, you turn your sword against them and help us to punish these wicked men. You will then have the honor of having supported the accession of the rightful heir. You will not only become noble and rich, but also be highly esteemed. Surely that is better than getting involved in such a wicked crime!"

"You are absolutely right," Tu'an Yi said.

"Do you think you can carry this off?" Zhui Chuan asked.

"If you have any concerns about my loyalty," Tu'an Yi proclaimed, "let us swear a blood covenant!" He slaughtered a chicken and they smeared their mouths with blood.

When Tu'an Yi left, Zhui Chuan told Pi Zhengfu what had happened, and Zhengfu communicated this to Li Ke. They arranged that their own soldiers would be mobilized and primed to set out on the day of the funeral.

On the appointed day, Li Ke announced that he was too ill to attend the obsequies. Tu'an Yi then spoke to Dongguan Wu: "All the grandees with the exception of Li Ke will be attending the funeral. Heaven must want him dead! Let me take three hundred soldiers to surround his mansion and kill him."

Dongguan Wu was very pleased. All that happened, however, was that Tu'an Yi pretended to surround Li Ke's house with the three hundred soldiers. Li Ke added verisimilitude to these events by sending a messenger to go to the tomb site and announce that he was under attack. Xun Xi was alarmed and asked what was going on, but Dongguan Wu simply said, "We heard rumors that Li Ke was planning to take advantage of the current situation to launch a coup, so we have sent one of our clients with a few troops to place him under temporary house arrest. If our efforts succeed, you will get credit for putting down a rebellion. If they do not, you will not take any of the blame."

Xun Xi felt as if he had been stabbed to the heart. He carried out the remainder of the funerary rites in a daze. He sent the forces under the command of the "Two Wus" to help in the attack, while he himself assisted the Honorable Zhuozi to preside over his first court, in the hope that this would put the best possible gloss on the matter. Dongguan Wu's troops were the first to arrive at the Eastern Market. Tu'an Yi came forward to meet him. With the excuse of needing to report on the progress of their plan, he came right up close, got Dongguan Wu into a headlock, and broke his neck. The army was thrown into complete chaos. Tu'an Yi then shouted: "The Honorable Chonger has already arrived at the foot of the city walls in command of an allied army! Let us punish the corrupt and wicked people responsible for the terrible death of poor Shensheng and welcome Chonger as our new ruler. Anyone who supports this should come with me! Anyone against it can go home!"

When the army heard that Chonger had been proclaimed their new ruler, they all leaped up and were happy to obey his orders. When Liang Wu heard that Dongguan Wu had been murdered, he immediately rushed to court, for it was his intention to flee into exile with Xun Xi and the Honorable Zhuozi. However, Tu'an Yi came in hot pursuit. Li Ke, Pi Zhengfu, and Zhui Chuan all arrived at the same time, each in command of his own troops. Liang Wu realized that he would not be able to escape, so he drew his sword and tried to cut his own throat, but before he could kill himself, Tu'an Yi wrested the sword from his grasp and took him prisoner. Li Ke then raised his saber and cut him in two pieces. Just at that moment Grandee Gong Hua, the general in command of the army of the left, arrived at the head of his own army to assist them. They cut their way through the palace gates together, with Li Ke leading the way, a naked blade in his hand. The soldiers followed him, and the palace servants scattered in terror.

Xun Xi remained calm and hugged Zhuozi to his chest with his left arm, while holding his right arm so that his sleeve hid the boy's face. Zhuozi was whimpering with fear. "What crime has this child committed?" he demanded. "Kill me instead! I beg that you will leave His Late Lordship's son alive!"

"And where is Shensheng now?" Li Ke retorted. "Was he not also one of His Lordship's sons?" He turned his head to look at Tu'an Yi, and said, "What are you waiting for?"

Tu'an Yi grabbed the boy from Xun Xi's grasp, threw him down upon the steps, and crushed him to death with a single stamp from his foot. Xun Xi was furious; wrenching his sword from its scabbard, he launched an attack on Li Ke. He too was beheaded by Tu'an Yi. They then fought their way through the palace, only to discover that Lady Li Ji had already fled to seek sanctuary with Lady Jia Jun. However, Lady Jia Jun shut the door on her and refused to help, so she went to the rear gardens, where she threw herself into the lake from the top of the bridge and drowned. Li Ke ordered that her body be exposed in the marketplace. Lady Li Ji's younger sister had never been favored, nor had she held any power at court, in spite of the fact that she gave birth to the Honorable Zhuozi. Therefore they did not kill her, but she was imprisoned in one of the side rooms in the palace. They murdered every member of the "Two Wus" family and that of the actor, Shi.

A bearded old man wrote a poem bewailing what happened to Lady Li Ji:

> What was the point of murdering Shensheng
> To allow a child to take over these lands?
> But both mother and child were killed in their turn,
> Just as described in the song: "The Pleasures of Idleness."

There is another poem that bemoans the fact that Xun Xi upheld his lord's stupid commands and thus established two concubines' sons in power, to the detriment of his posthumous reputation. This poem runs:

> Surely it is not right to follow the stupid orders of a misguided ruler,
> And yet he stubbornly insisted on remaining loyal until death.
> What happened to the intelligence that planned the bribing of the
>   Duke of Yu?
> Thus a ruler and a minister ended up waiting to die together.

Li Ke summoned all the ministers to court to discuss the situation with them. "The two base-born children are now dead. Of all the sons of His Late Lordship, Chonger is the cleverest and he is also the most senior. He should become our next ruler. All those grandees who agree with me should sign their names to this document."

"For this matter to be accomplished, we will need the help of Grandee Hu Tu," Pi Zhengfu reminded him.

Li Ke immediately sent someone with a chariot to fetch him. Hu Tu refused to go, saying: "My two sons followed the Honorable Chonger into exile with the Di people. If I now play any role in bringing him back to the country, I will become an accessory after the fact in the assassinations of Xiqi and Zhuozi. I am an old man anyway. Chonger will only come back if mandated to do so by all the grandees of our country."

Li Ke seized the brush and was the first to sign his name to the document. He was followed by Pi Zhengfu, Gong Hua, Jia Hua, Zhui Chuan, and more than thirty other grandees—in fact not all of the junior people who wanted to sign were able to. They awarded Tu'an Yi the office of a senior knight and ordered him to take this official letter of appointment to the Di, and to escort the Honorable Chonger back to the country.

When Chonger noticed that Hu Tu had not signed, he became suspicious.

"They want to bring you back, so why don't you go?" his supporters demanded. "Do you want to stay in exile forever?"

"You don't understand," Chonger said. "There are many other potential heirs, not just me. Besides which, although the two boys have both been killed, their supporters are still out there. What is the point of going back if I am just going to be forced into exile again? If Heaven wishes to bless me, surely it will not leave me stateless."

Hu Yan was worried that his reputation would be irreparably damaged if Chonger were seen to take advantage of Lord Xian's death to launch a coup, so he urged him not to go. The Honorable Chonger apologized to the envoy, and said: "I fled into exile after offending against my father, so during his lifetime I was unable to perform the duties of a son, and after his death I have not been able to mourn him according to the proper rites. In the circumstances, surely it is not appropriate for me to take advantage of the chaos in Jin to take over the country. The grandees will have to establish one of His Lordship's other sons, because I do not want anything to do with this situation."

Tu'an Yi reported back with this message, and Li Ke wanted to send another envoy. However, Grandee Liang Yaomi now spoke up: "Any of His Lordship's sons will do as our next ruler, so how about Yiwu?"

"Yiwu is a greedy and unpleasant man," Li Ke said. "Since he is greedy, he is untrustworthy, while his unpleasant character means that people do not love him. Chonger is a much better choice."

"But he is cleverer than any of His Lordship's other sons, is he not?" Liang Yaomi said. The company all agreed, so Li Ke had no choice but to send Tu'an Yi to help Liang Yaomi bring the Honorable Yiwu home.

. . .

The Honorable Yiwu had been living in Liang, where the Earl of Liang had given him the hand of his daughter in marriage. While Yiwu was staying with his in-laws, he was on watch day and night for developments in Jin, in case there was some kind of opportunity that would allow him to go home. When he heard that Lord Xian had died, he immediately ordered Lü Yisheng to attack the city of Qu and hold it for him. Xun Xi was so busy with other matters of state that he could not deal with this. Then Yiwu heard that Xiqi and Zhuozi had both been murdered and that the grandees had sent someone to bring Chonger home. Lü Yisheng told the Honorable Yiwu about the document that they had prepared. Yiwu then discussed the situation with Guo She and Xi Rui, because he was planning to dispute the succession. Suddenly Liang Yaomi and his entourage turned up to welcome Yiwu back, so he slapped his hand against his forehead and said, "Heaven has snatched the country out of Chonger's grasp and given it to me!" He could not overcome his delight.

Xi Rui came forward and said: "Chonger has certainly not given up his claim to the title, so his refusal is highly suspicious. You must not trust him! The grandees are all still in power inside the state, and yet they are bringing you back from exile to make you the ruler, so they will be expecting lavish rewards. The most important ministers in the government of the state of Jin are Li Ke and Pi Zhengfu. You will have to give them massive bribes, or your position will be in great danger. As the saying goes, when a man walks into the tiger's den, he had better be carrying a sharp spear. If you want to return to your country, my lord, you will have to have the assistance of a strong foreign power. Of the states bordering on Jin, Qin is by far the strongest. You should send an envoy to humbly beg for Qin for help in installing you in power. If Qin agrees, then you can go home."

Yiwu followed his advice and agreed to give Li Ke one million *mu* of land in Fenyang, while Pi Zhengfu would get seven hundred thousand *mu* in Fukui. This was all set out in writing, and then the document was sealed. He ordered Tu'an Yi to go back to Jin to report on the situation, while he kept Liang Yaomi behind, because he wanted him to take a letter to Qin to announce that the grandees of the state of Jin wanted to establish him as their new ruler.

Lord Mu of Qin spoke about this to Jian Shu: "I am the only person in the world who can bring an end to the civil war in Jin; that has been proclaimed by the dream given to me by God on High. I have heard that Chonger and Yiwu are both brilliant young men, so I should choose one to install in power. But which one is best?"

"Chonger is living with the Di, while Yiwu is in Liang," Jian Shu said. "These two places are both nearby, so Your Lordship could send someone to condole with them on the death of their father. That way you can learn something of their personalities."

"That would be good," Lord Mu agreed.

Thus it came about that he sent the Honorable Zhi to offer formal condolences first to Chonger and then to Yiwu. When the Honorable Zhi arrived among the Di people, he had an audience with the Honorable Chonger at which he expressed his condolences, just as he had been instructed by the Lord of Qin. When the ceremony had been completed, Chonger withdrew. The Honorable Zhi then sent a message by the gatekeeper to say, "You should be thinking about how to take advantage of this situation to get back home. His Lordship would be happy to help you in return for a small douceur."

Chonger reported this to Zhao Cui, who said, "If your own people want you back, that is one thing. It is something quite different if you are installed by a foreign power."

Chonger went out and had an audience with the ruler of Qin's envoy at which he said: "His Lordship has been kind enough to send official condolences to me even though I am in exile, but he has humiliated me by his second message. Having been expelled from my country, I have no treasure to offer him—friendship is all that I have left. My father has only just died; under the circumstances, how could I be plotting a coup?"

He threw himself upon the ground and wept, kowtowed, and withdrew; from start to finish, he did not say a single word that could possibly be construed as indicating any selfish ambition. The Honorable Zhi realized that Chonger would not be playing along, and he was deeply impressed by his noble character, so he sighed in admiration and left.

Next he went to condole with Yiwu in Liang. When the ceremony was over, Yiwu said to the Honorable Zhi, "You, sir, received His Lordship's order to come and condole with me, so do you have any further instructions for me?"

The Honorable Zhi then tried the line about "taking advantage of this situation to get back home" on him, and Yiwu kowtowed and thanked him. Afterwards he went in and reported this to Xi Rui, saying, "Qin has agreed to install me in power."

"What is Qin hoping to get out of it?" Xi Rui asked. "They are going to want something from us. You had better be prepared to bribe them with a large tranche of land."

"Won't giving them a large area of land harm Jin?" Yiwu inquired.

"Until such time as you have returned to your own country as ruler," Xi Rui explained, "you are just an ordinary subject of the Lord of Liang, and you do not own so much as a foot of land in Jin! What is the problem with giving them something that actually belongs to someone else?"

Yiwu then had a second audience with the Honorable Zhi. Clasping hold of his hand, he said: "Li Ke and Pi Zhengfu have both promised to support my accession. I intend to reward both of them generously for this. If, thanks to His Lordship's support, I am able to take control of the state altars of Jin, I will give five cities beyond the Yellow River to Lord Mu to add to his eastern border. I am happy to give the Lord of Qin all the former territory of Guo, as far south as Mount Hua and extending right up to the border at Xieliang, and yet this will only requite one tiny part of His Lordship's generosity to me."

He took a document to this effect out of his sleeve with an appealing expression on his face. The Honorable Zhi went through the motions of refusing, but Yiwu said, "I have here forty ingots of gold and six pairs of white jade pendants, which I would like to give to your entourage. I hope that you will speak well of me to His Lordship. Indeed, I will never forget your kindness to me."

The Honorable Zhi then accepted all his gifts.

A historian wrote a poem, which reads:

The Honorable Chonger was virtuous and mourned the death of his father.
The Honorable Yiwu was vicious, and so he was thrilled by these events.

Simply by observing the way in which they received the condolences
    offered,
You can tell which of them would succeed and which would fail!

The Honorable Zhi returned with this document to show Lord Mu,
and he described his audience with the two young men.

"Chonger is a much more noble character than Yiwu, so I will
install him," Lord Mu announced.

"Is Your Lordship planning to install a new ruler in Jin because you
feel sorry for this country?" the Honorable Zhi inquired. "Or is it
because you want to make yourself famous?"

"Why should I care in the slightest what happens in Jin?" Lord Mu
said in puzzlement. "I just want to make myself famous."

"If Your Lordship were feeling sorry for Jin," the Honorable Zhi
explained, "you would want to select the best possible ruler to install
in power. If your primary intention is to become famous, then you had
better choose an ignoble character. In both instances you are putting a
new ruler in place, but a brilliant man would outshine you, whereas a
stupid person would always be in your debt. Which of the two is more
beneficial for you?"

"You have really opened my eyes!" Lord Mu exclaimed. He ordered
Noble Grandson Qi to take a force of three hundred chariots out to
install Yiwu in power.

. . .

Lord Mu of Qin's principal wife, Lady Mu Ji, was the younger sister of
Scion Shensheng of Jin. From a very young age, she had been brought
up in the palace of Lord Xian's second wife, Lady Jia Jun, and she was
a most noble and virtuous woman. When she heard that Noble Grandson Qi was going to install Yiwu in power in Jin, she wrote a letter for
him which said:

When you become the ruler of Jin, you must treat Lady Jia Jun well.
Your brothers and uncles who have fled into exile to avoid the troubles
in Jin are all innocent of any crime, so you should allow them all to
come home. If in the future they achieve great things, this will only
bring greater glory to you. Let them protect the borders of our state.

Yiwu was afraid of offending Lady Mu Ji, so he did exactly as she
instructed him. Meanwhile, Li Ke and Pi Zhengfu asked permission

from the senior minister Hu Tu to take charge of the ceremonies of appointing a new marquis. They arranged that the officials would prepare the carriages to go to collect Yiwu at the border of Jin. Upon his entry into the capital city of Jiang, Yiwu was formally installed as Lord Hui of Jin, and this year was proclaimed the first year of his rule. The first year of Lord Hui of Jin's rule was also the second year of the reign of King Xiang of Zhou. The residents of the capital had long admired Chonger's noble character, and they were hoping that he would become their next ruler. Now Yiwu had replaced Chonger and they were very disappointed.

When Lord Hui was established, he appointed Hu Tu and Guo She senior grandees and Lü Yisheng and Xi Rui as mid-level grandees, while Tu'an Yi became a junior grandee. The remaining ministers all kept their old offices. After the government of Jin had been reorganized, Noble Grandson Qi of Qin remained behind, because he insisted on the five cities west of the Yellow River being handed over. Lord Hui could not bear to lose them, so he summoned his officials for a meeting to discuss the situation.

At this meeting, Guo She stared meaningfully at Lü Yisheng. He then came forward and said: "The reason why Your Lordship wanted to bribe Qin was that you had not yet been able to return to your country, so the land that you offered them was actually not yours to give. Now you have been installed in power and the country is yours. If you don't give this land to Qin, what can they do about it?"

"Your Lordship has only just come to power," Li Ke reminded him, "so it would not be a good idea for you to betray the trust of a powerful neighboring state. You had better give them the land."

"Losing those five cities is like losing half the state of Jin," Xi Rui said. "Even though Qin is militarily very powerful, they certainly would not be able to wrest these lands from us by force. Besides which, His Late Lordship began his military campaigns from that territory—we cannot just abandon them!"

"Since you knew that those were His Late Lordship's heartlands, why on earth did you agree to hand them over?" Li Ke demanded. "Having agreed, will you not anger Qin greatly when you refuse to give them? Besides which, our former lord founded the country at Quwo, a very small parcel of land, but he then strengthened his government and was eventually able to conquer a number of other small states, thus becoming great. If Your Lordship were to reform the government and maintain good relations with your neighbors, there is nothing to worry about in losing these five cities."

Xi Rui sighed and said, "Li Ke isn't speaking up on behalf of Qin, but because he wants his one million *mu* of land in Fenyang and is afraid that Your Lordship is not going to give them to him. He wants Qin to use as a precedent."

Pi Zhengfu elbowed Li Ke in the ribs and he did not dare to say another word.

"If I don't hand over these cities, then I betray my word," Lord Hui said, "but if I do hand them over, then I am seriously weakening my position. How about I just give them one or two cities?"

"If you present them with one or two cities," Lü Yisheng said, "first of all, you have not completely kept your word, and secondly, it might well provoke open conflict with Qin. How about you try apologizing to them?"

Lord Hui ordered Lü Yisheng to write a letter apologizing to Qin. This letter said:

> Originally I promised to give five cities west of the Yellow River to Your Lordship. Now I have been so fortunate as to be able to return and take control of the state altars. Remembering your great kindness to me, I want to fulfill my promise. However, my senior ministers all said: "Your lands are the territory of our former rulers. When you were in exile, how could you unilaterally agree to give them away to someone else?" I argued with them, but they did not accept my position. I hope that you will agree to a slight delay. I will never dare to forget your generosity to me.

"Who will go on my behalf to apologize to the state of Qin?" His Lordship asked. Pi Zhengfu was willing to go, and so Lord Hui agreed to this.

Li Ke's original idea was to make the Honorable Chonger the next ruler of Jin, but Chonger refused to come back, and Yiwu offered generous bribes in his efforts to return to the country, so Li Ke followed the wishes of the majority and set about seeing to Yiwu's accession. Who could have guessed that once Yiwu was installed as Lord Hui, he would refuse to hand over any of the lands that he had promised, and would employ only his personal friends such as Guo She, Lü Yisheng, and Xi Rui in senior government positions, thereby alienating all the old officials who had served in the previous regime? Li Ke found himself in a situation that he simply could not accept. When he encouraged Lord Hui to give the land to Qin, this was clearly said with the good of the country at heart, but Xi Rui interpreted it as being for his own selfish reasons. He was careful not to put his rage into words and tried to appear calm, but in actual fact he was furious. When he walked out of the palace gates, the mask slipped and he looked murderous. When Pi Zhengfu went on his mission to Qin, Xi Rui and his cronies were worried that he was involved in some kind of plot with Li Ke, so they secretly sent people to spy on him. Pi Zhengfu had anticipated the possibility that Xi Rui would send someone to check up on him, so he deliberately did not go to say goodbye. Li Ke sent someone to fetch Pi Zhengfu because he wanted to speak to him, but at that time he had already left the city. Li Ke chased after him but could not catch up with him.

Naturally, someone reported this news to Xi Rui. He had an audience with Lord Hui and presented his opinion: "Li Ke hates Your Lordship because you have taken away his power in the government and refused to give him the fields in Fenyang. Now when he heard that Pi Zhengfu had been sent on a diplomatic mission to Qin, he set off in hot pursuit, so he must be plotting something. I have always understood that Li Ke was a close friend of the Honorable Chonger and never intended to see Your Lordship succeed to the title. If he is indeed plotting a coup with Chonger, what are you going to do to stop him? You had better force him to commit suicide before he brings disaster down upon you."

"Li Ke put me in power," Lord Hui said. "What excuse can I now give for killing him?"

"Li Ke assassinated both Xiqi and Zhuozi," Xi Rui reminded him, "and he murdered Xun Xi, the man who received your father's dying commands. These are terrible crimes! You may be privately grateful for his assistance in ensuring your accession, but that should not prevent you from punishing him for his murders in the interests of justice. No enlightened ruler ever neglected the interests of justice in favor of some private gratitude. I request that you give me the order to punish him."

"Please do!" said Lord Hui.

Xi Rui went to Li Ke's house and told him: "The Marquis of Jin has commanded me to come and see you. His Lordship said, 'If it were not for you, I would never have succeeded to the title, and so I have always been cognizant of the enormous assistance that you have given me. However, you assassinated two lords and murdered one senior grandee, which really puts me in a very difficult position. I have now taken up the mandate of our former lords, so I cannot neglect the interests of justice because of my personal gratitude. Therefore I wish you to commit suicide.'"

"If those people had not died, would His Lordship be in power now?" Li Ke demanded. "Now you want me to take the blame, so how can I escape disaster? I accept my fate!"

Xi Rui attempted to force the issue. Li Ke drew his sword and paced around, shouting, "Heavens! I am innocent! Loyalty has now become a crime! If the dead do indeed have awareness, how can I face Xun Xi?" He then killed himself by cutting his throat.

Xi Rui went back and reported this to Lord Hui, who was very pleased.

A bearded old man wrote a poem, which reads:

> Given that working for the Honorable Yiwu got him killed,
> Would it not have been better to die with Scion Shensheng?
> He should have known that sitting on the fence would not work,
> And made his reputation even worse than that of Xun Xi!

Do you want to know what happened next? THE STORY CONTINUES . . .

The Fight for Lady Xia Ji

Chapter Eight

*Lord Ling of Chen uses underwear to make
a joke at court.*

*An unfortunate remark to Xia
Zhengshu causes many deaths.*

The Honorable Pingguo, the son of Shuo, Lord Gong of Chen, succeeded to his father's title and was installed as Lord Ling in the sixth
year of the reign of King Qing of Zhou. He was a frivolous and silly
man, without any of the awe-inspiring characteristics that a ruler
needs. His only interests were alcohol and women; his only pursuit
was of enjoyment. He paid no attention whatsoever to the government
of the country. There were two grandees whom he particularly favored:
Kong Ning and Yi Xingfu. Both encouraged and assisted him in his
drunken debauchery. The ruler and his two subjects found themselves
to be birds of a feather; there was no restraint in their words or actions.
At this time there was one wise minister at the Chen court, a man
named Xie Ye, who was loyal and upright, and who dared to speak his
mind on every occasion. The Marquis of Chen and his cronies were
scared stiff of him. There was also a certain Grandee Xia Yushu. His
father was the Honorable Shaoxi, the son of Lord Ding of Chen.

*The Honorable Shaoxi had the style name Zixia; therefore. his
descendants used the word Xia as their surname, though sometimes they
were also called the Shaoxi clan.*

The Xia family held office as minister of war in the state of Chen as
a hereditary prerogative, and they enjoyed the revenues of a fief at
Zhulin. Grandee Xia Yushu was married to Lady Xia Ji, the daughter
of Lord Mu of Zheng. Lady Xia Ji had a face like an almond with

cheeks of coral; her slanted phoenix eyes were topped by elegantly curved eyebrows. She was as beautiful as Lady Li Ji or Lady Xi Gui, and as seductive as Da Ji or Lady Wen Jiang. She seemed to hook the soul of every man who saw her out of his body, causing him to go raving mad. There was a further remarkable thing about her: at the age of fifteen, she had dreamed that she saw a man dressed in a hat covered with stars and a robe of feathers who proclaimed that he was an immortal from the realms above. When they engaged in sexual relations, he instructed her in the skills of sucking out a man's essence and moving his *qi,* so that every time she had sex, not only would she enjoy great pleasure, she would also be able to use her partner's *yang* to boost her own *yin,* thereby never growing old. This is the so-called Plain Girl's Fighting Technique.

Before she was married, Lady Xia Ji engaged in an incestuous relationship with Lord Ling of Zheng's older half-brother, born to a concubine mother: the Honorable Man. Within three years the Honorable Man had died in his prime. Later on she married Xia Yushu and gave birth to a son named Zhengshu. Xia Zhengshu, styled Zinan, was only twelve years of age when his father became sick and died. Lady Xia Ji was having an affair, so she left Zhengshu behind in the capital where he could receive instruction from his teachers, while she herself went to live in Zhulin.

Kong Ning and Yi Xingfu were both acquainted with Xia Zhengshu from their dealings at court, and, having spied on his beautiful mother, they each conceived the idea of seducing her. Lady Xia Ji had a maid named Hehua, wise in the ways of the world, who played a key role in introducing her mistress to suitable lovers. One day Kong Ning was out hunting beyond the suburbs with Xia Zhengshu, whereupon they journeyed as far as Zhulin and spent the night in his house. Kong Ning put a bit of thought into how to seduce Hehua first. He gave her a hairpin and a pair of earrings and then begged her to present him to Her Ladyship. Having seduced her too, he left, having stolen her brocade vest to wear under his own clothes. He paraded round in front of Yi Xingfu, showing off about it. That made Yi Xingfu envious, and so he offered generous bribes to Hehua as well, to put him in contact with Her Ladyship. Lady Xia Ji had already noticed how tall and handsome Yi Xingfu was and was deeply attracted by him, so she sent Hehua to arrange a secret meeting between them. Yi Xingfu had invested in some aphrodisiacs in the hope of pleasing Lady Xia Ji, and she loved him twice as much as Kong Ning.

Yi Xingfu said to Lady Xia Ji, "Grandee Kong has the brocade vest that you gave him, and now I hope that you will give me something too as a sign of your affection."

"He stole my brocade vest," Lady Xia Ji said with a laugh. "I did not give it to him." Then she whispered in his ear, "Although I have slept with both of you, do you really think that I can't tell which one is better?"

She took off her green silk underpants and gave them to him. Yi Xingfu was very pleased. From this time onwards, Yi Xingfu came and went in great secrecy, and Kong Ning naturally found himself somewhat left out. Yi Xingfu had once been envious because Kong Ning got the brocade vest, but now that he had her green silk underpants, he could vaunt his position in front of Kong Ning. Kong Ning went in secret to visit Hehua and discovered that Yi Xingfu was having an affair with Lady Xia Ji. He was very jealous, but had no idea of how to get back at him. Then he thought of a plan: the Marquis of Chen was a greedy and debauched man who had long heard tell of Lady Xia Ji's remarkable beauty. He had mentioned her several times and would obviously like to number her among his many conquests.

"If he starts having an affair with her too, the Marquis of Chen is sure to be grateful to me for making it possible. However, His Lordship suffers from a disease in his private parts which medical textbooks call the 'Fox Stink' or 'Armpit Effluvium'; Lady Xia Ji is not going to like that at all. I will act as a go-between and try and strike up a relationship between the two of them, thereby making sure that I come out on top. At the very least, Yi Xingfu will find himself being ignored a little, which will be an adequate penalty for the jealousy he has made me suffer. What a plan! What an excellent plan!"

He went alone to see Lord Ling, and as they were gossiping, he casually mentioned that Lady Xia Ji was the most beautiful woman in the world.

"I too have long heard her name mentioned," Lord Ling said, "but she must now be over forty. Surely she is long past her prime!"

"Lady Xia Ji is exceptionally well-versed in the bedroom arts," Kong Ning explained, "and her face has preserved all its beauty. To look at her you might think her seventeen or eighteen years old! She is also unusually skilled in sexual techniques. If you try her, I can guarantee that you will lose your heart to her."

Lord Ling felt desire coursing through his veins, his face turning purple. "Can you arrange for me to meet Lady Xia Ji?" he asked. "I promise I will not forget how helpful you have been!"

Kong Ning presented his opinion: "The Xia family live at Zhulin, a place well-known for its magnificent bamboos and trees, so you can go there to admire them. If you announce tomorrow morning that you are going to visit Zhulin, the Xia family will be sure to arrange a banquet in your honor. Lady Xia Ji has a maid named Hehua, who knows all about her mistress's amorous adventures. I will communicate Your Lordship's wishes to her. That way, everything can easily be arranged."

"I am relying on you to make this happen," Lord Ling said with a laugh.

The following day, he ordered his chariot to be prepared and traveled to Zhulin in plain clothes. Only Grandee Kong Ning was allowed to accompany him. Kong Ning had already sent a letter on ahead to Lady Xia Ji instructing her to make suitable preparations. He also made sure that Hehua was aware of what was in the wind, so that she would be ready to play her role. Lady Xia Ji was not the kind of woman to be flustered by having to entertain a nobleman at such short notice, and every arrangement was made well ahead of time. Lord Ling thought about nothing except Lady Xia Ji: as far as he was concerned, this trip was all about the conquest of a famous beauty. As the saying goes, an affair with a beautiful woman is everything, and makes even the most magnificent scenery meaningless. Within a short time, they arrived at the Xia family mansion.

Lady Xia Ji came out to greet them wearing her official robes. She invited His Lordship to take the seat of honor in the main hall, then bowed, and said politely: "My son, Zhengshu, is away from home. Not knowing that Your Lordship intended to honor us with a visit, he is not present to receive you." Her voice, like the fluting of an oriole, was utterly delightful to listen to. Lord Ling looked at her: she really was divinely beautiful! Among all the concubines in his six palaces, there was no one who could compare.

"I happened to be passing and thought that I would visit your mansion," Lord Ling declared. "I do hope that I am not disturbing you."

Lady Xia Ji straightened her robe and said, "It is a great honor to be able to receive Your Lordship in my humble home. I have prepared some simple snacks and wine, but I do not dare to present them to you."

"Since you have already put your cooks to this trouble," Lord Ling returned, "let us not bother with a formal banquet. I have heard that your mansion has an exceptionally beautiful garden attached to it, which I would very much like to see. How about serving the meal there, Your Ladyship?"

"Since the death of my husband," Lady Xia Ji replied, "the garden has become overgrown and desolate. I am afraid that you will not enjoy it, my lord. Let me apologize now for its poor condition!"

Lady Xia Ji's modest and respectful replies made Lord Ling even more anxious to seduce her. He ordered Lady Xia Ji: "Change out of your formal robes and show me around your garden!"

Lady Xia Ji then removed her official robes, revealing herself in a simple dress, like pear blossom below the moon or plum petals in the snow. She really was exceptionally lovely. Her Ladyship led the way into the garden. Although it did not cover a huge area, it contained elegant pine trees and fine cypresses, unusual rocks and rare plants— there was a lake to one side and several painted pavilions scattered here and there. In the middle of the garden, there was a belvedere placed on a high promontory; its pillars were painted red and its beams hung with silk, all very beautiful and refined: this was where the banquet would be held. Rooms were set aside for the servants to be entertained as well. Behind this belvedere was a covered walkway winding up and down, leading to a separate cluster of buildings; these were the bedrooms. There was also a stable in the garden, where fine horses were raised. West of the garden, there was an area of open ground, which was used for target archery.

Lord Ling looked at everything, and then a banquet was served in the belvedere. Lady Xia Ji had arranged the seating in order of precedence, so when Lord Ling told her to sit down beside him, she declined politely.

"How can Your Ladyship refuse to sit down in your own house?" Lord Ling asked. He ordered Kong Ning to sit on his right hand side and Lady Xia Ji to sit on his left. "Today let us make none of the distinctions between ruler and subject, but just enjoy ourselves!"

While he was drinking, Lord Ling never took his eyes off her, and Lady Xia Ji returned his glances. His Lordship was a heavy drinker at the best of times, and with Kong Ning sitting beside him and encouraging him, he poured the wine down his neck without noticing how much he was consuming. As the sun set behind the western hills, the servants brought in lamps and washed the drinking cups before pouring in new wine. Lord Ling was now very drunk and lay slumped across his seating mat, snoring.

Kong Ning whispered to Lady Xia Ji, "His Lordship has heard a great deal about how lovely you are and came here today because he is hoping to enjoy you. You cannot refuse."

Lady Xia Ji smiled and said nothing. Kong Ning made the necessary arrangements quickly; he went out to tell the servants to go to bed, then he went to sleep himself. Lady Xia Ji had a brocade coverlet and embroidered pillow taken to the belvedere. She herself went off to bathe in perfumed waters in preparation for receiving His Lordship's amorous advances. She made Hehua stay behind and look after him.

A short time later, Lord Ling awoke. As he opened his eyes, he asked, "Who are you?"

"I am Hehua, my lord," she said, sinking to her knees. "Her Ladyship ordered me to take care of you." Accordingly, she offered him some sour plum hangover soup.

"Who made this soup?" Lord Ling asked.

"I did," Hehua replied.

"If you are serving me plum soup, does that mean you are also ready to serve as my go-between?"

Hehua pretended that she did not understand what he was talking about, and said, "I have never been a go-between before, but I do know how to run errands and take messages. However, I do not know who has taken Your Lordship's fancy."

"Her Ladyship has sundered my soul!" Lord Ling exclaimed dramatically. "If you can arrange this for me, I will reward you generously."

"Her Ladyship is a widow so I am afraid she cannot join your harem," Hehua replied. "However, if you do not object to the idea, an affair might be possible . . ."

Lord Ling was delighted and immediately ordered Hehua to carry a lamp and light his way. By twists and turns, they made their way to the women's quarters. Lady Xia Ji was sitting alone beside a lamp, as if she were waiting for someone. When she suddenly heard the sound of footsteps, she made as if she was about to call out, but Lord Ling was already inside the room. Hehua carried the silver lamp away. Lord Ling did not bother to say anything; he just wrapped his arms around Lady Xia Ji and carried her towards the bed, stripping her of her clothes along the way. Her skin was so soft and delicate, and yet her body was burning with desire. When he penetrated her, he could have sworn that she was a virgin. Lord Ling was amazed and asked her about it.

"I know how to look after myself," Lady Xia Ji explained. "Even though I have given birth to a child, after three days I was as good as new."

Lord Ling sighed and said, "If I encountered a genuine goddess, she would not be as lovely as you!" Lord Ling's sexual techniques were far inferior to those of either Kong Ning or Yi Xingfu, in addition to which he had an unpleasant disease, so there was no pleasure to be gained by sleeping with him. On the other hand, he was the ruler of a country and hence in a position of great power, so Lady Xia Ji did not dare to complain. She pretended to enjoy his fumbling, and Lord Ling thought that he was engaged in an earth-shattering romance.

They slept until cockcrow, and then Lady Xia Ji shook Lord Ling awake.

"Having met you," Lord Ling told her, "I look upon the women of my six palaces as so much dross. However, I do not know if you have any feeling in your heart for me."

Lady Xia Ji was concerned that Lord Ling already knew about her affairs with Kong Ning and Yi Xingfu, so she said, "I would not dare to deceive Your Lordship. After my husband died, I was not able to control myself, and I ended up having a number of affairs. Now that I have served Your Lordship, I will refuse all other relationships in the future. If I betray my word, you can punish me as you wish!"

"Tell me who your other lovers are," Lord Ling said cheerfully. "I do not want you to conceal any of them."

"My lovers are Grandee Kong and Grandee Yi," Lady Xia Ji said. "No one else!"

"No wonder that Kong Ning praised your unusual sexual prowess," Lord Ling said. "How could he have known if he had not experienced it himself?"

"I apologize," Lady Xia Ji said humbly. "Please forgive me!"

"Kong Ning did a wonderful thing in recommending you," Lord Ling stated. "I am grateful to him, have no doubts about that! I want to see you regularly in the future, to continue our affair. You can do whatever you like the rest of the time, and I would not dream of interfering with you."

"If you come here often, my lord, will you not be able to see me regularly?" Lady Xia Ji asked coquettishly.

A short time later Lord Ling got up, and Lady Xia Ji removed her own undershirt and gave it to him to wear. "When you look on this shirt, my lord," she said, "you can imagine that you are looking at me!" Hehua picked up a lamp and led His Lordship back to the belvedere the same way that they had come.

When it got light, breakfast was laid out in the main hall. Kong Ning ordered the servants to prepare the carriages. Lady Xia Ji invited Lord Ling to take the seat of honor and asked if he had slept well. The cooks presented the viands, and everyone ate and drank their fill. When the meal was over, Kong Ning drove His Lordship back to court. The officials knew that the Marquis of Chen had spent the night out in the countryside, so they had all assembled at the inner door of the palace to ask after him. Lord Ling gave orders: "No court will be held today." He went straight in through the main door of the palace. Yi Xingfu dragged Kong Ning off to one side and asked him where His Lordship had spent the night. Kong Ning could not lie, so he told him the truth.

Yi Xingfu realized that Kong Ning was at the back of all of this, so stamping his foot, he burst out: "How could you monopolize His Lordship's favor in this way!"

"His Lordship is really thrilled," Kong Ning replied. "However, next time I will leave it to you to make the recommendation."

The two men laughed heartily and went their separate ways.

· · ·

The following day, Lord Ling held court in the morning. Once the ceremony was over, the ministers dispersed. His Lordship summoned Kong Ning into his presence and thanked him for recommending Lady Xia Ji. He also summoned Yi Xingfu and asked him, "You should have let me in on this secret much earlier. How could you keep it to yourselves?"

Kong Ning and Yi Xingfu both said, "There is no secret."

"She told me about it herself," Lord Ling said. "There is no need for you to lie."

"I guess you could compare this to a subject acting as a taster for his lord, or a son for his father," Kong Ning replied. "If we were not sure that she was wonderful, how could we dare to recommend her to Your Lordship?"

Lord Ling laughed and said, "Not so. Supposing that a bear's paw was served, I think letting me have first taste would not hurt anyone." Kong Ning and Yi Xingfu both burst out laughing, and His Lordship continued: "You may have gotten there first, but unlike the pair of you, I have a memento of the occasion." He took out the undershirt and showed it to them. "This was a present from her. What have you two got to say about that?"

"I have my own memento," Kong Ning told him.

"What did she give you?" Lord Ling asked.

Kong Ning loosened his clothing to reveal his brocade vest, and said, "Lady Xia Ji gave me this. It is not just me either, Yi Xingfu also has something."

"So what do you have?" Lord Ling inquired teasingly.

Yi Xingfu took out the green silk underpants and showed them to His Lordship. Lord Ling laughed heartily. "All three of us have a token of our victory on our persons. Someday we should all go to Zhulin together for an orgy!"

Word that the lord and the two grandees were making disgusting jokes together in the main hall spread beyond the palace gates, thereby angering an upright minister beyond measure. This man, Xie Ye, gritted his teeth and shouted: "Court is where the laws and regulations are determined. If such wickedness is to be countenanced, the state of Chen will collapse at any moment!" He straightened his robes and grabbed his staff of office before heading in through the gates to confront them.

Kong Ning and Yi Xingfu were afraid of Xie Ye's direct reproaches, and seeing him barge in without any announcement, they knew that he was going to remonstrate with them. Therefore, they bade hasty farewells to Lord Ling and left. Lord Ling was just about to leave his throne when Xie Ye stormed in and grabbed him by the sleeve. He knelt down and said: "I have heard that a vassal should respect his ruler and that men and women should maintain a proper segregation. Now you have caused a widow to lose her chastity, and what is more, you and your boon companions boast of your wicked exploits, encouraging each other to go even further. It is completely inappropriate that such vile things should be discussed at court—you have destroyed every vestige of honesty and shame, violating our traditions. Your subjects no longer respect you, no woman is safe—our moral order has collapsed! A lack of respect leads to dissolution, dissolution leads to chaos, and chaos leads to the ruin of the country. You must reform!"

Lord Ling could feel the sweat breaking out on his forehead. Covering his face with his sleeve, he said, "Say no more! I regret everything that I have done!"

Xie Ye said goodbye and walked out of the palace gates. Kong Ning and Yi Xingfu were standing out there, attempting to find out what was going on inside. When they saw Xie Ye marching out in a rage, they tried to hide in the crowd. However, Xie Ye had already spotted them and called the two men forward, upbraiding them to their faces: "When a ruler does a good deed, his subjects should publicize it; when a ruler does something wrong, his subjects ought to conceal that fact. Now you not only behave badly but encourage His Lordship to do likewise and make sure that everyone far and wide has heard of your wicked deeds. What does that look like? Are you not ashamed of yourselves?"

The two men had nothing to say, so they just apologized weakly.

When Xie Ye had left, Kong Ning and Yi Xingfu went to see Lord Ling, and they told him of Xie Ye's parting shot: "His Lordship must never go to Zhulin again!"

"Are you going to go back?" Lord Ling asked.

"Xie Ye was complaining about your behavior, my lord, and that has nothing to do with us," they said. "We can go again, but you can't!"

"I would rather annoy Xie Ye than give up my pleasures there," Lord Ling said crossly.

"If you go back again, my lord, I am afraid that you will find it difficult to withstand Xie Ye's tongue-lashing," they pointed out. "What are you going to do?"

"Do you have a plan for silencing Xie Ye?" His Lordship asked.

"If you want to shut Xie Ye up," Kong Ning said, "you are going to have to prevent him from opening his mouth."

Lord Ling laughed at that: "His mouth is his own. How am I supposed to stop him from opening it?"

"I know exactly what Ning means," Yi Xingfu said. "If he is dead, he won't be able to speak. Why don't you just give orders, my lord, to have Xie Ye killed? That way you can enjoy yourself without restraint!"

"I could not possibly do that!" Lord Ling exclaimed.

"How about I send an assassin after him?" Kong Ning suggested.

Lord Ling nodded and said, "Do whatever you like!"

The two men then said goodbye and left the palace, going somewhere private to discuss the matter. They hired an assassin, ordering him to lie in ambush on the main road to wait until Xie Ye went to court, then he leapt out and killed him. The people of Chen believed that the marquis was behind this assassination, for they were unaware of the two grandees' role in the conspiracy.

A historian wrote a poem about this:

> Every principle of virtue was humbled into the dust in Chen;
> The ruler and his subjects proclaimed their vices proudly.
> Their official hats and robes were polluted by women's underwear,
> They behaved as if the court had moved its home to Zhulin.
> How brave was Xie Ye!
> He alone remained as straight as an arrow, speaking his mind.
> Though he died, his reputation was unsullied,
> As loyal as Guan Longfeng or Prince Bigan!

After Xie Ye was murdered, neither ruler nor ministers were afraid of anyone anymore, so they would regularly go together to Zhulin. The first couple of times they went in secret, but as it became a common occurrence they made no pretense of trying to hide. The people of the capital composed the song "Zhulin" to criticize them. This song runs:

> Why does His Lordship go to Zhulin?
> He follows Xia Nan.
> If he is in Zhulin,
> He follows Xia Nan!

Xia Zhengshu's style name was Zinan. The people who composed this song were loyal subjects who deliberately chose not to mention the name of Lady Xia Ji. Instead they spoke of "Xia Nan," suggesting that His Lordship went to visit the son rather than the mother.

. . .

The Marquis of Chen was a worthless man, and with the full and active support of Kong Ning and Yi Xingfu, he paid no attention to the demands of propriety or any sense of shame. What is more, Lady Xia Ji was good at arranging things to everyone's satisfaction, so they came to an agreement whereby the three men would share her, enjoying themselves together. They saw nothing to be surprised at in their mode of living. Xia Zhengshu gradually grew up and became aware of his mother's behavior, which cut him to the heart. However, an open breach was impossible because of the Marquis of Chen's noble position, so there was really nothing he could do. Every time he heard that the Marquis of Chen was going to visit Zhulin, he made some kind of excuse not to be present, on the principle that what the eye does not see, the heart does not grieve after. This debauched foursome thus found themselves unrestrained by Xia Zhengshu's presence. Time flew like an arrow until Zhengshu was eighteen, by which time he had grown up into a handsome and strapping young man, a fine warrior and impressive archer. In order to please Lady Xia Ji, Lord Ling appointed him to the office formerly held by his own father, which gave him complete control over the army. When Zhengshu had finished offering thanks for His Lordship's benevolence, he went back to Zhulin to see his mother, Lady Xia Ji.

"How terribly kind of His Lordship!" she said. "You must do your utmost to fulfill the demands of your office and take responsibility for the security of the state. Do not worry about what is going on at home!"

Zhengshu said goodbye to his mother and returned to court to take up his new office.

. . .

It happened that one day Lord Ling of Chen was visiting Zhulin with Kong Ning and Yi Xingfu and they stayed overnight at the Xia family mansion. Xia Zhengshu came home especially in order to hold a banquet in Lord Ling's honor, to thank His Lordship for his kindness in allowing him to inherit his father's office. Since her son was present, Lady Xia Ji did not dare to come out and keep the men company. As they got drunk, His Lordship and his boon companions were making their usual smutty jokes, waving their hands about and stamping their feet. Xia Zhengshu was disgusted by their appearance and withdrew to the far side of the screens, where he listened in secret to what they were saying.

"Zhengshu is a handsome young man and he looks a little like you," Lord Ling joked with Yi Xingfu. "Are you sure he is not your son?"

Yi Xingfu laughed and said, "The sparkle in Zhengshu's eyes reminds me of Your Lordship. I think that he is your son."

Kong Ning then broke into the conversation. "His Lordship and Grandee Yi are both far too young to be his father. However, there are lots of possible candidates for the paternity of that little bastard. I bet even Lady Xia herself can't remember who it really is!"

The three men clapped their hands and roared with laughter. It would have been a good thing if Xia Zhengshu had not heard this. However, since he did, his anger and humiliation were indeed hard to bear. As the saying goes, rage and disgust are born deep within! He went and quietly locked Lady Xia Ji in her chambers, then slid out of one of the side gates and instructed his guards, "I want you to surround the mansion and prevent the Marquis of Chen, Kong Ning, and Yi Xingfu from leaving."

The officers accepted these orders and shouted out their instructions. The Xia mansion was now completely cut off from the outside world.

Xia Zhengshu now donned his armor and clasped a cloak around his neck. With a sword in his hand, he led the strongest of his private guard on an attack through the main gate of the residence. "Arrest the rapists!" he shouted.

Lord Ling of Chen was still cracking foul jokes, laughing and drinking, but Kong Ning realized that something was terribly wrong and shouted, "My lord! Zhengshu has tricked you into coming here. He is leading his soldiers in an attack. Run!"

"The front gate is surrounded," Yi Xingfu screamed. "Let us try the back!"

The three men had spent a lot of time in the Xia mansion and knew the place very well. The Marquis of Chen thought of going to the women's quarters, to beg Lady Xia Ji to save him. When he discovered that the door to that part of the residence was locked, it only added further terror to his panic. Now he ran in the direction of the garden, with Xia Zhengshu in hot pursuit. His Lordship remembered that the stables on the east side were surrounded by a low wall that he would be able to climb over, so he ran in that direction.

"You are not going anywhere!" Xia Zhengshu shouted. He drew his bow and sent an arrow whistling after him, but it did not hit him. When the Marquis of Chen got to the stables, his first idea was to find somewhere to hide, but the frightened horses started to neigh. Running back as quickly as he could, he came within range of Xia Zhengshu. He shot a second arrow, and this time it killed him. How sad that the Marquis of Chen should rule for fifteen years only to die so ignominiously in a stable yard!

Master Qian Yuan wrote the following poem, expressing sympathy with Xia Zhengshu for assassinating his ruler:

This lord and his ministers were one more lascivious than the last;
In their disgusting debauchery they showed not the slightest sense of
    shame.
Even though he knew that he would be punished for it,
At least he gave vent to his anger and feelings of humiliation.

When Kong Ning and Yi Xingfu saw the Marquis of Chen heading eastwards, they knew Zhengshu would chase after him, so instead they ran westwards towards the archery ground. Just as they had anticipated, Zhengshu went after the marquis of Chen. Kong Ning and Yi Xingfu then managed to squeeze out through a dog-flap. Not daring to go home, they fled penniless to the kingdom of Chu.

Do you want to know what happened next? READ ON.

Chapter Nine

After remonstrance from his ministers, King Zhuang of Chu restores order in Chen.

Having married Lady Xia Ji, Wu Chen flees to Jin.

After shooting dead the Marquis of Chen, Xia Zhengshu led his troops into the capital city. He gave out that the Marquis of Chen had been struck down by a violent illness after drinking too much wine and died. According to His Lordship's dying wishes, Scion Wu was to succeed him: he took the title of Lord Cheng. Lord Cheng loathed Xia Zhengshu, but he was too powerful to control, so he had to endure the situation in silence. Xia Zhengfu was afraid that the other feudal lords might try to punish him, so he forced the new Marquis of Chen into going to pay court to Jin, in order to cement the alliance between their two states.

As it happened, an ambassador from the kingdom of Chu had been ordered to go and make a blood covenant with the Marquis of Chen at Chenling. Before he had even arrived, he heard about the murder and turned back. It was at this time that Kong Ning and Yi Xingfu arrived in exile in Chu. When they had an audience with King Zhuang, they kept completely quiet about the vices that they and His Late Lordship had been engaged in, simply saying, "Xia Zhengshu launched a coup and assassinated Pingguo, the Marquis of Chen." This accorded exactly with what the ambassador had said.

King Zhuang summoned his ministers to discuss this situation. There was a hereditary grandee of the kingdom of Chu named Qu Wu, styled Ziling, who was the son of Qu Dang. This man was very handsome and skilled in all the arts of war as well as literature, but he had one flaw: he was excessively libidinous and an expert in techniques for improving longevity and sexual performance. A few years earlier he had been sent on a mission to the state of Chen, during which time he had met Lady Xia Ji and seen how beautiful she was. He had also heard of her skills in bed and how she never seemed to grow old, for which he admired her greatly. When he heard that Xia Zhengshu had assassinated his ruler, he decided to take advantage of this situation to steal Lady Xia Ji, so he encouraged King Zhuang to raise an army and attack Chen.

The Grand Vizier, Sunshu Ao, also said: "We must punish this murder in Chen!"

King Zhuang agreed. This happened in the ninth year of the reign of King Ding of Zhou, which was the first year of Lord Cheng of Chen's rule.

King Zhuang began by sending a formal declaration of intent to the state of Chen:

> The king of Chu says to you: A member of the Xia family has assassinated his ruler, something which both gods and men hold in abomination. You cannot punish him, so I will do it for you. He is the only person guilty of this crime, so everyone else can rest assured that they will not be harmed.

When this text reached the Chen capital, everyone blamed Xia Zhengshu and was perfectly happy to see him punished by Chu. As a result, there was no plan forthcoming for resisting the enemy.

King Zhuang of Chu personally took control of the three armies, which were headed by the senior generals Prince Yingqi, Prince Ce, and Qu Wu. They raced to the Chen capital with the speed of lightning, without encountering the slightest opposition. In order to maintain order among the populace, strict orders were given to avoid causing trouble. Xia Zhengshu knew that the people of Chen had turned against him, so he fled to Zhulin. At that time Lord Cheng of Chen had still not returned from the state of Jin.

Grandee Yuan Po discussed the situation with the other ministers: "The king of Chu is here to punish the guilty on our behalf. He is not planning to execute anyone other than Xia Zhengshu. We had better arrest Zhengshu and hand him over to the Chu army, then send an ambassador to ask for a peace treaty, for that way we will preserve the state altars safe and sound. That would be the best plan."

The other ministers all agreed with him. Accordingly, Yuan Po ordered his son, Qiaoru, to lead the army to Zhulin and arrest Xia Zhengshu. Before Qiaoru could set out, the Chu army had already arrived below the walls of the capital. The government of Chen had ceased to function effectively many years earlier, and the marquis was abroad, so the people of the capital opened the gates of their own accord and welcomed the Chu army. King Zhuang led his troops into the city in good order.

When Grandee Yuan Po and his colleagues were brought before King Zhuang, His Majesty asked, "Where is Zhengshu?"

"At Zhulin," Yuan Po replied.

"You are all subjects of His Late Lordship," King Zhuang pointed out. "Why have you let this traitorous bastard get away with murder? Why didn't you punish him?"

"It is not that we did not want to punish him," Yuan Po explained. "We were not powerful enough."

Immediately King Zhuang ordered Yuan Po to lead the way as the main body of the army advanced towards Zhulin under the command of His Majesty himself. Prince Yingqi stayed behind with his forces, camped inside the city walls.

Xia Zhengshu had collected all his family's portable wealth, with the intention of going into exile in the state of Zheng with his mother, Lady Xia Ji. Just moments before they were due to set off, the Chu army surrounded their mansion at Zhulin and arrested Zhengshu. King Zhuang ordered that he be placed in a prison cart. "Why don't I see Lady Xia Ji?" he asked. He had his officers search the mansion, and they found her in the garden.

Lady Xia Ji bowed twice before King Zhuang and said, "With my country in chaos and my family ruined, my life is now in your hands, Your Majesty. If you allow me to live, I will happily serve you as a slave."

Lady Xia Ji was so beautiful and her voice so elegant that King Zhuang found himself bewitched by the very sight of her. He said to his generals, "Even though there are many women in my harem, there are few who are as lovely as Lady Xia Ji. I would like to take her into my own household as a concubine. What do you think?"

"You must not do that!" Qu Wu remonstrated. "You turned the army against Chen, Your Majesty, in order to punish Xia Zhengshu for his crime. If you now take Lady Xia Ji into your harem, it shows that you only really care about her beauty. It is righteous to punish the guilty, but taking a woman into your household like this would be wicked. You must not start righteously and end up in the wrong. This is not the kind of thing that a hegemon would do."

"You are absolutely right!" King Zhuang exclaimed. "I would not dare take her in the teeth of your advice. However, she really is amazingly lovely, and if she crosses my path again, I am afraid that I will not be able to control myself."

Prince Ce was standing by the king's side throughout this exchange, and he too was deeply struck by Lady Xia Ji's beauty. When he realized that King Zhuang was not going to keep her for himself, he knelt and said, "Although I am now middle-aged, I have never been married. Please give her to me as my wife."

Again, Qu Wu remonstrated: "You must not agree to this, Your Majesty!"

"Why don't you want me to marry Lady Xia Ji?" Prince Ce demanded angrily.

"This woman is ill-starred," Qu Wu declared. "Let us look at the evidence: she brought the Honorable Man of Zheng to an early grave, caused the murder of Xie Ye, the assassination of the Marquis of Chen, the execution of her son, the exile of Grandees Kong Ning and Yi Xingfu, and the destruction of the state of Chen. What more proof of her evil nature do you want? There are many beautiful women in the world, so why do you have to pick this disgusting creature who will cause you nothing but regrets?"

"If it is indeed as you say, that is horrifying!" King Zhuang exclaimed.

"In that case I won't have her," Prince Ce said. "So far you have said that His Majesty cannot marry her and I cannot marry her. Are you planning to take her on yourself?"

"No! I wouldn't dare!" Qu Wu protested.

"Everyone fights over things that don't have an owner," King Zhuang said thoughtfully. "If I remember correctly, Sirdar Xiang Lao has recently lost his wife. I will give her to him as a second one!"

At this time, Xiang Lao was out on campaign with the auxiliaries. Now King Zhuang summoned him and gave Lady Xia Ji into his care. The couple thanked His Majesty for his benevolence and withdrew.

Prince Ce put the whole business out of his mind. However, when Qu Wu remonstrated with King Zhuang and prevented Prince Ce from taking the woman over, it was with the intention of getting her himself. When King Zhuang bestowed her upon Xiang Lao, Qu Wu said to himself, "What a shame! What a loss!" Then he considered the matter further: "How can such an old man cope with a woman like that? Within six months to a year, she is going to be a widow and fresh arrangements will have to be made."

Qu Wu had his own plans for the woman but he said nothing whatsoever about them. King Zhuang spent one night at Zhulin and then went back to the capital city of Chen. He entered the city in state with Prince Yingqi. King Zhuang ordered that Xia Zhengshu should be taken out of the Li Gate in chains and torn to pieces by chariots.

A historian wrote a poem:

The Lord of Chen brought his doom upon himself by wickedness
    and lust,
Nevertheless it was wrong of Xia Zhengshu to assassinate him.
King Zhuang's attack came like timely rain;
Above the Si River, the feudal lords could see his pennants flying.

Less than a year after Lady Xia Ji of Chen married Sirdar Xiang Lao, her husband was sent on campaign in Bi. This allowed Lady Xia Ji to embark upon an incestuous relationship with her stepson, Heiyao. When Xiang Lao died in battle, Heiyao was so besotted with Lady Xia Ji that he did not even go and collect his father's body for burial—this was much criticized by the people of the capital. Lady Xia Ji felt humiliated by all the gossip that this caused, so she made the excuse that she would like to go and collect her husband's body herself, but in fact she was hoping to go home to Zheng. Qu Wu now bribed her servants to carry the following message to her: "I have heard so much about you that it has awakened my deepest interest—if you return to the state of Zheng, I will join you there as soon as I can, that we may get married."

In addition to that, he sent a further message to Lord Xiang of Zheng: "Her Ladyship would like to return home. Would you send someone to meet her?" Lord Xiang of Zheng then did indeed send an ambassador to escort Lady Xia Ji.

King Zhuang of Chu questioned his ministers about this development: "Why should Zheng send someone to collect Lady Xia Ji?"

Qu Wu was the only person to try to answer him: "Her Ladyship has expressed the wish to collect Xiang Lao's body for burial. Zheng must be aware of this and imagine that she will succeed, so they have sent someone to meet her."

"The body is in Jin," King Zhuang said in puzzlement. "What on earth has it got to do with Zheng?"

"Xun Ying is Xun Shou's beloved son," Qu Wu replied, "and he is at present a prisoner in Chu. His father is worried sick about him. Xun Shou has been appointed as deputy general in command of the New Central Army, and he is a close friend of Grandee Huang Shu of Zheng. Xun Shou is going to employ Huang Shu as an intermediary, to try and get Chu to release Ying from custody. He would be happy to exchange the bodies of Prince Guchen and Sirdar Xiang Lao to ensure the return of his son. Ever since the battle of Bi, the ruler of Zheng has been terrified lest Jin come and punish him. He is going to try and use this opportunity to establish a better relationship with Jin. That is what is actually going on here."

While he was still speaking, Lady Xia Ji arrived at court to bid His Majesty farewell and report that she was going home to Zheng. Her tears fell like rain as she said, "If I cannot find my husband's body, I swear I will never return to Chu!"

King Zhuang felt sorry for her and allowed her to leave.

· · ·

When Lady Xia Ji had gone, Qu Wu wrote a letter to Lord Xiang of Zheng begging his permission to marry her. Lord Xiang did not know that both King Zhuang of Chu and Prince Yingqi had once hoped to marry this woman; he thought that this would be an excellent match because Qu Wu was an important minister in the kingdom of Chu, so he accepted his betrothal gifts, and no one in Chu was any the wiser. Meanwhile, Qu Wu sent another messenger to Jin to take a letter to Xun Shou, instructing him to offer to exchange the two bodies for Xun Ying, just as he had said. Xun Shou accordingly got in touch with Huang Shu, begging him to act as an intermediary. King Zhuang was determined to get back the remains of his son, Prince Guchen, so he sent Xun Ying home to Jin. Afterwards, Jin returned the two bodies to Chu. The people of Chu believed that every word Qu Wu had said was true and did not suspect him of any ulterior motive.

Later on, when the Jin army attacked Qi, Lord Qing of Qi requested assistance from Chu. However, Chu was engaged in national mourning following the death of King Cheng and hence could not mobilize their army. Subsequently, they heard that the Qi army had suffered a terrible defeat and Guo Zuo had made a blood covenant with Jin.

"Qi has made this alliance with Jin because we failed to protect them," King Gong of Chu declared. "This does not reflect their real wishes. I am going to attack Lu and Wey on Qi's behalf to expunge the humiliation that has been inflicted upon them. Who will convey my intentions to the Marquis of Qi?"

"I will go!" Qu Wu shouted.

"Your route will take you through the state of Zheng," King Gong said. "You had better inform the Zheng army that we expect them to arrive at the borders of Wey in support of Qi in the first week of the tenth month. You can also tell the Marquis of Qi that this is the date we have set!"

Qu Wu accepted this command and went home. On the pretext of visiting Xinyi to collect taxes, he gathered up his household and all his property, to the tune of more than a dozen carts, and sent them out of the capital. He himself set off afterwards, driving his light chariot in the direction of Zheng, speeding along as fast as he could, in accordance with his mission from the king of Chu. On his arrival, he married Lady Xia Ji in a ceremony conducted at the official guesthouse. The joy the couple felt can readily be imagined!

There is a poem that testifies to this:

> This beauty was a famous whore,
> Her affairs were notorious wherever she went.
> This precious pair made the perfect couple,
> It is hard to know which one of them was worse.

When they were in bed together, Lady Xia Ji asked Qu Wu, "Have you informed the king of Chu about this?"

Qu Wu explained that both King Zhuang and Prince Yingqi had both wanted to marry her, concluding with the words: "I went to a lot of trouble in order to be able to get my hands on you. Now that we are married, I regard that as my crowning achievement! However, I do not dare go back to Chu. Tomorrow we will have to find somewhere else to live, a place where we can grow old together. Wouldn't that be wonderful?"

"Now I understand," Lady Xia Ji said. "But if you don't go back to Chu, how will you complete your mission to the state of Qi?"

"I am not going anywhere near the state of Qi!" Qu Wu declared. "Right now, the only state that can deal with Chu on equal terms is Jin. You and I are going there!"

The following morning, having written a letter of explanation, he instructed his servants that they should deliver it to the king of Chu. Then Qu Wu and Lady Xia Ji fled into exile in the state of Jin.

. . .

Lord Jing of Jin was still feeling profoundly humiliated by the defeat that he had suffered at the hands of the Chu army, so when he heard that Qu Wu had arrived, he said happily, "This man really is a gift from Heaven!" He immediately appointed him to the position of a grandee and gave him the lands of Xing as his fief. Qu Wu then decided to give up using the surname Qu and took the name of Wu instead, with the personal name Chen.

Today he is better known by this later name: Wu Chen.

He took up residence in the state of Jin.

. . .

Meanwhile, King Gong of Chu had received Wu Chen's letter. He opened and read it.

> When the ruler of Zheng offered me Lady Xia Ji's hand in marriage, I was unfortunately not able to refuse. I was afraid that Your Majesty would be angry about this, so I have temporarily taken up residence in the state of Jin. As for the embassy to Qi, you will have to find someone else to send. I do apologize for all the trouble that I am causing!

King Gong was furious when he read this letter. He summoned Prince Yingqi and Prince Ce and ordered them to read it too.

"Jin and Chu are hereditary enemies," Prince Ce said. "Now he has gone over to Jin, he has utterly betrayed us. We must punish him!"

Prince Yingqi was struck by a different aspect of the matter: "Hei-yao committed incest with his stepmother, and that is a crime. You ought to punish him too!"

King Gong followed this advice. He sent Prince Yingqi to take his soldiers to confiscate everything the Qu clan owned, while Prince Ce took his troops to arrest Xiang Heiyao and execute him. The property of these two aristocratic clans was then partitioned by the two princes. When Wu Chen heard that his family had been executed, he wrote a letter to the two princes:

> You may claim to be serving His Majesty, but in fact you are just greedy and sycophantic swine. Having killed so many innocent people, I am looking forward to the day when I see you starving to death in the gutter!

Prince Yingqi and his brother kept the contents of this letter a secret, and did not mention it to the king of Chu. Wu Chen came up with a plan for Jin whereby they would develop an alliance with the kingdom of Wu. He went as a military advisor to that kingdom, to train their troops in chariot warfare. His son Huyong ended up staying behind in Wu as a government advisor, to keep avenues of communication open. As a result, the power of the kingdom of Wu grew day by day as they picked off all of Chu's subordinate states in the east. It was at this point that their ruler, Shoumeng, first adopted the title of king. They raided the Chu border area constantly, not allowing them a moment's peace.

A historian wrote a poem about this:

> Why begrudge someone else possession of a lascivious woman?
> As the whole court fought to marry her, brother turned against
> brother.
> Thus the kingdom of Wu was able to fight for hegemony,
> And Chu could only regret losing an able minister!

Later on, when Wu Chen died, his son Huyong started to use the surname Qu again. Qu Huyong spent the rest of his life in the service of the kingdom of Wu, eventually becoming the prime minister, entrusted with the most important affairs of state. However, this all happened much later on.

. . .

After Wu Chen defected to the state of Jin, King Gong of Chu launched a major attack on that state. When the king of Chu moved his army into position just outside the enemy camp and then went into battle formation, he thought that this would be a most unexpected move for them, whereby they would be thrown into confusion. What he was not expecting was total silence and a complete lack of movement. He asked Pasha Bo Zhouli about this. "The Jin army is sitting behind their fortifications without moving. You are a Jin person, so you must have some idea of what they are up to?"

"Why don't you get onto a battle tower and have a look for yourself, Your Majesty?" Bo Zhouli suggested.

The king of Chu then climbed the mobile tower, and Bo Zhouli stood by his side. "The Jin army is rushing about, some heading left and some heading right," the king said thoughtfully. "What are they doing?"

"They are collecting the army officers together," Bo Zhouli said.

"Now a group of them has gathered by the Central Army," the king noted.

"They are discussing a plan together," Bo Zhouli said.

The king of Chu looked out into the distance and remarked, "Now they are putting up a tent. What is that for?"

"That means they are going to report their decision to the ancestors of our ruling house," Bo Zhouli informed him.

Looking out again, His Majesty observed, "Now they are taking the tent down."

"That means that they are going to give orders."

Staring into the distance, His Majesty said, "What on earth are they doing? Why is there so much dust?"

"They don't have enough space to go into battle formation, so they are closing up their wells and food storage areas in order to make room to fight."

The king looked out again. "Horses are being hitched to chariots, and soldiers are getting on board."

"They are going to go into battle formation."

A little bit later, the king inquired, "Why are the people who climbed onto the chariots getting off again?"

"Since they are about to do battle," Bo Zhouli responded, "they are praying to the gods."

Looking out, the king said: "The Central Army seems to be exceptionally strong; is His Lordship present?"

"The Luan and Fan families have sent their forces to fight side by side with the Marquis of Jin. This is an enemy that you do not want to underestimate."

When the king of Chu had placed himself in full command of the situation inside the Jin camp, he issued his own warnings to his troops and planned the attack for the following day. Miao Benhuang, who had surrendered from the Chu army, stood in attendance on the Marquis of Jin and informed him: "Ever since the death of Sunshu Ao, there have been big problems in the Chu army. The so-called crack troops of the Royal Guard have been in service for too long; there are many of them who are now too old to fight. Furthermore, the generals in command of the armies of the left and right hate each other. You should be able to defeat Chu in one battle."

A bearded old man wrote a poem:

> Chu employed Bo Zhouli, once an aristocrat in Jin,
> Jin employed Miao Benhuang, who originally came from Chu.
> It is hard enough to find a really talented man,
> You don't want to lose them to an enemy country!

That day, the two armies both kept to their encampments, holding firm and not fighting. The Chu general, Pan Dang, was practicing his archery in the rear camp, hitting the middle of the target with three successive arrows. The other generals present all praised his marksmanship. Then Yang Yaoji arrived, and the generals said, "The best archer we have is here!"

"In what way is my archery inferior to yours?" Pan Dang asked crossly.

"You have just hit the middle of an archery target," Yang Yaoji told him. "That is nothing to be particularly proud of. I can send an arrow through a willow at one hundred paces."

The assembled generals asked him, "What do you mean by sending an arrow through a willow at one hundred paces?"

"If you send someone to mark a single willow leaf, I will shoot an arrow through that leaf at one hundred paces," Yang Yaoji told them. "That is my target."

"There are a great many willow trees round here," the generals said. "Would one of them be suitable?"

"Why not?" Yang Yaoji asked.

The generals exclaimed happily: "Now we are really going to get to see some fine shooting!" They picked out a single leaf that was marked with a black spot, and Yang Yaoji moved one hundred paces away and drew his bow. No one saw where the arrow went; however, when the generals went to inspect the target, they saw that the arrow had pierced the leaf, the point having struck the mark exactly.

"That is just a coincidence," Pan Dang declared. "In my opinion, it is only when you can hit the marks on three leaves in succession that you can be considered a truly great archer."

"I am not sure that I can do it," Yang Yaoji said thoughtfully. "However, I am willing to give it a try."

Pan Dang marked three different leaves, hanging down at different levels, with the numbers one, two, and three. Yang Yaoji took note of their position, then moved back one hundred paces. He had three arrows, which were also numbered one, two, and three. He hit each target with the correct arrow one after the other without the slightest mistake. The generals present all clapped their hands and exclaimed, "What an amazing archer you are, Mr. Yang!"

Pan Dang could not prevent himself from feeling a certain shock, but he was nevertheless determined to try and show off his own skills. Therefore, he said to Yang Yaoji, "Your archery is deeply impressive! However, when killing a man, you need real strength behind the bow. I can pierce several layers of armor with a single shot—let me show you gentlemen what I mean."

"We would love to see that!" the generals all exclaimed.

Pan Dang ordered several soldiers in armor to take it off, and he piled them up in five layers. The generals said, "Surely that is enough," but Pan Dang added another two layers, making seven in total. The generals present thought to themselves, "Seven layers of armor is almost a foot thick—how can an arrow pass through that?" Pan Dang had these seven layers hung from an archery target. He too stood one hundred paces away and grabbed his black lacquer bow, nocking his wolf-tooth arrow to the string. His left hand was held as hard as if he were pushing back Mount Tai; his right hand was as gentle as if he were holding a baby. He stood firm, and then put all the force at his command into the arrow. He released the bow with a shout: "Hit!" No one saw the arrow arch up into the air; no one saw it come down again. All the generals had their eyes fixed on the target, and then with one voice they started to shout: "How amazing! How wonderful!" With the force that Pan Dang had put behind that arrow, he had managed to pierce seven layers of armor. The arrow had nailed them to the target, piercing straight through.

Pan Dang looked very pleased with himself. He instructed an officer to take down the armor but leave the arrow in place, so that it could be shown round the army camp.

"Don't move it," Yang Yaoji said. "I would like to have a go!"

"Why not?" the generals said.

Yang Yaoji picked up his bow and made as if to shoot, then he stopped. The generals asked: "Why do you not shoot?"

"There is nothing special about whacking an arrow through many layers of armor," Yang Yaoji declared. "I have another idea." When he had finished speaking, he drew his bow and shot.

The shout rose up: "Beautiful!" This arrow moved neither up nor down, not to the left or to the right; it simply curved along exactly the same trajectory that General Pan Dang's arrow had carved through the air and tracing it straight into the target. Yang Yaoji's arrow split the first one, following the hole that it had drilled through the seven layers of armor. When they saw this, the generals were truly amazed. Even Pan Dang had to admit that this was a remarkable thing to be able to do. He sighed and said, "You really are a great archer, Mr. Yang! I do not even come close!"

Master Qian Yuan wrote a poem:

There are many archers who have shot down birds or sent an arrow
    through a rat;
Hitting a willow leaf at one hundred paces is a much rarer feat!
To shoot an arrow through many layers of armor is nothing to be
    amazed about;
For every powerful man, there is someone even stronger!

The following day at the fifth watch, the two armies sounded their drums and moved their armies forward. Lord Li of Jin wore a helmet topped with a plume made of pheasant feathers and battle dress consisting of a red brocade gown with a design of coiling dragons and serpents. A precious sword hung from his waist, and he grasped a great spear in his hand. Furthermore, he was riding in a battle chariot decorated with gilded bronze panels. Luan Shu held his position on the right and Shi Xie held his position on the left, as they threw open the gates to the army camp and fell upon the Chu soldiers drawn up in tight formation. Who could have imagined that there would be a marshy patch of ground located right in front of the Chu army? In the faint predawn light, it was impossible to see clearly. The Marquis of Jin's charioteer whipped up his horses and sent them charging into battle, driving the wheels of the chariot straight into the mud, so that the horses found it impossible to move. Luan Qian got down from the chariot as quickly as he could. Standing in the mud, he used every ounce of strength to lift up the body of the chariot with his two bare hands. As the chariot came free, the horses moved forward; step by step they dragged the vehicle out of the quagmire. After this narrow shave, both sides collected their forces and returned to camp.

At dawn the following day, General Luan Shu of Jin ordered the gates to be opened so that they might do battle again. The senior general, Wei Yi, reported to Luan Shu: "Last night I dreamed that the moon floated high in the sky, whereupon I drew my bow and shot at it. Just as my arrow hit the center, a beam of golden light shone down. I was in a great hurry to get away from it, but my foot slipped and I became bogged down in the marshy patch in front of the encampment. That gave me such a shock that I woke up. I wonder if this is an auspicious omen or not."

Luan Shu thought about this carefully for a moment, and then said: "Relatives of the Zhou ruling house are represented by the sun, other ruling houses by the moon. If you shot the moon and hit it, that must refer to the king of Chu. However, mud comes from the mixing of earth and water. You stepped backwards and got stuck in the mud— that is not an auspicious omen! You had better be very careful!"

"If we can defeat Chu, I don't care if I die!" Wei Yi said.

Luan Shu then agreed that Wei Yi could go out in advance of the main body of the troops. King Gong of Chu gave orders to whip up his chariot and headed off towards the front lines. Wei Yi noticed this maneuver and, shaking off Mirza Xiang, set off in pursuit of the king of Chu. He let fly a single arrow, which struck the king of Chu in his left eye. Pan Dang fought him off while supporting the king of Chu inside the chariot. The king of Chu endured the pain of plucking out the arrow himself; his eyeball came out on the point of the arrow and dropped to the ground. A foot-soldier picked it up and handed it back to him. "This is Your Majesty's eyeball. It should not just be thrown away!" The king of Chu took it from him and dropped it into his quiver.

The Jin army realized that Wei Yi had pulled off a remarkable feat, so they now attacked all together. Prince Ce led his own forces to defend against this, thereby allowing King Gong of Chu to escape. By this time the king of Chu was as furious as he had ever been in his life, and he quickly shouted for General Yang Yaoji to get him out of there. When Yang Yaoji heard the summons, he came immediately. The king of Chu handed him two arrows and said, "The man who shot me was wearing a green robe and had a heavy beard; I want you to take revenge for me, general! With your remarkable skills, I am sure you do not need any more arrows than this!"

Yang Yaoji ordered a fast chariot to take him within range of the Jin army. He immediately caught sight of a man wearing a green robe, who had a heavy beard, whom he recognized as Wei Yi. "Who do you think you are, you bastard?" he shouted "How dare you shoot at His Majesty!" Wei Yi was just about to respond when he was struck by Yang Yaoji's arrow. It hit him in the neck. He fell back upon his bow case and died. Luan Shu ordered that his soldiers recover the body. Meanwhile, Yang Yaoji had returned the remaining arrow to the king of Chu. He announced: "According to Your Majesty's commands, I have shot and killed the general with a beard, wearing a green robe." King Gong was very pleased. He personally presented him with a brocade robe and one hundred wolf-tooth arrows. The whole army took to calling him "One Arrow Yang" since he did not need a second one to hit the target.

There is a poem which testifies to this:

> Whipping up his horses, the chariot sped into battle.
> At first sight the Jin troops felt their blood run cold.
> Where everyone else had failed to kill this famous general,
> Yang Yaoji returned in triumph, having downed him with one shot!

. . .

Let us now turn to a different part of the story. Prince Ce of Chu was an alcoholic. Once he started, he would not stop until he had drunk one hundred calabashes dry; once he got drunk, he would not wake up for days. King Gong was well aware of this failing, and every time they went out on campaign, he would warn his servants to keep him off the drink. During the tense standoff between Jin and Chu, because he had such an important role to play, he did not touch a drop of any kind of liquid all day.

On the day when the king of Chu returned to the camp having had his eye shot out, he was feeling both angry and deeply humiliated. Prince Ce came forward and said, "Both armies are now exhausted. Let us rest tomorrow! Let your ministers have time to come up with a new plan of campaign, so that we can expunge the humiliation inflicted upon Your Majesty!"

Prince Ce bade His Majesty farewell and returned to the Central Army. He sat in his tent until the middle of the night, trying and failing to come up with a plan. One of his servants, a man named Gu Yang, was very much favored by His Royal Highness, who kept him constantly about his person. When he saw that the commander-in-chief was looking troubled and exhausted, Gu Yang took out the triple-distilled *meijiu* that he had secreted away and warmed one bottle before presenting it to the prince. When Prince Ce smelled the liquid, he was startled, and said, "Is this alcoholic?"

Gu Yang knew that His Royal Highness wanted a drink, but was afraid that his servants might report it to the king. Therefore, he lied and said, "It is not alcoholic. This is a pepper soup."

Prince Ce understood exactly why he was saying this and downed the cup in a single gulp. He felt its sweet fragrance spread through his mouth and was more delighted than he could say. "Is there any more pepper soup?" he asked.

"There is," Gu Yang assured him.

Since he was claiming that it was entirely innocuous, this time he served a whole bowl to His Royal Highness. Prince Ce was feeling absolutely parched anyway. He remarked, "This pepper soup is delicious! How thoughtful of you to prepare it for me!" As soon as the bowl arrived, he drained it in one swallow and asked for more, until he had no idea how many bowls he had drunk. He was now too sodden with drink to be able to stand up, so he was lolling against his seating mat.

The king of Chu was informed that Jin would do battle at cockcrow, and they had received reinforcements from Lu and Wey. He immediately sent one of the palace servants to summon Prince Ce and discuss a plan for countering the enemy attack. He had no idea that Prince Ce was now so drunk that he was comatose! They shouted at him, but he did not respond; they tried to lift him up but couldn't. The smell of alcohol was overpowering. Realizing that he was drunk again, they went back to report this to the king of Chu. His Majesty sent a dozen messengers to the commander-in-chief in succession, trying to wake him up. The more they tried to wake Prince Ce, the sounder he seemed to sleep. The servant, Gu Yang, said tearfully, "I love the commander-in-chief, and that is why I gave him something to drink. I had no idea that I would cause such a disaster! When the king of Chu finds out, he will probably order my execution. I had better run away now!"

When the king of Chu realized that Prince Ce was not coming, there was nothing that he could do about it. He had to order the Grand Vizier, Prince Yingqi, to discuss strategy with him instead. Prince Yingqi had never been close to Prince Ce. He now presented his opinion: "I told you that the Jin army was very powerful and that if we fought them we could not be assured of victory. That is why in our initial discussions I opposed this campaign. This was all Prince Ce's idea. Now he is too drunk to continue the campaign—I have no plan to offer. Why don't you stand down your army overnight and head for home? That way, at least we will not suffer the humiliation of sustaining a second such defeat!"

"If we were indeed to do that and leave the prince drunk in his tent with the Central Army, he would be taken prisoner by Jin," the king of Chu said. "That would also be a humiliation for our country." He summoned Yang Yaoji and said, "You are a very fine archer. It will be your mission to bring His Highness home safe and sound." He secretly gave orders to strike camp and leave.

Yang Yaoji was left behind alone to cover the retreat, and he thought to himself, "There is no saying when His Royal Highness will wake up." He gave orders to the servants to lift Prince Ce and tie him onto the back of a chariot with leather straps. His troops then headed off. Yang Yaoji and the three hundred archers he had with him retreated slowly. Prince Ce of Chu only woke up fifty *li* into the journey. He realized that he had been tied up, so he shouted: "Who has trussed me up like this?"

"You were drunk," his servants told him, "and General Yang was worried that you would not be able to keep your footing on a moving chariot, so he tied you up in this way." They immediately cut the leather thongs off him.

Prince Ce was bristling with rage. "Where are we going?" he asked.

"We are on the way home," his servants informed him.

"Why are we going home?"

"Last night the king of Chu sent many messengers to try and get you, but you were so drunk that you were dead to the world. The king of Chu was afraid that if the Jin army attacked us, there would be no one to lead the defense, so he had no choice but to stand down the army!"

Prince Ce wept bitterly. "Gu Yang might as well have killed me!" He immediately called for Gu Yang, but he was long gone and no one knew where.

King Gong of Chu moved his army two hundred *li,* but since there were no signs of pursuit, he then started to relax. He was afraid that Prince Ce might be so frightened of punishment that he would commit suicide, so he sent an envoy to tell him: "The failure of this campaign rests solely with me, the king. It is not your fault."

Prince Yingqi was afraid that Prince Ce might fail to commit suicide, so he sent a messenger to tell him: "You know the law: a defeated general deserves the death penalty. His Majesty cannot bear to order your execution, but do you really think you can ever face the Central Army again?"

Prince Ce sighed and said, "The Grand Vizier is correct when he blames me for this defeat. In the circumstances, how can I survive?" He promptly hanged himself. The king of Chu was devastated by this news. These events occurred in the eleventh year of the reign of King Jian of Zhou.

If you want to know what happened next, THE STORY CONTINUES . . .

The Orphan of the Zhao Clan

Chapter Ten

After the siege of the Lower Palace,
Cheng Ying hides an orphan.

Having executed Tu'an Gu, the Zhao
clan rises again.

Let us now turn to another part of the story. After Zhao Chuan murdered Lord Ling of Jin at the Peach Garden, he was protected from any consequences by his uncle, the prime minister, Zhao Dun. Meanwhile, Lord Ling's younger brother was installed as the new marquis, taking the title of Lord Cheng. Subsequently, Lord Cheng's son came to power as Lord Jing. He was very fond of Tu'an Gu, and the two of them would go out hunting and then spend time drinking together, just like in the time of Lord Ling. Tu'an Gu did not get along at all with Zhao Tong, Zhao Tuo, or his older brother Zhao Yingqi. He slandered them, accusing them of corruption and sedition, forcing them into exile in Qi. Lord Jing could do nothing to prevent this. It was around this time that Mount Liang suddenly collapsed for no reason, blocking the waters of the Yellow River for three days before they worked their way past the obstruction. Lord Jing ordered the Grand Astrologer to perform a divination about this. Tu'an Gu bribed the Grand Astrologer to give the reading that this was because punishments had not been meted out to the right people.

"I have never punished anyone," Lord Jing said in surprise, "so why would it say that I am not punishing the right people?"

Tu'an Gu presented his opinion: "When the oracle speaks of punishments not being meted out to the right people, it could mean that the innocent are suffering, but it could also mean that people who ought to be punished are escaping scot-free. Zhao Dun assassinated Lord Ling in the Peach Garden; this is written in our historical records. This is an unforgivable crime, and yet your father, Lord Cheng, not only did not execute him, he entrusted the government of the country to him. This situation has carried on to the present day—the sons and grandsons of this traitor fill the court. Is this how you warn later generations against following their example? I have heard that Zhao Shuo, Zhao Tong, and Zhao Tuo are all engaged in treasonous conspiracies, backed by their powerful clan. Mount Liang crumbled because Heaven wants you to punish the murder of Lord Ling—this is the crime of the Zhao family!"

Lord Jing had already been deeply offended by the arrogance shown by Zhao Tong and Zhao Tuo, so he was swayed by Tu'an Gu's words. Therefore, he discussed the matter further with Han Jue.

"I do not think that Zhao Dun can be held responsible for what happened at the Peach Garden," Han Jue said thoughtfully. "Furthermore, every generation of the Zhao family has done great things in the service of the state. I do not understand why you doubt the loyalty of the descendants of such a great minister merely at the word of some jumped-up little jack-in-office!"

Lord Jing could not make up his mind what to do. He asked Luan Shu and Xi Yi about it. The two of them had already received full instructions from Tu'an Gu as to what to say. They stuck to the script and would not admit any positive achievement by any member of the Zhao clan. Lord Jing was now convinced that every word Tu'an Gu had said was the truth. He therefore proclaimed Zhao Dun guilty of murder and instructed Tu'an Gu: "You deal with this! All I ask is that you do not alarm the people of the capital!"

Han Jue knew that Tu'an Gu was up to something, so that very night he went to the Lower Palace to warn Zhao Shuo and tell him to get ready to flee.

"My father prevented the late Lord Ling from carrying out his threat to execute him, and the only thing he gained thereby was an evil reputation," Zhao Shuo said. "Tu'an Gu has received an order from His Lordship to kill me; how could I dare to run away? However, my wife is pregnant and will give birth any day now. It does not matter if she gives birth to a daughter, but if Heaven blesses us with a son, the ancestral sacrifices of the Zhao clan may yet continue. In that case, I beg you to save the baby. Even if I die, at least let my son survive!"

Han Jue spoke through his tears. "I know that everything I have achieved is thanks to your father's assistance; Zhao Dun treated me as if I were his own son. I am afraid that today there is nothing I can do to help you—I cannot cut off the bastard's head! Given that it is His Lordship's order, I have no choice but to obey! This wicked man has been holding back his resentment for a long time: now the floodgates have burst and we are on the verge of a cataclysm! There is nothing I can do to stop it. But why don't you go send your wife secretly into the palace now, before the troops arrive? At least there she should be safe. When your son is grown, that is the day for revenge!"

"I will do just as you suggest," Zhao Shuo said. The two men dried their tears and said goodbye.

Zhao Shuo secretly made the following agreement with his wife, Lady Zhuang Ji: "If you give birth to a daughter, then I want her to be named Wen, meaning 'cultured.' If you give birth to a son, then I would like him to be named Wu, or 'martial.' Cultured people are completely useless, but a martial son will avenge us!"

The only person who knew about this was Cheng Ying, Zhao Shuo's close associate. He smuggled Lady Zhuang Ji out the back door and into a covered carriage, which he then conveyed to the palace of Jin, where he placed her in the care of her mother, Lady Cheng, the Dowager Marchioness of Jin. The bitterness and pain that the couple felt in parting does not need to be described.

. . .

When it got light, Tu'an Gu ordered armed guards to surround the Lower Palace. He had the document that Lord Jing had written concerning the Zhao clan's crimes suspended from the main gate, and put out the word that he had received His Lordship's orders to punish the guilty. He then executed Zhao Shao, Zhao Tong, Zhao Tuo, and Zhao Zhan, together with all their family: young and old, male and female. Bodies lay everywhere in the main halls of the house, and the blood poured down the steps and soaked the courtyards. When they counted the dead, they discovered that Lady Zhuang Ji was missing.

"Her Ladyship is not a source of concern," Tu'an Gu said. "The problem is that I have heard that she is expecting a baby. If by some mischance she were to give birth to a boy, leaving this villainous spawn alive would simply be storing up trouble for the future!"

Someone reported, "A covered carriage entered the palace in the middle of the night."

"That must be Lady Zhuang Ji," Tu'an Gu decided. Immediately he presented his opinion to the Marquis of Jin. "The traitor's family has now been executed, but Her Ladyship has now gone to the palace. I beg you to make a decision on the matter!"

"Mother loves my older sister," Lord Jing said. "You cannot possibly expect me to do anything to harm her!"

Tu'an Gu then presented his opinion: "Her Ladyship is pregnant. If she were to give birth to a boy and we let this last remnant of the traitor's family survive, when he grows up he will take revenge upon us. We will just see a repeat of the murder at the Pear Garden. You need to think about this very carefully!"

"If the baby is a boy, kill him!" Lord Jing commanded.

Tu'an Gu sent out spies to keep watch day and night for any news of Lady Zhuang Ji's baby. A couple of days later, Lady Zhuang Ji did indeed give birth to a son. The dowager marchioness gave instructions to everyone in the palace to pretend that the baby was a girl. Tu'an Gu did not believe this, so he sent a nurse from his own household into the palace to inspect the child. Lady Zhuang Ji was terrified and discussed the matter with her mother, the dowager marchioness. They decided to say that the baby girl had died. At this time Lord Jing of Jin spent all his time sunk in drunken debauch, and the government of the state was entrusted to Tu'an Gu, leaving him free to do exactly as he pleased. Tu'an Gu suspected that the baby was neither female nor dead, so he personally escorted maids from his own household to search the palace from top to bottom.

Lady Zhuang Ji tied the baby under her own voluminous robes and prayed to Heaven: "If Heaven is determined to destroy the Zhao clan, let my son wake up and cry. If the Zhao family is destined to continue, let my baby remain silent!"

When the maids dragged Lady Zhuang Ji out of her rooms so that they could be searched, they discovered nothing. The baby tied under his mother's clothing did not make a sound. Although Tu'an Gu had searched the palace from one end to the other, he remained suspicious.

Someone suggested: "Perhaps the orphan has already been smuggled out of the palace!"

Tu'an Gu had the following reward posted on the gates: "Anyone who reports the location of the orphan will be rewarded with one thousand pieces of gold. Anyone who knows his whereabouts and conceals this information will be punished according to the law on hiding a traitor, and his whole family will be executed!" He also ordered that anyone going in or out of the palace should be interrogated.

. . .

Zhao Dun had two particularly close subordinates: Gongsun Chujiu and Cheng Ying. When the pair of them first heard that Tu'an Gu had surrounded the Lower Palace, Gongsun Chujiu suggested that they should go and rescue them.

"That man is claiming that he is simply carrying out His Lordship's orders," Cheng Ying replied. "He says he is punishing traitors. If we go there he will just kill us, which will not help the Zhao family at all!"

"I know it won't help," Gongsun Chujiu wailed, "but they are in danger and I cannot bear to just stand by and watch!"

"Her Ladyship is pregnant," Cheng Ying informed him. "If she gives birth to a son, the two of us can support him. If she gives birth to a daughter, it will not be too late to die for our master then."

When they heard that Lady Zhuang Ji had given birth to a daughter, Gongsun Chujiu wept and said, "Does Heaven really want bring the Zhao clan to an end?"

"I don't believe it," Chen Ying declared. "Let me make further investigations."

He gave lavish bribes to one of the palace maids, who then took a letter through to Lady Zhuang Ji. Her Ladyship knew of Cheng Ying's strong sense of loyalty and honor, so she smuggled out a message consisting of a single word: "Wu." Cheng Ying was thrilled: "Her Ladyship has given birth to a boy!"

When Tu'an Gu searched the palace without finding the baby, Cheng Ying said to Gongsun Chujiu: "The orphan of the Zhao family is in the palace but they have not found him, thank Heaven! However, they will not be able to keep his existence a secret for much longer. The minute word gets out, that bastard Tu'an Gu is going to be back for another search. We must come up with a plan to get him out of the palace and hide him somewhere far away—that is the only way to keep him safe!"

Gongsun Chujiu was sunk in deep thought for a time, then he asked Cheng Ying: "It will be difficult to save the orphan, but it would also be hard to die. Which do you think is worse?"

"In this situation, getting yourself killed is easy. It is saving the orphan that is going to be difficult."

"You take the difficult job," Gongsun Chujiu proposed, "and I will take the easy one."

"Do you have a plan?"

"We will find some other baby and pretend that he is the orphan of the Zhao clan," Gongsun Chujiu said. "I will take that baby to Mount Shouyang; you can then go to the authorities and tell them where the child is hidden. Once that bastard Tu'an Gu has got his hands on the pretend orphan, the real one will be able to escape."

"Swapping the babies is easy," Cheng Ying agreed. "However, we must find a way to get the real orphan out of the palace, so that we can keep him safe."

"Of the generals serving in the Jin army, Han Jue has always been the closest to the Zhao family," Gongsun Chujiu said thoughtfully. "He could be entrusted with the task of smuggling the baby out of the palace."

"My son was born at about the same time as the orphan," Cheng Ying said. "He can replace him. After all, if we are discovered to have been involved in the conspiracy to hide the orphan, our whole families will be executed anyway." Then he burst into tears: "It is unbearable, though, that my son should have to die before me!"

"You are doing the right thing," Gongsun Chujiu said angrily. "Why are you crying?"

Cheng Ying then dried his tears and left. That very night, he carried his son in his arms and placed him in the hands of Gongsun Chujiu. Immediately afterwards he went to have an audience with Han Jue. First, he showed him the message with the word "Wu"; then, he explained what he and Gongsun Chujiu had planned.

"Her Ladyship is complaining about feeling ill, so I have been commanded to find her a doctor," Han Jue explained. "If you can persuade that criminal lunatic Tu'an Gu to head off on a wild-goose chase round Mount Shouyang, I have a plan for how to get the orphan out of the palace."

Cheng Ying started to spread the word: "If the minister of justice, Tu'an Gu, wants to lay hands on the orphan of the Zhao clan, why is he messing around in the palace?"

When one of Tu'an Gu's subordinates heard this, he asked, "Do you know where the orphan of the Zhao clan is?"

"Give me a thousand pieces of gold and I will tell you," Cheng Ying said. The man took him to meet Tu'an Gu, who began by asking his name.

"I am Cheng Ying," he replied. "Gongsun Chujiu and I used to work for the Zhao family. When Her Ladyship gave birth to a boy, she had one of her women take him out of the palace and instructed us to hide him. I was afraid that sooner or later someone would find out and go to the authorities. He would then be rewarded with a thousand pieces of gold, but my whole family would be executed. That is why I have come to hand myself in."

"Where is the orphan now?" Tu'an Gu demanded.

"Send your entourage away," Cheng Ying said, "and I will tell you." Tu'an Gu immediately ordered his servants to withdraw.

"He is hidden deep in Mount Shouyang," Cheng Ying whispered. "If you hurry you will be able to catch him; otherwise, in a few days' time he will be taken to the state of Qin. I am afraid that you are going to have to go yourself, sir, for so many people owe a great deal to the Zhao family and might be tempted to let the child go. This is not a task that you can entrust to anyone else."

"You are coming with me!" Tu'an Gu said. "If you are telling the truth, you will receive great rewards. If you are lying, I am going to kill you!"

"I have just come from the mountains," Cheng Ying told him, "and I am practically starving. Please give me something to eat!" Tu'an Gu had him served food and wine. When Cheng Ying had finished eating, he told him that they needed to be on their way as quickly as possible.

Tu'an Gu led his own force of three thousand armed guards in the direction that Cheng Ying indicated, heading straight for Mount Shouyang. Once they had traveled a few *li,* the road began to get narrower and more difficult. They saw a small thatched cottage located overlooking the stream, its wicker gate firmly closed. Cheng Ying pointed to it and said, "That is where Gongsun Chujiu has the orphan hidden." When Cheng Ying knocked on the door, Gongsun Chujiu came to greet him. Seeing how many soldiers there were, he made as if to run away and hide. Cheng Ying shouted, "There is nowhere to go! The minister of justice already knows that you have the orphan here and has come to collect him. Hand him over immediately!" Before he had finished speaking, the guards had laid violent hands upon Gongsun Chujiu and dragged him in front of Tu'an Gu.

"Where is the orphan?" he demanded.

Chujiu tried to deny the whole thing: "I know nothing about it."

Tu'an Gu gave orders that the hut be searched. There was a very strong lock on one of the doors; the soldiers broke it open and went into the room. It was pitch dark, but they could hear the sound of a baby crying hysterically, coming from a bamboo-frame bed. They carried the baby out and discovered that he was wrapped in fine embroidered silk clothes: this was certainly the child of a noble family. When Gongsun Chujiu caught sight of the baby, he tried to snatch it away from them, but he was held back by his bonds and could not move.

"You bastard, Cheng Ying!" he cursed. "When the Lower Palace was surrounded, I wanted us to die together. It was you who said that Her Ladyship was pregnant and that if we died there would be nobody to protect the orphan! Her Ladyship entrusted her son to the two of us, so we hid in these mountains. We plotted this together! Now you are so greedy for the reward of one thousand pieces of gold that you have gone to the authorities and told them everything! It doesn't matter if I get killed, but I have betrayed Zhao Dun's trust in me!" He cursed on and on, using the worst swear words that he could.

Cheng Ying looked deeply ashamed and humiliated. He said to Tu'an Gu: "Why don't you kill him?"

Tu'an Gu shouted his order: "Behead Gongsun Chujiu!" He lifted up the baby and dashed him against the ground. The baby gave a sobbing sound and died. How sad!

An old man wrote a poem:

Even in the midst of the palace, no member of the Zhao family was
   safe;
They were lucky that Cheng Ying put his own son in the orphan's
   place.
Tu'an Gu was determined that he would not escape his net,
But he could not have imagined Gongsun Chujiu's trick!

When Tu'an Gu headed to Mount Shouyang to capture the orphan, the capital was rocked by rumors. There were some people who were pleased at the rise of the Tu'an family, while others bewailed the fall of the Zhao clan. In the absence of the minister of justice, the palace guards did not bother with questioning people. Han Jue ordered one of his most trusted confidantes to dress up as a doctor and enter the palace to treat Her Ladyship's illness. The one-word message that he had been given by Cheng Ying, "Wu," was pasted inside his medicine chest. When Lady Zhuang Ji saw that, she knew exactly what was afoot. After he had checked her pulse, he asked her some questions about her health before and after giving birth. Lady Zhuang Ji's attendants on this occasion were all servants devoted to her interests, and they immediately placed the baby inside the chest. The baby started to cry. Lady Zhuang Ji placed her hand on top of the medicine chest and prayed: "Zhao Wu! Zhao Wu! More than a hundred innocent members of our family are dead—you are the only survivor! When you leave the palace, you must not cry!"

When she finished speaking, the baby gradually stopped crying. When they left the palace, there was no one there to interrogate the "doctor." Once Han Jue had the orphan in his possession, he felt as if he had been given an invaluable treasure, and hid him away in the most secluded part of his mansion in the care of a single wet nurse. Even his closest relatives knew nothing about what was going on.

· · ·

When Tu'an Gu returned to his mansion, he gave Cheng Ying the reward of one thousand pieces of gold. Cheng Ying refused to take it.

"You went to the authorities because of this reward," Tu'an Gu said, "so why do you now refuse it?"

"I worked for the Zhao family for a long time," Cheng Ying explained. "Now I have killed the orphan to save my own skin—I have already behaved unforgivably! What would it look like if I were also to accept this enormous reward? If you really appreciate the small contribution that I have made, let this money be used to bury the dead Zhaos properly. At least I can show them this last bit of respect."

Tu'an Gu was very pleased about this: "You really are a good man! There is no problem with letting you collect the bodies of the Zhao family for burial. If you want to use this money for the funeral, you can."

Cheng Ying then bowed and took the reward. He collected the bones of each family member and had them formally encoffined; afterwards, they were buried in graves arranged around the tomb of Zhao Dun. Once that was done, he went back again to thank Tu'an Gu. He wanted him to stay behind and work for him, but Cheng Ying burst into tears and said, "A moment's greed and fear of death led me to commit a terrible injustice. I cannot bear to stay another moment in Jin and face the people here. Let me go and make my living somewhere far away." Cheng Ying bade farewell to Tu'an Gu, before going to have an audience with Han Jue. The general entrusted the orphan and his wet nurse to Cheng Ying's care. Cheng Ying treated him as if he were his own baby son. They went away to live hidden in Mount Yu.

Later on people called this place the Hidden Mountain, to commemorate the fact that the orphan of the Zhao clan was concealed here.

. . .

Three years later, Lord Jing of Jin was out hunting in Xintian when he noticed that the land was very fertile and the waters sweet, so he moved his capital there. The officials all came to court to offer their congratulations to His Lordship. Lord Jing held a banquet in honor of his senior ministers in the inner palace. As it began to get dark, his servants lit the lamps. Suddenly a strange gust of wind came roiling through the main hall, forcing people away with its icy blast. Those present were all panic-stricken. A short time later, the wind fell. Lord Jing was then the only person present to see the ghost that walked in: a tall man with long hair that trailed upon the ground. He clenched his fist and shouted: "Heaven! What crime had my sons and grandchildren committed that you should murder them like that? My complaints have been heard by God on High and so I have come to take your life!" When he had finished speaking, he struck Lord Jing with a bronze cudgel.

"Save me!" Lord Jing screamed. He drew his sword and tried to strike at the ghost, but in his panic all he managed to do was to slice through his own fingers. The ministers present had no idea what was going on, but in spite of all the confusion, they managed to overpower His Lordship and wrench the sword out of his grasp. Lord Jing spat a mouthful of blood before crumpling to the floor, unconscious. The palace eunuchs lifted him up and carried him into his bedchamber, but it was a long time before they were able to bring him round. The ministers eventually dispersed, deeply concerned about what had happened. Lord Jing was now too ill to get out of bed.

One of his entourage suggested: "The Great Shaman from Sangmen can see ghosts even in broad daylight—why don't we summon her?"

The Great Shaman arrived in response to the Marquis of Jin's summons and was taken directly into His Lordship's chamber. She immediately announced that it was haunted.

"What does the ghost look like?" Lord Jing asked.

"It is a tall man with long, unbound hair," the Great Shaman replied. "He beats his breast and looks deeply enraged!"

"That is exactly the same as what I saw!" Lord Jing exclaimed. "He claims that I murdered his innocent children and grandchildren. I wonder who this ghost could be!"

"How about, it is a minister who did great things in the service of your ancestors," the Great Shaman suggested, "only to have his sons and grandsons murdered by you in a particularly cruel and appalling way?"

Shocked, Lord Jing said, "Do you think this really is the ancestor of the Zhao clan?"

Tu'an Gu was standing to one side and immediately presented his opinion: "This shaman once worked for the Zhao family, and now she is taking advantage of this situation to complain about what happened to them. Do not believe a word she says, Your Lordship!"

Lord Jing was silent for a long time; then he asked another question: "Can you exorcise this ghost?"

"This ghost is so angry that an exorcism will be of no use," the Great Shaman declared.

"Does that mean that I am going to die?" asked Lord Jing.

"I will tell you the truth even at the risk of my own life," the Great Shaman responded. "In your current state of health, I am afraid that Your Lordship will not live to taste this year's freshly harvested barley!"

"The barley is only a month from harvest!" Tu'an Gu exclaimed. "Even though His Lordship is ill, his mind is still perfectly clear: it is not possible that he will die any day now! If His Lordship does live to eat fresh barley, I am going to kill you!"

He did not wait for Lord Jing to give the order, but shouted at the servants to throw the shaman out.

After the Great Shaman left, Lord Jing's condition worsened. Every doctor in Jin was called in to consult, but none of them were able to recognize the condition that was killing him, and they did not dare prescribe any drugs.

Grandee Wei Yi's son, Wei Xiang, spoke to the ministers: "I have heard that there are two famous doctors in Qin: Gao He and Gao Yuan. They are trained in the tradition of the great Bian Que. They understand the principles of human anatomy and have had great success in treating all kinds of diseases, and they have both been appointed as court physicians in Qin. These are the only people who can cure His Lordship's illness. Why don't I go and ask them to come here?"

"Qin is an enemy state," the ministers responded. "Why on earth would they send their best doctors to help cure His Lordship?"

"Neighboring countries ought to help in times of trouble," Wei Xiang replied. "Even though I am not a talented man, I am prepared to go and try to persuade them to let their doctors come to Jin."

"If you can do that," the ministers said, "we will all be deeply grateful to you."

. . .

That very day, Wei Xiang packed his bags and set off for Qin at full speed, traveling day and night. Lord Huan of Qin asked the reason for his journey. Wei Xiang respectfully said, "My lord is suffering from a terrible illness. I have heard that your country has two excellent doctors—Gao He and Gao Yuan—both of whom can bring the dead back to life. I have come especially to beg you to save my lord's life."

"The state of Jin has repeatedly defeated our army in unprovoked attacks," Lord Huan returned. "We may have fine doctors, but why would we want to save your lord?"

"You are wrong!" Wei Xiang said sternly. "Qin and Jin are neighboring countries—in the past our Lord Xian and your Lord Mu were allies and relatives by marriage, and our states remained on good terms from one generation to the next. Your Lord Mu put our Lord Hui in power; then your invasion caused the battle of Hanquan. Next he put Lord Wen in power; then your side betrayed the covenant at Fannan. The reason that this alliance has not endured is all the fault of

Qin! After Lord Wen died, your Lord Mu made a terrible mistake and tried to bully our little Lord Xiang, sending your army to Mount Xiao and attacking our subordinate states. Any defeat and humiliation that you suffered there, you brought upon yourselves! We captured the generals of your three armies, but we did not execute them, and in the end they were pardoned. The response Qin made to this was to betray your promise and steal our royal office! In the reigns of Lord Ling and Lord Kang, when we invaded Chong, you responded by immediately attacking Jin. When our Lord Jing tried to punish Qi, you ordered Du Hui to raise an army to rescue them. When you are defeated, you lack basic discipline; when you are victorious, you do not know when to stop. If anyone is responsible for breaking our alliance and making us into your enemies, it is Qin! Please consider: Is it Jin that has caused trouble for Qin? Or Qin that has caused trouble for Jin? Now His Lordship is terribly ill and he wants to borrow a qualified doctor from your country. The other ministers all said, 'Qin hates us and they will not agree.' I said, 'No. The ruler of Qin may have done many things wrong in the past, but perhaps he now regrets this! My mission is to use the doctors as an excuse to reaffirm the long-standing good relationship between our two countries.' If you do not agree, my lord, all that will happen is that you confirm our ministers' poor opinion! Neighboring countries ought to assist each other in time of trouble, but you are refusing to do so! Doctors try and save people's lives, but you, my lord, are preventing them! Let me say that I think this a very bad idea."

Lord Huan of Qin was rendered acutely uncomfortable by Wei Xiang's incisive analysis. He felt an increasing admiration for the man, and said, "You are quite right to criticize me, sir. I have no choice but to grant your request." He immediately ordered the court physician, Gao Yuan, to go to Jin. Wei Xiang bowed and thanked His Lordship. He and Gao Yuan then departed from Yongzhou, traveling day and night in the direction of the Jin capital.

There is a poem that testifies to this:

Having once been allied by marriage, they have now become enemies,
Sitting by and enjoying the moments when the other suffers disaster.
If it were not for Wei Xiang's persistence and eloquence,
Would this famous doctor ever have set out for Jin?

By this time, Lord Jing of Jin was critically ill; day and night he watched for the Qin doctors, but they did not come. One day he had a dream in which two little boys jumped out of his nose. One child said, "Gao Yuan of Qin is one of the most famous doctors of our times. If he comes here and starts his treatment, we are going to be very seriously injured. How can we avoid him?" The second little boy said, "If we hide above the heart and below the top of the ribcage, there is nothing that he can do about us!" A short time later, Lord Jing screamed in agony because of the terrible pain in his chest. He was uncomfortable whether he sat up or lay down.

A short time later, Wei Xiang arrived with Gao Yuan. When he entered the palace, he began by feeling His Lordship's pulse. When that was done, Gao Yuan declared, "I can do nothing about this disease!"

"Why not?" Lord Jing asked.

"This disease is lodged above your heart and below the top of your ribcage," Gao Yuan replied. "Under such circumstances, I cannot get at it with moxabustion, and acupuncture will not work either. Even if I were to try and use drugs, they would not reach it. I am afraid that this is the will of Heaven!"

Lord Jing sighed and said, "What you have said accords exactly with my dream. You really are a wonderful doctor!" He gave him a large present of money and had the doctor escorted back to the state of Qin.

· · ·

There was a young eunuch named Jiang Zhong. Exhausted by the work of looking after Lord Jing, he fell asleep in the morning. He dreamed that he carried Lord Jing on his back and the two of them flew off into the sky. When he woke up, he told the other servants about this. Even Tu'an Gu, coming to the palace to ask after His Lordship's health, heard about the dream. He congratulated Lord Jing and said, "Heaven represents light and disease represents darkness. If you fly up into the sky, it means that you are going to move towards the light, leaving darkness behind you. You will soon recover from this illness, my lord!"

The Marquis of Jin was feeling somewhat better that day, and when he heard these words he was absolutely delighted. Suddenly a report came in: "The superintendent of farms has come to present freshly harvested barley.

Lord Jing announced that he would like to taste some. He ordered his cooks to take half of it and pound it up to make porridge for him. Tu'an Gu was still furious about the complaints that the Grand Shaman of Sangmen had made concerning the violent deaths of the innocent members of the Zhao clan, so he presented his opinion as follows: "The shaman said that Your Lordship would not live to taste the barley harvested this year. You have now proved her wrong, my lord, so let us summon her and show her how mistaken she was."

Lord Jing did as he suggested and summoned the Grand Shaman of Sangmen to the palace. Tu'an Gu shouted at her: "Here is the fresh barley! Do you think His Lordship is going to be unable to eat it?"

"That remains to be seen," the shaman replied.

Lord Jing changed color.

"How dare you curse His Lordship?" Tu'an Gu screamed. "Behead this woman immediately!" He shouted at his entourage to drag the shaman away.

The shaman sighed and said, "Because of my ability to foretell the future, I have brought disaster down upon my own head. Is that not tragic?"

The servants brought back the dead shaman's head to present to His Lordship just as the cooks sent in the porridge. It was exactly midday. Lord Jing was just about to taste the dish, when suddenly he felt the onset of a bout of diarrhea gripping his guts. He shouted to Jiang Zhong: "Lift me onto the privy!" As he was placed on the privy seat, he felt a terrible pain around his heart. He was not able to keep his balance and fell into the privy. Jiang Zhong lifted him out, paying no attention to the disgusting filth, but Lord Jing had already died.

He did not live to taste the newly harvested barley. The death of the Great Shaman of Sangmen, who had accurately foretold his fate, can be laid entirely at the door of Tu'an Gu.

The senior minister Luan Shu led the other officials to assist the scion Zhoupu in taking charge of the funeral. Afterwards he took the title of Lord Li of Jin. Everyone was discussing Jiang Zhong's dream, in which he had taken His Lordship on his back and flown up into the sky—this seemed to correspond with the fact that he had lifted Lord Jing out of the privy. Thanks to this connection, Jiang Zhong was selected to be one of the human sacrificial offerings in Lord Jing's tomb.

If right at the beginning, Jiang Zhong had said nothing about his dream, this horrible fate would not have befallen him. You can bring great harm upon yourself by speaking incautiously—this is something to be on guard against!

. . .

Later on, after Lord Li was murdered with poisoned wine, Lord Dao was established as the new Marquis of Jin. Ever since Lord Jing had been killed in an attack by a powerful ghost, the state of Jin was riven with gossip about the unjust fate of the Zhao clan. However, thanks to the good relationship that still pertained between Tu'an Gu and the Luan and Xi families, Han Jue remained completely isolated. For this reason he did not dare to speak out about the deaths of so many innocent people.

When Lord Dao appointed Han Jue as commander-in-chief of the Central Army, he came to court ostensibly to thank His Lordship for his kindness, but in fact this gave him an opportunity to speak privately to Lord Dao: "There are many of us here at court who keep our positions thanks to the meritorious service of our ancestors. However, when it comes to performing great deeds in the service of the state of Jin, there is no one who can compare to the Zhao clan. Zhao Cui served Lord Wen, Zhao Dun served Lord Xiang—both of them were totally loyal and worked incredibly hard to make our country powerful and our rulers respected by their peers. Unfortunately, Lord Ling lost control of the government and trusted the wicked Tu'an Gu: he plotted the murder of Zhao Dun, and it was only by going into exile that he was able to escape. Lord Ling was later murdered at the Pear Garden by mutinous soldiers. When Lord Jing was established, he too favored Tu'an Gu. Although Zhao Dun was by that time dead, Tu'an Gu still pretended that the Zhao family were involved in murder and sedition, and punished them for their so-called crimes. He killed the entire Zhao clan, and right up to the present day the people of Jin are still in uproar over this. Luckily, a single member of the Zhao family, the orphan Zhao Wu, has survived. Today, my lord, you have been rewarding the virtuous and punishing the wicked, instituting great reforms in the government of Jin. Surely you are not going to forget to reward the great deeds of the Zhao family."

"I remember hearing my late father speak about this," Lord Dao said thoughtfully. "Where is the orphan now?"

"When Tu'an Gu was searching everywhere for the orphan of the Zhao clan, two old retainers of the family got involved," Han Jue explained. "One was called Gongsun Chujiu and the other Cheng Ying. Gongsun Chujiu pretended that he had smuggled the orphan out of the city, for which he was executed—this allowed Zhao Wu to escape. Later on Cheng Ying took the orphan to hide at Mount Yu, where they have been living for the last fifteen years."

"Can you summon him back for me?" Lord Dao asked.

"Tu'an Gu is still here at court," Han Jue pointed out. "You must keep this secret, my lord!"

"I will!" Lord Dao said firmly.

Han Jue bade His Lordship farewell and left the palace. Driving himself in a chariot, he went to find Zhao Wu in his place of hiding at Mount Yu. On the way back, Cheng Ying drove the chariot. When he returned to the capital, everything about the city was completely different, and his feelings were deeply pained. Han Jue took Zhao Wu into the palace, where he had an audience with Lord Dao. The Marquis of Jin kept him hidden inside the palace, while announcing that he himself was unwell. The following morning, Han Jue led the officials into the palace as part of a formal delegation to ask after His Lordship's health, and Tu'an Gu was also present.

"Do you know why I am feeling so ill?" Lord Dao asked. "Those who have performed meritorious deeds should be reported to the ruler. However, in one case this has not happened, and I am most unhappy about it!"

The ministers kowtowed and asked, "Who has performed a meritorious deed without it being reported?"

"Zhao Cui and Zhao Dun both performed great deeds in the service of our country, so how can their ancestral sacrifices be cut off?" Lord Dao asked.

"The entire Zhao clan was murdered fifteen years ago," the ministers replied in chorus. "Although you may still admire the great deeds that they did, my lord, there is no one left to take charge of their family sacrifices!"

Lord Dao called on Zhao Wu to come out and had him bow to the generals present. "Who is this young man?" they asked.

"This is the real orphan of the Zhao clan: Zhao Wu," Han Jue explained. "The child who was killed was in fact the son of Cheng Ying, one of the Zhao clan's retainers."

Tu'an Gu was horror-struck, and collapsed to the ground as if drunk. He could not find a single word to say.

"This is all Tu'an Gu's fault," Lord Dao declared. "If today the Tu'an clan gets off scot-free, how will the souls of his innocent victims in the Underworld ever be appeased?" He shouted to his guards: "Arrest Tu'an Gu, drag him out, and behead him!"

Afterwards he commanded Han Jue and Zhao Wu to take their soldiers to Tu'an Gu's house and surround it, killing everyone inside regardless of age or sex. Zhao Wu asked permission to sacrifice Tu'an Gu's head on the grave of his father, Zhao Shuo. Everyone in the country was delighted by the fall of Tu'an Gu.

Master Qian Yuan wrote a poem about this:

> First Tu'an Gu killed the entire Zhao clan,
> Today the Zhao clan gets to execute them.
> Since the wheel turned completely in only fifteen years,
> They did not have to wait too long for their revenge.

After Lord Dao of Jin executed Tu'an Gu, he summoned Zhao Wu to court, where a capping ceremony was held, marking his advent into manhood. Afterwards he appointed Zhao Wu as minister of justice, replacing Tu'an Gu. All the lands and emoluments that had previously been held by the Zhao clan were now returned to him. In appreciation of what Cheng Ying had done, the Marquis of Jin also wanted to appoint him as an officer in the army.

"I could not die before the orphan of the Zhao clan had been restored to his rightful heritage," Cheng Ying said. "Now his family has been avenged and his official position confirmed, but that is no reason for me to become greedy for titles and riches! I let Gongsun Chujiu die alone, now it is time for me to join him in the Underworld to report our success!"

He then committed suicide by cutting his throat. Zhao Wu cradled his body and wept bitterly. He begged Lord Dao for permission to bury him with full honors. He was interred at Mount Yunzhong with Gongsun Chujiu, in a tomb known as the Grave of the Two Righteous Gentlemen. Zhao Wu wore mourning clothes for three years, just as he would for his own father, to show his appreciation for all that Cheng Ying had done for him.

There is a poem which testifies to this:

Fifteen years were spent in hiding far away,
Thus the baby lived to revenge the deaths of his innocent parents.
Cheng Ying and Gongsu Chujiu were both righteous men;
Since they both died, who cares which one of them went first?

Do you want to know what happened next? THE STORY CONTINUES . . .

The Downfall of the Kingdom of Wu

Chapter Eleven

King Fuchai of Wu forgives Yue in the teeth of all remonstrance.

King Goujian of Yue racks his brains for ways in which to serve Wu.

In the second month of the twenty-sixth year of the reign of King Jing of Zhou, King Fuchai of Wu, having completed his period of mourning for his grandfather, reported this to the ancestral temple. He then raised an enormous army, appointing Wu Zixu as the senior general, with Bo Pi to assist him. They set out from Lake Tai and traveled along a network of waterways to attack Yue. They defeated the Yue army in a series of battles, and King Goujian of Yue retreated to the fastnesses of Mount Kuaiji. When he counted how many soldiers he had left, there were just over five thousand men. King Goujian sighed and said, "My late father never suffered a defeat as appalling as this one in the thirty years of his reign! I should have listened to Fan Li and Wen Zhong—it is my own fault that things have reached this pass!"

Grandee Wen Zhong presented the following plan: "The matter has now reached crisis level! However, if you can get a peace treaty, all is not lost!"

"Wu will not accept a peace treaty," King Goujian said. "What can I do?"

"The chancellor of Wu, Bo Pi, is a greedy and lascivious man," Wen Zhong replied. "He is jealous of the ability of his colleagues and begrudges other people any success that they may achieve. He may serve at court with Wu Zixu, but they are not united in either ambition or interests. The king of Wu is afraid of Wu Zixu, but he is very fond of Bo Pi. If I were to go privately to his camp and establish relations with him on a friendly footing, agreeing on the process by which a peace treaty will be negotiated, he can discuss this with His Majesty. The king of Wu will certainly listen to his advice. By the time that Wu Zixu finds out what is going on and tries to stop it, it will be too late."

"When you go and see Bo Pi, what will you give him as a bribe?" King Goujian asked.

"The most obvious thing missing from any army is women," Wen Zhong answered. "If I present him with some lovely ladies, Heaven may even now bless the kingdom of Yue, in which case Bo Pi will do what we tell him."

King Goujian then sent a messenger under cover of darkness to the capital, ordering his wife to select eight beautiful women from his harem, dress them up in their finest robes and jewelry, and convey them to Chancellor Bo Pi's camp, together with twenty pairs of white jade discs and one thousand ingots of gold. Grandee Wen Zhong went that very same night to request an audience with the chancellor. At first Bo Pi refused, but when he sent his servant to find out what was going on and the man reported that the Yue envoy had arrived with gifts, he summoned him in.

Bo Pi received Grandee Wen Zhong sitting down, with his legs splayed out in front of him. Grandee Wen Zhong knelt down and said, "My king, Goujian, is a young and foolish man, who has proved unable to serve your country the way that he should—that is why he has been guilty of great offenses against you. His Majesty regrets everything but knows that it is already too late! He would be happy to become a vassal of the kingdom of Wu, but he is afraid that the king of Wu will remember his crimes and refuse to accept this. Knowing of your great virtue and success, Chancellor, as such a close advisor of His Majesty the king, my ruler ordered me to kowtow at the gates to your army camp. If you will speak up for His Majesty and ensure his survival, your kindness will be rewarded with a never-ending stream of gifts." He then presented the list of presents on offer.

"The kingdom of Yue is going to be crushed any day now," Bo Pi said angrily, "in which case everything to be found in Yue will soon belong to Wu! Why are you trying to bribe me with these trinkets?"

Grandee Wen Zhong again came forward and said, "Even though the Yue army has been defeated, there is still an elite force of five thousand men holed up on Mount Kuaiji. They will fight until the very end! If they are not victorious, they are planning to set fire to the treasury and storehouses before making their way into exile abroad by secret routes. Do you really think that Wu is going to be able to just take everything over? And even supposing that Wu does manage to get its hands on everything, the majority will simply be appropriated by the royal palace. You, Chancellor, will get perhaps ten or twenty percent of the booty, but even that will have to be shared with the other generals. If you were to preside over the successful conclusion of a peace treaty with Yue, His Majesty would not be the king of Wu's vassal, he would be yours! His Majesty has promised to present tribute in spring and autumn every year—it would go to your mansion before anything went to the royal palace! You would be the only person to benefit from Yue's largesse, and this you would not have to share with the other generals! Besides which, even animals fight desperately when forced into a corner. It is very hard to say who will win when the Yue army does battle with their backs to the walls of the capital!"

Everything that he had said seemed to speak right to Bo Pi's heart. He could not stop himself from nodding and smiling. Now Grandee Wen Zhong pointed to the reference to beautiful women in the list of gifts. "These eight women were all drawn from the palace of the kings of Yue. If any more beautiful women can be found among our people and if His Majesty is able to return to his kingdom alive, he will do his very best to search them out to replace the inferior examples already presented to you."

Bo Pi stood up and said, "I am deeply touched by the fact that you came to me, sir. I have no intention of taking advantage of your desperate situation to bring harm to you. I will take you to see His Majesty tomorrow morning, so that the discussions over the terms of the peace treaty can begin." He accepted all the gifts that were on offer and had Grandee Wen Zhong stay in his encampment, where he was treated with all the ceremony due to a guest from his host.

The following morning the pair made their way to the main camp, to have an audience with King Fuchai of Wu. Bo Pi was the first to enter His Majesty's presence, where he paved the way by explaining that King Goujian of Yue had sent Grandee Wen Zhong to ask for a peace treaty.

"The enmity between myself and the king of Yue is such that the two of us cannot share the same sky!" King Fuchai bellowed with rage. "How could I possibly accept a peace treaty with them?"

"Have you forgotten the words of Sun Wu, Your Majesty?" Bo Pi replied. "'Weapons are evil things. You can use them for a short time but not for long.' Even though Yue has committed terrible crimes against Wu, they have now accepted that we have conquered them: the king of Yue has asked permission to be your vassal and the queen of Yue has agreed to become your slave. All the treasure and wealth of the kingdom of Yue will be presented as tribute to the Wu palace, and what King Goujian asks of Your Majesty in return is that the sacrifices to his ancestors be allowed to continue. If you accept the surrender of the kingdom of Yue, it will make you rich. If you pardon Yue for the crime they have committed, it will make you famous. If you become both rich and famous, Wu can become hegemon. If you wish to waste your soldiers' lives on trying to punish Yue to the hilt, you will force King Goujian to set fire to his ancestral temples, kill his wife and children, throw all his gold and jade into the Zhe River, and fight to the death with his remaining five thousand men. We may succeed in killing them, but do you think that can be done without costing of the lives of many of your own soldiers? If we slaughter their people, what benefit do you think we will obtain from having captured their kingdom?"

"Where is Grandee Wen Zhong now?" King Fuchai asked.

"He is waiting outside the tent for your summons."

King Fuchai ordered him to come in for an audience. Grandee Wen Zhong came forward, walking on his knees. He restated exactly what he had said before, but in much humbler terms.

"Your king and queen have agreed to become my vassals," His Majesty said. "Are they prepared to come with me to the kingdom of Wu?"

Wen Zhong kowtowed and said, "They are already your vassals—it is entirely up to you whether they live or die. How could they dare to refuse to serve Your Majesty?"

"If Goujian and his wife are willing to go and live in the kingdom of Wu," Bo Pi explained, "even though in name you will have pardoned Yue, in actual fact you will have taken it over completely! What more could you possibly ask for, Your Majesty?"

King Fuchai agreed to the peace treaty. Right at the beginning of their conversation, someone had dashed over to report what was happening to Wu Zixu. He hurried over to the main camp, where he saw Bo Pi and Grandee Wen Zhong standing beside His Majesty. With fury writ clear across his face, Wu Zixu questioned the king of Wu: "Have you already agreed to make peace with Yue?"

"Yes," the king said.

"You cannot do this!" Wu Zixu shouted at the top of his voice. "You must not do this!"

Wen Zhong was shocked into taking a couple of steps backward. He listened in silence as Wu Zixu remonstrated with King Fuchai: "Yue and Wu are neighbors, but such is their enmity that they cannot coexist. If Wu does not destroy Yue, Yue will destroy Wu. If we were to launch a victorious attack over the states of say, Qin or Jin, even if we conquered their territory, we would not be able to live there; even if we captured their chariots, we would not be able to make use of them. However, if we were to attack Yue and conquer them, we would be able to occupy their lands and sail in their boats. Such a great benefit to our country cannot be given up! Furthermore, they were responsible for the death of your grandfather, our former king! If you do not destroy Yue, how can you requite the oath that you swore to avenge him?"

The words that King Fuchai had been planning to speak were now stuck in his throat—he could not find a single thing to say. He turned a glance of mute appeal to Bo Pi. The chancellor came forward and presented his opinion: "You are mistaken in what you say, Prime Minister. When our founding kings established the Zhou confederacy, both water and land were divided up—Wu and Yue were created as riverine states while Qi and Jin were land-based states. Some were given land to live on and others boats to ride in. You have said that Wu and Yue cannot coexist. Now Qin, Jin, Qi, and Lu are all land-based states, and they could easily take over each other's territory and ride in each other's chariots: why have these four states not become one? When you speak of the circumstances of our former king's death as something that must be avenged, you are absolutely right! However, your enmity with Chu ran even deeper. Why did you first try to destroy Chu and then agree to make peace with them? The king and queen of Yue have now both agreed to serve Wu, so why are you trying to kill them? You seem to be happy to garner a reputation for benevolence and generosity for yourself, while leaving His Majesty to be seen as a harsh and cruel monarch—I really do not think that a genuinely loyal minister would behave in this way!"

"You are right, Chancellor," King Fuchai said happily. "Have the prime minister go away. We will wait until tribute has arrived from the kingdom of Yue, and then everyone shall have their share."

Wu Zixu was so enraged by this that he went quite white. "I really regret not getting rid of Bo Pi when I had the chance," he snarled. "How can I possibly work with this sycophantic worm?" Muttering angrily to himself, he walked out of the tent. He told Grandee the Royal Grandson Xiong, "Yue will spend the next decade building up their manpower and resources, and another decade on training. The royal palace at Wu will be overrun within twenty years."

Royal Grandson Xiong was shocked, but did not really believe what Wu Zixu was saying. Wu Zixu mastered his anger and returned to his encampment.

. . .

Leaving his officials behind to govern the country, King Goujian headed off into captivity in Wu, accompanied only by Fan Li. Forced to part at the mouth of the Yangtze River, ruler and ministers shed tears. The king looked up at the sky, and said with a sigh, "Death is something that many people fear. However, when I hear mention of death, I do not find myself in the least bit afraid." He got into a boat and headed off. Those who were left behind bowed down in tears along the banks of the river, but the king of Yue did not look back even once.

There is a poem which testifies to this:

As the slanting sun sinks behind the mountains, the sail is unfurled,
The wind whips up the spring waves, rolling back towards his
    homeland.
Today the oars pull His Majesty away from the sandy bank,
When will he find himself crossing this river again?

The queen of Yue took her place in the prow of the boat, whereupon she burst into tears. She noticed that there were a number of birds catching little shrimp on the mudflats along the riverbank, flying backward and forward. She invested their movements with a deeper meaning, seeing in them a likeness to her own situation. She began to sing through her tears:

"The crows and the cormorants fly up in the sky,
Flapping in the frozen air.
They gather on the islands and sandbanks,
They soar into the clouds on powerful wings.
They peck at the shrimps, they drink the waters,
They come and go just as they please!
What have I done that I deserve this punishment?
What crime have I committed that I must suffer in this way?
The wind blows my boat towards the west—
When will I come back again?
My heart feels as if it has been cut in two!
My tears roll down my cheeks!"

When King Goujian of Yue heard his wife's sad song, he was deeply moved. He forced himself to smile in the hope that this would cheer her, and said, "Once my wings are ready, I am going to fly away. There is nothing to worry about!"

. . .

When the king of Yue crossed the border into Wu, he sent Fan Li on ahead to meet the chancellor Bo Pi at Mount Wu. He presented him with yet more gold and silk, and women.

"Why has Grandee Wen Zhong not come?" Bo Pi inquired.

"He is busy safeguarding the capital on behalf of my master," Fan Li explained. "We could not both come!"

Chancellor Bo Pi followed after Fan Li to meet the king of Yue. King Goujian thanked him heartily for his assistance in preserving the kingdom intact, whereupon Po Bi promised to do everything in his power to ensure that His Majesty returned home one day. This assuaged the most urgent of the king of Yue's fears. Bo Pi commanded his troops to take the king of Yue, in chains, into the heartlands of Wu. There he was taken to have an audience with King Fuchai. King Goujian bared his shoulders in a gesture of surrender and prostrated himself at the foot of the stairs leading up to the main audience hall. The queen of Yue followed his example. Fan Li passed the list of treasures and people being presented to His Majesty up to the king.

The king of Yue bowed twice and kowtowed, with the words: "Your vassal from the Eastern Sea, Goujian, being entirely ignorant of my own weaknesses, committed the crime of invading your territory.

Thanks to Your Majesty pardoning the dreadful offense that I have committed and allowing me to serve you as a vassal, I have been able to preserve my life for the time being. I cannot overcome my sense of amazed gratitude and hence I kowtow to you in sincere appreciation."

All this time, Wu Zixu was standing by His Majesty's side, his eyes burning like hot coals. Now he stepped forward, and said in a voice like thunder: "When you see a bird flying in the azure sky, you want to pick up your bow and shoot it, let alone when you see it sitting in your own courtyard! King Goujian is a dangerous man! Now he is like a lobster in a pot—you should give the cooks the order to dispatch him! The reason why he is flattering and fawning on you, Your Majesty, is because he is hoping to avoid execution. If he leaves here alive, it will be like allowing a tiger to return to its mountain or a whale to get back to its ocean. You will never be able to get him again!"

"The appalling consequences of executing someone who has already surrendered to you can sometimes ruin the lives of three generations," King Fuchai said. "It is not because I have some particular affection for the state of Yue that I forgive them—it is because I do not want to be punished by Heaven!"

"Wu Zixu is excellent at coming up with plans to cope with sudden emergencies but understands nothing about how to bring peace to the country," Bo Pi declared. "Your Majesty speaks as a magnanimous ruler should!"

Wu Zixu realized that King Fuchai was completely taken in by Bo Pi's sycophantic words, so there was no point in remonstrating further. He withdrew, boiling with anger. King Fuchai accepted the tribute offered by the kingdom of Yue and ordered Royal Grandson Xiong to construct a stone chamber next to the tomb of King Helü. King Goujian and his wife were shut up inside, stripped of their official regalia, given rough clothes and wild-thorn hairpins to wear, and told to look after His Majesty's horses. Bo Pi secretly provided them with food and drink, ensuring that they did not actually starve. Every time the king of Wu went out on a journey, King Goujian was required to hold a whip and walk in front of his carriage. The people of Wu would all point at him and say, "That is the king of Yue!" King Goujian's only reaction was to lower his head.

There is a poem which testifies to this:

Let us sigh over the torments of a fallen hero.
Every nerve and fiber suffered under this torture.
Far away from Yue and with little news from home,
He looked back at the Yangtze River as tears coursed down his cheeks.

During the two months that King Goujian lived in the stone chamber, Fan Li was constantly by his side, never moving more than a couple of paces away. Suddenly one day, King Fuchai summoned the king of Yue into his presence. King Goujian knelt down and then prostrated himself on the ground before him, with Fan Li taking up position behind him.

"I have heard it said that a clever woman would not agree to marry into a ruined family, while a famous sage would refuse to work for a doomed state," the king of Wu said to Fan Li. "King Goujian has behaved with great wickedness, bringing his country to destruction—you are both my slaves now, master and man, and spend your time imprisoned in a single room. Surely that is very humiliating. I am prepared to pardon you any offense you have committed against me. If you will agree to draw a line under the past and start afresh, leaving the service of Yue and pledging your allegiance to Wu, I can assure you of an honored position in my government. Leave all these regrets and problems behind you and join me to become rich and noble! What do you think of my proposal?"

All this time the king of Yue, lying flat on the floor, was racked with sobs, for he was terrified that Fan Li might indeed agree to follow Wu. However, Fan Li simply kowtowed and responded: "I have heard it said that a minister from a ruined country should refrain from speaking about matters of state, while the general who has led his army into a defeat should refrain from talking about bravery. I have proved disloyal and untrustworthy since I have failed to keep the king of Yue on the straight and narrow, thus offending so seriously against Your Majesty. We have been so fortunate as to escape execution thanks to your clemency. I am happy to serve you with alacrity whenever it is required. Since I have everything that I could possibly wish for, how could I think about becoming rich and noble?"

"If you do not change your mind," King Fuchai said, "you are going to have to go back to the stone chamber."

"As Your Majesty wishes," Fan Li replied.

King Fuchai got up and went back to the palace. Meanwhile King Goujian and Fan Li returned to the stone room, where the king of Yue changed into coarse short trousers and a peasant's headcloth, so that he could start mashing up the feed that would be given to the horses. His wife, dressed in ragged clothing, went off to draw water, shovel dung, and sweep the ground clear. Fan Li himself chopped firewood and tended the stove, baking his face to a cinder. From time to time, King Fuchai would send people to spy on them, but when they saw both ruler and minister working hard, without the smallest sign of resentment or anger in their faces and never saying a word of complaint, they imagined this meant that they had given up hope of ever returning home. Consequently their surveillance became very slack.

· · ·

One day, King Fuchai climbed the Gusu Tower. In the distance, he caught sight of the king and queen of Yue squatting down next to a pile of horse dung, while Fan Li stood on the left hand side, holding a fly whisk. Clearly all the proprieties between a husband and wife, not to mention the respect due to a ruler from his subject, were still being observed. King Fuchai turned his head towards Chancellor Bo Pi and said, "The king of Yue ruled what is really only a tiny country, Fan Li was just a perfectly ordinary gentleman, but even in circumstances like these they have never forgotten their proper roles. I really have a lot of admiration for them."

"One can admire them and also feel sorry for them," Bo Pi responded.

"You are absolutely right," King Fuchai said. "I really can't bear to watch them carry on like this. Since they have clearly understood the error of their ways and turned over a new leaf, why shouldn't I pardon them?"

"I have heard that countries that have behaved without proper virtue can never be successfully restored," Bo Pi replied. "Your Majesty really is the equal of any sage-king! Not only do you feel sorry for people in adversity, you are even prepared to show clemency to Yue. I am sure that in the future you will be lavishly repaid for your kindness! It is entirely up to Your Majesty to decide their fate!"

"Order the Grand Astrologer to select an auspicious date," King Fuchai said, "and we will allow the king of Yue to go home."

Bo Pi sent one of his servants to visit the stone chamber in the fifth watch, to inform King Goujian of the good news. The king of Yue was delighted and reported this to Fan Li.

"I would like to perform a divination about it," Fan Li said. "Today is Wuyin day, and you heard the news in Mao hour. Wu represents imprisonment; furthermore, when Mao is reduplicated, it can overcome Wu. The line reading is: 'The Heavenly Net is spread in all directions; each one of the myriad creatures is injured thereby. Good luck will turn to disaster.' Even though you have been told you will be released, there is nothing to be pleased about in this news." King Goujian's joy now turned to sorrow.

When Wu Zixu heard that King Fuchai was proposing to pardon the king of Yue, he immediately rushed to the palace and had an audience with His Majesty: "In the past evil King Jie of the Xia dynasty imprisoned Tang and refused to execute him, while the wicked King Zhou of the Shang dynasty held the future King Wen prisoner and did not kill him. However, when the Will of Heaven changed, the disaster that Tang and Wen had suffered turned out to be a great blessing for them. Thus Jie was replaced by Tang and the Shang dynasty was destroyed by the Zhou. Today you hold the king of Yue at your mercy, and yet you consistently have refused to execute him—you are going to suffer the same disaster as that which afflicted the Xia and the Shang dynasties!"

King Fuchai was convinced by Wu Zixu's words that he ought to kill the king of Yue and sent someone to summon him. Chancellor Bo Pi again managed to get word to King Goujian ahead of time. He was very shocked at this new turn of events and discussed what to do with Fan Li.

"Do not be afraid, Your Majesty!" Fan Li said. "King Fuchai has held you prisoner for three years now. If he has managed to put up with your continued existence all these years, why should he not be able to endure another day? I am sure that you are not in any danger when you go to see him."

"The only reason that I have been able to survive all this time is thanks to your excellent advice," King Goujian declared.

He went to the city to have an audience with the king of Wu. He stayed there for three days, and the whole of this time King Fuchai did not summon him to court. Eventually, Bo Pi came out of the palace to see him and informed him that, by order of the king of Wu, he should return to his stone chamber. King Goujian found this whole episode quite peculiar and asked what was going on.

"His Majesty was led astray by Wu Zixu's emotive language and decided that he wanted to execute you," Bo Pi explained. "That is why you were summoned. However, His Majesty has lately developed influenza and does not feel like leaving his bed. I went into the palace to ask after King Fuchai's health and took the opportunity to tell him: 'If you are suffering ill health, you should perform virtuous actions. Right now, the king of Yue is on tenterhooks, waiting outside the gates of the palace for you to decide whether you are going to execute him or not. His fear and resentment will certainly have reached Heaven. If you wish to preserve your health, Your Majesty, you should let him go back to the stone chamber. Once you have recovered, you can think about what you want to do with him.' His Majesty listened to what I had to say and agreed that you should be allowed to leave the capital." King Goujian expressed his deep gratitude for his intercession.

Another three months went by with King Goujian living in the stone chamber, during which time the king of Wu continued to feel very unwell, finding it impossible to recover his health completely. King Goujian asked Fan Li to perform a divination about it. When Fan Li laid out the hexagrams, he said, "The king of Wu is not going to die. On Yisi day he will gradually start to recover, and by Renshen day he will be back to full health again. I would recommend that you ask to see His Majesty. If you are granted permission to have an audience with him, you should taste his stool and look carefully at the color of his face. After that you can bow twice and congratulate His Majesty, announcing the dates by which he will recover. If he does indeed get better as we expect, he is sure to feel very grateful to you. Then you can look forward to receiving a pardon shortly."

King Goujian wept, and said, "Even though I have no particular talents, I have been called upon to take my place facing south and rule as a king. How can I endure the humiliation of having to taste another man's urine and diarrhea?"

"When the evil King Zhou of the Shang dynasty imprisoned the future King Wen of Zhou at Youli," Fan Li reminded him, "he killed his son Boyikao, cooked his flesh, and served it up to him. The future King Wen had to endure the terrible torment of eating the flesh of his own son. If you want to achieve great things, you have to rise above ordinary considerations. The king of Wu is a man too weak for his own good, and he lacks the decisiveness that makes a great leader. He has already expressed his willingness to pardon you, but all of a sudden things went wrong. If you do not do this, how do you think you are going to get yourself into his good graces?"

That very day, King Goujian of Yue went to Chancellor Bo Pi's mansion. When he saw the chancellor, he said, "It is the natural order of things that a vassal should be upset when his lord it ill. I have heard that His Majesty has now been sick for a very long time and there seems to be no improvement in his condition, which has made me most uneasy. I find that I cannot eat or sleep for worry. Next time that you go to visit His Majesty to inquire after his health, I would like to go with you, to show the care and concern that befits a subject."

"Since you feel that way about it," Bo Pi said, "I will be sure to convey your message to His Majesty."

The chancellor went into the palace to have an audience with the king of Wu. He hinted that King Goujian was very distressed at hearing about his ill health and mentioned that he would very much like to see His Majesty. King Fuchai was not feeling at all well and appreciated King Goujian's good wishes, so he agreed to see him.

Bo Pi led King Goujian into the king of Wu's bedchamber, and King Fuchai forced himself to open his eyes. "You have come to see me?" he said.

King Goujian kowtowed and replied, "Your humble prisoner heard that you are not feeling well; on obtaining this news, it was as if my heart was being torn in two! I was determined to come and see how you are."

While he was speaking, King Fuchai felt the urgent pain of the onset of another bout of diarrhea and waved at his visitor to leave the room.

"When I was living by the Eastern Sea," King Goujian remarked, "I once had occasion to speak to a famous doctor, who was able to diagnose his patient's condition from the appearance of urine and stools." He folded his hands respectfully and went to stand by the door to the bedchamber. The servants brought a chamber pot to the bed and assisted King Fuchai into place. When they were about to withdraw, King Goujian lifted the lid off the chamber pot and picked up a piece of His Majesty's stool with his bare hand before kneeling down to taste it. The servants present were all holding their noses. King Goujian then entered the bedchamber again and kowtowed, saying, "Let me bow twice and congratulate Your Majesty. You will begin to get better on Yisi day, and by Renshen day in the third month, you will have made a full recovery."

"How can you be so sure?" King Fuchai asked.

"The famous doctor that I mentioned just now informed me that stools should have the same taste as the grain that the patient eats," King Goujian explained. "If the flavor is in harmony with the season of the year, the patient will survive. If the flavor is contrary, the patient will die. Just now I made so bold as to taste Your Majesty's stool, and the flavor was both bitter and sour. That is entirely appropriate to the spring season, so that is how I made my deduction."

King Fuchai was very pleased: "What an amazing man you are, Goujian! It is often said that a vassal should serve his ruler as a son would serve his father, but it is not often that you see a man prepared to taste someone else's diarrhea in order to make a diagnosis!"

All this time, Chancellor Bo Pi was standing by the king of Wu's side. King Fuchai asked him, "Could you do that?"

Bo Pi shook his head and said, "Even though I am very fond of Your Majesty, I could not do a thing like that."

"It is not just you," the king said. "I am sure that not even my own son, the crown prince, would be prepared to do the like!"

He immediately gave orders for King Goujian to leave the stone chamber and move to somewhere more comfortable: "As soon as I am fully recovered," he said, "I will send you home." King Goujian bowed and thanked His Majesty for his magnanimity. From this time on he was living in a house just like everyone else, though he carried on looking after horses as before.

King Fuchai did indeed gradually recover from his illness, exactly to the timetable that King Goujian had given. His Majesty was most impressed by the loyalty that the king of Yue had shown on this occasion, and so when he was able to attend court once more, he gave orders that a banquet should be prepared at the summit of the Wen Tower and summoned King Goujian to attend. The king of Yue pretended that he had no idea what was going on and went dressed as a prisoner. When King Fuchai heard this, he commanded that he be given a bath and dressed in suitable official robes. King Goujian refused time and again, before finally agreeing. Once he had dressed formally, he went in to have an audience with His Majesty, at which he bowed twice and kowtowed. King Fuchai hurried forward and lifted him to his feet. Then he gave the following orders: "The king of Yue is a most virtuous and magnanimous man: otherwise, how could he have survived many years of humiliation the way that he has? I am going to release him from captivity, pardon him for his crimes, and allow him to go home. However, today the king of Yue will sit facing north, and my ministers should treat him as an honored guest!"

He bowed and gestured to the king of Yue to sit down. All the grandees present lined up beside him and then took their seats. Wu Zixu realized that His Majesty had completely forgotten the sorrows that he had suffered at the hands of the king of Yue and was proposing to treat his enemy as a guest of honor. He was so angry that he could not sit still, and walked out in a huff.

Bo Pi came forward and said, "Your Majesty has seen fit to extend clemency concerning a crime committed by a man of much merit. I have often heard it said that similar sounds harmonize with one another, while men of a like temperament will come to each other's aid. At today's banquet it is only too appropriate that the magnanimous have stayed behind while the fractious and quarrelsome have seen fit to walk out. The prime minister is a very brave man, it is true, but perhaps he felt himself too humiliated by the example before him to remain in his seat?"

King Fuchai laughed and said, "You are absolutely right, Chancellor!"

The wine circulated three times. Fan Li and the king of Yue both got up and raised their goblets to toast King Fuchai with the following words: "Your August Majesty, your magnanimity spreads across the land like the warm winds of spring, your kindness is without compare, and your virtue is daily renewed! Ah! May your glorious reign never end, may you live ten thousand years, and may you govern the kingdom of Wu forever! Let all those within the four seas unite behind you, may the aristocrats of the Central States submit and pay court to you! Let us lift our goblets brimming with wine and wish Your Majesty a myriad blessings!"

The king of Wu was delighted. That day they got drunk together. Finally, King Fuchai ordered Noble Grandson Xiong to escort the king of Yue to a guesthouse: "Within three days, I will escort you back to your country."

However, the following morning, Wu Zixu had an audience with King Fuchai, at which he said: "Yesterday you held a banquet in honor of your mortal enemy; what do you expect to gain from that? King Goujian harbors just as much loyalty to you as a tiger or wolf would, no matter how respectful and friendly he may appear. You seem to care more for a moment's flattery, Your Majesty, than you do for the fact that in the future this man may very well bring about your destruction! You are setting aside loyal advice in order to pay heed only to those who flatter and fawn on you—you are prepared to help your greatest enemy for the sake of a fleeting reputation for mercifulness. Your actions can be compared to placing a feather on top of burning coals and hoping it will not burn, or throwing an egg from a great height and imagining that it will not break. Do you really think that he is going to forgive you for what you have done to him?"

"When I was bedridden for three months thanks to that horrible disease, you did not say one nice thing to me to cheer me up in all that time," the king of Wu retorted. "That shows your lack of loyalty to me! You did not give me one nice present: that shows your lack of kindness! What is the point of having someone around who is neither loyal nor kind? The king of Yue has left his country and come all this way to serve me; he has given me everything he owns and works for me like a slave. That shows his loyalty! When I was ill, he tasted my diarrhea without the slightest sign of disgust or resentment. That shows his concern! If I were to listen to your biased opinions, Prime Minister, and execute this excellent man, I am sure that I would be asking for punishment from Heaven!"

"You seem determined to misunderstand the true nature of the situation, Your Majesty!" Wu Zixu shouted. "When a tiger tries to conceal its strength, it is because it is about to attack you. When a fox crouches down, it is getting ready to pounce. The king of Yue hates you because he has been forced to come to Wu as a vassal: how can you not grasp that? When he tasted your diarrhea, it was so that he would be able to kill you in the future! If you persist in ignoring his true intentions, you are going to fall into his wicked trap! That will cause the destruction of the kingdom of Wu!"

"You are wasting your breath, Prime Minster!" King Fuchai returned. "My mind is made up!" Wu Zixu realized that there was no point in remonstrating more, so he withdrew, sunk in gloom.

On the third day, the king of Wu ordered that a banquet be held outside the Snake Gate, and he personally escorted the king of Yue out of the capital. The Wu ministers all raised their cups and toasted King Goujian. The only person who did not attend was Wu Zixu. King Fuchai said to the king of Yue, "I have now pardoned you, and you may go home. However, I want you to remember our kindness and forget any enmity that you might feel."

The king of Yue kowtowed and said, "You have very graciously taken pity on my lonely and isolated state, Your Majesty, and that is how I have been able to return to my kingdom alive. I promise that I will do my very best to repay you in this life and the next! May Heaven bear witness that I am telling the truth! If I ever betray Wu, may the Bright Spirits punish me!"

"Since you have sworn on your honor as a gentleman," King Fuchai said, "I am sure that I can trust you. You should be on your way. Off you go! Off you go!"

King Goujian bowed twice, knelt down, and prostrated himself on the ground, with tears streaming down his cheeks. He seemed unable to tear himself away from the king of Wu's company. King Fuchai had to help the king of Yue into his chariot himself. Fan Li seized the reins, and the queen too bowed twice and thanked His Majesty for his kindness. When all three of them were safely ensconced on their chariot, they set off southward. This occurred in the twenty-ninth year of the reign of King Jing of Zhou.

A historian wrote a poem about this:

> The king of Yue's position was once like that of a lobster in a pot;
> No one could have imagined that he would leave Mount Kuaiji alive.
> How stupid was King Fuchai, unable to foresee the future,
> Opening the net to allow this whale to escape.

When King Goujian of Yue was released from imprisonment, he was determined to exact revenge, and to this end he worked extremely hard, day and night, living a very austere life. When he was so tired that his eyes would start to close, he would wake himself up by pricking himself with a thorn. When his feet got cold but he wanted to continue working, he would simply put them in water. In the winter, he was often to be found holding a lump of ice; in the summer, he could be seen huddled next to a roaring fire. When he was so exhausted that he absolutely had to get some rest, he would lie down on a heap of straw, without even using a pillow or blanket. He kept a gall suspended next to wherever he was sitting or lying, so that he could taste it prior to eating or drinking anything. In the middle of the night he would burst out crying, after which he would wail and moan, and the memory of what happened at Mount Kuaiji always spurred him on.

Because so many people had died in his disastrous campaign against Wu, King Goujian was very much worried that the population might collapse. To counteract this, he passed a law making it illegal for a young man to marry an old woman, or for an old man to marry a young wife. Furthermore, the parents of any girl left unmarried at seventeen or boy unmarried at twenty would be punished. When a woman got pregnant and was about to give birth, she could report this to local officials, who would arrange for her to have medical attention. If a son was born, she would receive a pot of wine and a dog; if it was a daughter, she would receive a pot of wine and a pig. In the event of a woman giving birth to triplets, two of them would be raised at state expense. Should a woman give birth to twins, one of them was raised at state expense. If anyone in the capital died, His Majesty would try to pay a personal visit of condolence; every time King Goujian left the palace, he would be followed by a cart loaded down with food. In the event of meeting a child, His Majesty would give a present of food and ask its name. When it was time to plough the fields, the king of Yue would take a turn himself. The queen of Yue, meanwhile, was busy weaving. The two of them made every effort to ensure that they shared the suffering and hard work that was their people's lot.

Given that they had decided to remit taxes for seven years, the king and queen of Yue had no meat to eat with their meals nor any new clothes. However, they were extremely punctilious about one thing—not a month went by without an envoy being sent to Wu. Men and women were sent out into the mountains to collect wild nettles which were then woven into fine ramie cloth: this was intended for presentation to the king of Wu. Before they had time to send it, King Fuchai, delighted with all the efforts that the king of Yue had made to please him, sent an ambassador to increase the size of his fief. King Goujian collected one hundred thousand lengths of ramie cloth, one hundred vats of honey, five sets of fox furs, and ten boats built of bamboo as a thank-offering for this increased grant of land. King Fuchai was very pleased and presented the king of Yue with a set of feather regalia. When Wu Zixu heard what had happened, he announced that he was feeling too unwell to be able to attend court.

• • •

Grandee Wen Zhong went into the palace to have an audience with King Goujian of Yue: "I have heard it said that a bird is killed by grain, no matter how high it flies, while a fish is killed by bait, no matter how deep it dives. If you want to take revenge on Wu, Your Majesty, you must first make use of the things that they enjoy, because that is how you get control of their fates."

"Even if we are able to make use of the things they enjoy," King Goujian said, "how does that help us to control their fate?"

"There are seven techniques that you can use to destroy Wu," Wen Zhong replied. "The first is by giving them property, which pleases both ruler and ministers. The second is by paying a high price for their grain, thereby destabilizing their markets and emptying their reserves. The third is through the use of beautiful women, who lead them astray and make them forget their original ambitions. The fourth lies in giving them fine materials and excellent craftsmen, encouraging them to waste their money on building fancy palaces. The fifth is through sowing the seeds of suspicion by flattery and persuasion, causing dissension in the ranks when any plan is discussed. The sixth is forcing loyal ministers to commit suicide, thereby depriving the king of support. The seventh is accumulating your own resources and training your own troops, so that when the time comes, you can take advantage of their disarray."

"Excellent!" King Goujian exclaimed. "What is the first technique that we should use?"

"The king of Wu has just announced that he wants to rebuild the Gusu Tower," Wen Zhong replied, "and so we should present them with the finest timbers culled from our most famous mountains."

Having done this, King Goujian wanted to move on to the next stage of the plan. He told Wen Zhong: "The king of Wu needs some singers and dancers for his palace, because without beautiful women, he is not going to be distracted from the business of government. That is the next thing that I want you to do for me!"

Do you want to know how Grandee Wen Zhong achieved this? READ ON.

Chapter Twelve

Having fallen into the trap laid by Yue, Xi Shi is much favored at the Wu Palace.

Having killed King Fuchai, the ruler of Yue proclaims himself hegemon.

King Goujian of Yue decided to search out beautiful women from across his country in order that they could be presented to the king of Wu. Wen Zhong suggested the following plan: "Let me take one hundred of your servants, Your Majesty, in particular astrologers and persons who perform divinations by inspecting the face, and have them go and ply their skills among the people. As they wander around the country, let it be their job to make a note of the names and places of residence of any particularly beautiful young women whom they see, and then the final selection can be made from the girls in this group. I am sure that you do not have to worry that you will not be able to find anyone suitable."

King Goujian followed this plan, and in the next six months the existence of more than twenty beautiful women was reported to him. King Goujian had his people go out and make a second triage, which resulted in the selection of two exceptionally lovely girls, whose portraits were submitted to the palace for approval. Who were these two girls? One was Xi Shi and the other was Zheng Dan. Xi Shi was the daughter of a firewood cutter on Mount Zhuluo. There were two villages on this mountain—an eastern one and a western one—and most of the residents were members of the Shi family, so given that this girl came from the western village, she was called Xi or "Western" Shi to distinguish her. Zheng Dan also came from the western village and was a neighbor of Xi Shi. Given that they lived overlooking the river, every day they would go down to the water's edge to do their washing. The two girls were both unusually pretty; their reflections in the water were as beautiful as lilies floating across the waves.

King Goujian ordered Fan Li to buy each of them from their families with one hundred ingots of gold. He dressed them in fine silk gowns and had them ride in a carriage curtained on all sides. The people of the capital heard about their superlative beauty and fought to be allowed to see them—they all came out of the city in order to welcome them, creating a horrendous traffic jam on the roads. Fan Li made Xi Shi and Zheng Dan stay at a guesthouse, and put out the word: "Anyone who wants to see these two beauties will have to pay a copper coin." He set up a counter at which the money could be handed over, and in a trice his moneybox was full. The two gorgeous young women climbed up to a little red-painted pavilion where they stood looking out, leaning against the railings. Looking up at them from below, they seemed to float in mid-air like goddesses. They lived outside the suburbs for three days, during which time they earned a huge amount of money, which was all collected by the treasury to fill the state coffers. Afterwards, King Goujian personally escorted the pair of them to their new residence in Tucheng, where he had arranged for senior court entertainers to instruct them in the arts of singing and dancing. Having mastered the arts of seduction, not to mention their instruction in other disciplines, they were sent to the Wu capital. This happened in the thirty-first year of the reign of King Jing of Zhou, which was also the seventh year of the reign of King Goujian.

. . .

In all, the king of Yue had the beautiful women whom he had collected instructed for three years. When they had completed their training, he had them dressed up in pearl-encrusted crowns and they then drove through the city streets, riding in fine carriages, whereupon their perfume could be smelled far and wide. He had the prime minister, Fan Li, convey them both to the kingdom of Wu. Accordingly, Fan Li sought an audience with King Fuchai, at which he bowed twice and kowtowed. Then he said, "Your humble servant living by the Eastern Sea, Goujian, is deeply appreciative of the kindness that you have always shown him. Unfortunately, it has not been possible for him to bring his wife and concubines to Wu to serve you in person. Instead, he has searched his entire kingdom and found these two lovely girls who can sing and dance for your pleasure, so he ordered me to take them to Your Majesty's palace that they may serve you."

King Fuchai looked at the pair and thought that they might as well be a pair of goddesses visiting from the skies above—he felt slightly drunk.

Wu Zixu remonstrated: "I have heard it said that the Xia dynasty was ruined by Mo Xi, the Shang dynasty was destroyed by Da Ji, and the Zhou dynasty was brought to its knees by Bao Si. Beautiful women cause disaster to the countries in which they live; you cannot accept them, Your Majesty!"

"It is human nature to enjoy sex!" King Fuchai exclaimed. "Goujian did not dare to keep these women for himself but sent them to me—that proves that he is completely loyal to Wu! I do not understand why you are always so suspicious, Prime Minister!" He decided to take the gift.

The two women were so superlatively beautiful that King Fuchai came to love and favor them to the exclusion of all others. However, Xi Shi was the more bewitchingly attractive of the pair, and so she was always given the lead role when they were asked to sing or dance. She was sent to live at the Gusu Tower, where she monopolized the king's affections: whenever she went in or out, she was treated with the same ceremony as would have been shown if she were genuinely the queen. Zheng Dan was left behind at the Wu Palace. She was very jealous of the favor shown to Xi Shi and became depressed at her failure, resulting in her early death. King Fuchai was upset about this and buried her at Mount Huangmao, where he established a shrine in her honor. This happened somewhat later on.

King Fuchai loved and favored Xi Shi so much that he ordered Royal Grandson Xiong to build a residence just for her—the Lodging Beauties Palace at the top of Mount Lingyan. The gutters were made of bronze and the balustrades of jade, each room being hung with pearls and precious gems: all for the delectation of this entrancing woman. On top of the mountain there were the Enjoying Flowers Pool, the Enjoying the Moon Pool, and the King of Wu's Well. The waters drawn here are very fresh and pure. Sometimes Xi Shi would look into the water to find herself mirrored there and do her makeup; King Fuchai stood by her side and arranged her hair himself. There was also a cave known as Xi Shi's Cave—supposedly King Fuchai of Wu would sit there with his favorite. Outside the cave there was a stone with a small indentation in it: this was commonly called "Xi Shi's footprint." His Majesty would sometimes play the *qin* with Xi Shi on top of the mountain.

The Qin Tower is to be found there now.

He ordered people to go to Mount Xiang to plant fragrant flowers, then he boated there with Xi Shi and her ladies to pick them.

Even today, south of Mount Lingyan, there is a canal that runs as straight as an arrow, which was the old site of the Picking Flowers Waterway.

There was also the Lotus-Picking Canal, running southeast of the city of Jun; the king of Wu and Xi Shi picked lotus blossoms there. They dug a deep waterway running north-south through the capital city and sailed there on a boat with silken sails—that is why people called it the "Brocade Sail Canal."

Gao Qi wrote a poem about this place:

When the king of Wu was alive, a myriad flowers blossomed here;
Painted boats were moored by these islands, as musicians played.
When the king of Wu died, a myriad flowers fell here;
As the sounds of singing faded, these islands were left barren and
    bare.
Flowers have bloomed and flowers have fallen in every spring of every
    year;
How many people have seen them blossom over the course of
    millennia?
When you see the bare branches reflected in the river waters,
Remember the countless petals that have crumbled into dust!
Centuries of wind and rain have swept over this weed-covered tower,
As the sun sets, the golden orioles sing their heartbreaking song.
No one comes here now to admire the beautiful flowers blossoming,
Since for so many years there have been no flowers to see!

To the south of the city there was the Long Island Park, which was where the pair of them went hunting. There was also the Fishing Village, where they went fishing, and the Duck Village, where they kept ducks. Chickens were raised at Chicken Bank, and wine was made at the Wine Village. There is also the South Cove at the Dongting Islands, which was where she went to avoid the heat of summer.

This cove is more than ten li in length and has mountains on three sides, with access only from the south.

The king of Wu said, "This is where we can escape the summer heat," so this place became known as Escaping the Summer Cove.

Zhang Yu wrote a poem titled "The Song of Gusu Tower:"

A myriad flowers bloom at the Lodging Beauties Palace.
Xi Shi appears at the Gusu Tower.
Her pink skirt and green sleeves float on the breeze,
Her body seems so frail it can hardly stand against the wind.
Looking out at the rivers of the distant Yangtze delta,
Two distant green dots mark the Dongting Islands in Lake Tai.
Although she turns her head, she finds it hard to drag her eyes away;
She hopes to see His Majesty shoot down a deer.
As the sun sets behind the walls of the city, the crows find a place to
    roost;
As the performance ends below the hall, the pear trees bloom.
None of the passers-by walking on the opposite bank even notice
The threatening glint of Yue's drawn swords.

After Xi Shi came to live with him, King Fuchai of Wu took up permanent residence at the Gusu Tower. Throughout the year he would go hunting whenever he felt like it, ordering a troupe of musicians to follow him and play for his amusement. He was enjoying himself far too much to be bothered with any official business. He would allow Chancellor Bo Pi and Royal Grandson Xiong to attend him, but if Wu Zixu asked for an audience, he would refuse to see him.

. . .

When King Goujian heard that the king of Wu favored Xi Shi so much that he was spending every day enjoying himself in her company, he discussed the next stage of his plan with Grandee Wen Zhong.

"I have heard it said that the people are the foundation of the state and that their most important consideration is food," Wen Zhong replied. "This year the harvest has been poor, and so the price of grain is already rising. You should ask for food aid from Wu, to save our people from starvation. If Heaven has indeed abandoned them, they will be stupid enough to agree."

King Goujian commanded Wen Zhong to take lavish gifts with which to bribe Chancellor Bo Pi so that he would arrange an audience with the king of Wu. The king of Wu did indeed agree to give him an audience at the palace attached to the Gusu Tower. Wen Zhong bowed twice, then said, "The marshlands of Yue often suffer from unseasonal floods and droughts. This year the harvest has been very poor and the people are suffering from starvation. His Majesty begs you for ten thousand bushels of grain from your storehouses to relieve the famine that is now imminent. We will pay you back when next year's harvest is ripe."

"The king of Yue is my vassal," King Fuchai declared. "That means that starvation among his people it is no different from famine in Wu. How could I possibly begrudge the grain that will save you?"

By this time Wu Zixu had been informed of the arrival of an ambassador from Yue, so he came hot-foot to the Gusu Tower to ask for an audience with King Fuchai. When he heard that His Majesty had agreed to give them the grain, he immediately remonstrated: "No! You must not do that! In the current situation, either Wu will conquer Yue or vice versa. I have observed the Yue ambassador, and he is here not because his country is genuinely suffering from famine and needs the food, but because he is hoping to clear out our stocks of grain. If you give it to them, they will not become closer allied. If you do not give it to them, they cannot possibly hate you any more than they already do. It would be better to refuse."

"When the king of Yue was a prisoner in this country," King Fuchai retorted, "he walked in front of my horse every time I went out—there is no one in the world that has not heard of that! Now I have restored his country's independence, a gift comparable to being reborn, and he sends a constant stream of tribute to me. Why should I worry that he might betray me again?"

"I have heard that the king of Yue works from early in the morning until late at night, showing enormous care and concern over his people, and gaining the services of every knight that he can," Wu Zixu said. "He wants his revenge on Wu! If you send him this grain, it will just help him achieve that! I am afraid that any day now we will be able to see deer walking through the ruins of the Gusu Tower!"

"The king of Yue has already accepted a position as my vassal. What kind of vassal would attack his own lord?"

"Tang attacked the wicked King Jie of the Xia dynasty, Wen attacked the evil King Zhou of the Shang dynasty—are they not instances of a vassal attacking his lord?"

Chancellor Bo Pi was standing by the king of Wu's side. Now he shouted, "That is most rude of you, Prime Minister! Are you meaning to compare His Majesty with King Jie and King Zhou?" Then he presented his opinion to King Fuchai: "I have been informed that the text of the covenant sworn at Kuiqiu specifically forbade refusing to hand over grain in time of famine, when you should be feeling sympathy for your neighbor's suffering. Furthermore, has the kingdom of Yue ever failed to offer you all the tribute you desire? Next year when the harvest is ripe, you can ask them for several times this amount of grain in recompense. It will cause no damage to Wu and will show our virtue to Yue. What are you worried about?"

King Fuchai then agreed to give Yue the ten thousand bushels of grain. He said to Grandee Wen Zhong, "I am going against the express advice of my ministers in sending this grain to Yue. You are going to have to repay it next harvest. Please do not break your word!"

Grandee Wen Zhong bowed twice, kowtowed, and said, "How could we fail to keep to our agreement, when you feel such great sympathy for Yue that you have helped us in time of famine?"

Wen Zhong returned home to Yue with the ten thousand bushels of grain. King Goujian was delighted. The other ministers all shouted out: "Long life to His Majesty!" The king of Yue had the grain parceled out to feed the very poorest of his people, who in turn praised His Majesty's generosity.

The following year, there was a bumper harvest in the kingdom of Yue. King Goujian asked Grandee Wen Zhong, "If I do not pay back the grain that I received from Wu, I will be breaking my promise to them. If on the other hand I do pay it back, I will be benefiting Wu to the detriment of Yue. What should I do?"

"You should pick the finest quality of grain and steam it," Wen Zhong told him, "and then hand it over to them. If they are sufficiently impressed by the grain that we send them, they will keep it for use as seed, in which case our plan will succeed."

The king of Yue followed this advice and used grain that had already been precooked to repay Wu, in exactly the same quantities as he had been given. King Fuchai sighed and said, "What a trustworthy man the king of Yue is!" When he noticed that the grain they had sent was somewhat larger than normal, he said to Bo Pi: "The soil in Yue is very fertile, and so the grain grown there is of exceptionally high quality. We ought to hand it out to our people for use as seed."

The grain sent by Yue was distributed and planted throughout the country, only for them to discover that it did not sprout. The kingdom of Wu suffered a terrible famine because of this. King Fuchai of Wu remained under the impression that something must have gone wrong with the planting, because he did not know that the grain had been steamed. Grandee Wen Zhong's plan was cruel indeed! This took place in the thirty-sixth year of the reign of King Jing of Zhou.

· · ·

When King Goujian heard that the kingdom of Wu was suffering from a famine, he wanted to raise an army and attack Wu. Wen Zhong remonstrated: "The time is not yet ripe. They still have loyal ministers at court."

King Goujian asked the same question of Fan Li, who replied, "Soon the time will come for your revenge. You should be training your army in combat techniques, Your Majesty."

"Do we have all the equipment that we need?" the king of Yue asked.

"A good general needs well-trained troops," Fan Li replied. "Well-trained troops need proper equipment, be that swords and spears, or bows and crossbows. However, without training and practice, they simply will not be able to use their weapons properly. I have heard that there is a girl who lives in the southern forests of Yue who is an exceptionally fine swordswoman. In addition, there is a man from Chu called Chen Yin, who is a very good archer. Your Majesty ought to recruit the pair of them into your service." The king of Yue sent out two envoys, loaded with rich gifts to be presented to both of them, and they proceeded to train his army for him.

· · ·

Subsequently, King Fuchai had the loyal minister Gongsun Sheng beaten to death with an iron cudgel for criticizing him. When the king of Wu tired of Wu Zixu's constant remonstrance and complaints, he ordered him to commit suicide, presenting him with the sword named *Black* with instructions to cut his own throat. It was in this same year that King Goujian of Yue discovered that King Fuchai of Wu had given himself up to the pleasures of wine and women, paying no attention at all to matters of government. To make things worse, Wu had endured successive years of poor harvests, and anger was spreading among the populace. He decided to mobilize all the soldiers within his borders and launched a massive attack on Wu. When they left the suburbs, His Majesty happened to notice a large frog on the road, which glared and puffed out its chest as if angry at the passers-by. King Goujian was struck by this, and he bowed over the bar of his chariot.

"Whom are you showing such respect to?" his entourage asked.

"I thought that angry frog looked like a fierce warrior," King Goujian explained. "That is why I bowed to it."

The soldiers said amongst themselves, "His Majesty shows respect even to an angry frog. We have received many years of specialized training—how can we allow ourselves to be shown up by a frog?" After this they competed with each other in showing reckless courage.

King Goujian issued the following order to his troops: "If there is a father and son in this army, then let the father go home; if there is an older and a younger brother in this army, then let the older brother go home; if there is anyone who has their parents living but no siblings, you should go home to care for them. If there is someone who is too sick to be able to fight, stand forward and you will be given medicine and special food."

The soldiers appreciated the care and concern that His Majesty showed them, so their shouts of acclamation resounded like thunder. When they arrived at the mouth of the Yangtze River, those who had committed crimes while under arms were executed, to show the strictness of military law. This ensured that discipline was maintained.

. . .

When King Fuchai of Wu heard that the Yue army had attacked, he mobilized his entire army and came out to intercept them on the river. The Yue army was camped on the south side of the river; the Wu army was camped on the north side. The king of Yue divided his army into two camps, to the left and right; Fan Li was in command of the Army of the Right, Wen Zhong was in command of the Army of the Left. His Majesty had personal command of six thousand soldiers of aristocratic background—they formed the Central Army.

The following day, they were going to fight a battle at the river. Therefore, as dusk began to fall, His Majesty ordered that the Army of the Left should cross the river in silence, moving fifty *li* upstream, where they had orders to wait until needed to attack the Wu army. When the drums were sounded in the middle of the night, they were to advance, but not before. King Goujian also ordered the Army of the Right to cross the river some ten *li* away, again moving in silence. They were to wait until the Army of the Left had joined battle, then they were to move upstream in a pincer attack. At this time, each was to sound its large drums, so that they would be able to locate each other by the noise. In the middle of the night, the Wu army suddenly heard the sound of battle drums reverberating through the sky, and they realized that the Yue army had launched a surprise attack. Although they made haste to light their torches, they were still not able to see clearly what was going on. The sound of drumming could now be heard far in the distance as the two armies responded, on their way to join the encirclement.

King Fuchai was horrified. He immediately gave orders that the army be divided and units moved to intercept the enemy. He was not anticipating that King Goujian would secretly lead the six thousand men under his own command, without making a sound, to attack Wu's Central Army under cover of darkness. At this time it was still not yet light, and they found themselves completely overrun by the Yue army. There was absolutely no way that the Wu forces could resist their onslaught; having suffered a terrible defeat, they began to run away. King Goujian led his three armies in close pursuit, and when they reached the Li Marshes, the two sides did battle again. Yet again, the Wu army was defeated. In total, they fought three times and were defeated three times; the famous generals Prince Gucao and Wumen Chao were both killed, while King Fuchai fled home through the night, closing the gates of the capital city behind him. King Goujian advanced his troops from Mount Heng. They built a fortress outside the Xu gate, which they called the Yue Citadel, as their base of operations during the siege of Wu. After King Goujian had laid siege to the city for some time, the people of Wu began to really suffer. Bo Pi made ill health the excuse for staying at home.

King Fuchai sent Royal Grandson Luo, stripped to the waist in a gesture of surrender, to crawl forward and beg the king of Yue for a peace treaty: "His Majesty treated you very badly in the past when you were holed up at Mount Kuaiji, but in the end he did not refuse to make a peace treaty. Now you have raised an army and placed yourself in a position where you can kill him. All he asks is that you pardon him, just as he forgave you."

King Goujian was deeply moved by his words, and was just about to grant his request when Fan Li said, "Your Majesty has worked so hard for this for the last twenty years. Surely you are not going to give it all up now and settle for a peace treaty?" The king of Yue decided to refuse to make peace.

Ambassadors came and went from the Wu capital seven times, but Wen Zhong and Fan Li were adamant that no peace treaty could be accepted. They sounded the drums and attacked the city, but by this time the people of Wu were in no condition to fight any more. Wen Zhong and Fan Li discussed entering the city by breaking open the Wu gate. However, that very night they saw an apparition of the head of Wu Zixu on top of the southern city wall. It appeared as big as a cartwheel, with its eyes sparkling and its hair blowing in the breeze. The glowing lights that shone around it could be seen for ten *li*. The Yue generals were all terrified by this, so they made camp temporarily. That very night a violent storm blew through the south gate, with powerful gusts of rain. Thunder rolled through the heavens, interspersed with sudden bolts of lightning. The wind picked up sand and even pebbles, throwing them around with the force of crossbow bolts. Many of the Yue soldiers were hit, suffering injury and in some cases even death. Their boats slipped their moorings, as it proved impossible to keep them tied up fast. Fan Li and Wen Zhong were in a panic, so they bared their chests and braved the lashing rain to go to the south gate and kowtow in apology. After a long time, the wind began to die down and the rain ceased. Wen Zhong and Fan Li both lay down and dozed, as they waited for dawn to break.

In their dreams, Wu Zixu drove up in a plain chariot drawn by snow-white horses, wearing a magnificent official hat and robe, looking just as he had done when he was alive. He said to them: "I knew that sooner or later the Yue army would arrive, and that is why I begged that my head should be hung from the east gate to the city, so that I could observe your attack on Wu. Instead, the king of Wu placed my head on the south gate. However, I still feel a sense of loyalty to this country, so I could not bear for you to enter the capital beneath my skull. That is why I conjured up the wind and rain, to force your army to leave. It is Heaven's will that Wu should be destroyed by Yue—how can I possibly prevent it? If you want to enter, you can go through the east gate and I will show you the way! I will pierce the city wall in order to allow you free passage."

The two men reported their identical dreams to the king of Yue, who had his soldiers dig a canal from the south to the east of the city. When this canal reached a particular point between the Snake and the Artisan's Gates, there was a sudden flood of water from Lake Tai, which came pouring through the Xu Gate. The towering force of the waters ripped a huge hole in the enceinte wall, as countless bream and even porpoises rode into the city on the crest of the waves. Fan Li said, "Wu Zixu is showing the way for us!" He ordered his soldiers to enter the city immediately.

Later on, this hole was converted into a proper gate, known as the Bream and Porpoise Gate. Because many water caltrops grew in the nearby waters, it was also sometimes known as the Water Caltrop Gate. The river that flows past this place is the Water Caltrop Stream. This is where Wu Zixu revealed his numinous powers.

When King Fuchai heard that the Yue army had entered the city and Bo Pi had already surrendered, he fled to Mount Yang with Royal Grandson Luo and his three sons. As they sped through the night, His Majesty became both hungry and thirsty, to the point where he found he could no longer even see clearly. His companions gave him raw grain to eat, which they just cut from the plant and presented to him. King Fuchai chewed on it, then lay down on the ground in order to drink the water from a stream. Meanwhile, King Goujian led a thousand of his men in pursuit of the king of Wu and surrounded him in several concentric circles. King Fuchai composed a letter, which he attached to an arrow and shot over to the Yue army. An officer collected it and took it to His Majesty. Wen Zhong and Fan Li opened and read this missive, which read:

> I have heard that when the last cunning rabbit is caught, the loyal hunting dog is doomed. Once the enemy state has been overrun and destroyed, the advisors who plotted this will also be killed. Why do you not allow Wu to survive, that you too may be left with some room to maneuver?

Wen Zhong composed his reply, attached it to an arrow, and shot it back:

Wu has committed six terrible mistakes. First, you executed the loyal minister Wu Zixu. Secondly, you killed Gongsun Sheng despite his excellent advice. Thirdly, you listened to the flattery and fawning of Chancellor Bo Pi, employing him in positions far too senior for his abilities. Fourthly, you attacked the states of Qi and Jin repeatedly, when they had done nothing wrong. Fifthly, you attacked your neighbor Yue time and time again. Sixthly, although Yue was responsible for the death of your grandfather, the late king, you did nothing to punish us; instead you pardoned us and allowed us to bring disaster down upon you now. You have made these six terrible mistakes and yet you still hope to survive; is that likely? In the past, Heaven delivered Yue into your hands and yet you did not take it; now Heaven has delivered Wu into our hands. Do you really think that we are going to go against the wishes of Heaven?

When King Fuchai received this letter and read its description of his six mistakes, he said with tears in his eyes, "I did not execute King Goujian of Yue; I forgot my duty to avenge the death of my grandfather; I have been an unfilial child! This is the reason why Heaven has abandoned Wu!"

"Let me go and speak to the king of Yue again and beg him for mercy!" Royal Grandson Luo requested.

"I do not hope to restore my country," King Fuchai said. "However, if they would be prepared to let us act as a buffer state, serving Yue from one generation to the next, I would be happy with that!"

Royal Grandson Luo went to the Yue army, where Wen Zhong and Fan Li refused to allow him to enter. King Goujian, watching from a distance, noticed the Wu envoy leaving in tears. He felt sorry for him, so he sent a messenger to the king of Wu to say: "Remembering how kind you have been to me in the past, I will send you to live at Yongdong and give you five hundred families to support you for the rest of your life in the style to which you have been accustomed."

King Fuchai held back his tears and replied, "If Your Majesty would but show clemency to Wu, we will happily become your subordinate state. But if I am to have my country destroyed and my ancestral temples razed, what would five hundred families avail me? I am far too old to get used to being an ordinary subject; I will simply have to die!" The Yue envoy left.

King Fuchai of Wu was still unwilling to commit suicide. King Goujian of Yue discussed this with Wen Zhong and Fan Li. "Why don't the two of you simply arrest and execute him?"

"Given that we are subjects," they replied, "we cannot possibly execute a king! If you want him dead you are going to have to order it yourself, Your Majesty. It should be done immediately, for the longer this drags on, the worse it will be!"

King Goujian walked out at the head of his army, the sword *Shining* in his hand. He sent someone to tell the king of Wu: "No one lives forever; sooner or later we all have to die! Are you really going to force me to turn my troops against you?"

King Fuchai sighed several times and looked in all directions. Then he spoke with tears running down his cheeks: "I killed my loyal minister Wu Zixu and the innocent Gongsun Sheng—my death is long overdue!" He said to his entourage: "If the dead do indeed have awareness, how am I to face Wu Zixu and Gongsun Sheng in the Underworld? Please cover my face with three layers of cloth that I will never have to see them again." When he had finished speaking, he drew the sword hanging by his side and cut his throat. Royal Grandson Luo took off his coat and covered the king of Wu's body with it. Then he untied his belt and hanged himself. King Goujian gave orders that King Fuchai be buried with the honors due to a marquis at Mount Yang.

. . .

When the king of Yue entered the city of Gusu in triumph, he took up residence in the palace of the kings of Wu, and his officials all offered him their congratulations, including Bo Pi. Bearing in mind all that he had done for the king of Yue in the past, his expression showed that he thought his position to be assured. King Goujian asked him, "You were the chancellor of the kingdom of Wu; how could I dare to ask you to serve me? Your king is dead and buried at Mount Yang. Why don't you follow him?"

Bo Pi looked ashamed of himself and withdrew. King Goujian ordered one of his knights to arrest the man and kill him, together with his entire family. "I want to make it clear that Wu Zixu was a loyal minister!" he said. Afterwards, King Goujian gave orders to calm the people of Wu, then took his army north across the Yangtze and the

Huai Rivers to meet the rulers of Qi, Jin, Song, and Lu at Shuzhou. He also sent an ambassador to offer tribute to Zhou. By this time, King Jing of Zhou was dead and Crown Prince Ren had just succeeded to the throne under the title of King Yuan. His Majesty sent an envoy to bestow an official robe and crown on the king of Yue, together with a jade baton and jade disc, a vermilion lacquer bow, and black lacquer arrows. He ordered him to assume the title of eastern hegemon. King Goujian accepted His Majesty's commands, and the aristocrats all sent ambassadors to congratulate him.

At this time, Chu had just destroyed the state of Chen, and, impressed by the might of the Yue army, they too sent an ambassador to resume diplomatic relations. King Goujian gave the lands he held north of the Huai River to the kingdom of Chu; he gave one hundred *li* of land east of the Si River to the state of Lu; and he returned all the land that Wu had captured from Song to its original owner. The aristocrats were delighted with this and offered their allegiance to King Goujian, showing him all the respect due to a hegemon. The king of Yue returned to Wu, whereupon he ordered his people to build the Congratulations Tower at Mount Kuaiji, as a sign that the humiliation of being besieged there had now finally been expunged. He held a banquet at the Patterned Tower at the Wu palace, at which he made merry with all his ministers. The ministers feasting together on top of the tower were delighted and laughed heartily. The only person who did not look pleased was King Goujian himself.

Fan Li stifled a sigh and said, "The king of Yue is not willing to share his glory with his ministers. His paranoid and jealous personality now stands revealed!" A few days later, he said farewell to the king of Yue: "I have heard it said that a subject should die to save his ruler from humiliation. In the past, you suffered dreadfully at Mount Kuaiji, Your Majesty. The reason why I did not die at the time was because I hoped that by enduring it all, we might one day see Yue rise again. Now you have conquered Wu, so if you are prepared to spare me the execution I deserve, I beg permission to leave your service and grow old amid the rivers and lakes."

King Goujian was very upset; his tears ran down and soaked his robe. "I owe everything that I have today to your efforts," he said. "I have been thinking about how to repay you for all that you have done, and you now tell me that you want to abandon me! If you stay, I will share my country with you, but if you leave, I will have your wife and children tortured to death!"

"It is I who deserve to be executed," Fan Li declared. "What crime have my wife and children committed? Their lives are in your hands, Your Majesty, and no longer my concern!"

That night, he got into a light skiff and sailed out of Lady Qi's Gate, traversing the Yangtze delta and entering the Five Lakes. The following day, His Majesty sent someone to summon Fan Li, but he had already left. The king of Yue was deeply upset at this news. He asked Wen Zhong, "Should I go after him?"

"Fan Li is a remarkably devious man," Wen Zhong replied. "There is no point in trying to chase him down."

When Wen Zhong left the court, someone handed him a letter. When he opened it, he discovered that it was written in Fan Li's handwriting. It said:

> Do you not remember what the king of Wu said? "When the last cunning rabbit is caught, the loyal hunting dog is doomed. Once the enemy state has been overrun and destroyed, the advisors who plotted this will also be killed." The king of Yue has a long neck and a sharp beak-like mouth; such a person can endure humiliation, but is jealous of other people's success. You can go through great trouble with him, but you cannot enjoy the fruits of peace together. If you do not leave immediately, you will not be able to avoid disaster!

When Wen Zhong finished reading the letter, he wanted to talk to the person who had brought it, but he had already disappeared. Wen Zhong was unhappy about the whole thing but he did not really believe what Fan Li had written to him. He sighed and said, "Surely Fan Li is overreacting!"

A couple of days later, King Goujian stood down his armies and went home to Yue, taking Xi Shi with him. The queen of Yue secretly ordered someone to take her out of the harem. Tying a heavy stone to her, they threw Xi Shi into the river to drown.

"This thing comes from a doomed country," Her Majesty declared. "Why should we keep it?"

Luo Yin wrote a poem proclaiming Xi Shi's innocence:

> Every country goes through the cycle of rise and fall,
> Why should anyone blame this disaster on Xi Shi?

Even if Xi Shi was responsible for the destruction of the kingdom
    of Wu,
Who do we blame for the collapse of Yue?

King Goujian did not reward anyone for their role in the destruction of Wu, nor was anyone given so much as a foot of land as a fief.
He kept his old ministers at a great distance, seeing them very rarely.
Wen Zhong now thought seriously about what Fan Li had said, and so
he did not attend court, claiming poor health. There was a member of
the king of Yue's entourage who particularly disliked Wen Zhong, so
he slandered him to His Majesty: "Wen Zhong is angry because he
thinks you did not reward him the way he deserves. That is why he
does not come to court."

The king of Yue knew how capable Wen Zhong was, but since the
defeat of Wu, he had nothing for him to do. He became afraid that one
day, Wen Zhong would cause trouble for him, in which case there
would be little he could do to stop him. He wanted to get rid of him
but could not find a suitable excuse. At this time there was a serious
rift between Lord Ai of Lu and the Jisun, Mengsun, and Zhongsun
families. The Marquis of Lu wanted to borrow an army from Yue and
get rid of the three clans once and for all. With this in mind, Lord Ai
made the excuse that he wanted to pay court to Yue and arrived in
person. However, King Goujian was so worried about the possible
threat posed to him by Wen Zhong that he refused to mobilize his
army. Lord Ai eventually died in exile in the kingdom of Yue.

Suddenly one day, King Goujian decided that he wanted to visit
Wen Zhong and inquire after his health in person. Wen Zhong stum-
bled out to greet His Majesty, looking terribly sick. The king undid his
sword and sat down. "I have heard people say that an ambitious knight
is not concerned about his own death," he said, "he is worried that his
policies will not be implemented. You came up with seven stratagems
to destroy the kingdom of Wu; after I had used three of them, Wu was
in ruins. What should I do with the other four?"

"I have no idea what you should do with the other four," Wen
Zhong replied.

"How about you take those four policies and use them in the
Underworld to destroy King Fuchai's predecessors?" the king of Yue
suggested. When he had finished speaking, he got into his carriage

and left. The sword that he had taken off was still lying on his seat. Wen Zhong picked it up and looked at it. The word *Black* was written on the scabbard. This was the sword that King Fuchai had given to Wu Zixu for him to cut his throat. Wen Zhong raised his head to the sky and sighed: "Ever since antiquity, people have said that the greatest virtue goes unrewarded. I did not listen to what Fan Li said, and now I find myself at the mercy of the king of Yue; how stupid is that!" Afterwards, he laughed at himself: "For the next hundred generations, everyone who talks about me will compare me with Wu Zixu. How can I complain?" He committed suicide by falling on the sword. When the king of Yue heard that Wen Zhong was dead, he was extremely pleased and buried him on Mount Wolong. One year after his funeral, a tidal wave swept over this land and hit the mountain, breaking the tomb open. Someone saw Wu Zixu and Wen Zhong riding one after the other on top of the waves.

Today, when the waters crash on the Qiantang tidal bore, the incoming waters are said to represent Wu Zixu; the outgoing waters are Wen Zhong.

An old man wrote the following poem in praise of Wen Zhong:

How loyal was Grandee Wen Zhong, such a marvelous administrator!
He destroyed Wu in just three moves, he himself died at the behest of Yue.
He was not prepared to leave with Fan Li; he preferred to die like Wu Zixu!
For a thousand years his rage has been unappeased, as the waves of the tidal bore crash!

King Goujian died after twenty-seven years in power, in the seventh year of the reign of King Yuan of Zhou. His sons and grandsons all claimed hegemony in their turn.

Do you want to know what happened next? THE STORY CONTINUES...

Rival Students of the Master of Ghost Valley

Chapter Thirteen

After saying goodbye to the Master of Ghost Valley, Pang Juan descends the mountain.

In order to escape from disaster, Sun Bin pretends to have gone mad.

In the vicinity of Yangcheng in the Zhou royal domain, there was a place known as Ghost Valley. The mountains were very high and the forest very dense, sunlight never penetrated, and you might imagine that no one could possibly live there—that is why it was called Ghost Valley. However, it was the abode of a recluse who called himself the Master of Ghost Valley. According to tradition, his real name was Wang Xu. He was a contemporary of Lord Ping of Jin, and he had studied medicine and cultivated the Way in the Yunmeng Mountains in company with Mo Di from the state of Song. In the end Mo Di abandoned his family and announced that he wanted to travel round the world helping people and saving them from danger. Wang Xu stayed behind, living in hiding in Ghost Valley; over time, people started to talk about the Master of Ghost Valley, who was supposed to be incredibly wise, trained in many different branches of learning, so that no mere mortal could compare. What did he know? He was learned in mathematics and in astronomy; furthermore, he could divine the future with uncanny accuracy. He was also trained in the military arts, in the Six Strategies and Three Plans, whereby he could respond to any emergency and array his troops so that not even a god could find a way to break through his lines. He had also studied the arts of rhetoric and was learned in many different things, so he could speak of underlying principles and taking advantage of situations.

When he spoke, his logic and arguments were impeccable. He had also learned medicine, so that he could cultivate his own body and nourish it with the right foods, preventing disease and extending his own lifespan to the point of becoming an immortal.

Since the Master of Ghost Valley could indeed have become an immortal, why did he stay on this earth? It was because he wanted to recruit a number of brilliant disciples so that they could become immortals at the same time—that is the reason why he stayed at Ghost Valley. To begin with, he would occasionally go to the city and perform divinations for people: the accuracy of his predictions of good luck and bad was uncanny. As a result, gradually people began to want to study with him. The Master would consider the personality of his would-be disciples and then instruct them in the branch of study that was most suitable. This would train them in learning that would be of great use to the country and also allow them to develop the qualities that could allow them to become immortals. Nobody knew how many years he had spent in Ghost Valley or how many disciples he had. The Master never turned anyone away who wanted to study with him, but if they decided to leave, he would not try to keep them.

The story goes that a couple of his most famous disciples were there at the same time: Sun Bin from Qi and Pang Juan from the kingdom of Wei. Sun Bin and Pang Juan were sworn blood brothers, and they both studied military arts. Having spent some three years familiarizing himself with the arts of war, Pang Juan thought that he had made great advances. It so happened that one day he went to draw water and happened to go down to the foot of the mountain, where be heard some travelers discussing how the kingdom of Wei was offering large rewards to recruit men of talent, since they were hoping to hire new senior ministers and generals. Pang Juan decided to cash in on this. He resolved to say goodbye to the Master and go down the mountain to seek his fortune in the kingdom of Wei. However, on reflection he was worried that the Master would not let him leave. He vacillated, unable to decide whether to speak or not. The Master knew exactly what was going on from just one look at his face. He said laughingly, "Your time here is up. Why don't you go down the mountain to seek fame and fortune?"

When Pang Juan heard the Master's words, his feelings were assuaged. Falling to his knees, he said, "That is exactly what I was thinking, but I am not sure whether I will achieve my ambitions."

"Pick a wild flower for me," the Master said, "and I will perform a divination on your behalf."

Pang Juan went down the mountain and looked for wild flowers. This was in the dog days of the sixth month, so while the trees were growing well, the wild flowers that bloom in the mountains were nowhere to be seen. Pang Juan hunted high and low, spending ages to try and find one of these plants, but all he found was a vine. He ripped it out of the ground, roots and all, thinking that he had found what he was looking for and could present it to the Master. Then suddenly the thought struck him: "This plant is weak and weedy—it would not be auspicious." He threw it on the ground and kept on looking. The strange thing is that there was not a single other plant to be seen for miles around, so in the end he had to go back and put the one that he had found earlier into his sleeve. He returned and told the Master, "There are no flowers on the mountain."

"In that case, what is that you have in your sleeve?"

Pang Juan could not conceal it; he had to hand it over. Having been ripped from the ground, it had wilted in the sun, as a result of which it was now half-dead.

"Do you know the name of this plant?" the Master said. "This is the horse-bell flower. It puts out twelve flowers in each floret; that is the number of years that you will enjoy success. You picked it in Ghost Valley, and now it is wilted in the sun; if you combine the character for *ghost* with that for *wilting*, it makes the word *Wei*. You will find success in the kingdom of Wei."

Pang Juan was silent, but he was marveling inwardly. The Master continued: "You had better be careful about bullying. If you make someone else suffer, they will punish you for it; you are warned! Let me give you a message to remember: 'Success will come with a Ram. Death will come with a Horse.'"

Pang Juan bowed twice and said, "I will keep your teachings in mind at all times, Master!"

When he was about to leave, Sun Bin escorted him down the mountain. "We are sworn blood brothers," Pang Juan declared, "and have promised that we will share wealth and honor with one another. If this journey brings me success, I will recommend you for office too. That way the two of us will be able to work together as colleagues."

"Is this true?" Sun Bin asked.

"If I am lying, may I die under the hail of ten thousand arrows!" Pang Juan said.

"Many thanks for your generous intention. There was no need for you to swear such an oath." The two of them said goodbye in tears.

When Sun Bin returned to the mountain, the Master noticed his tear-stained face. "Are you sad that Pang Juan has gone?" he asked.

"How could I fail to be sad," Sun Bin replied. "He is my classmate!"

"Do you think that Pang Juan will make a great general?" the Master asked.

"He has received your teaching for so long, Master, how could he fail?"

"No! No!" the Master said.

Sun Bin was shocked and asked what he meant. The Master of Ghost Valley was silent. A couple of days later, he said to his disciples, "Last night I was disturbed by the sounds of rats—do you think you could all take it in turns to guard my room and chase these vermin away for me?" His disciples obeyed.

One night when it was Sun Bin's turn, the Master took a scroll out from under his pillow, and said: "These are the thirteen chapters of *The Art of War* written by your grandfather, Sun Wu. He presented them to King Helü of Wu, and His Majesty used these stratagems to defeat the Chu army. King Helü was very fond of this book, but he did not want it to become known to everyone, so he had an iron casket made and hid what he thought was the only copy of this book inside one of the roof beams at the Gusu Tower. That copy was destroyed when the Yue army burned the tower. However, I was a great friend of your grandfather, and he gave me another copy of his book, which I have annotated personally. All the secrets of military strategy are recorded here, but I have never taught them to anyone. Since you have impressed me as a kind and generous person, I have decided to give this book to you."

"My parents died when I was still a small child," Sun Bin said, "and thanks to the many political problems of recent years, my family has become dispersed. I knew that my grandfather had written a book, but nothing more. Since you know this book so well, Master, why did you not teach it to Pang Juan rather than leaving it for me alone?"

"A good person who obtains a copy of this book can use it to help others," the Master of Ghost Valley said. "A bad person who obtains this book could bring disaster down upon humanity. Pang Juan is not a good man, and I am not going to give it to him!"

Sun Bin carried the book back to his own room and studied it day and night. Three days later, the Master asked for the original text back. Sun Bin took it from his sleeve and handed it over to the Master. The Master asked him questions about particular chapters, and Sun Bin replied without the slightest hesitation. In reciting the text, he did not leave out a single word. The Master said happily, "Your intelligence and powers of concentration remind me very much of your grandfather."

. . .

To turn now to another part of the story: After Pang Juan said goodbye to Sun Bin, he went directly to the kingdom of Wei. He used his knowledge of military strategy to seek service with the prime minister, Wang Cuo, who recommended him to King Hui. At the moment that Pang Juan entered the court, a cook was serving King Hui from a dish of braised lamb, as His Majesty raised his chopsticks. Pang Juan said happily to himself, "There you are! 'Success will come with a Ram!'"

King Hui was impressed by Pang Juan's appearance and put his chopsticks down. Getting up to meet him, he welcomed him politely. Pang Juan bowed twice, whereupon King Hui helped him up, asking him about the nature of his studies. Pang Juan replied, "I am one of the Master of Ghost Valley's disciples. I have learned a great deal to do with military strategy." He pointed to the map as he launched into his exposition, going into great detail.

"My country has Qi to the east, Qin to the west, Chu to the south, and Han, Zhao, and Yan to the north," King Hui said. "All are of about equal strength. Now Zhao has just stolen Zhongshan off us, and we have not yet avenged this insult; what plan can you suggest?"

"If you do not appoint me as a general, Your Majesty," Pang Juan said, "there is nothing to be done. However, if you put me in charge of the army, I will train them so well that they are guaranteed to win every battle they fight and achieve success in every attack. You will unite the whole world under your own control, not just these six kingdoms!"

"That sounds very fine," King Hui said, "but surely it will be difficult to achieve?"

"I have recommended myself for this position because I can control these other countries on the palm of my hand," Pang Juan assured him. "If I fail, you can execute me!"

King Hui was delighted and appointed him as commander-in-chief, combined with the position of military advisor. Pang Juan's son, Pang Ying, and his nephews, Pang Cong and Pang Mao, were all appointed as junior generals. Pang Juan trained his troops and then invaded the two small states of Wey and Song, obtaining repeated victories in both cases. The rulers of Song, Lu, Wey, and Zheng all agreed to pay court to Wei in rotation. When the Qi army invaded, Pang Juan succeeded in stopping their advance. He thought he was the finest general alive and could not stop himself from becoming haughty and proud.

. . .

At this time Mo Di was traveling around various famous mountains, and he happened to pass by Ghost Valley to visit his old friend. He met Sun Bin, and the two of them got into conversation, getting along extremely well with one another.

"You have already completed your studies," he said to Sun Bin, "so why don't you leave here and make a name for yourself? Why should you waste your time hidden away here?"

"I have a friend and fellow student named Pang Juan who went to take up office in Wei," Sun Bin explained. "We agreed that when he got a job, he would recommend me too. That is why I am waiting."

"Pang Juan has already been appointed as a general," Mo Di said. "Let me go to Wei and find out what he is up to."

He then said goodbye and left, heading straight for the kingdom of Wei. He quickly discovered that Pang Juan was a very arrogant man, who made the most extravagant claims about his own abilities without the slightest blush, and it was quite clear that he had absolutely no intention of recommending Sun Bin for office. Therefore Mo Di put on rustic clothing and sought a personal interview with King Hui of Wei.

King Hui knew Master Mo by reputation, and so he came down the steps of the palace to welcome him, asking him about military strategy. Mo Di spoke of the underlying principles of any military campaign, and His Majesty was extremely impressed. He hoped to be able to recruit him into his service. Mo Di firmly refused. "I am used to living in the mountains and would not be happy in an official robe and hat. However, I am acquainted with the grandson of the great Sun Wu. His name is Sun Bin, and he would make a truly fine general. I simply cannot even begin to compare with him. At present he is living in seclusion in Ghost Valley. Why don't you summon him, Your Majesty?"

"If this Sun Bin studied at Ghost Valley, then he must have had the same master as Pang Juan," King Hui remarked. "Which of the two is better?"

"Even though Sun Bin and Pang Juan studied together," Mo Di replied, "Sun Bin is the sole inheritor of his grandfather's *The Art of War*. There is nobody in the whole world that can match him—Pang Juan is nothing!" After this, Master Mo said goodbye and left.

King Hui immediately summoned Pang Juan and asked him, "I have been told that you have a fellow student named Sun Bin who is the only person to have inherited Sun Wu's secret teachings, and that he is a man of the most remarkable talents. Why have you not recommended him to me?"

"I am perfectly aware of Sun Bin's abilities," Pang Juan replied, "but he is a man of Qi, and his family has been based there for many generations. If he were to take office in Wei, you can be sure that he would still put Qi's interests first. For that very reason, I did not dare to mention him."

"A knight will die for the man who understands him," King Hui declared. "Surely it cannot be right that we only employ people from our own kingdom."

"If you want to summon Sun Bin, Your Majesty," Pang Juan replied, "I will write to him immediately."

Although he did not say so, he was very unhappy about this development. "Control of the Wei army is at present entirely in my hands," he said to himself. "If Sun Bin comes here, he will steal my thunder. However, since the king of Wei has given me a direct order, I would not dare to openly disobey him. I will have to wait until he arrives and then come up with some plan to get rid of him, to stop him from being promoted to a senior position. That would also work!"

He drafted a letter, which he showed to King Hui. His Majesty sent an ambassador directly to Ghost Valley to present Pang Juan's letter to

Sun Bin, riding in a fine chariot drawn by four horses and laden with gifts of gold and white jade.

When Sun Bin opened the letter, this is what he read:

> I have been lucky enough to have had an audience with the king of Wei, and he has appointed me to a senior government position. I have never forgotten the agreement we made when we said goodbye. Today I have specially recommended you to the king of Wei, and so he has sent this chariot to collect you. Let us join forces in making the country great!

Sun Bin showed this letter to the Master of Ghost Valley. The Master realized that Pang Juan must have already held high office for some time, and yet it was only now that he wrote to suggest that he would recommend Sun Bin for office. Furthermore, there was no mention in the letter of any good wishes being extended to his former teacher. This proved that he was a complete good-for-nothing, but the Master could not be bothered to get angry about it. However, he was concerned that with Pang Juan's arrogant and jealous character, if Sun Bin went to join him, would he not cause trouble for him? He felt inclined to not allow him to go. On the other hand, he realized that it would be difficult to resist the express command of the king of Wei and that Sun Bin himself was desperate to go. That being the case, it would be hard to stop him. He decided to send Sun Bin to pick a flower on the mountain, which would function as a divination of whether he should proceed. At this time it was the ninth month, and Sun Bin noticed that there was a vase on the Master's table with a single yellow chrysanthemum in it. He took it out of the vase and presented it to the Master, before putting it straight back in the vase.

The Master made his pronouncement: "This flower was cut before you picked it, so it is already damaged. It is a characteristic of this kind of flower that they can endure the cold and will not wither even when struck by frost—even though this plant has been damaged, it is not a particularly bad omen. Furthermore, it has been placed in a vase to allow people to enjoy it. This vase is made of gilded metal, of the same kind as would be used for a bell or sacrificial vessel—in other words, having braved cold winds and frost, it has finally been appreciated. This flower has experienced two pluckings, which means that you are unlikely to achieve your ambitions in the short term, but you returned it to its vase, which means that you will finally make your name once you have returned to the home of your ancestors. I am going to change your name, in the hope that it may improve your luck."

He decided that he would change the character *Bin* in Sun Bin's personal name, from the character that means "guest" to the one that dictionaries tell us is the name of a form of punishment—to have the kneecaps cut off. The Master of Ghost Valley changed his name because he knew that one day he would suffer this punishment, but he could not tell his disciple that. Was he not a truly remarkable man?

An old man wrote a poem:

A flower was plucked to determine his fortune;
This proved to be more efficacious than any oracle-bone divination.
Though you may laugh at modern fortune tellers,
That is simply because they do not have the Master of Ghost Valley's
    skills.

When he was about to set out, the Master of Ghost Valley gave him a silk brocade bag with the words: "If you ever find yourself caught in a terrible crisis, you can open this and have a look."

Sun Bin bowed and said goodbye to the master, then followed the king of Wei's messenger down the mountain, where he got into the waiting chariot. When Sun Bin arrived in the kingdom of Wei, he took up lodgings in Pang Juan's mansion. Sun Bin thanked Pang Juan for his kindness in recommending him for government service, which seemed to please him. Sun Bin then recounted how the Master of Ghost Valley had changed his name.

"That is a horrible meaning!" Juan said in a shocked tone of voice. "Why did you change it?"

"I would not dare to disobey the Master's orders," Sun Bin declared.

The following day the pair went to court together and had an audience with King Hui. His Majesty walked down the steps to greet them and treated them with the greatest respect. Sun Bin bowed twice and presented his opinion: "I am just a peasant, and yet Your Majesty has treated me with such excessive kindness; I am overwhelmed!"

"Master Mo informed me that you are the only person to have received of Sun Wu's secret teachings," King Hui said. "I have been awaiting your arrival as a thirsty man longs for drink. Now you are here, and it is time for you to bring peace to the world!" He turned to ask Pang Juan: "I wish to appoint Sun Bin as my deputy military strategist, with the same powers as you to command the army. What do you think?"

"Sun Bin and I are not only fellow students but also close friends," Pang Juan replied. "He is my sworn older brother. Surely it is not acceptable that he should be appointed as my deputy. Why don't you make him a minister without portfolio? When he has made some contribution to this country, I will resign my position in his favor and happily accept office under his command."

King Hui agreed to this and appointed Sun Bin as minister without portfolio, rewarding him with exactly the same emoluments as Pang Juan received.

The position of minister without portfolio served to sideline Sun Bin, while also ensuring that he did not have to be treated with the same ceremony as an honored guest. While it seemed to show Pang Juan's respect, in fact he suggested this because he did not want to have his military command shared with Sun Bin.

From this time on, the two men had little to do with one another.

Pang Juan thought to himself, "Sun Bin has received this special instruction, but I have not yet seen any sign of it. I must find a way to force him to show his hand."

He had tables set out for a banquet, and as the wine circulated, he turned the conversation to the subject of military strategy. Sun Bin answered every question without the slightest difficulty, but when it was the turn of Sun Bin to challenge Pang Juan to cite the chapter and verse of his sources, Pang Juan had no idea where they had come from. He asked deviously, "Are they by any chance from Sun Wu's *The Art of War?*"

Sun Bin was completely unsuspicious, and said, "Of course."

"Although I was lucky enough to have received instruction from the Master of Ghost Valley, I simply did not study hard enough and have forgotten much of what I did learn. If you would let me read your book, I will pay you back in the future."

"The version I studied includes the Master's annotations and explanations, so it is somewhat different from the original text. The Master allowed me three days to learn it and then took it away again. I do not actually possess a physical copy."

"Do you still remember every word?"

"It is all there in my memory."

Pang Juan was even more determined to study this text, but, at that moment, he had no idea how he was going to set about it.

. . .

A couple of days later, King Hui decided to test Sun Bin's abilities, so he held a demonstration of martial arts at the training ground. He wanted Sun Bin and Pang Juan to demonstrate battle formations. Pang Juan put his troops in position, and then Sun Bin took one look, after which he could name the formation and explain how to defeat it. Afterwards, Sun Bin arranged the troops in a formation which Pang Juan simply could not identify. He privately consulted Sun Bin on the subject.

"This is the 'Reversible Eight Gates' formation," Sun Bin explained.

"Is there a further move?" Pang Juan asked.

"If it is attacked, you can easily move into 'Snake' formation," Sun Bin replied.

Pang Juan thought about this and then went back to report to King Hui: "Sun Bin has arranged the 'Reversible Eight Gates' formation; it can be transformed into the 'Snake' position."

When the demonstration was over, King Hui asked Sun Bin what he had done, and it was exactly as Juan had said. King Hui was now under the impression that Pang Juan was every bit as brilliant as Sun Bin, and he was delighted by this.

Pang Juan returned to his mansion and thought, "Sun Bin is a much more brilliant man than I. If I do not get rid of him, I will end up being surpassed by him." He came up with a plan. So, one day when he met Sun Bin, he happened to mention to him privately, "All your family are back in the state of Qi. Since you have now accepted government office in the kingdom of Wei, why don't you send someone to bring them here so that they too can enjoy your present prosperity?"

Sun Bin burst into tears and said: "Even though we studied together, you really don't understand my position. My mother died when I was four, and my father died when I was nine. After that, I was brought up by my uncle, Sun Qiao, who served Lord Kang of Qi as a grandee. When Lord Kang had his position usurped by the Tian family and he was forced into exile by the sea, all his ministers were either transported or executed. My family ended up being scattered to the four winds. My uncle and cousins, Sun Ping and Sun Zhuo, fled to the

Zhou Royal Domain, taking me with them. There we encountered a famine year, and they sent me to work as a servant for a family living at the north gate of the Zhou capital; I do not know where they went. When I grew up, I happened to overhear one of the neighbors talking about the brilliance of the Master of Ghost Valley, and I came to admire him very much. That is why I went off all by myself to study with him. Through these years I have received no communication from any member of my family. What relatives could I bring here to live with me?"

"Surely you still care about your home town and the ancestral tombs." Pang Juan said.

"Men are not animals—how could I forget where I came from? When we were saying goodbye, the Master said, 'You will finally make your name once you have returned to the home of your ancestors.' However, now I am working for the Wei government, so it would not be suitable to mention such an ambition again."

Pang Juan sighed and pretended to agree: "You are absolutely right. A real man makes his reputation where he can. Why should he have to stay at home?"

Things started to happen about six months later, by which time Sun Bin had completely forgotten this earlier conversation. One day on his way home after attending court, he suddenly bumped into a man with a thick Shandong accent, who asked him, "Are you Sun Bin, the minister without portfolio?"

Sun Bin invited him into his mansion and asked who he was.

"My name is Ding Yi," the man said, "and I come from Linzi. I was on a business trip to the Zhou Royal Domain, so your cousin asked me to take a letter to you at Ghost Valley. When I got there, I heard that you had accepted government office in the kingdom of Wei, so I came here to find you." When he had finished speaking, he handed over the letter. Sun Bin picked it up in his hands. He broke open the seal and read the contents:

This letter is addressed to Sun Bin by his cousins Ping and Zhuo. It is now three years since our family was overtaken by disaster and we found ourselves forced into exile. We went to work as tenant farmers in the state of Song, where our father became ill and died. We have suffered so much, far from home and all by ourselves. Luckily, His Majesty has now decided to offer an amnesty for all earlier offenses and informed us that we can go back, and we would like you to go with us. Let us reestablish our clan! We have heard that you have been studying in Ghost Valley and are sure that you will have done well. You have a great future ahead of you. We write this letter to inform you of our news and will entrust it to someone to take to you. Please make your plans to return home as soon as possible! We hope to see you again soon.

When Sun Bin got this letter, he thought that it was true and burst into tears.

"Your cousins told me that I should encourage you to return home as soon as possible," Ding Yi said. "It is not right that relatives should be parted."

"I hold a government position in Wei," Sun Bin explained. "I can't just leave."

He treated Ding Yi to a banquet and served him wine, while he wrote his reply. He began by expressing his wish to return home, and then he continued: "Since I have taken up a position in the government of Wei, I cannot return right now. Let me wait until my position here is secure, and then I will try and find a way to go home."

He gave Ding Yi a gold ingot to cover his travel expenses. He took the reply and left after saying goodbye. What Sun Bin did not know was that this man was no Ding Yi. Instead, he was one of Pang Juan's most trusted subordinates, Xu Jia. Once Pang Juan had discovered Sun Bin's background and the names of his relatives, he had been able to forge this letter purporting to be from Sun Ping and Sun Zhuo. He instructed his subordinate, Xu Jia, to pretend to be a merchant from Qi named Ding Yi and sent him to see Sun Bin. Since Sun Bin had become separated from the rest of his family at a very young age, he did not even know what their handwriting looked like. That is why he thought this letter was true.

Having obtained a reply by trickery, Pang Juan imitated Sun Bin's handwriting and forged an additional couple of lines at the end:

Although I am at present serving in the government of the kingdom of Wei, I have never forgotten where I come from. Every day I think of ways to get home. If the king of Qi were to give me a job, I would do my very best to repay his kindness.

There is a poem that testifies to this:

Although they were once classmates, he used his subordinate to get
  rid of him,
Who would have guessed that his trickery would have such terrible
  consequences?
A forged letter set a dreadful trap:
Sun Bin's life hung by a thread!

Pang Juan went to court and sought a private audience with King Hui. Having sent away His Majesty's entourage, he presented the forged letter and said, "Sun Bin is intending to betray Wei to Qi, and he has recently been in secret communication with an envoy from that country. I was able to obtain part of their correspondence by having my men intercept and search the messenger outside the suburbs."

When King Hui had finished reading the letter, he said, "Sun Bin is still greatly attached to his own country, but surely that does not mean that I cannot give him a senior government position here. Why should I not make use of his talents?"

"Sun Bin's grandfather was a great general who served the king of Wu," Pang Juan replied, "but he went home to Qi in the end. Who can forget where his family comes from? Even if you give Sun Bin a senior appointment, he will care most about Qi and will not be capable of doing his best for Wei. Besides which, Sun Bin is not inferior to me—if he is appointed as a general by Qi, sooner or later they will end up in competition with Wei. Were that to happen, it would be a disaster for Your Majesty. You had better kill him."

"Sun Bin came here in answer to my summons," King Hui said, "and he has not done anything wrong. If I were to kill him now, I am afraid people would accuse me of being a bad ruler."

"You are absolutely right, Your Majesty," Pang Juan replied. "I will go and talk to Sun Bin. If he is willing to stay in the kingdom of Wei, let him be appointed to a senior position. If not, then you can send him to me for punishment. I will deal with him myself."

When Pang Juan had said farewell to King Hui, he went to see Sun Bin, and asked, "I have heard that you have recently received a letter from your family; is that true?"

Sun Bin was a very straightforward kind of person, and so he was not suspicious at all at this. He simply answered, "I have." He explained how the letter called for him to go back to his old home town.

"It has been such a long time since you saw any member of your family . . . you must be desperate for a reunion. Why don't you go to the king of Wei and ask for leave for two or three months, so that you can go home and visit your ancestral tombs? Once that is done, you can come back again."

"I am afraid that His Majesty will be suspicious of my intentions and refuse my request."

"Why don't you ask him?" Pang Juan suggested. "I will be there to support you."

"I would appreciate that very much," Sun Bin assured him.

That night, Pang Juan returned to the palace to have a second audience with King Hui, and presented his opinion. "In accordance with Your Majesty's orders, I went to see Sun Bin. He is simply not willing to stay in this country and was angry at the mere suggestion. If he sends in a request for leave in the near future, you should punish him for the crime of secretly communicating with the Qi ambassador." King Hui nodded his head.

The following day, Sun Bin did indeed present a memorial, in which he requested a month's leave in order to go to Qi and visit his ancestral tombs. King Hui was furious when he saw this document, and wrote across the top: "Sun Bin has already engaged in treasonous commerce with the Qi ambassador, and that is why he now asks to go home. He is clearly intending to betray the kingdom of Wei, turning his back on the trust that I have always shown him. He is hereby stripped of his official rank with immediate effect. Let him be taken to the office of my military advisor for punishment."

The military officials, having received this order, arrested Sun Bin and took him to the military advisor's office to see Pang Juan. When he caught sight of him, Pang Juan pretended to be shocked: "What are you doing here?" The officials reported King Hui's orders. When Pang Juan received them, he said to Sun Bin, "I will go and speak to His Majesty on your behalf. I will not let you suffer such a terrible injustice."

When he had finished speaking, he gave orders for his charioteer to whip up the horses and go and see King Hui. He presented his opinion as follows: "Although Sun Bin is guilty of secret communication with the Qi ambassador, this is not a crime that merits the death penalty. In my humble opinion, he should be punished with penal tattooing and having his kneecaps cut away. In that case he will never be able to return to his old home town. He will be kept alive, but it will prevent him from causing trouble in the future. Surely that would be best. However, I would not dare to make such a decision on my own authority, so I have come to you to ask for directions!"

"I think that is an excellent suggestion," King Hui said.

Pang Juan said goodbye and drove back to his office. "The king of Wei is absolutely furious and he was quite determined to have you executed," he told Sun Bin. "I begged and pleaded with him, which has at least served to save your life. However, you will have your kneecaps cut away and your face tattooed—this is the law of the kingdom of Wei, and I am afraid that there is nothing that I can do about it."

Sun Bin sighed and said, "The Master of Ghost Valley said: 'Even though it has been damaged, it is not a particularly bad omen.' Today, at least I will keep my head on my shoulders! This is all thanks to your efforts, and I will never forget what I owe you!"

Pang Juan called in the executioner, who tied Sun Bin down and then cut away his bony kneecaps. Sun Bin screamed and fainted away. It was a very long time before he recovered consciousness. Afterwards, his face was pierced with needles as they pricked out the words "Secret Communication with an Enemy Country" and rubbed ink into the wounds. Pang Juan pretended to be crying as he packed medicinal herbs onto Sun Bin's knees and wrapped them with bandages. He ordered people to carry him into the archives building, where he said what he could to cheer the man up, giving him good food and encouraging him to rest. After about a month, the wounds on Sun Bin's knees had pretty much healed, but without his kneecaps he could not move his legs properly—naturally, he would never be able to walk again. He could only sit with his legs stretched out in front of him.

An old man wrote a poem:

> When he changed his name, he knew that disaster would strike.
> Why did he wait until Pang Juan tried to destroy him?
> How stupid of Sun Bin to be so naively loyal:
> Just because he survived, he felt thankful to Pang Juan!

Sun Bin was now a cripple and was very unhappy to think that he was entirely dependent upon Pang Juan for receiving three meals a day. Pang Juan begged for the text of Sun Wu's *The Art of War* with the Master of Ghost Valley's commentary and explanations and Sun Bin naturally agreed. Pang Juan provided him with wooden strips and asked him to write it out, but Sun Bin had so far only managed to get down one-tenth of the whole text. At this point, Pang Juan ordered a slave named Cheng'er to look after Sun Bin. This Cheng'er saw how much the innocent Sun Bin had suffered and felt deeply sorry for him. Now Pang Juan summoned the slave into his presence and asked him how many lines Sun Bin could write in a day.

"General Sun's two legs are crippled, and so he spends most of his time resting," the slave explained. "It is difficult for him to sit for long. He can only write two or three paragraphs a day."

"If it is that slow, when will he ever finish?" Pang Juan said angrily. "I want you to make him hurry up."

Cheng'er withdrew and asked one of Pang Juan's personal servants about this: "The general wants Mr. Sun to write this text out for him, but why does he have to keep harassing him on the subject?"

"You don't understand," the servant replied. "Although the general appears to be very fond of Mr. Sun on the surface, in fact he is deeply jealous of him. The only reason he kept him alive was because he was hoping to obtain this book from him. Once he has written it all out, he won't be getting any more food or water, but don't tell anyone about this!"

When Cheng'er heard this news, he secretly informed Sun Bin. The latter was dreadfully shocked: "How heartless Pang Juan has turned out to be! How can I possibly let him get his hands on *The Art of War?*" Then he thought to himself, "If I don't carry on writing it out, he is sure to be furious with me. My life is really hanging by a thread!"

He thought and thought, trying to come up with some way to get himself out of this predicament. Suddenly the idea struck him: "When the Master of Ghost Valley said goodbye to me, he gave me a silk brocade bag and said, 'If you are ever in real danger, you can open it up and have a look.' Now is the time!" He opened up the silk bag and took out a piece of yellow silk. On it were written the words: "Pretend to be mad."

"So that is the answer," Sun Bin said.

That very evening, when his meal was set out, Sun Bin was just about to pick up his chopsticks when suddenly he buckled up and made as if to vomit. After some time, he went into fits. Glaring around him, he shouted, "Why are you trying to poison me?"

He swept all the crockery onto the floor and then picked up the wooden strips he had been writing and threw them into the fire. Rolling around on the floor, he cursed and screamed. Cheng'er did not realize that this was all pretend, so he rushed off to report this to Pang Juan. The next day, Pang Juan came to see for himself. Sun Bin was lying on the floor laughing heartily, his face covered with spittle, and then all of a sudden he burst into tears. Pang Juan asked him, "Why were you laughing? Why did you then cry?"

"I was laughing at the idea of the king of Wei wanting to kill me when I have a hundred thousand soldiers at my disposal," Sun Bin cackled. "What can he do to me? I was crying because without me, the kingdom of Wei has no competent generals!" When he had finished speaking, he again opened his eyes wide and stared at Pang Juan. Kowtowing over and over again, he shouted, "Master of the Ghost Valley, save me!"

"It is me, Pang Juan!" he shouted. "Don't you recognize me?"

Sun Bin grabbed hold of Pang Juan's robe and would not let go. He was shouting, "Save me, Master!" Pang Juan ordered his entourage to pull him free. He spoke privately to Cheng'er: "When did General Sun get so sick?"

"Last night," Cheng'er said.

Pang Juan got back into his chariot, his mind churning with suspicion. Since he was afraid that he might be pretending to be mad, he decided to test him: he ordered his servants to drag Sun Bin into a pigpen full of shit. Sun Bin lay there in the muck, his hair down over his face. Afterwards Pang Juan sent a servant with wine and food to trick him into revealing himself: "I am so sorry to see you suffer the punishment of having your kneecaps removed when you are innocent of any crime. I bring you this wine as a token of my respect. Pang Juan does not know anything about it."

Sun Bin knew that this was another of his little schemes, so he looked at the servant with furious eyes and cursed him. "Are you here to poison me too?" he screamed, upsetting the wine and food all over the ground. The servant then threw some dog shit and lumps of mud into the pen, and that Sun Bin did eat. Afterwards he went back to report to Pang Juan, who said, "If he really is mad there is nothing to be worried about."

After this he relaxed his surveillance of Sun Bin, allowing him to go in and out. Sometimes he would leave in the morning and come back at night, sleeping in the pigpen. Sometimes he would go out and simply not return, spending the night in the marketplace. Sometimes he seemed really cheerful and full of laughter, and other times he would wail and scream. The people in the marketplace knew that this was Sun Bin, the minister without portfolio, and they were very sorry to see him so crippled and sick, so there were many who gave him food and drink. Sometimes he would eat it and sometimes not, but he kept on saying crazy things all the time. There was nobody who realized that he was actually pretending to be insane. Pang Juan told the local officials that they should report Sun Bin's position every day just before dawn, because he was still checking up on him.

Do you know what happened next to Sun Bin? READ ON.

Chapter Fourteen

Tian Ji leads his forces to victory at Guiling.

At Maling, Pang Juan is shot to pieces by crossbows.

At this time, Master Mo Di was traveling in Qi and stayed at the house of Tian Ji. His disciple Li Hua arrived from Wei, and Mo Di asked him, "Has Sun Bin done well in Wei?"

Li Hua reported how Sun Bin had ended up having his kneecaps cut off. Master Mo Di sighed and said, "I originally wanted to help Sun Bin by recommending him for office, but all I have done is harm him!" He told Tian Ji all about how talented Sun Bin was and how Pang Juan had been jealous of him. Tian Ji went on to mention this to King Wei of Qi: "This man has remarkable talents and he has suffered a great deal in government service abroad—it is such a shame!"

"Why don't I send some troops to bring Master Sun home?" King Wei suggested.

"Pang Juan would not allow Sun Bin to serve in the government of Wei," Tian Ji replied. "Do you think it is likely that he would let him take office in Qi? If you want Sun Bin to come here, there are certain things that you have to do to keep his travels a secret, for that is the only way he will get here alive."

King Wei accepted his suggestions and ordered his minister without portfolio, Chunyu Kun, to go to Wei to find Sun Bin while pretending to be taking a present of tea to their king. Chunyu Kun accepted the mission and arranged for a cartload of tea to be prepared. Armed with his official credentials, he arrived in the kingdom of Wei. Li Hua accompanied him, disguised as a servant.

On arrival in the Wei capital, Chunyu Kun had an audience with King Hui in accordance with the orders he had received from the king of Qi. King Hui was delighted, and allowed Chenyu Kun to stay in an official guesthouse. When Li Hua saw that Sun Bin was acting crazy, he did not attempt to speak to him. Instead, he went back secretly in the middle of the night to talk to him. Sun Bin was sitting with his back resting against a well-head. When he caught sight of Li Hua, he opened his eyes wide, though he remained silent. Li Hua said with tears in his eyes, "How much you have suffered! I am Li Hua, a disciple of Master Mo Di. My master has told the king of Qi all about you, and His Majesty has expressed the greatest admiration. Chunyu Kun is here, not to present a tribute offering of tea, but to get you back to Qi. We will avenge the punishment they inflicted on you!"

Sun Bin was now in floods of tears. After a long time, he replied, "I have been anticipating that I would end up dead in a ditch—I could never have imagined that I would have the opportunity that you offered me today! However, Pang Juan is a very suspicious man, and I am afraid that it will not be easy to wrest me from his clutches. What shall we do?"

"I have a plan," Li Hua replied. "Do not worry, sir. On the day we are due to leave, someone will come to collect you."

They agreed that this was the only time that they would meet, so as not to arouse suspicion.

. . .

The following day, the king of Wei held a banquet in Chunyu Kun's honor. Discovering that he was a very learned man, he gave him generous gifts of gold and silk. Afterwards Chunyu Kun said goodbye to the king and was about to set off, when Pang Juan invited him to another farewell banquet at Changting. The night before, Li Hua had concealed Sun Bin inside a covered carriage, while his servant, Wang Yi, put on his clothes. With tousled hair and mud plastered all over his face, he looked just like Sun Bin. The guards made their usual report, and Pang Juan was completely unsuspicious. Chunyu Kun went out to Changting and enjoyed his banquet with Pang Juan. Afterwards he said goodbye and set off: Li Hua speeded on ahead with the covered carriage, and Chunyu Kun himself brought up the rear. After a couple of days, Wang Yi made his escape and joined them. By the time that the guards discovered Sun Bin's filthy clothes lying in a heap on the ground, he was already long gone. They immediately reported this to Pang Juan, who wondered whether he might not have fallen into the well and drowned. When the people he sent to drag the well found no body there, they searched everywhere but without discovering any trace of him. Being afraid that the king of Wei would blame him for this, he ordered his entourage to send in a report saying that Sun Bin had drowned. He had no idea that he was safe and sound in Qi.

Once Chenyu Kun had carried Sun Bin across the border, he arranged for him to be given a bath. When they approached Linzi, Tian Ji himself came ten *li* out of the city to welcome them. He mentioned his arrival to King Wei, who had a comfortable carriage sent to collect him and bring him to court. The two men discussed military matters, and King Wei wanted to appoint him to an official position. Sun Bin refused: "I have achieved nothing, so it would not be appropriate to receive a title. If Pang Juan hears that I have been given an official appointment in Qi, it will provoke his jealousy. It would be better to keep my presence here a secret for the time being and wait until there is something for me to do. Then I can show my mettle."

King Wei agreed and sent him to live in Tian Ji's household, where he was treated as an honored guest. Sun Bin wanted to Li Hua to convey his thanks to Master Mo Di, but the two of them disappeared without even saying goodbye. Sun Bin was very upset about this. He also sent someone to try and find Sun Ping and Sun Zhuo, but all the information that had been given in the letter was wrong. Then he realized that this too was part of Pang Juan's trickery.

King Wei of Qi amused himself in his free time by gambling with other members of the royal family over horseback archery. Tian Ji did not own any particularly strong horses, so he repeatedly lost money. One day, Tian Ji invited Sun Bin to go with him to the archery ground to watch the shooting. Sun Bin realized at once that the horses were simply not strong enough to be able to get far, and Tian Ji did indeed lose three ends. Afterwards he spoke privately to Tian Ji: "When you go back to shoot tomorrow, I can guarantee that you will win."

"If you can indeed guarantee victory for me," Tian Ji said, "I will ask His Majesty to put up a stake of one thousand pieces of gold."

"Do so, sir."

Tian Ji said to King Wei: "I lost in today's shooting, but tomorrow I am prepared to beggar myself over a single competition. Let the stake be one thousand pieces of gold on each end." King Wei agreed with a laugh.

The next day, all the members of the royal family arrived at the archery ground in fancy ornamented carriages. There were also a couple of thousand ordinary people present as spectators.

"What are you going to do to guarantee my victory?" Tian Ji asked. "One thousand pieces of gold is riding on each end, and that is a lot of money!"

"His Majesty owns the very finest horses in the kingdom of Qi," Sun Bin explained, "so if you want to beat him with the second-rate, that will be very difficult. However, there is a stratagem to counter this. You both have to change horses for each end. I want you to use your worst horse in competition against his best horse. Use your best horse in competition against his second-best horse and your second-best horse against his worst horse. Although you will lose one end, there are two that you will win."

"That is very clever!" Tian Ji declared. He had his gold saddle and silk brocade caparison put on his worst horse, pretending that it was in fact his best. He and King Wei then went out to shoot their first end. The horse proved to be very poor, and Tian Ji lost one thousand pieces of gold. King Wei laughed heartily.

"There are two more ends to go," Tian Ji reminded him. "If I lose them too, you can laugh at me then."

In the second and third ends, Tian Ji's horses won, just as had been anticipated. Thus he gained back all that he had lost and another thousand pieces of gold besides. Tian Ji presented his opinion: "The victory that I obtained today is not thanks to my horses. It was made possible by Master Sun's advice." He explained just what had happened.

King Wei sighed and said, "Even in this little matter, you can see just how clever Master Sun is!" He redoubled the respect with which he treated him and gave him countless presents. No more of this now.

• • •

Having crippled Sun Bin, King Hui of Wei tasked Pang Juan with reconquering Zhongshan. Pang Juan presented his opinion: "Zhongshan is far from Wei but close to Zhao. Rather than competing with them for lands far away, we would do better to capture territory located near to us. Let me attack Handan for you, Your Majesty, and thus avenge the loss of Zhongshan."

King Hui agreed to this. Pang Juan led an army of five hundred chariots out of the city and attacked Zhao, laying siege to Handan. The official in charge of the city, Pi Xuan, was defeated in one battle after the other and sent a report to this effect to Lord Cheng of Zhao. He sent an envoy to present the lands of Zhongshan to Qi in return for assistance. King Wei of Qi was aware of how brilliant Sun Bin was, so he appointed him as commander-in-chief. However, Sun Bin refused: "I have suffered a crippling punishment, so if you were to employ me to take charge of your army, it would look as if the kingdom of Qi is lacking in men of real ability, thus making us a laughingstock to the enemy. Please appoint Tian Ji as general."

King Wei did indeed appoint Tian Ji as the commander-in-chief. Sun Bin became chief military advisor instead. He spent his time sitting inside a battle chariot, thinking up their next move, and his name was not made public.

Tian Ji wanted to lead his army to rescue Handan, but Sun Bin stopped him: "The generals in Zhao cannot possibly defeat Pang Juan—before we have even reached Handan, the city will already have fallen. You had better station your troops mid-route and announce your intention of attacking Xiangling. That will force Pang Juan to turn back, and then you can attack him. Victory is certain!"

Tian Ji followed his advice. At this time, since the help that the people of Handan were waiting for had not arrived, Pi Xuan had to surrender the city to Pang Juan. The general sent a messenger to report his victory to the king of Wei. However, just as he was about to advance his troops, he was suddenly informed that Qi had sent Tian Ji to take advantage of his absence to attack Xiangling.

"If Xiangling falls, the capital is in danger!" he said in alarm. "I must go back to rescue my base." He immediately stood down the army.

When they were twenty *li* from Guiling, they encountered the Qi army. Sun Bin had already discovered which route the Wei army would use and made his own preparations. He opened by sending the junior general, Yuan Da, to throw three thousand soldiers in their way to provoke battle. One of Pang Juan's nephews, Pang Cong, was in command of the vanguard—he launched himself into the fray. Having crossed swords about twenty times, Yuan Da pretended to be defeated and started to flee. Pang Cong was afraid that there might be some kind of ambush ahead, so he did not dare to chase him. He returned and reported this to Pang Juan. The latter shouted at him: "If you are so scared of a junior general that you do not dare to try and capture him alive, how are you going to deal with Tian Ji?" He ordered the main body of the army to set off in pursuit.

When they arrived at Guiling, they could see that the Qi troops ahead of them were already in battle formation. Pang Juan leaned on the railing of his chariot and inspected it—this was the "Reversible Eight Gates" formation that Sun Bin had used all that time ago in the kingdom of Wei. Pang Juan was now suspicious and thought to himself, "How does Tian Ji know this battle formation? Can it be that Sun Bin has managed to make his way home to Qi?"

He gave orders for his own men to go into formation. Now they saw the battle standard of General Tian fluttering above the Qi army, as a battle chariot pulled out from the line. Tian Ji, in full armor and holding a painted spear in one hand, was standing on top of it. Tian Ying, holding a halberd, was in place on his right.

"Can a responsible Wei general come forward to speak?" Tian Ji shouted.

Pang Juan drove his own chariot forward and responded: "Qi and Wei have always been allies, while Wei and Zhao are enemies. What has that to do with Qi? I think it is a very bad idea for you to abandon the alliance between us to team up with our enemies."

"Zhao has presented the lands of Zhongshan to His Majesty, and so our king ordered me to come and rescue them," Tian Ji replied. "If you would be prepared to hand over a couple of commanderies to us, our army will withdraw immediately."

Pang Juan was furious. "This battle formation is called 'Reversible Eight Gates,'" he shouted. "I studied under the Master of Ghost Valley, and there is nothing you can do to baffle me! Even small children in my country could recognize that!"

"Since you recognize it," Tian Ji retorted, "would you dare to attack it?"

Pang Juan was now starting to sweat, but if he said that he would not attack, it would make him look bad. Hence, he replied in a loud voice, "Since I know what it is, why shouldn't I be able to attack it?"

Pang Juan now instructed Pang Ying, Pang Cong, and Pang Mao as follows: "I remember Sun Bin talking about this battle formation, and I think I know how to defeat it. However, this particular formation is easy to move into 'Snake' position: if you attack the head, then the tail fights back; if you attack the tail, then the head fights back; and if you attack the middle, you get caught in a pincer movement—the attacker is immediately in trouble. I am now going to go and fight this formation. Each of you is in command of your own army, and I want you to watch as it changes. You must then move forward in a simultaneous attack. This will ensure that the head and tail cannot help each other and the formation can be broken."

When Pang Juan had given his instructions, he led his own vanguard of five thousand men forward to attack the initial formation. However, once he had burst through their lines, he was only able to orientate himself according to the eight flags marking direction. This being the case, the enemy kept moving them around, until he was completely confused and had no idea where he was. He attacked this way and that, but encountered a forest of weapons in all directions and simply could not find a way out. He could hear the sound of drumming and bells chiming, and there was shouting on all sides. Standing in among all the other generals' flags was one bearing the name Sun. Pang Juan was appalled: "The cripple has indeed managed to make his way to Qi. I have fallen into his trap!"

It was just at this critical moment that Pang Ying and Pang Cong fought their way in and rescued Pang Juan. Every single one of the five thousand men he had led into battle was dead. When he asked after Pang Mao, he was informed that he had been killed by Tian Ying. All in all, they had lost more than twenty thousand men. Pang Juan was deeply shocked.

This particular battle formation, based on the eight trigrams, corresponds to the eight directions; together with the central position, it is formed by nine divisions of troops. This formation sees the troops arranged in a square. When Pang Juan attacked, two of these divisions split off to prevent anyone outside from trying to rescue him. The remaining seven divisions moved into a circular formation. It was this which confused Pang Juan. Later on in the Tang dynasty, Li Jing, Duke of Wey, used this particular formation as the basis for his "Snowflake" formation, whereby the troops started off in a circle.

There is a poem that testifies to this:

This particular battle formation can undergo remarkable transforma-
    tions;
Although the Master of the Ghost Valley knew this, he taught it to few.
Pang Juan knew that it could transform into "Snake,"
But he did not know the subtle changes between "Square" and "Round."

*Today southeast of Tangyi County there is a place called "Ancient
Battlefield." This is where Sun Bin and Pang Juan fought.*
    When Pang Juan realized that Sun Bin was over with the Qi army,
he became very frightened. He discussed this development with Pang
Ying and Pan Cong. They decided to abandon their camp and flee.
That very night, they made their way back to the kingdom of Wei.
Tian Ji and Sun Bin discovered that the enemy camp was empty and
went home to Qi in triumph. This happened in the seventeenth year of
the reign of King Xian of Zhou. King Hui of Wei decided that Pang
Juan's success in the capture of Handan canceled out his defeat in the
battle of Guiling. Meanwhile, King Wei of Qi had been so impressed
by Tian Ji and Sun Bin that he entrusted them with absolute power
over his army. Zou Ji was afraid that in the future one or the other of
them would replace him as prime minister, so he secretly discussed
what to do with one of his clients, Gongsun Yue. He was determined
to replace Tian Ji and Sun Bin in His Majesty's favor. By coincidence,
it was just at this moment that Pang Juan sent someone to Zou Ji's
house with a bribe of one thousand pieces of gold, wanting him to get
rid of Sun Bin. Since this was exactly what Zou Ji wanted himself, he
ordered Gongsun Yue to pretend to be a member of Tian Ji's household, and sent him to knock on the door of a fortune teller in the middle of the night, armed with ten pieces of gold. "General Tian Ji has
ordered me to request a divination from you," he announced.
    When the hexagram had been laid out, the diviner asked, "What do
you want to know?"
    "My master is a member of the Tian royal family," Gongsun Yue
said. "He has control over the army, and his power strikes awe into
enemy countries. He is plotting a coup and wants to know if it will be
successful."
    The diviner was horrified, and said, "That is treason! I would not
dare to perform such a divination!"

"If you do not want to perform the divination, that is quite alright," Gongsun Yue said, "but if you know what is good for you, you must not tell anyone about this!"

Once he had gone, Zou Ji's men arrived and arrested the fortune teller. They accused him of performing a divination for the traitor, Tian Ji. "Even though someone did come to me," the diviner said, "I did not perform a divination for them."

Zou Ji rushed to court and informed King Wei of what Tian Ji had wished to have a divination about—he brought the fortune teller along to prove it. King Wei now became suspicious and had his people watching Tian Ji's movements every day. When Tian Ji found out what had happened, he immediately resigned on the grounds of ill health. This assuaged King Wei's animosity. Sun Bin also resigned his position as military advisor. The following year, King Wei of Qi died. Prince Bijiang inherited the throne, taking the title of King Xuan. Since King Xuan was aware of Tian Ji's innocence and Sun Bin's abilities, he restored both of them to their old positions.

. . .

Going back a little now, when Pang Juan heard that Tian Ji and Sun Bin had been stripped of their offices by the kingdom of Qi, he said happily, "Now I can take over the whole world!" It was around this time that Lord Zhao of Han destroyed the state of Zheng and made his capital there. The prime minister of Zhao went to Han to offer congratulations and invited them to take part in a joint campaign against Wei, whereby they would partition their territory equally between them after their final victory. Lord Zhao of Han agreed to this, sending back the following message: "Unfortunately, we have just suffered a famine. We will have to wait until next year before we can take our army out on campaign."

When Pang Juan heard this news, he said to King Hui, "I have discovered that Han is plotting to assist Zhao in an attack on us. We should take advantage of the fact that their alliance has not yet stabilized to attack Han. That will put an end to their conspiracy."

King Hui agreed to this. He appointed Crown Prince Shen as the commander-in-chief and Pang Juan as senior general, and they advanced on the state of Han in a truly massive show of force. When they were traveling through Waihuang, a commoner named Xu Sheng requested an audience with the crown prince.

"Since you have asked to see me, sir, what do you have to say?" the crown prince asked.

"You are here today, Your Highness, in order to attack Han," Xu Sheng said. "I have a method which will ensure you victory every time you fight. Would you like to hear it?"

Crown Prince Shen replied, "I would be delighted!"

"Do you think anywhere in the world is richer than Wei? Do you think your position is more important than that of a king?"

"I do not," Crown Prince Shen replied.

"Now you have made yourself general, Your Highness, and attacked Han. If you succeed, you will not be any richer and your position will still not be as important as that of His Majesty the king. On the other hand, if you lose, what will happen then? You are lucky enough to be in a situation where one day you will enjoy the honors of a king without ever having to go to war—that is my method for ensuring your ultimate victory."

"Excellent!" the crown prince declared. "I will follow your advice and stand down my army immediately."

"Even though you think that my advice is good," Xu Sheng replied, "you are not going to be able to put it into practice. When one man cooks a pot of food, many people get to taste the soup. There are a huge number of people who are hoping to get a mouthful of Your Royal Highness's soup. You may want to go home, but will they let you?" He said goodbye and left, whereupon the crown prince issued an order to stand down the army.

"His Majesty has entrusted the command of three armies to you," Pang Juan said. "If you stand down your troops before you have even fought a single battle, what is the difference between that and being defeated?"

The other generals were also unwilling to return empty-handed. Crown Prince Shen could not make up his mind what to do, so he led the army forward until they arrived at the Han capital.

· · ·

Lord Ai of Han sent someone to report this emergency to Qi, begging them to send an army to help him. King Xuan of Qi assembled all his ministers and asked them, "Should I assist Han? Would this be a good idea?"

The prime minister, Zou Ji, said, "If Han and Wei are fighting, that is good for their neighbors. We should not try and help them."

Tian Ji and Tian Ying said, "If Wei defeats Han, then Qi will suffer disaster next. We ought to assist them."

Sun Bin was the only person present to remain completely silent. "You have not said a word, military advisor," King Xuan remarked. "Surely it cannot be that both options are wrong?"

"That is in fact the case," Sun Bin replied. "The kingdom of Wei makes much play of its military might. Last year they attacked Zhao, and this year they have invaded Han. Surely Qi will not escape their attention forever! If we do not go to the rescue, we will be abandoning Han to enrich Wei—therefore, those who have spoken out against assistance are wrong. Wei is now attacking Han, and if we save them before they have been seriously weakened, we are going to get our troops killed in order to spare theirs. Han will suffer little, and we will suffer much—that is why those who have spoken in favor of going to the rescue are also wrong."

"If that is so, what should I do?" King Xuan asked.

"My advice, Your Majesty, is that you begin by promising assistance to Han in order to improve their morale," Sun Bin replied. "Once Han knows that help from Qi is on the way, they will resist Wei with all their might. Similarly, Wei will attack Han with everything that they have got. We will wait until Wei is exhausted and then lead our army out to attack them in order to rescue Han. That way, we can achieve a great result with little expenditure of effort. Surely this is better than the two suggestions previously on offer."

King Xuan clapped his hands, and said "Good." He made his promise to the Han ambassador: "The Qi army will be on its way to help you immediately."

Lord Zhao of Han was delighted, and resisted the incursion by the Wei army with all the forces at his command. They fought some five or six battles, and Han did not win a single one. Again he sent an ambassador to Qi to hurry up their relief troops. Yet again Qi appointed Tian Ji as commander-in-chief and Tian Ying as his deputy. Sun Bin was the military advisor. They took an army of five hundred chariots to rescue Han. As before, Tian Ji was planning to advance straight to

Han, when Sun Bin said, "No! No! When we went to rescue Zhao, we did not set foot inside their territory. Now we are going to rescue Han; what on earth do we want to go there for?"

"What do you think we should do?" Tian Ji asked.

"If you want to put an end to all of this, we are going to have to attack something that they cannot afford to lose," Sun Bin replied. "Right now, our target is the Wei capital."

Tian Ji followed his advice. He gave orders to the three armies to march on Wei. Meanwhile Pang Juan, having defeated the Han army in one engagement after the other, was now pressing close on the new capital. Now suddenly he received an urgent dispatch from home. This read: "Qi has invaded us again. You must return immediately!" Pang Juan was horrified and gave orders to leave Han and return to Wei. The Han army did not go in pursuit of them.

Sun Bin knew that Pang Juan would soon arrive. He said to Tian Ji: "The armies of the Three Jins are very brave and tough—they despise Qi. Since the Qi army has a reputation for cowardice, a good general would make use of this to maneuver the enemy into a disadvantageous position. *The Art of War* says, 'If you race one hundred *li* after profit, the general will get himself killed; if you race fifty *li* after profit, half the army will not make it.' Our army has now penetrated deep into Wei territory, so we should pretend to be weak to trick them."

"How exactly do we trick them?" Tian Ji asked.

"Today we will light one hundred thousand cooking fires," Sun Bin explained. "Starting tomorrow, we will gradually reduce the number. They will see the number of fires decreasing and so they will imagine that our troops are afraid of having to do battle and so many of them have deserted. They will chase after us, trying to take advantage of that. They will be rendered more arrogant, but they will also be exhausted. We can then use my plan to defeat them." Tian Ji followed his advice.

Pang Juan's army was moving southwest. The general knew that the Han troops had been defeated time and time again, and he had been looking forward to the next stage of the advance. Now, since Wei had been invaded by Qi, he had been robbed of his victory and was furious about this. When he arrived at the Wei border, he discovered that the Qi army had already retreated. He gave orders to have their campsite cleaned up and noticed that it had been laid out on the most massive scale. He tasked someone with counting up the number of cooking fires and learned that there were one hundred thousand of them in total. He said in amazement, "I had no idea there were so many of them. We should not underestimate the enemy!"

The following day they arrived at the site of their next camp. On checking the number of fires, they discovered that there were more than fifty thousand. The following day, they only counted thirty thousand. Pang Juan clapped his hand against his forehead. "How lucky the king of Wei is!"

"We have not even engaged the enemy yet," Crown Prince Shen said. "Why are you so happy?"

"I always knew the people of Qi are cowards," Pang Juan replied, "but it appears that having entered Wei territory, more than half of their army has deserted in the space of just the last three days. How could they dare to fight us?"

"People from Qi are full of tricks," the crown prince said. "You need to be very careful."

"Tian Ji has met his match today!" Pang Juan declared. "Although I am not a talented man, I reckon I can go and capture him alive. That will wipe out the humiliation I suffered at Guiling."

He gave the following orders: twenty thousand picked troops, together with the two divisions under the command of Crown Prince Shen, were to march off on the double. The infantry was all to remain behind, with Pang Cong, advancing at their own pace.

Sun Bin immediately sent someone to spy on what Pang Juan was up to. The report came back: "The Wei army has already passed Mount Shalu and they are pressing forward, traveling day and night." He traced out their journey with his finger on a map and realized that they would reach Maling at dusk. The road there passed between two mountains, traveling through a very deep valley with extremely steep sides. This was perfect for an ambush. The woods growing along the sides of the road were very dense. Sun Bin indicated one huge tree to be spared and then had all the others felled. They were laid across the road to block it. A piece of bark was stripped off the one remaining tree on the east side, and here he wrote with a piece of charcoal the six words: "Pang Juan died below this tree." Then he signed this message: "The military advisor, Sun Bin." He ordered generals Yuan Da and Dugu Chen to take five thousand archers each and lie in ambush to the left and right of the road. He instructed them: "When you see a fire lit below that tree, you are to open fire in unison." He also gave orders that Tian Ying should take ten thousand men and lie in ambush three *li* from Maling. He was to wait until the Wei army had passed and then attack them from behind. Once everyone knew what they had to do, he and Tian Ji took the main body of the army and made camp a considerable distance away. They would respond to the situation as it developed.

. . .

When Pang Juan heard that the Qi army was not far ahead, he was furious that he could not overtake them in a single bound. However, he restricted himself to hurrying his men along. When they arrived at Maling, the sun was setting over the western mountain. It was the last week in the tenth month, and there was no moon. His advance guard reported: "There are cut trees blocking the road, so it will be difficult for us to proceed."

"The Qi army must have been terrified that we would be coming up behind them," Pang Juan shouted, "so that is why they have done this."

He ordered his troops to move the trees out of the way. Suddenly, raising his head, he noticed that a piece of bark had been stripped off the one remaining tree. He could make out some writing but it was simply too dark to read. He ordered his soldiers to light a torch to illuminate it. As his officers all came forward with lighted torches. Pang Juan could now read exactly what it said. He exclaimed, "I have fallen into that crippled bastard's trap!"

Immediately he shouted at his men: "Retreat as quickly as you can!" Before he had even finished speaking, Yuan Da and Gudu Chen's troops, who had been lying in ambush, saw the flames, and ten thousand crossbows fired in unison. The bolts fell like rain, and the army was thrown into utter confusion. Pang Juan was so severely injured that he knew he would not survive this encounter. He sighed and said, "How much I regret not killing that cripple. All I have done is make the brute famous!" He then drew his sword and committed suicide by cutting his throat. Pang Ying was also shot dead by a single bolt in this encounter. The number of Wei soldiers killed was truly incalculable.

A historian wrote a poem:

In the past it seemed such a cunning scheme to forge the letter;
Today, a further crafty plan saw ten thousand crossbows fired.
In your dealings with your friends, you should be loyal and just;
Do not imitate Pang Juan, whose evil ways brought about his own
    death!

In the past, when Pang Juan was about to leave Ghost Valley, the Master told him, "If you make someone else suffer, they will punish you for it." Pang Juan forged a letter to get Sun Bin into trouble: that resulted in his kneecaps being cut off. Now he was in turn tricked by Sun Bin, thanks to his scheme of reducing the number of cooking fires. The Master of Ghost Valley also said, "Death will come with a Horse." In the end he died at Maling, which means "Horse Hill." Pang Juan held office in Wei for twelve years, right up until the moment of his death—this corresponds to the twelve flowers. From this we can see how miraculously accurate the Master of Ghost Valley's divinations were.

Do you know what happened next? THE STORY CONTINUES . . .

The Family Troubles of
the King of Qin

Chapter Fifteen

*Having hatched a cunning plan, Lü Buwei
sends Prince Yiren home.*

*Fan Wuqi circulates criticism in an attempt to
punish the king of Qin.*

Royal Grandson Yiren of Qin was sent as a hostage to Zhao. He was
one of the younger sons of the Lord of Anguo. The Lord of Anguo was
better known as Prince Zhu, styled Zixi, the crown prince to King
Zhaoxiang of Qin. The Lord of Anguo had more than twenty sons, all
of them the children of his concubines. Not a single one was born of
the crown princess as his legitimate heir. His Lordship's favorite concubine, who originally came from Chu, was given the title of Lady
Huayang. She too had no children. Royal Grandson Yiren's mother
was a Lady Xia Ji, whom the crown prince did not love and who died
young. It was for this reason that Royal Grandson Yiren was selected to
go as a hostage to Zhao, without communication with his family for a
very long time. When the Zhao army was defeated in battle by Qin, the
king decided to vent his fury on his hostage. He decided to kill Yiren.

One of his ministers remonstrated: "Yiren is not an important
member of the royal family, so killing him won't change anything. It
will just give Qin an excuse to attack us and put an end to any peaceful
resolution in the future."

The king of Zhao had still not calmed down entirely from his anger,
and so he sent Yiren to live at the Zong Tower. He ordered Grandee
Gongsun Qian to take charge of guarding him, keeping a close eye on
his movements while cutting down the emoluments he received. Not
only did Royal Grandson Yiren not have a carriage to use; he found

that he now did not even have enough money for his daily needs. This caused him to become sunk in depression.

It was at this time that he met a man named Lü Buwei from Yangdi. His father was a merchant, who spent his days traveling from one country to another, buying things cheap and selling them at a considerable markup, accumulating great reserves of wealth. Lü Buwei happened to be visiting Handan where he caught sight of Royal Grandson Yiren on the road. He was a very striking-looking man—even when poor and friendless, he never lost his aristocratic air. Lü Buwei was impressed and asked one of the passers-by, "Who is that man?"

"That is the son of the crown prince of Qin, the Lord of Anguo," the man replied. "He is a hostage here in the kingdom of Zhao. Since the Qin army has repeatedly invaded our borders, the king wanted to kill him. Although he has escaped being put to death, he is now being held under close guard at the Zong Tower, and they don't support him anymore, as a result of which he has become very poor."

Lü Buwei sighed and said to himself, "This is a remarkable business opportunity!"

He went home and asked his father, "What is the profit we expect from our agricultural investments?"

"Ten percent."

"What profit do we expect from our trade in pearls and precious stones?"

"One hundred percent."

"What kind of profit do you think we could expect if we established a king and took control of his country?"

His father laughed and asked, "Where could we find such a king? The profits would be one thousand percent, ten thousand percent—incalculable!"

Lü Buwei expended one hundred pieces of gold on making friends with Gongsun Qian. As the two of them became increasingly close, he was able to visit Royal Grandson Yiren. Pretending to know nothing about him, he asked who he was, and Gongsun Qian told him the truth.

One day, Gongsun Qian invited Lü Buwei to a drinks party. "Since you have invited no other guests and Royal Grandson of Qin is here," Buwei said, "why don't you ask him to join us?"

Gongsun Qian followed his suggestion. He introduced Yiren to Lü Buwei, and they sat down on the same mat and started drinking.

When they were all somewhat tipsy, Gongsun Qian got up in order to go to the privy. Lü Buwei now said in a low voice to the royal grandson, "The king of Qin is getting old. The crown prince loves Lady Huayang, but she does not have any children of her own. You have more than twenty other brothers, but there is none who is obviously more favored than the others. Why don't you ask to be allowed to return to the kingdom of Qin and, when you are there, seek to ingratiate yourself with Lady Huayang, maybe even becoming her adopted son? In that case, in the future, you might hope to become the king of Qin yourself!"

Yiren replied, almost in tears: "Do you think I don't want to go home? Every time I hear people talk about my home country, it is like my heart is being sliced open with a knife! I have no idea how I am going to get away from here!"

"Even though my family is poor," Buwei told him, "we can offer you one thousand pieces of gold towards the expenses of your journey to the west. Let me go and persuade the crown prince and Lady Huayang to rescue you and bring you home. How would that be?"

"If you can make that happen," Yiren said, "I will share my future wealth and honors with you."

When they had just finished speaking, Gongsun Qian came back. He asked, "What were you talking about?"

"I asked the royal grandson what the price of jade is like nowadays in Qin, and he was apologizing because he does not know," Lü Buwei said.

Gongsun Qian was not at all suspicious. He ordered that more wine be poured, and, having enjoyed themselves heartily, the party finally broke up. After this, Lü Buwei and Royal Grandson Yiren often met one another, and he gave the latter five hundred gold pieces in secret, instructing him to buy some servants and make some useful friends. Yiren gave gold and silk to Gongsun Qian and his household, until they all felt they were practically like family and were not at all suspicious of what he might be up to.

Lü Buwei used another five hundred pieces of gold to buy various expensive jewels and other treasures. Having bade farewell to Gongsun Qian, he headed off to Xianyang. He discovered that Lady Huayang had an older sister who was also married in Qin, so he began by bribing some of her family servants to communicate the following message to her: "Royal Grandson Yiren is stuck in Zhao, but he very much misses Her Ladyship and asked me to bring her various presents to show his filial love. This little gift is from the royal grandson to his aunt." He presented her with a box of gold and pearls.

Lady Huayang's older sister was delighted and came out into the main hall of the house in person, where she had an audience with Lü Buwei from the far side of a curtain. "It is very kind of the royal grandson to send you all this way," she said. "Having spent all this time in Zhao, does he really miss his home so much?"

"I live opposite to the royal grandson and we often talk to one another," Lü Buwei explained. "I might say that I know him very well indeed. He misses Her Ladyship day and night. Having lost his own mother as a small child, he has come to feel that Lady Huayang is like his real mother. He would love to be able to come home to see her again, to fulfill the demands of his filial duty!"

"How has the Royal Grandson fared in Zhao?"

"The Qin army had repeatedly attacked the kingdom of Zhao," Lü Buwei replied. "Each time, the king of Zhao has threatened to execute the Royal Grandson. Fortunately, he has been able to survive thanks to the representations of ministers and other people. That is the reason that he is so desperate to go home!"

"Why do the ministers and people of Zhao try and protect him?"

"The royal grandson is a remarkably filial and fine young man," Lü Buwei replied. "Every time that it is the birthday of the king of Qin, the crown prince, or Her Ladyship, or indeed New Year's Day or any other festival, the Royal Grandson performs full ritual lustrations and then burns incense while bowing to the west and praying for blessings for you all. Everyone in Zhao knows that he does this. He is also very studious and treats wise men with great respect—he has acquired many clients and advisors from other kingdoms. Wherever you go in the world, you will hear people talking about what a remarkable man he is. That is the reason why everyone has gone to such lengths to save his life!"

When he had finished speaking, Lü Buwei presented further rare items to the value of about five hundred pieces of gold: "Since the royal grandson cannot come back to serve Her Ladyship in person, he hopes that these little gifts will show his filial love for her. Please, would you give them to your sister on his behalf?"

Lady Huayang's older sister ordered a senior member of her household to entertain Lü Buwei with food and wine while she went to the palace to speak to Her Ladyship. When Lady Huayang saw these treasures, she thought that the royal grandson must really care about her, and she was very pleased. Her sister went back to report this to Lü Buwei, who asked, "How many children does Her Ladyship have?"

"She is childless."

"I have often heard people say that a woman who relies on her beauty for her position will find that love fades as she gets older," Lü Buwei remarked. "At the moment, Her Ladyship is the crown prince's favorite, but she has no children of her own. In these circumstances, she ought to select the most filial of his sons to adopt as her own. That way, in the fullness of time, he can become king and she will never lose power. Otherwise, if the crown prince's love does fade as she gets older, it will be too late! Now Yiren is a very clever and filial young man, and he is deeply attached to Her Ladyship. He knows that as things stand, he has no hope of ever becoming king. However, were Her Ladyship to promote him to the position of heir apparent, would she not be loved in Qin from one generation to the next?"

Her sister again reported these words to Lady Huayang. "He is quite right," she said.

Accordingly one night, when she and the Lord of Anguo had been drinking together perfectly happily, she suddenly burst into tears. The crown prince was surprised and asked her what the matter was.

"Although I have been lucky enough to join your harem," Lady Huayang sobbed, "I have never been so fortunate as to have children. Of all your sons, Yiren is by far the most intelligent, and he is much admired by all the foreign ambassadors and advisors who come and go from Zhao—they cannot praise him enough. If I were to adopt him and he became your heir, I would have someone to rely on."

The crown prince agreed to her request.

"You have said yes now," Her Ladyship pouted. "But when your other concubines start nagging you, you will forget all about it."

"If you don't trust me, I will write my promise down," the crown prince told her.

He took a jade tablet and scratched four words upon it: "Yiren is my heir." He broke the tablet in half and they each kept one part of it as proof.

"Yiren is in Zhao," Lady Huayang said. "When will we bring him home?"

"I will find an opportunity to mention this to His Majesty," the crown prince assured her.

At this time King Zhaoxiang of Qin was furious with Zhao, so when the crown prince spoke to His Majesty, he did not listen. Lü Buwei knew that His Majesty was very fond of the queen's younger brother, the Lord of Yangquan, so he bribed his servants and asked to be allowed to have an audience with His Lordship. He began his persuasion as follows: "You, sir, have committed a crime deserving of the death penalty. Did you know that?"

The Lord of Yangquan was horrified. "What crime have I committed?" he asked.

"You have arranged for your entire household to receive important government posts," Lü Buwei said. "You enjoy rich emoluments, your stables are packed with the finest of horses, your harem is stuffed with the most beautiful of women—but where are the rich, noble, and powerful members of the crown prince's household? His Majesty is already an old man. When he passes away, the crown prince that will come to the throne, and his household will certainly be filled with resentment towards you. Your situation will then be precarious indeed!"

"What should I do?" the Lord of Yangquan asked.

"I have a plan that could mean that you could live out your natural life span in complete security: as safe as Mount Tai," Lü Buwei declared. "Do you want to hear it?"

The Lord of Yangquan knelt down and invited him to speak. "His Majesty is getting on in years, and the crown prince does not have a legitimate heir," Lü Buwei continued. "Now, Royal Grandson Yiren is a wise and filial man whose conduct has won glowing praise from the other kings, and yet he is at present living as a hostage in Zhao, hoping day and night to be allowed to return home. You should ask the queen to speak to the king about bringing Yiren home, and have the crown prince appoint him as his heir. In that case Yiren will go from having nothing to being the future monarch; the crown prince's wife, Lady Huayang, will go from having no children to having a wonderful adopted son; the crown prince and the Royal Grandson will both be most grateful to the queen, and your own noble position will be preserved from one generation to the next without the slightest impairment!"

The Lord of Yangquan went down the steps and bowed to show his respect. "I am very grateful for your advice," he said.

He immediately reported what Lü Buwei had said to the queen. Her Majesty then spoke to the king of Qin about it. "When the people of Zhao beg for a peace treaty," he said, "I will bring my grandson home."

The crown prince summoned Lü Buwei and asked him, "I would like to bring Yiren home to Qin and make him my heir, but His Majesty will not allow it. Do you have a good plan to suggest?"

Lü Buwei kowtowed and said, "If you indeed intend to make him your heir, Crown Prince, I would not begrudge spending every penny I have. If I were to bribe the people in power in Zhao, I am sure I can save him."

The crown prince and Her Ladyship were both delighted and gave three hundred ingots of gold to Lü Buwei. This he was to hand over to Yiren, to pay for the expenses of his household. The queen gave him a further two hundred gold ingots. Lady Huayang also prepared a whole trunk of clothes for Yiren, and gave Lü Buwei one hundred gold ingots to keep for himself, since she wanted to appoint him as the Grand Tutor. He was to take the following message to the royal grandson: "Any minute now we will get you out of there. Don't worry." Lü Buwei said goodbye and left.

There is a poem which testifies to this:

> This idle merchant cared only about profit:
> Now a few treasures bought him a royal grandson.
> He was able to make a childless woman have her own son,
> Convincing her to requite filial piety with an adoption.

When he arrived back in Handan, he went first to see his own father and tell him what had happened. His father was delighted. The following day he prepared presents and went to see Gongsun Qian. After that, he had an audience with Royal Grandson Yiren, at which he repeated exactly what the queen and Lady Huayang had said to him and presented him with the five hundred ingots of gold and the clothes. Yiren was very pleased. He said to Lü Buwei, "I will keep the clothes, but you, sir, should take the gold. Even though I need money, I have put you to a lot of trouble and expense. If I ever get to go home, there is nothing I will not do for you."

. . .

It was about this time that Lü Buwei took a beautiful woman named Zhao Ji, who was good at singing and dancing, into his household. When he discovered that she was two months pregnant, he came up with a plan: "When the Royal Grandson Yiren goes home, sooner or later he will become king. If I present this woman to him, she may give birth to a boy, who will be my own flesh and blood. If this boy eventually becomes king himself, then the Ying clan will be replaced on the throne by the Lü family. That is something that would be worth bankrupting us all to achieve!"

He invited Royal Grandson Yiren and Gongsun Qian to his house for drinks. The tables were groaning with the finest of delicacies, and the most delightful tunes were played by the musicians. When the wine circulated and they had become a little drunk, Lü Buwei announced: "I have recently acquired a new concubine who is good at singing and dancing. I would like her to come out and offer a toast; I hope you don't mind." He commanded the maids to go and bring Zhao Ji out.

"Why don't you pay your respects to my honored guests?" Lü Buwei said.

Zhao Ji walked forward a couple of steps and then fell to her knees on the carpet and kowtowed. Royal Grandson Yiren and Gongsun Qian quickly made respectful bows in return. Lü Buwei ordered Zhao Ji to take a gold cup and toast each of the men in turn. When it came to Yiren, he raised his head and looked at her, only to see that she was indeed very lovely.

How to describe her?
Her tresses billowed out, floating as lightly as a cicada's wing;
Her eyebrows were clearly marked in a beautiful wave-like curve.
Her lips were painted in a lovely cherry-red cupid's-bow;
Her pearly teeth shone like brilliant white jade.
When she gave her seductive laugh,
You could imagine that she was Bao Si bewitching King You.
When she danced on her tiny feet,

You might think that this was Xi Shi beguiling the ruler of Wu.
You could never have enough of watching her seductive ways;
You could paint her portrait a thousand times and never catch her
    charm.

When Zhao Ji had offered a toast to each of them, she shook loose
the long sleeves of her gown. Taking up a position on the carpet, she
began to dance. Her body moved with sinuous grace, and her sleeves
arced through the air like rainbows. She spun like a feather being tossed
on the wind, and she seemed so light as to be almost insubstantial, like
mist or fog. It was all so delightful that Gongsun Qian and Yiren were
completely bewitched. They sat there in a trance, their mouths agape,
sighing with admiration. When Zhao Ji had finished dancing, Lü Buwei
ordered her to pour large goblets of wine and toast everyone again. His
two guests drained their cups in a single draft. When she had finished
serving them wine, Zhao Ji withdrew into the women's quarters. The
host and guests continued to drink, enjoying themselves very much.

Gongsun Qian got very drunk indeed and fell asleep where he sat.
Royal Grandson Yiren was thinking about Zhao Ji. Pretending to be
much drunker than he really was, he said to Lü Buwei, "I wish you
would give her to me as my wife—after all, I am here as a hostage on
my own and I spend my time alone. Having her would make me very
happy. I don't know how much it would cost to buy her. I would refund
you however much you spent on her in the first place."

Lü Buwei pretended to be angry, and said, "I invited you here and
had my womenfolk come out to meet you because I wanted to show
you my respect. How can you try and steal her from me?"

Yiren was very uncomfortable at the direction the conversation
had taken. Falling to his knees, he said, "Since I am so lonely in my
present situation, I was so desperate that I actually considered trying
to take your concubine away from you! Treat it as drunken babbling
. . . Please don't be angry!"

Lü Buwei rushed forward and helped him to his feet. He said, "In
order to make it possible for you to go home, I have spent every penny
of my family's wealth without regret. Why should I begrudge you a
woman? However, she is very young and easily embarrassed, so I am
afraid that she will not simply do your bidding. If she is willing, I will
escort her to your residence so she can serve in your bedchamber."

Yiren bowed twice and expressed thanks. He waited until Gongsun Qian had woken from his drunken stupor, and then the two of them went home in their carriage.

That night, Lü Buwei said to Zhao Ji, "The royal grandson from Qin loves you very much and would like to marry you. What do you think?"

"I have already lost my virginity to you," Zhao Ji said, "and I am carrying your baby—how could I leave you to marry someone else?"

"If you spend the rest of your life with me, you will never be more than the wife of a merchant," Lü Buwei hinted. "However, the royal grandson will be king of Qin one day. If you obtain his favor, you will certainly become his queen. If the baby you are carrying is a boy, he will naturally become crown prince. You and I will then be the father and mother of a future king of Qin, and we will be rich and powerful beyond our wildest dreams. If you have ever really loved me, then please follow my advice, but do not let anyone know what we are doing!"

"Your plan is indeed a great one," Zhao Ji said. "How could I dare to refuse to carry it out? However, given that we love each other, it is difficult indeed to be parted!" As she spoke she began to cry.

Lü Buwei soothed her: "As long as you love me, in the future when Qin is ours, we can still be husband and wife, this time never to be parted. Wouldn't that be wonderful?" The two of them then swore a solemn oath and then spent the night together with redoubled affection, which does not need to be described.

· · ·

The following day, Lü Buwei went to visit Gongsun Qian, to apologize for treating him rudely the night before.

"Actually," Gongsun Qian explained, "the Royal Grandson and I were just about to go to your residence to thank you for yesterday's entertainment. You really didn't need to come here in person." A short time later, Yiren came in and the two of them expressed their gratitude.

"Your Royal Highness was kind enough to mention that you did not think my concubine too ugly and that you would like her to serve you," Lü Buwei said. "I have spoken to her about it and she has already agreed. Today is a suitably auspicious day, and so I am going to escort her here immediately."

"Even if you ground my bones to powder," Yiren declared, "it would be difficult for me to repay you!"

"If there is going to be a marriage," Gongsun Qian said happily, "I will be the official matchmaker!" He ordered his servants to prepare a wedding banquet. Lü Buwei bade them farewell and left. That evening, he sent Zhao Ji round in a closed carriage, and she began her life with the Royal Grandson Yiren.

An old man wrote a poem:

> In an instant a new fancy or an old love may be snuffed out;
> When the candles in the bridal chamber gutter it is time to enjoy
>   oneself.
> When this scion of the royal house stole the throne,
> Who could have known it was for the son of Lü Buwei?

When Royal Grandson Yiren obtained Zhao Ji, he was extremely happy and loved her very much. After they had been together for about a month, Zhao Ji told him, "Since I have been lucky enough to serve you, I have become pregnant with your child." Yiren did not know the ins and outs of this and thought that this was his own child, so he was even more delighted. Zhao Ji married Yiren when she was two months pregnant, so she was expecting to give birth to the baby at nine months. However, time passed and nothing happened. Given that she was pregnant with the future First Emperor of China—a man who would change the destiny of the world—it is not surprising that his birth was heralded by unusual signs. So it was not until one year after she became pregnant that she finally gave birth to a baby boy. When he was born, a glowing red light filled the room and a myriad of birds came flapping in to view the baby. At birth he had a prominent nose and large eyes, a square forehead, and double pupils. He had already cut a couple of teeth, and there was a pattern like the scales of a dragon on his back. When he began to scream, the sound was so loud that it could be heard throughout the entire city. He was born on New Year's Day in the forty-eighth year of the reign of his great-grand-father, King Zhaoxiang of Qin.

The Royal Grandson Yiren was thrilled and said, "I have heard that someone who will achieve remarkable things is always heralded by strange signs at the time of their birth. This child has a most unusual appearance and he is born on New Year's Day—in the future it will be he who rules a united China." He named the baby Zheng, or "United Rule." Later on Zheng did indeed become the king of Qin. He unified the other six kingdoms and became the First Emperor of China. Of course, when Lü Buwei heard that Zhao Ji had given birth to a boy, he too was secretly delighted.

· · ·

In the fiftieth year of the reign of King Zhaoxiang of Qin, Zheng turned three years old. At this time the Qin troops were pressing ever closer in their siege of Handan. Lü Buwei said to Yiren, "The king of Zhao might well try to take his anger out upon you again, Your Royal Highness! What are you going to do? You had better run away to the kingdom of Qin to get away from all of this."

"I will do whatever you suggest, sir," the Royal Grandson Yiren said.

Lü Buwei collected a total of six hundred pounds of gold. He used three hundred pounds to bribe the general in command of guarding the South Gate. The following message was attached: "My family originally comes from Yangdi. We came here on business, but unluckily we got caught up in the siege by the Qin army which has dragged on for many days. I really miss my home, and I have now given you every last penny to distribute among your men. I hope you will help me by letting my family leave the city and go back to Yangdi. I will never forget this kindness!"

The general agreed to let him go. Lü Buwei presented another one hundred pounds of gold to Gongsun Qian and announced that he was going home to Yangdi. He said that he wanted Gongsun Qian to talk to the officers at the South Gate on his behalf. Since the general, officers, and men had already been bribed, they were happy to agree. Lü Buwei told Royal Grandson Yiren that he should secretly make arrangements to send Zhao Ji and the baby to live with her parents.

On the appointed day, he held a banquet for Gongsun Qian. He said, "I am going to be leaving the city in three days' time. I am holding this party to say goodbye!" He made sure that Gongsun Qian got so drunk that he could not move. The soldiers and guards present all ate and drank to their hearts' content until they were so stuffed that they simply went to sleep. At midnight, the Royal Grandson Yiren mingled with the other servants, dressed in simple clothes, to follow Lü Buwei and his father as they walked out of the South Gate. The general there, not knowing what was really going on, unlocked the gate and let them out of the city. In actual fact, the Qin army's main camp was located outside the West Gate. However, because the South Gate was on the road to Yangdi and Lü Buwei was claiming that he wanted to go home, he had to leave that way. The three men and their servants raced through the night in a wide circle, trying to make their way over to the Qin army.

At dawn, they were taken prisoner by a party of Qin soldiers out on patrol. Lü Buwei pointed to Yiren and said, "This is a Royal Grandson from Qin who has been held hostage in Zhao. He has managed to escape from Handan and is on his way home. You had better do everything in your power to help him!"

The patrol got off their horses to let the three men ride and took them to the main camp. When the general there heard who they were, he invited them to come in and have an audience. He gave Yiren a suitable hat and robe to change into and held a banquet in his honor.

"His Majesty is here to view our progress in person," he said. "His traveling palace is not ten *li* from here." He prepared a carriage and horses and had them escorted there.

When King Zhaoxiang saw Yiren, he could not contain his delight. "The crown prince misses you day and night," he said. "Heaven has enabled you to escape from the tiger's jaws! You must go back to Xianyang immediately, so that your parents can stop worrying about you!"

Yiren said goodbye to the king of Qin. He got into a carriage with Lü Buwei and his father and headed for Xianyang. Someone had already reported this development to the crown prince, the Lord of Anguo. He said to Lady Huayang, "My son has arrived." The two of them took their seats in the main hall to wait for him.

"Lady Huayang is originally from the kingdom of Chu," Lü Buwei said to Yiren, "and you are just about to be adopted as her son. You must wear Chu dress when you go to see her, to show how affectionately you feel towards her."

The Royal Grandson Yiren followed this advice and immediately changed his clothes. When he arrived at the East Palace, he bowed first to the Lord of Anguo and then to Her Ladyship. With tears running down his face, he said, "I feel deeply unfilial for having been separated so long from my family—I could do nothing to show my love and affection to you. I hope that you can forgive me!"

Her Ladyship noticed that Yiren was wearing a Chu hat on his head and boots made from wildcat fur, while his robe had short sleeves and his belt was made of leather. She was very surprised, and exclaimed: "You have been living in Handan! Why are you dressed like someone from Chu?"

Yiren bowed and said, "I have missed you day and night, Mother, and that is why I had a set of Chu clothes made specially to represent my love for you."

"I am originally from the kingdom of Chu," Lady Huayang said happily. "Of course you are my son!"

"In the future, my boy," the Lord of Anguo said, "you can take the name of Prince Chu."

Yiren bowed and thanked him. The Lord of Anguo went on to ask, "How were you able to come home?"

The prince explained how the king of Zhao had wanted to execute him and how he had been saved by Lü Buwei's spending his entire fortune on bribes. The Lord of Anguo summoned Lü Buwei and spoke kindly to him: "If it were not for you, sir, my wise and filial son might well have been killed! Let me reward you with two hundred acres of farmland from the estates attached to the East Palace, a mansion, and fifty ingots of gold to keep the wolf from the door. When His Majesty returns to his kingdom, I am sure that you will receive even greater titles and emoluments."

Lü Buwei thanked the crown prince for his kindness and withdrew. Afterwards, Prince Chu moved into Lady Huayang's palace.

. . .

When King Zhaoxiang of Qin died, Lord Anguo came to the throne. Three days later, he was dead, poisoned by Lü Buwei. Then Prince Chu came to the throne as King Zhuangxiang, and Zheng became crown prince. King Zhuangxiang was on the throne for three years, and then he too was murdered by Lü Buwei to allow his own son to become king of Qin. At this time, the king of Qin's younger half-brother, Ying Chengjiao, the Lord of Chang'an, was seventeen years old and had just been appointed to a military command. He knew nothing about warfare, and so when his orders arrived, he summoned General Fan Wuqi to discuss the matter. Fan Wuqi loathed Lü Buwei for having seized control of the country by astutely presenting a concubine to the king, so having asked permission to send away all the servants, he told His Lordship all that had happened in considerable detail: "His Present Majesty is not in fact the son of the late king—you are the legitimate heir to the throne. If Lü Buwei has put you in command of the army, it is because he harbors evil intentions towards you. No doubt he is afraid that if the truth comes out, you will try and get rid of our present monarch. That is why he pretends to favor and promote you, when in fact what he is trying to do is to get rid of you. Lü Buwei goes in and out of the place without any let or hindrance; he and the queen dowager are continuing their adulterous relationship: the whole family is in this together! The only person they are afraid of is you, my lord. If you are lucky, you will merely find yourself stripped of all your honors. If you are unlucky, you are going to be executed. Henceforward the kingdom of Qin will be ruled by the Lü family! Everyone in the capital knows that this is true. You must make plans to deal with the situation!"

"If you had not told me," the Lord of Chang'an said, "I would not know anything about this. What should I do?"

"You have a fine army under your command," Fan Wuqi declared. "If you were to circulate placards proclaiming the crime committed by these wicked people and exposing the imposture practiced on His Late Majesty, what loyal subject of Qin would fail to support you as the rightful heir to the throne?"

His Lordship drew his sword, flushing bright red with excitement. "For a man, death is nothing!" he exclaimed. "How can I bend the knee before the son of a mere merchant? I hope that you will help me get rid of these people!"

Fan Wuqi then drafted the text for these placards:

The Lord of Chang'an announces the following to the people: Within any monarchy, a guaranteed succession within a single family is of paramount importance; any attempt to overthrow the ruling house is a crime of the blackest kind. The Marquis of Wenxin, Lü Buwei, was originally a merchant from Yangdi, but now he is the uncrowned king in Xianyang—this is because our present king, Zheng, is not the son and heir of His Late Majesty but Lü Buwei's own child! He began by presenting a pregnant concubine to seduce the late king, and now we have ended up under the rule of a wicked impostor. The bloodline of our kings has been sullied! He has used his gold to buy his way into power, and his ultimate aim has always been to pervert the realm!

There is a reason why two of our kings died before their time—are we going to let him get away with it? He has been in power now through the reign of three monarchs: who will stop him? The man currently presiding over the court is not the real king; a member of the Lü family has been imposed on us as a royal Ying! His Majesty has given his real father enormous power—although he is officially merely a minister, in fact he governs the country. The state is in danger! The gods are angry! As the real heir to the throne, I want to punish these wicked men! Any soldier is welcome to join my righteous cause. Any member of the public can throw in his lot with mine, secure in the knowledge that by doing so, they are supporting the Ying house. When you see this text, prepare your weapons, hitch up your chariots, and come and join me!

Fan Wuqi had the text circulated in all directions. There were many people in Qin who had heard the story of how Lü Buwei gained royal favor by presenting his concubine to His Majesty, but reading of how she had been pregnant at the time and given birth to an imposter prince, they believed that every word of it was true. The only reason they did not rise up was because they were too frightened of Lü Buwei. However, they were hoping that someone would get rid of him.

. . .

At this time a comet was sighted in the east, then it moved to the north, and finally to the west. Diviners said that this was an omen of a military uprising in the country. This caused people to become very nervous. Fan Wuqi recruited able-bodied young men from the counties close to Tunliu into his army and attacked the cities of Changzi and Huguan—his military might was visibly increasing. Zhang Tang realized that the Lord of Chang'an was now in open rebellion against the throne, and he rushed back to Xianyang under cover of darkness to report this uprising. When Zheng, king of Qin, saw the text of the placards, he was absolutely furious and summoned Lü Buwei to discuss the matter.

"The Lord of Chang'an is far too young to organize something like this," Lü Buwei pointed out. "It must be Fan Wuqi's doing. He is a brave man but pretty stupid. If you send the army out, Your Majesty, I am sure that you will be able to capture him alive. There is really nothing to worry about."

He appointed Wang Jian as the senior general, with Huan Yi and Wang Ben commanding the left and right vanguards. With a force of one hundred thousand men, they set off to put down the Lord of Chang'an's revolt. The Lord of Chang'an was terrified by this development.

"Your position today, my prince, is like a man riding a tiger," Fan Wuqi said. "Getting on is hard enough, but getting off is even worse. However, you have the forces of three cities at your disposal, an army of not less than one hundred and fifty thousand men. If they fight on home ground, it is not at all certain who will win and who will lose. There is nothing to be so frightened about!"

He arranged his troops into battle formation at the foot of the city walls and waited. Wang Jian put his troops into formation opposite him. He said to Fan Wuqi, "What has our country done to offend you that you incite the Lord of Chang'an to rebel?"

Fan Wuqi leaned out from his chariot and said, "The king of Qin is in actual fact the illegitimate son of Lü Buwei: everyone knows that! My family has worked for the government for generations—how can I just sit by and watch while everything that the Ying family built up with their own sweat and blood is stolen by the Lü family? The Lord of Chang'an is the true heir to our royal house, and that is why I am supporting him. If you still remember all that you owe to His Late Majesty, general, why don't you support this righteous cause and attack Xianyang, killing these wicked people and getting rid of the usurper? If you were to help the Lord of Chang'an to become king, you will certainly be enfeoffed as a marquis and enjoy great wealth and honor. Wouldn't that be wonderful?"

"The dowager queen was pregnant for an unusually long time when she gave birth to His Present Majesty, but he is certainly the son of our former king," Wang Jian retorted. "You have been spreading seditious rumors and illegally gathering troops—these are crimes that will see your entire family killed! Now you are trying to disturb the morale of my army with your wicked and baseless gossip. When I get my hands on you, I am going to rip you to pieces!"

Fan Wuqi was furious at this and opened his eyes wide as he bellowed with anger. Grabbing a long sword, he charged straight at the Qin army. When the soldiers saw his reckless courage, they simply could not withstand him. Fan Wuqi charged first to the left and then to the right, moving as if there were nobody else present on the field of battle. Wang Jian signaled to his troops to surround him. Although they did so on a number of occasions, each time Fan Wuqi was able to cut his way out. The Qin army suffered terrible losses.

In the evening, both sides recalled their troops. Wang Jian made camp at Mount Sangai. He thought to himself, "Fan Wuqi is a remarkably brave man, and it will be extremely difficult to deal with him. We need a plan to destroy him." He asked the people present in his command tent, "Is anyone here acquainted with the Lord of Chang'an?"

The junior general, Yang Duanhe, originally a native of Tunliu, said, "I used to be a member of the Lord of Chang'an's household."

"I am going to write a letter and give it to you," Wang Jian said. "I want you to take it to the Lord of Chang'an. It will urge him to surrender to the court before he gets himself killed."

"How am I supposed to get into the city?" Yang Duanhe asked.

"You must wait until we are engaged in battle," Wang Jian instructed him. "You are to take advantage of the moment when they recall their troops to smuggle yourself into the city dressed as one of their soldiers. When the attack on the city has reached a critical point, you should go and ask for an audience with the Lord of Chang'an. That way, the situation will be sure to change in our favor."

Yang Duanhe agreed to follow this plan. Wang Jian then wrote out a letter in front of the assembled company and sealed it. This he handed over to Yang Duanhe for him to keep until the moment was ripe. Next he summoned Huan Yi and ordered him to take his army to attack the city of Changzi. Likewise, Wang Ben was commanded to lead his troops to attack the city of Huguan. Wang Jian himself would assault Tunliu, so that these three cities could be attacked simultaneously and one would not be able to go to the help of the others.

. . .

Fan Wuqi said to the Lord of Chang'an, "We must take advantage of the fact that they have divided their forces to win a decisive victory. Otherwise, if we lose Changzi and Huguan, the situation will move in favor of the Qin forces. In that case they will be much more difficult to defeat!"

The Lord of Chang'an was still little more than a child, and he was frightened. "You planned all of this, general," he sobbed, "and you are in charge. Please don't get me into trouble!"

Fan Wuqi selected an army of battle-hardened soldiers, one hundred thousand men strong. He opened the gates of the city and sent them out to fight. Wang Jian pretended to give way and withdrew ten *li*. He made camp at Mount Fulong. Fan Wuqi returned to the city in triumph. By this time, Yang Duanhe had managed to mingle with his troops, and he marched back in with them. Given that he was originally a native of this city, it was easy for him to find a relative who would give him a place to stay.

On his return, the Lord of Chang'an asked Fan Wuqi, "If Wang Jian does not withdraw his army, what are we going to do?"

"Today's battle has already blunted their ardor," the general replied. "Tomorrow I am going to take my entire army out to fight, and our task will be to capture Wang Jian alive. Then we can march straight on Xianyang and put you on the throne. That is my greatest wish."

Do you want to know who won and who lost? READ ON.

Chapter Sixteen

Ai Lao uses a faked castration to bring the Qin palace to chaos.

Mao Jiao removes his clothes to remonstrate with the king of Qin.

Having withdrawn his army ten *li,* Wang Jian instructed them to build a huge rampart around the camp and dig deep ditches. Troops were dispatched to defend any points of danger, and they were not allowed to go out to fight under any circumstances. He sent twenty thousand soldiers to go and help Huan Yi and Wang Ben, to urge them to capture their objectives as soon as possible. Fan Wuqi sent out his whole army day after day, yet the Qin army simply did not respond. General Fan decided that Wang Jian must be frightened. Just as he was debating the possibility of dividing his army to go and rescue Changzi and Huguan, suddenly one of his mounted spies reported: "The two cities have already fallen to the Qin army!" Fan Wuqi was horrified. He immediately made camp outside the city, in order to encourage the Lord of Chang'an to feel some confidence.

When Huan Yi and Wang Ben were informed that Wang Jian had moved his camp to Mount Fulong, they took their troops there to join him. They said, "The two cities have already returned to the fold. We have left some of our soldiers there to guard them and maintain order."

"Tunliu is now isolated," Wang Jian said happily. "All we need to do now is to capture Fan Wuqi alive, and that will put an end to this matter."

Before he had even finished speaking, one of the soldiers guarding the camp reported: "General Xin Sheng is outside the gates to the encampment with an order from the king of Qin."

Wang Jian escorted him back to the command tent and asked the general why he had come.

"First, His Majesty is very mindful of the suffering his armies have experienced on this campaign, so he sent me here with special rewards for everyone," Xin Sheng explained. "Secondly, the king of Qin hates Fan Wuqi and asked me to take the following message to you: 'You must capture this man alive because I want to behead him with my own sword, to assuage my anger!'"

"Since you are here, general," Wang Jian remarked, "you could be very useful!" He ordered the rewards to be distributed among his troops. Then he commanded Huan Yi and Wang Ben to each take their army and lie in ambush on either side. He instructed Xin Sheng to take five thousand cavalry and go forward to provoke battle, while he himself took the main body of the army to get ready to attack the city.

· · ·

When the Lord of Chang'an heard that they had lost the cities of Changzi and Huguan, he sent someone to summon Fan Wuqi back to the city immediately to discuss the situation.

"Any minute now, we are going to have to fight the decisive battle," Fan Wuqi said. "If we lose, I will take you north to seek sanctuary in Zhao or Yan, creating an alliance among the other kings to launch a joint attack on Qin and execute the usurper! That way we can bring peace to the kingdom."

"Please be careful!" the Lord of Chang'an whimpered.

Fan Wuqi went back to his encampment. One of the mounted spies reported: "The king of Qin has recently appointed a new general, Xin Sheng, and he is on his way here to provoke battle."

"He is a poor strategist of no particular repute," Fan Wuqi sneered. "I will get rid of him straightaway."

He led his army out of the encampment and went forward to engage with Xin Sheng's troops. Having fought a couple of encounters, Xin Sheng started to pull back. Fan Wuqi charged forward recklessly. He had gone about five *li* when Huan Yi and Wang Ben ordered their troops waiting in ambush into action. Fan Wuqi suffered a terrible defeat and turned his army back as quickly as he could. However, by that time Wang Jian's troops were already in position at the foot of the walls of Tunliu. Fan Wuqi hurled himself into battle, cutting a bloody swathe through the enemy forces. When the defenders on the city walls opened the gates to let him in, Wang Jian brought all his troops together to besiege the city, and the fighting reached a new peak of ferocity. Fan Wuqi patrolled the walls day and night, without the slightest sign of exhaustion.

At this time, Yang Duanhe was already in place inside the city. Realizing that the situation was now critical, he went under cover of darkness to ask for an audience with the Lord of Chang'an: "I have something top secret to inform His Lordship."

When the Lord of Chang'an discovered that his visitor was a former member of his household, he happily called him in. Yang Duanhe had the servants sent away, and then he said, "You know how strong the Qin army is, my lord. Even the forces of the other six states combined cannot defeat them. If you are determined to fight them all on your own, you are bound to get into serious trouble!"

"Fan Wuqi says that His Majesty is not actually the son of the late king," the Lord of Chang'an said. "He got me into this. It was not my idea."

"Fan Wuqi is very brave, but also very stupid, and he does not seem to care how many people he gets killed," Yang Duanhe said. "That is why he has dragged you into this mess. Although he has circulated his placards round every county and commandery, there has been no response. General Wang Jian is now attacking the city very fiercely. When the city falls, do you think you will be able to survive?"

"I was thinking of running away to Yan or Zhao and creating an alliance with them," the Lord of Chang'an explained. "Do you think that would work?"

"Tell me," Yang Duanhe demanded, "which of the six kingdoms is not afraid of Qin? Whichever country you go to, when Qin asks for you to be extradited, they will arrest you and hand you over. In such circumstances, how can you hope to stay alive?"

"What do you think I should do?" the Lord of Chang'an asked.

"General Wang knows that you have been led astray by Fan Wuqi. He wrote a secret missive and asked me to give it to you."

He presented this to His Lordship, and Ying Chengjiao, the Lord of Chang'an, broke the seal and read it:

> Your Lordship is the brother of His Majesty the king, and you hold the title of a Marquis of Qin. Why are you listening to malicious gossip and

getting involved in matters that are much more serious than you can possibly understand? You have brought disaster down upon yourself, and I find this very regrettable. However, we all know that the architect of this misery is Fan Wuqi. If you can execute him and present his head to the army, while submitting to arrest yourself, I promise that I will speak up on your behalf to His Majesty. If you fail to do this immediately, the consequences will be on your own head!

When the Lord of Chang'an read this, he burst into tears. Weeping, he said, "Fan Wuqi is a loyal and upright gentleman. How could I bear to kill him?"

Yang Duanhe sighed and said, "That is what is known as being as weak as a woman. If you are not going to do what you are told, I am going to leave."

"I want you to stay with me for the time being," the Lord of Chang'an whimpered. "Do not go far away! You are going to have to wait for me to think about what you have said and then we will speak again."

"Don't tell anyone what we have been talking about!" Yang Duanhe instructed him.

The next day, Fan Wuqi drove his chariot to the palace to have an audience with the Lord of Chang'an. "The Qin army is very powerful and the people are panicking," he explained. "The city will fall any day now. Let us go into exile in Yan or Zhao. Once we are in a place of safety, we can think about what to do next."

"My family is all in Xianyang," the Lord of Chang'an said. "If we now go far away to live in some foreign country, will they take us in?"

"Other countries have suffered a great deal from Qin's violent attacks," Fan Wuqi told him. "You do not need to worry about whether they will take us in or not!"

Just as they were talking, a report came in: "The Qin troops by the South Gate are trying to provoke battle!" Fan Wuqi tried repeatedly to make him hurry up: "If you don't go now, Your Highness, you will not be able to leave." The Lord of Chang'an hesitated, unable to make up his mind.

Fan Wuqi had no choice but to strap his sword to his side and get onto his chariot, speeding in the direction of the South Gate. Having made his way out of the city, he fought yet another engagement there with the Qin army. Yang Duanhe encouraged the Lord of Chang'an to climb up onto the walls and watch the progress of the battle. All he could see was that Fan Wuqi was fighting desperately and the Qin army was pressing ever closer. Since General Fan could not resist the enemy onslaught, he raced back to the city, shouting, "Open the gates!" Yang Duanhe was standing next to the Lord of Chang'an, brandishing his sword. He shouted back, "His Lordship has already surrendered the city! You are on your own now, General Fan! Anyone who dares to open the city gates will be beheaded!" He took a flag out of his sleeve— on it was the word "Surrender." Since His Lordship's servants were all old friends of Yang Duanhe, they immediately ran this flag up the pole, without so much as waiting for a sign of assent from the Lord of Chang'an. He just stood there weeping.

"There is no point in trying to help a weakling!" Fan Wuqi said with a sigh.

By this time, the Qin troops had encircled him in several concentric rings. As the king of Qin had specifically ordered them to capture him alive, they did not dare to simply shoot him full of arrows. Fan Wuqi hacked a bloodstained path through the surrounding soldiery and headed off for exile in Yan. Even though Wang Jian pursued him, he did not catch up with him. Yang Duanhe ordered the Lord of Chang'an to open the gates and allow the Qin army into the city. While His Lordship was held prisoner in the official guesthouse, Xin Sheng went back to Xianyang to report news of the victory to His Majesty and ask what he wanted done with the Lord of Chang'an. The dowager queen of Qin went to see His Majesty with her hair unbound, begging for clemency to be extended to His Lordship. She also pleaded with Lü Buwei to speak up for him.

"If this traitor is not punished," the king of Qin said crossly, "I am going to find my whole family plotting against me!"

He sent an envoy to order Wang Jian to have the Lord of Chang'an publicly beheaded at Tunliu. All the Qin soldiers and officials who had joined in his rebellion were to be executed. The entire population of the city was to be moved to Linzhao. He also put a price on Fan Wuqi's head—anyone who captured him alive would be rewarded with a fief of five cities. When the envoy arrived in Tunliu with the king of Qin's orders, the Lord of Chang'an heard that he would not be pardoned, so he hanged himself in the guesthouse. Wang Jian ordered that the head be cut off the corpse and suspended above the city gate. Tens of thousands of soldiers and officials were also executed. Then the inhabitants of the city were forced to move, leaving Tunliu entirely empty. This happened in the seventh year of the reign of Zheng, King of Qin.

An old man wrote a poem about this:

When your fields are invaded by weeds, it is right to reach for the hoe.
Nevertheless, it is a good idea to consider the bigger picture.
The siege of Tunliu changed nothing for the better,
Yet the punishments meted out to those involved would fill a book.

· · ·

Let us now turn to another part of the story. Thanks to his sexual prowess and military air, Lü Buwei was much loved by Dowager Queen Zhuangxiang. He came and went from the women's quarters of the palace without the slightest hindrance. When he realized that the king of Qin had grown up and was very clever, he started to get frightened. However, there was nothing that he could do about the fact that Dowager Queen Zhuangxiang was becoming more and more lecherous and would summon him at all hours of the day and night to come to the Sweet Springs Palace. Lü Buwei was worried that if one day their affair came to light he would be in serious trouble. He wanted to present someone to Her Majesty to replace himself, but finding someone who would satisfy her requirements was not so easy. He heard that there was a man working in the marketplace called Lao Da who was famous for the huge size of his penis. He was the object of much fighting among the lascivious local women. In the Qin language, a person who acted immorally was called *Ai*, and so this man was known to everyone as Lao Ai. When Lao Ai came to the attentions of the authorities thanks to his adulterous affairs, Lü Buwei pardoned him and took him into his household as a retainer. It was the custom in the kingdom of Qin to celebrate for three days after the end of the harvest, to mark the end of their labor. This was also a time when all kinds of different entertainers would ply their trade. Anyone with any skill, who could do something that others could not, would show it off during these three days. Lü Buwei had a wheel made of paulownia wood and ordered Lao Ai to stick his penis through the hole in the middle. Even though the chariot wheel spun round, his penis suffered no injury. This made the people in the marketplace fall about laughing. The dowager queen heard about it and made discreet inquiries of Lü Buwei—she seemed most interested.

"Would you like to meet this man, Your Majesty?" Lü Buwei asked. "I can make time to arrange it."

The dowager queen giggled and did not reply. Then after a long pause, she said, "Surely you are joking. How can an outsider possibly enter the palace?"

"I have a plan," Lü Buwei said. "I will get someone to rake up his old crimes and condemn him to castration. If you then bribe the executioner, Your Majesty, he will pretend to carry out the castration, and after that, Lao Ai can enter the palace as a eunuch working here. That way, you can enjoy him on a long-term basis."

"That is a wonderful plan!" the dowager queen exclaimed happily.

She gave Lü Buwei one hundred pieces of gold. He then secretly summoned Lao Ai and told him what was intended. Lao Ai was a man with strong sexual urges, who was naturally happy to pleasure a lady of such high rank. Lü Buwei ordered someone to accuse him of adultery yet again, and this time he was condemned to castration. The one hundred pieces of gold were given to the executioner and other officials, who used a donkey's penis and its blood to pretend that the penalty had indeed been carried out. They plucked his beard to make him look like a eunuch. Meanwhile, the executioner arranged for the donkey's penis to be put on show so that everyone would believe that Lao Ai had indeed been castrated. Everyone who heard news of these events was most surprised. Having undergone this faked castration and had his appearance changed so that he looked like a eunuch, Lao Ai joined the other palace servants. The dowager queen had him allocated to her palace and ordered him to serve her overnight. She was very satisfied with the experience and thought him ten times better as a lover than Lü Buwei. The following day, she gave lavish rewards to Lü Buwei to thank him for all his hard work. He, on the other hand, was simply happy to have escaped.

The dowager queen lived with Lao Ai as if they were man and wife. When she got pregnant, she was afraid that she would not be able to keep it a secret, and so she announced that she was ill. She instructed Lao Ai to bribe a diviner with gold, and he said that the palace had become infested with evil spirits and the dowager queen needed to go at least two hundred *li* to the west to get away from them. The king of

Qin was very unhappy about his mother's relationship with Lü Buwei, so he was delighted to see her gradually spending less and less time with him. He wanted to put a complete stop to their relationship, so he said, "Yongzhou is located two hundred *li* to the west of Xianyang. The palaces and halls are still well-maintained from when it was the capital of Qin. You can go and live there."

So it happened that the dowager queen traveled to Yongzhou in a carriage driven by Lao Ai. Having left Xianyang, they moved into the former royal palace known as the Dazheng Palace. Lao Ai and the dowager queen were now able to give free rein to their affection. In the space of two years, Her Majesty gave birth to two sons. She constructed a secret room where they were brought up. Her Majesty and Lao Ai agreed that when the king of Qin died, they would make one of their own children his successor. Although some people knew about this, they were too frightened to speak. The dowager queen claimed that Lao Ai had looked after her wonderfully when her son could not, and so he ought to be given an enfeoffment. The king of Qin could hardly refuse his mother's request, and so he invested Lao Ai as the Marquis of Changxin and gave him the lands of Shanyang.

Once Lao Ai had received this noble title, he became more and more arrogant and overbearing. Leaving on one side the gifts Her Majesty gave him every day, he went hunting or partying as the mood took him, using the palace, its contents, the chariots and horses as if they were his own personal belongings. Every matter, large or small, was decided by him. He had a household staff of several thousand people, not to mention the thousand and more men who had come to him in the hope of gaining an official position and agreed to remain as his retainers. He bribed many nobles and court officials to join his faction, and anyone who wanted to become powerful tried to gain his support. In many ways he was even more powerful than Lü Buwei himself.

Every year, the king of Qin had to perform sacrifices according to the rules laid down by his ancestors. Given that the dowager queen was living in Yongzhou, when the king went there for the suburban sacrifice, he would also go to see his mother. Once the ceremonies were over, he would stay at the Qi'nian Palace. Normally this sacrifice was performed in the spring, but this was changed because of the comet. When he was about to set off, His Majesty ordered General

Wang Jian to make sure the army was highly visible for the next three days in Xianyang, since he and Lü Buwei would be in charge of maintaining order in the capital. Huan Yi led thirty thousand men to make camp at Mount Qi. After this was done, His Majesty got into his chariot and set off.

At this time the king of Qin was already twenty-two years old, but he had not yet held the official capping ceremony that would mark his assumption of adulthood. The dowager queen gave orders that his capping ceremony would be held in the temple dedicated to Lord De, and she presented His Majesty with a fine sword. This was followed by five days of feasting for all the officials. The dowager queen joined His Majesty in hosting an enormous banquet at the Dazheng Palace. Perhaps it was because Lao Ai had enjoyed too much power and honor for too long that he brought trouble down upon himself. He had been betting and drinking with some of his cronies, and on the fourth day, it happened that he lost a whole series of bets, one after the other, with Grandee Yan Xie. He was drunk at the time and demanded that they start again from the beginning. Yan Xie—who was also drunk—refused. Lao Ai lunged forward and grabbed hold of Yan Xie, punching him in the face. Yan Xie refused to budge and managed to rip Lao Ai's hat off his head.

Lao Ai was furious. Glaring at the man, he yelled, "I am His Majesty's stepfather! How dare you fight with me, you pestiferous peasant!" Yan Xie was frightened and ran away. Purely by chance, he bumped straight into the king of Qin, who was leaving the palace after drinking a few toasts to his mother. Yan Xie threw himself on the ground and kowtowed, weeping and proclaiming that he deserved the death penalty. The king of Qin was not at all a stupid man. He did not say a word, but ordered his servants to pick him up and take him to the Qi'nian Palace where they could talk in private. Yan Xie informed His Majesty of how he had been punched in the face by Lao Ai, who had claimed to be the king's stepfather. He added, "Lao Ai is not really a eunuch. They pretended to castrate him and then he went to serve the dowager queen. They have two children who are living here in the palace. They have been plotting to usurp the throne."

When the king heard this, he was absolutely furious. He secretly sent someone with a military tally to summon Huan Yi, telling him to bring his troops to Yongzhou. However, the palace historian Si and Jie from the Palace Guard, two men who had received a great deal of money from Her Majesty and Lao Ai and hence were firm supporters of this precious pair, knew what was going on and rushed to Lao Ai's mansion to tell him all about it.

By this time Lao Ai had recovered from his drinking bout, and he was horrified. That night, he went to the Dazheng Palace to ask the dowager queen for an audience. He informed her of what had happened: "In the circumstances we had better assemble all our own guards and retainers to attack the Qi'nian Palace before Huan Yi arrives with his army. If we kill His Majesty, we will be able to survive this crisis."

"Will the palace guards obey my command?" she asked.

"Give me your seal!" Lao Ai demanded. "We can pretend that it is the proper royal one. Our excuse is going to be that the Qi'nian Palace has been attacked by rebels and His Majesty wants the palace guards to go and rescue him. They will have to obey."

The dowager queen was too flustered to understand quite what it was she was agreeing to. "Do so!" she said, handing her personal seal to Lao Ai. He then forged a document purporting to be from the king of Qin, to which he affixed the dowager queen's seal. Armed with this, he had the palace guards summoned. That his own retainers rushed to do his bidding goes without saying. The rebellion was set for the following day at noon. When everyone had assembled, Lao Ai, the palace historian Si, and Jie from the Palace Guard led their men to surround the Qi'nian Palace. The king of Qin climbed a tower and asked them what they were doing. They replied, "Lao Ai, Marquis of Changxin, says that the palace is under attack by rebels. We came here to rescue Your Majesty."

"It is the Marquis of Changxin that is the rebel," His Majesty retorted. "How could there be any trouble here at the palace?"

When the various divisions of the palace guard heard this, half of them simply went home. The other half showed their mettle by turning around and attacking Lao Ai and his retainers.

The king of Qin issued the following order: "Anyone who captures Lao Ai alive will be rewarded with one million pieces of gold. Anyone who kills him and brings me his head will be rewarded with five hundred thousand pieces of gold. Anyone who takes the head of a rebel will be promoted one grade. Whether you are commoner or slave, the rewards will be the same."

When this was announced, a number of eunuchs and stable boys rushed out to join the fray. When the people of Yongzhou heard that Lao Ai had rebelled, they too came running with whatever weapons they had at hand. Several hundred of Lao Ai's retainers were killed. When he realized that his men had been defeated, he forced his way out of the East Gate of the city, massacring anyone in his way. That meant that he ran straight into Huan Yi and his army coming the other way. Lao Ai was taken prisoner together with the palace historian and Jie of the Palace Guard. When they were thrown into prison, the truth quickly came out under interrogation. The king of Qin went in person to search of the Dazheng Palace. He found the secret chamber in which Lao Ai's two illegitimate children lived, and he had his servants put them in a sack and beat them to death. The dowager queen was devastated but did not dare to try and save them—she just shut herself up in her own chambers and wept. The king of Qin did not attempt to see his mother, but returned to the Qi'nian palace.

The officials from the prison presented Lao Ai's confession: "Lao Ai entered the palace after a faked castration. This was all planned by the Marquis of Wenxin, Lü Buwei. Lao Ai had more than twenty coconspirators, including the palace historian Si and Jie from the Palace Guard."

The king of Qin ordered that Lao Ai be pulled to pieces by chariots outside the East Gate of the city of Yongzhou. In addition, every member of his family to the third generation was put to death. The palace historian Si, Jie from the Palace Guard, and their ilk were all beheaded in public as a warning to others. Their retainers and everyone else who had fought for the rebels were to be executed. Those who had not actually participated personally in the rebellion but knew about it were exiled to Sichuan: that comprised some four thousand families. Since the dowager queen had allowed her personal seal to be used by the rebels, she could no longer remain the Mother of the Country. She was stripped of her titles and emoluments and sent to live at the Yuyang Palace.

This was the very smallest of the Qin traveling palaces.

Three hundred soldiers were detailed to guard her, and if anyone entered or left the palace, they were subject to searching inquiries. From this time onwards, the dowager queen was a prisoner. What a terrible fate!

An anonymous poem describes this:

For the Mother of the Country to have an affair is shocking enough;
She flaunted the two children born from this second relationship.
In spite of blatantly flouting the laws of Qin, she hoped to keep this a
secret;
By keeping within the women's quarters, she thought nobody would
know.

When the king of Qin had put down Lao Ai's rebellion, he returned to Xianyang. Lü Buwei was afraid of being punished, so he pretended to be ill because he did not dare to go to court. The king wanted to execute him and asked his ministers for their opinion. Many of the ministers were close friends of Lü Buwei, and so they all said, "He played a crucial role in putting His Late Majesty on the throne, and he has done great things in the service of our country. Furthermore, there is no evidence to support Lao Ai's accusations. You cannot condemn him on the basis of mere gossip."

The king of Qin accordingly pardoned Lü Buwei and did not execute him, but he did strip him of his office as prime minister and took away his seal of office. Since Huan Yi had done so well in capturing the traitors alive, he was given a larger fief and promoted. In the fourth month of this year, it suddenly became very cold and snow fell, resulting in many people freezing to death. The people all said, "The king of Qin has disowned the dowager queen, which means that a son has turned against his own mother. That is why we are afflicted by such abnormal weather."

Grandee Chen Zhong stepped forward and remonstrated: "There is nobody in this world who does not have a mother. You should bring Her Majesty back to Xianyang and continue treating her with filial piety. Things will then return to normal in a couple of days."

The king of Qin was furious. He ordered that Chen Zhong be stripped of his clothes and thrown on top of a heap of brambles. There he was beaten to death. Finally, he had his body hung from one of the palace watchtowers with the following message attached: "If there is anyone else who wants to speak up for the dowager queen, look at this!" Nevertheless, a procession of people wanting to remonstrate with His Majesty continued to arrive. The king of Qin immediately had them executed and put their bodies on display at the watchtower.

In all, twenty-seven people were killed in this way, and their corpses were piled up in a great heap.

. . .

It just so happened that at this time there was a man named Mao Jiao, originally from Cangzhou, who was visiting Xianyang. He was staying in a hostel, and the other people residing there chatted about this whole situation. Mao Jiao was appalled: "For a son to imprison his mother means that everything is topsy-turvy!"

He asked the owner of the hostel to heat some water. "I am going to have a bath, and then, tomorrow morning, I will go to the palace to remonstrate with the king of Qin."

The other people staying at the same hostel laughed and said, "The twenty-seven men who died were all trusted ministers. The king of Qin wouldn't listen to them and so they were killed one after the other. What do you think a commoner like yourself can achieve?"

"If nobody goes to remonstrate," Mao Jiao retorted, "the king of Qin will certainly not listen. If somebody does go, even though his twenty-seven predecessors have failed, it does not mean that the king of Qin will refuse to listen to him." The other men all mocked his stupidity.

The following morning, Mao Jiao asked the hostel owner for a full meal. The man grabbed onto his clothes to try and stop him from going, but Mao Jiao wrenched himself free and left. The other residents were sure that he was going to get himself killed, so they stared dividing up his clothes and baggage among themselves. When Mao Jiao arrived at the watchtower, he threw himself down next to the pile of corpses and shouted, "My name is Mao Jiao, and I come from the kingdom of Qi. I am here to remonstrate with His Majesty."

The king of Qin sent one of his eunuchs out to ask, "What do you want to remonstrate with His Majesty about? Is it something other than the dowager queen?"

"It is exactly about that matter that I have come," he declared. The eunuch went in to report, "It is another one come to remonstrate about the dowager queen."

"How about you warn him about the pile of corpses?" the king of Qin said.

The eunuch said to Mao Jiao, "Do you not see all these dead bodies lying around the watchtower? Are you really not afraid to die?"

"I have heard that there are twenty-eight lunar lodges in the sky," Mao Jiao returned, "and when they are reborn on earth, they become righteous men. So far, His Majesty has killed twenty-seven of them, so he is still missing one. I have come here to make up the numbers. Everyone, saint and sinner, dies sooner or later, so what is there to be afraid of?"

The eunuch went back to report this. The king of Qin said angrily, "How dare this lunatic disobey my orders!" He looked at his entourage. "Why don't you boil up a cauldron of water in the courtyard and cook him alive? I am not going to let him leave a whole corpse to join the others at the foot of the watchtower! Why should he get to make up the numbers?"

The king of Qin sat down with his hand on his sword, looking deeply forbidding. The spittle flecked his mouth as he shouted with ungovernable rage: "Bring the madman in and cook him!" The eunuch went out to summon Mao Jiao. Mao Jiao deliberately adopted a very slow movement as he walked forward, showing not the slightest inclination to hurry. The eunuch tried to make him speed up, but Mao Jiao responded, "When I have audience with the king of Qin, he is going to kill me! What is wrong with letting me delay that a bit?" The eunuch felt sorry for him and put a hand under his arm to help him along.

When Mao Jiao reached the steps, he bowed twice, kowtowed, and presented his opinion: "I have heard that every living thing must die sooner or later; every country will collapse at some point; and that once dead, you cannot return to life. An enlightened ruler thinks carefully about life and death, survival and collapse. I do not know whether Your Majesty is interested in this kind of subject or not."

The king of Qin was already looking somewhat calmer, and asked, "Do you have something that you want to say to me?"

"A loyal vassal does not fill his ruler's ears with empty flattery," Mao Jiao replied, "and an enlightened ruler does not do stupidly reckless things. If the ruler does something foolish and his vassals do not remonstrate, it means they have betrayed him. If his vassals give him loyal advice and the ruler does not listen, then he has let them down. You, Your Majesty, have done a terrible thing, and yet you do not know it. I have loyal advice to give you, but you don't want to hear. I am afraid that from this point onwards, the kingdom of Qin faces serious trouble!"

The king of Qin was silent for a long time. He was clearly calming down from his earlier rage. "What exactly are you talking about?" he said. "I would like you to explain."

"Do you want to conquer the whole world?" Mao Jiao asked.

"I do!" the king of Qin told him.

"Today, the reason why so many people respect Qin is not because you are so militarily powerful," Mao Jiao said, "but because Your Majesty is the finest ruler in the world. As a result, loyal vassals and brave knights have flocked to the Qin court. Now you have had your stepfather ripped to pieces by chariots, which is not benevolent. You had your two half-brothers put into sacks and beaten to death, which shows that you are lacking in fraternal love. You have forced your mother to go and live in the Yuyang Palace, which demonstrates that you are not filial. What is more, you have executed the men who tried to remonstrate with you and put their bodies on display at the foot of the watchtower. This is the kind of thing done by the evil last kings of the Xia and the Shang dynasties! You may want to conquer the world, but if you carry on like this, how can you expect anyone to give their allegiance to you? In the past, the sage-king Shun served his wicked stepmother with exemplary filial love, and he ended up becoming the supreme ruler of the country. Evil King Jie killed Longguan Feng and wicked King Zhou tortured Prince Bigan to death, and so everyone rebelled against them. Although I knew that I would die if I spoke out, I am even more afraid that after I am dead, there will be nobody else who dares to remonstrate with Your Majesty. In that case flattery and malicious gossip will increase day by day, the loyal will find they have no way to make their voices heard, you will become increasingly alienated from your people, and the other kings will rebel against your authority. How sad! Qin was on the point of unifying the entire country, and yet this great work failed because of you! Since I have now finished what I want to say, let me be boiled to death!"

At this point, he stood up, took of his clothes, and ran towards the cauldron. The king of Qin rushed down into the courtyard and grabbed hold of Mao Jiao with his left hand. With his right hand, he waved to his entourage: "Take the cauldron away!"

"You have already circulated an order, Your Majesty, warning people not to remonstrate with you," Mao Jiao said. "If you don't kill me, you will be breaking your word."

The king of Qin ordered his staff to remove the warning notice and had his eunuchs assist Mao Jiao back into his clothes. He made him take a seat and apologized. "Those who remonstrated with me before just told me that I was wrong; they did not explain why it was important. Heaven sent you to me to clear my mind! How could I dare to refuse to listen to your advice?"

Mao Jiao bowed twice, stepped forward, and said: "If you have really paid attention to what I said, you ought to go and collect the queen dowager as quickly as you can. As for the bodies at the foot of the watchtower, these were all your loyal ministers. Please allow them to be given a decent burial."

The king of Qin immediately ordered his officials to collect the twenty-seven corpses. Afterwards, he had Mao Jiao drive him to Yongzhou.

Master Nan Ping wrote a historical poem about this:

As twenty-seven corpses lay in a heap,
Mao Jiao took off his clothes and ran towards the cauldron.
If the fates take a hand, however severe the crisis, you will not die.
His reputation for loyal advice will be honored for ten thousand
     generations.

When they arrived at the Yuyang Palace, His Majesty first gave orders that his presence be reported. Then, crawling forward on his knees, the king of Qin sought an audience with the dowager queen. He kowtowed and wept bitterly. His mother also burst into floods of tears. His Majesty presented Mao Jiao to the dowager queen. That evening, the king of Qin stayed overnight in the Yuyang Palace. The following day, he helped Her Majesty into a grand carriage and then set off in her wake, with an escort of one thousand chariots and ten thousand cavalry. A huge number of people followed on foot. Everyone who saw this procession praised His Majesty for his filial piety. When they returned to Xianyang, a banquet was held in the Sweet Springs Palace. The mother and son celebrated happily together. The dowager queen had wine served and toasted Mao Jiao. "It is entirely due to your efforts, sir," she said gratefully, "that I have been able to see my son again." The king of Qin appointed Mao Jiao as the Grand Tutor, with senior ministerial rank.

Zheng, king of Qin, remained concerned about the possibility that Lü Buwei would resume his affair with the dowager queen, so he made him leave the capital and sent him back to his original home country south of the Yellow River. When the various other kingdoms heard that the Marquis of Wenxin had returned, they each sent ambassadors to meet him and ask him to join their administrations as prime minister. These envoys formed a constant stream along the roads. The king of Qin then became worried that he might indeed be given high office in a foreign country, which would be disastrous for them, so he wrote the following letter and sent it to Lü Buwei:

> What did you achieve in the service of the Qin state that merited a fief of one hundred thousand households? What place did you hold in the Qin ruling house that you deserved the titles you received? Qin has been generous to you indeed! It is your fault that the Lao Ai rebellion ever happened; however, I could not bear to have you executed and allowed you to go back to your own country. You have failed to appreciate my gesture and opened communications with ambassadors of various foreign powers. Nevertheless, I am not proposing to mistreat you in any way. I am going to move you and your entire family to Sichuan, where the revenues of the city of Bei ought to be enough to support you in the style to which you have been accustomed for the rest of your life.

When Lü Buwei read this letter, he said angrily, "I bankrupted myself in order to put His Late Majesty on the throne—what service could be greater than that? The dowager queen was married to me before she ever served King Zhuangxiang and I got her pregnant, so the present king of Qin is my son—who could be more closely related? Has His Majesty really completely turned against me?" A short time later he sighed and said, "I put His Majesty on the throne in order to enrich myself, I plotted to usurp the throne for my son, I committed adultery with the king's wife, I murdered His Late Majesty, I put an end to the ancestral sacrifices of the Ying family—no wonder Heaven has decided that my time is at an end! I should have died years ago!" He put poison in a cup of wine and drained it to the dregs. There were many members of his household who had been treated with great kindness by their master, so they secretly conveyed his body out of the house and buried it at the foot of Mount Beimang, in the same grave at his wife.

Do you want to know what happened next? THE STORY CONTINUES . . .

The Assassins Strike

Chapter Seventeen

Tian Guang cuts his throat after recommending Jing Ke.

Having presented a map, Jing Ke's assassination attempt throws the Qin palace into chaos.

Let us now turn to another part of the story. After Crown Prince Dan of Yan returned home, his hatred of the king of Qin was so great that he spent every coin in his coffers to gain a great number of retainers, hoping to plot his revenge against him. He obtained the services of brave knights like Xia Fu and Song Yi, and he treated these men with the greatest generosity. There was also a man named Qin Wuyang. At the age of thirteen, he had killed an enemy in the marketplace in broad daylight, and nobody present had dared to move a muscle. The crown prince pardoned him for his crime and had him join his household. After the Qin general Fan Wuqi had angered His Majesty, he had fled for his life to Yan, hiding deep in the mountains. When he heard how much the crown prince appreciated men of honor, he came out and gave his allegiance to him. Crown Prince Dan treated him as a senior retainer. He built a castle east of the Yi River in which the general could reside: this was called the Fan Mansion.

The Grand Tutor, Ju Wu, remonstrated as follows: "Qin is a country of wolves and tigers. They are gulping down one kingdom after another. Even if you are one of their allies, they may still attack you, not to mention if you harbor one of their most wanted criminals! What you are doing is like stroking a dragon the wrong way—you are sure to get hurt! Why don't you send General Fan to attack the Xiongnu and put him out of the way? Then you can ally with the Three

Jins to the west, Chu and Qi to the south, and the Xiongnu to the north. In that case you might be able to withstand Qin."

"The plan that you have suggested, Grand Tutor, is one that would take years to bring into effect," Crown Prince Dan exclaimed. "I am in a hurry and cannot wait that long! Furthermore, General Fan came to me when he was at the very end of his tether—I helped him because I felt sorry for him. I am not proposing to abandon General Fan somewhere out in the desert because I am afraid of Qin's military might! Even if this decision brings about my own demise, I am not going to change my mind. I hope that you can come up with some other plan to help me."

"For a weak country like Yan to fight the mighty Qin is like throwing a feather onto a stove," Ju Wu declared. "Of course it is going to get burned up! Or you could say it is like throwing an egg against a rock— it is going to smash! I am a stupid and ignorant man and cannot possibly help Your Royal Highness come up with a sensible plan. However, I am acquainted with a certain Master Tian Guang. He is exceptionally clever and extremely brave, not to mention being a man of great learning. If you are determined to take on Qin, my prince, you could not do better than ask Master Tian for help."

"I have never been introduced to Master Tian," the crown prince said. "I would like you to arrange a meeting for me."

"Your wish is my command," Ju Wu said.

He immediately drove his carriage to Tian Guang's house and announced: "Crown Prince Dan feels great admiration for you, sir, and he would very much appreciate your advice. Please do not refuse!"

"The crown prince is a member of the royal family," Tian Guang said, "so I would not expect him to come here in person. However, if he does not mind the fact that I am of humble status and would still like to receive the benefits of my advice, I will go and see him. How could I dare to refuse?"

"The crown prince is very lucky that you are prepared to meet him!" Ju Wu said. He and Tian Guang then rode in the same carriage as they traveled to the crown prince's palace. When Crown Prince Dan heard that Tian Guang had arrived, he went out in person to greet him. Seizing the reins, His Royal Highness helped Tian Guang down from the chariot; retreating backwards before him, he bowed twice as a sign of respect. Kneeling down, he brushed off the seat where the master was to sit. Tian Guang, now an old man, hobbled forward to the seat of honor. Those watching were all trying to stifle their laughter.

The crown prince sent his servants away and then stood up from his seat to speak. "In the situation in which we find ourselves today, Qin and Yan cannot coexist. I have heard that you are a wise and brave man, capable of developing unusual plans to deal with any crisis—can you save Yan from disaster?"

"I have heard it said that when a blood horse is in the peak of condition it can gallop one thousand *li* in a single day, but once it gets old, even a mule can overtake it," Tian Guang replied. "Grand Tutor Ju Wu knew what I was like in my prime, but he does not seem to realize that I have grown old."

"I know that you have spent a great deal of time traveling, sir, so do you know of some person whose wisdom and bravery is the equivalent of what you had when you were young?" Crown Prince Dan inquired. "Perhaps you could recommend such a man to us instead?"

Tian Guang shook his head. "That is very difficult . . . very difficult indeed. However, you have a number of fine retainers in your household, Your Highness. Perhaps I might be permitted to meet them?"

The Crown Prince immediately summoned Xia Fu, Song Yi, and Qin Wuyang and introduced them to Tian Guang, who looked at them one by one, asking their names. He then said to the crown prince, "I have inspected all of your retainers, Your Royal Highness, and not one of them is suitable. Xia Fu is a brave man, but the moment he gets angry his face turns red. Song Yi likewise is brave, but the moment he gets angry his face becomes set. Qin Wuyang is brave too, but when he gets angry he goes pale. If you show your temper on your face and other people notice it, how can you ever hope to achieve anything? I know of a man called Master Jing, who is extremely brave but never shows his emotions by even the slightest sign. He would seem to be better than anyone you can call upon."

"What is this Master Jing's name?" Crown Prince Dan asked. "Where does he come from?"

"Master Jing's full name is Jing Ke," Tian Guang explained. "Originally his surname was Qing—he is a descendant of Grandee Qing Feng of Qi. When Qing Feng fled to Wu, his family settled in Zhufang. When Chu executed him, his family fled to Wey and took up residence there. Jing Ke himself tried to seek service with Lord Yuan of Wey on the basis of his swordcraft, but Lord Yuan did not want to employ him. When Qin captured these lands and established the Dong Commandery, Jing Ke fled to Yan. It was at that point that he changed his surname to Jing. Everyone calls him Master Jing. He is a great drinker and has become very friendly with the musician Gao Jianli. They will go drinking together in the marketplace of the Yan capital. When they are drunk, Gao Jianli plays his lute and Jing Ke sings in harmony with his melody. When he has finished his song, he bursts into tears because he thinks there is no place for him in the world. This man is both clever and cunning—I could never have been his equal!"

"I have never had any dealings with this Master Jing," Crown Prince Dan said. "Please introduce me to him."

"Jing Ke is poor, and I pay for his wine," Tian Guang said. "He ought to listen to what I say."

Crown Prince Dan escorted Tian Guang to the gate of the palace and helped him into the carriage that he normally rode in himself. He ordered one of the palace eunuchs to act as charioteer. When Tian Guang got into the carriage, the crown prince instructed him: "What we have been discussing is an important matter of state. Do not mention it to anyone else."

Tian Guang laughed and said, "I would not dream of it!"

Tian Guang rode in his carriage to the wine shop where Jing Ke was drinking. Jing Ke and Gao Jianli were there together, half drunk. Gao Jianli was playing his lute. When Tian Guang heard the sound, he got down from his carriage and walked straight in, calling for Master Jing. Gao Jianli removed himself and his instrument. When Tian Guang and Jing Ke met, he invited the latter to come to his house, then said, "You always complain that there is nobody who understands your true worth. I have always agreed with you. However, I am old now and there is little that I can do about it. I cannot help you to achieve the things of which you are capable. You are a young man—do you intend to try your own strength?"

"I would love to prove what I can do," Jing Ke declared. "I have never met the right person to help me."

"Crown Prince Dan economizes on his own expenses in order to maintain the knights in his service," Tian Guang said. "Everyone in the kingdom of Yan knows that! Since His Royal Highness did not know of my age and poor state of health, he summoned me today to discuss matters of state. Since we are friends and I know just what you are capable of, I recommended you to His Royal Highness in my place. I hope that you will go immediately to the crown prince's palace."

"Since you have commanded me to do so, sir," Jing Ke said, "how could I refuse?"

Tian Guang wanted to give a spur to Jing Ke's ambitions, so he picked up his sword and said with a sigh: "I have heard it said that when a man has things to do, nothing and nobody should be allowed to stand in his way! Today, the crown prince discussed various matters with me that touch upon issues of national security and warned me not to mention them to anyone else. That means he suspects me. I could do nothing to help His Royal Highness with his troubles and instead find myself the object of his suspicions. I am going to use my death to absolve myself from blame. Please go at once to inform His Royal Highness of this." He then drew his sword and committed suicide by cutting his own throat.

Jing Ke wept at this tragedy. However, just at that moment a messenger arrived from the crown prince to ask if Master Jing was coming or not. Jing Ke realized that the crown prince was sincere in seeking his assistance and got into the carriage that Tian Guang had just used, heading for the crown prince's palace. The crown prince greeted Jing Ke just exactly as he had Tian Guang, but then he looked around and asked, "Has Master Tian not come with you?"

"Having heard your instructions," Jing Ke explained, "the master wanted to use his death to show that he would never divulge your secrets. He has committed suicide."

The crown prince threw up his hands in horror. Weeping, he exclaimed, "It is my fault that he is dead! How could I kill an innocent man?" It was a long time before he stopped crying. He asked Jing Ke to take the seat of honor and then, standing before him, he dropped to his knees to kowtow. Jing Ke hastily responded. "Master Tian Guang did me the honor of recommending you to my service," Crown Prince Dan said. "This may be said to be a blessing from Heaven. I hope that you will not refuse to come to my assistance."

"Why are you so frightened of Qin?" Jing Ke asked.

"Qin can be compared to a tiger or a wolf," Crown Prince Dan said. "No matter how much they eat, they are hungry for more. The king of Qin will not be satisfied until he has conquered every inch of land within the four seas and made every king submit to him in vassalage. Now the king of Han has already handed over all his lands and they have become a commandery of Qin, after which Wang Jian moved his armies to attack Zhao, taking their king prisoner. Now that Zhao is gone, Yan is going to be next. This is why I cannot sleep at night and why my food turns to ashes in my mouth."

"Is it your plan to raise the largest army that you can and fight to see who can win," Jing Ke asked, "or do you have some other intention?"

"Yan is a small and weak country," he replied, "which has repeatedly suffered incursions from enemy armies. Now Prince Jia of Zhao has declared himself king of Dai and wants us to join him in an alliance to defend against Qin. However, I am worried that even if I mobilize every single able-bodied man in the country, they will not be able to withstand just one of Qin's armies. Furthermore, although we are nominally allied to the king of Dai, we have yet to see whether he is as powerful as he says. Wei and Qi are now allied to Qin, and Chu is much too far away to help. Everyone is terrified of Qin's military might, and they are not prepared to ally against them. In my humble opinion, the only thing left to do is to obtain the services of some brave knight and send him on a mission to Qin armed with lavish gifts. Driven by his greed, the king of Qin will let the ambassador get close to him, and he can then take advantage of that moment to take him hostage. With the king of Qin as a hostage, he can be forced to disgorge all the land that he has conquered from other kingdoms. That would be the best plan, I think. Of course, the other option is to assassinate the king of Qin. Each of his generals has many troops under his command, and they will not be prepared to take orders from one another. Once the king of Qin is gone, his country will be ripped apart by civil war. That is a country where everyone is suspicious of everyone else. After the king is dead, we can join with Chu and Wei to reestablish Han and Zhao; united, we can destroy Qin. In that case, everything will go back to normal. It is up to you to say if you are willing to join in!"

Jing Ke was sunk in thought for a long time. Then he replied: "This is an important matter of state. I am afraid that I come from far too low a social level to be able to complete such a mission!"

Crown Prince Dan kowtowed and said, "My life is in your hands. Please do not refuse!"

Jing Ke insisted again that he was unworthy of such trust, but in the end he was forced to agree. The crown prince appointed Jing Ke as a senior minister and built him a mansion to one side of that which he had previously erected for Fan Wuqi. This place was known as Jing Castle. Crown Prince Dan visited him every day, holding a grand feast in his honor. He gave him chariots and horses, not to mention beautiful women and anything else he had set his heart on. He was always afraid of not doing enough for Jing Ke.

One day the two men were at the crown prince's palace and wandered around, admiring the lakes and other water features. There was a large turtle sitting by the water, and Jing Ke happened to shoot it with a clay shot. The crown prince promptly presented him with a shot of solid gold to replace the clay one. On another occasion they were out riding together, and the crown prince was riding a fine horse, capable of galloping a thousand *li* in a day. Jing Ke happened to mention that he thought horse liver delicious. A short time later the palace cooks presented him with a dish of liver; the horse that had been killed was Crown Prince Dan's mount. His Royal Highness told Jing Ke about how Fan Wuqi had offended the king of Qin and come to the kingdom of Yan. Jing Ke wanted to meet him, so the crown prince held a banquet on the Huayang Tower which the two men were invited to attend. He had his own concubine serve wine and then ordered her to play the *qin* to entertain his guests. Jing Ke caught sight of her beautiful pale hands and exclaimed, "How lovely!" When the banquet was over, His Highness had a eunuch present a jade box to Jing Ke. When he opened it and looked inside, he discovered the concubine's hands. This was done to make it clear to Jing Ke that the crown prince begrudged him nothing. Jing Ke sighed and said, "How generously His Highness has treated me! Only my death can repay him!"

· · ·

Jing Ke was always interested in discussing swordcraft with other people, but very rarely found anyone who knew more than he did. However, he greatly admired Ge Nie from Yuci, whom he believed to be a much finer swordsman than himself. The two men were extremely close friends. Now that Jing Ke had been treated with such kindness by Crown Prince Dan of Yan, he decided he should go west to take the king of Qin hostage. Therefore, he sent someone to ask Ge Nie if he would come to Yan to discuss the situation with him. Unfortunately, Ge Nie was out traveling and nobody knew exactly where he had gone; certainly he was not expected back in the near future. Crown Prince Dan knew that Jing Ke was a great knight, and so he always treated him with the utmost respect, not daring to suggest that it was time he was on his way. Then border officials suddenly reported: "The king of Qin has sent his senior general, Wang Jian, north to invade Yan. Jia, King of Dai, has sent an ambassador here to suggest that we join forces to guard Shanggu and prevent Qin from advancing any further."

Crown Prince Dan was horrified. He said to Jing Ke, "Any moment now, the Qin army will cross the Yi River. I know you want to help us, but at that point, will you be able to do anything to change the situation?"

"I have considered the matter deeply," Jing Ke replied. "If I embark on this mission without some special thing to put the king of Qin off guard, he will not let me get close to him. General Fan has deeply offended His Majesty, so the king of Qin put a price on his head of one thousand pounds of gold and a fief of ten thousand households. Qin is also desperate to lay hands on the lands of Dukang, which are so very rich. If I had the head of General Fan and a map of Dukang, I could present them to the king of Qin. He would certainly be delighted and grant me an audience. That would give me an opportunity to repay Your Highness for all your kindness to me."

Crown Prince Dan demurred: "General Fan came to me when he was in dire straits; how could I possibly kill him? The map of Dukang, though, I do not begrudge you."

Jing Ke knew that Crown Prince Dan could not bear to contemplate executing the general, so he went in private to see Fan Wuqi. "You have suffered much from the king of Qin," he said. "Your father and mother were tortured to death by him, together with the rest of your clan. Now he has offered a price on your head of one thousand pounds of gold and a fief of ten thousand households. How do you plan to avenge this, General?"

Fan Wuqi looked up at the sky and sighed deeply. With tears streaming down his face, he said, "Every time I think of Zheng of Qin, the pain penetrates into the very marrow of my bones. But even though I want to kill him, I would never be able to get even close."

"I have a suggestion," Jing Ke said, "which would at one and the same time resolve the political difficulties of the kingdom of Yan and allow you to take revenge on your enemy. Would you be prepared to hear it?"

Fan Wuqi immediately asked: "If you have a suggestion, why don't you tell me?"

Jing Ke hesitated, not saying a word.

"Why don't you speak?" Fan Wuqi demanded.

"I have a plan, but it is hard to put into words."

"If it will allow me to take revenge upon Qin, I do not care if your plan calls for my bones to be ground to dust," Fan Wuqi declared. "Why is it so difficult to tell me what you have in mind?"

"It is my plan to assassinate the king of Qin," Jing Ke explained, "but I am afraid that he will not let me approach. If I could present your head to Qin, the king would be delighted and grant me an audience. I can then grab hold of him with one hand and stab him in the chest with the other. That way, you can have your revenge, General, and Yan can escape destruction. What do you think?"

Fan Wuqi threw off his jacket. Then, waving his arms and stamping his feet, he shouted, "Day and night I have been racking my brains and never come up with a decent plan. Now I have finally heard something sensible!"

He drew the sword that hung by his side and cut his own throat. Although his neck was severed, his head was still attached to his body. Jing Ke picked up the sword and hacked through the spine.

There is a poem which testifies to this:

> When he heard this cunning plan, he was like a man possessed;
> His soul had already hastened off towards Xianyang.
> If Jing Ke had succeeded in his strategy to kill the king of Qin,
> Fan Wuqi would have had no reason to regret his violent death.

Jing Ke immediately sent someone to report to Crown Prince Dan: "I have the head of General Fan Wuqi."

When the prince got this news, he came as quickly as he could. Throwing himself across the body, he wept with great sadness. He gave orders that the general's corpse be buried with full honors. His head, however, was enclosed inside a wooden box.

"Have you found me a good dagger yet?" Jing Ke asked.

"For one hundred pieces of gold," Crown Prince Dan said, "I have bought a very sharp dagger, one foot eight inches long, from a Zhao person named Xu Furen. An artisan has treated the blade with poison. This has been tested, and anyone cut with this dagger suffers a hemorrhage, immediately bleeding to death. This weapon has been ready and waiting for you for ages, but I don't know when you plan to set off."

"My friend, Ge Nie, has not yet arrived," Jing Ke said. "I am waiting for him because I need him in support."

"Your friend seems to be very elusive, like a piece of seaweed floating on the ocean," the crown prince responded. "I have a number of brave knights in my household, of whom Qin Wuyang is by far the best. Perhaps he could go with you as your deputy?"

Jing Ke understood that the prince was desperate. He sighed and said, "If I am to go and attack the king of such a powerful country as Qin armed only with a dagger, I will not come back alive. The reason why I have been delaying is because I wanted to wait for my friend, who will ensure the success of our plan. However, since Your Highness is in a fever of impatience I had better be on my way!"

Crown Prince Dan wrote out a letter of credentials. Then he gave him the map of Dukang and Fan Wuqi's head, together with a thousand pieces of gold to cover the expenses of the journey. Qin Wuyang was to go with him as his deputy. On the day that they were to set out, Crown Prince Dan and all his retainers who knew what was afoot dressed in white robes and plain hats and congregated above the Yi River to hold a banquet in his honor. When Gao Jianli heard that Jing Ke was going to Qin, he came too, bringing a shoulder of pork and a large pot of wine. Jing Ke introduced him to Crown Prince Dan, and His Highness gave orders that they should all sit together. When the wine had circulated several times, Gao Jianli began to play his lute and Jing Ke sang. The music played was a sorrowful tune. The words of the song ran:

> The wind soughs, and the waters of the Yi River run cold;
> The hero leaves, but he will not return!

The melody was extremely sad, and all the men who had come there began to weep, as if they were attending a funeral. Jing Ke looked up at the sky and sighed. His breath came out in a puff; as it floated into the heavens, it transformed into a rainbow, piercing the sun. Everyone who saw this was absolutely amazed. Jing Ke now began to sing a martial air:

He who enters the tiger's lair or the haunts of dragons,
Has breath that will transform into rainbows in the air.

This song was very stirring, and the company felt themselves excited, as if they were about to engage in battle. Now Crown Prince Dan poured more wine into a goblet, and kneeling in front of Jing Ke, he presented it to him. Jing Ke drained the cup in a single draft. Grabbing hold of Qin Wuyang's arm, he jumped into a chariot. Whipping up his horses, he sped away and never turned back to look at those left behind. Crown Prince Dan climbed onto a hill so that he could watch them leave. He did not move until they were out of sight, as sad as if he had lost something. He returned to his companions in tears.

In the Jin dynasty, the recluse Tao Yuanming wrote a poem about this:

Crown Prince Dan of Yan built up a stable of knights,
In order to take revenge upon the powerful kingdom of Qin.
Having brought together hundreds of good men,
In the end fate brought him Jing Ke.
A gentleman is prepared to die for the sake of the man who
    understands him,
Thus Jing Ke took his sword and left the Yan capital.
As his horse neighed on the broad road,
Unhappy men came to see him off.
Beneath his hat, his hair bristled with energy,
His official garb masked his heroic bravery.
The farewell banquet was held by the Yi River,
The finest of heroes were seated there—
On one side, Gao Jianli played a sorrowful song on his lute;
On the other side, Jing Ke sang at the top of his voice.
The trees soughed as a tragic wind blew through their branches,
The waters crashed as cold waves were whipped up.
The first song moved everyone present to tears;
With the second song, brave knights leapt to their feet.
Although he knew that he would not return,
He left a great name for later generations.

When Jing Ke arrived in Xianyang, he discovered that the king of Qin was very fond of one of the cadets in the Palace Guard, a man named Meng Jia. Thus, Jing Ke began by bribing this man with one thousand pieces of gold to put in a good word for him with the king of

Qin. Meng Jia went to the palace, where he presented his opinion to His Majesty: "The king of Yan is so much in awe of Your Majesty's military might, that he does not dare to so much as raise an army in case it offended you. He would like to have his country incorporated into Qin by peaceful means, accepting a position comparable to a feudal lord under the Zhou dynasty. He will offer you tribute and accept his territory being divided into Qin-style commanderies and counties, providing that he is allowed to continue the sacrifices at the temples dedicated to his ancestors. However, he is too much frightened to come here in person, so he has sent an ambassador here, armed with the head of Fan Wuqi, a map of the lands of Dukang, and a letter with the personal seal of the king of Yan affixed. This ambassador, Jing Ke, is waiting even as we speak in an official guesthouse. Please give the command, your majesty."

When the king of Qin heard that Fan Wuqi had been beheaded, he was delighted. He put on full court dress and arranged for the most lavish ceremonies to be performed. Then he had the ambassador summoned to the palace at Xianyang for an audience. Jing Ke came forward with the dagger in his sleeve, holding the box that contained Fan Wuqi's head. Qin Wuyang held the box containing the map of Dukang. As they walked up the steps, Qin Wuyang was deadly pale and seemed to be shaking with fear. One of the servants asked, "Why are you so frightened?"

Jing Ke turned his head to look at Qin Wuyang and smiled. Stepping forward, he kowtowed and apologized to the king. "This man is Qin Wuyang, a barbarian from the remote northern regions. He has never in his life seen the Son of Heaven before, so he cannot help feeling nervous and behaving differently from normal. I do hope that Your Majesty will not be offended. Please let him complete his mission."

The king of Qin gave orders that only the chief ambassador from Yan should ascend to the main hall. His entourage shouted at Qin Wuyang to go down the steps. His Majesty gave orders that the head box be opened so that he could inspect the contents: it was indeed Fan Wuqi's head.

"Why didn't you kill this traitor years ago?" he demanded.

"After Fan Wuqi committed his crime against Your Majesty," Jing Ke replied respectfully, "he went and hid in the Gobi Desert. The king of Yan offered a reward of one thousand pieces of gold to get him. His original intention was to present him to Your Majesty alive, but being afraid that it might prove difficult to transport him all that way, he had his head cut off. Nevertheless, he hopes in some small way to assuage Your Majesty's anger." Jing Ke's voice was calm and his appearance friendly, so the king of Qin felt no alarm.

It was now time for Qin Wuyang to present the map. He bowed and knelt at the bottom of the steps. The king of Qin said to Jing Ke, "Get the map that this Qin Wuyang is holding and let me see it!"

Jing Ke took the box containing the map from Qin Wuyang's hands and personally presented it to the king. His Majesty spread the map open and began to study it. It was at this moment that Jing Ke's dagger fell into view and he could not hide it. In a panic, Jing Ke grabbed the king of Qin's sleeve with one hand while with the other he stabbed at his chest. Before the point of the dagger had pierced his skin, His Majesty wrenched himself free with a strength born from terror, tearing his sleeve.

It was the first week in the fifth month, so the weather was already quite warm. His Majesty was wearing an unlined fine silk jacket, which tore easily.

To one side of His Majesty's throne was a screen some eight feet in height. His Majesty leapt behind it, and the screen came crashing to the ground. Jing Ke chased after him, the dagger gripped in his hand. The king of Qin could not escape him, so he ran round and round the pillars of the room. By Qin law, it was illegal for anyone to enter the audience hall with a weapon. All the palace guards and military officials were arrayed outside the building, but without a direct order from the king, they did not dare to enter. Now that an assassination attempt was underway, His Majesty did not have time to call for his guards—his retinue had to fight Jing Ke off with their bare hands.

Jing Ke fought bravely, stabbing at all the men who came near him. The royal physician, Xia Wuju, used his medicine bag to swing at Jing Ke. He lifted his arm to ward off the blow, cutting the medicine bag in two. Even though Jing Ke fought ferociously and the people trying to defend the king of Qin could not deal with him, there were many of them and only one of him. This enabled the king of Qin to keep running from one side of the hall to the other, and Jing Ke could not get close to him.

The king of Qin was wearing a sword, a fine blade called *Ripple*, but when he wanted to draw his sword to fight back, it got stuck in the scabbard because it was so very long. A young eunuch screamed, "Why don't you put the sword behind you, Your Majesty, and then try to draw it?" The king of Qin realized the good sense of this and did what he suggested. When the sword was behind him, it came out perfectly easily. The king of Qin and Jing Ke were equally ferocious in attack, but the latter was armed with a dagger useful only for stabbing at close quarters, whereas the sword, being much longer, could be used at a greater distance. With the sword in his hand, the king of Qin felt much more confident. He charged forward and slashed at Jing Ke, inflicting a deep cut in his left thigh. Jing Ke fell back against one of the bronze pillars of the palace, unable to get up. All he could do was to throw his dagger at the king of Qin. The king leapt to one side and the dagger flew past his ear to embed itself in the bronze pillar with a shower of sparks.

The king of Qin attacked Jing Ke again. Jing Ke grabbed hold of the blade of the sword, losing three fingers in the process. Having been stabbed eight times, he leaned against the pillars and laughed, then cursed the king of Qin, his legs splayed out in front of him: "You are a lucky man! I wanted to just hold you hostage, forcing you to give back the lands that you have conquered from the other kings. Now the whole thing has gone wrong, and you have been able to escape. This must be the will of Heaven! Since Qin is so strong, you will soon conquer all the other kingdoms, but how long will you enjoy your own?"

The king of Qin's retainers forced their way forward to beat him to death. Qin Wuyang, standing outside the hall, realized that Jing Ke had launched his assassination attempt and tried to join in. He was immediately killed by the palace guards. This occurred in the twentieth year of the reign of Zheng, King of Qin.

How sad it is, after Crown Prince Dan had done so much for Jing Ke and sent him on this special mission to Qin, that he failed completely. Not only did he bring about his own death, but this also cost the lives of Tian Guang, Fan Wuqi, and Qin Wuyang. He even got the king of Yan and Crown Prince Dan killed too. Can it be that his swordsmanship was not as good as everyone thought it?

An old man wrote a poem:

> Armed only with a dagger, he entered the capital of Qin.
> Although brave, his swordsmanship failed him.

This hero did not return, the conspiracy collapsed;
Fan Wuqi should never have entrusted him with his head!

When it was all over, the king of Qin sat still for a long time, his eyes staring into space. Having recovered somewhat from the shock, he went over to look at Jing Ke. His eyes were wide open, staring, and filled with rage. The king of Qin was horrified. He ordered the bodies of Jing Ke and Qin Wuyang be removed and burned in the market-place, together with Fan Wuqi's head. Every member of this embassy from Yan was killed, and their heads were suspended from the city gates. Afterwards, His Majesty got into a carriage and drove to the inner palace. His womenfolk had by this time heard that an assassination had been attempted, and they all rushed forward to make inquiries. They had wine served to celebrate His Majesty's survival and help him recover from the shock.

There was a certain Lady Hu Ji, who had originally been a maid in the royal palace at Zhao, who had been selected to come to Qin when Zhao was conquered. She was much favored by His Majesty because of her skill as a musician, which saw her elevated to the position of a junior wife. The king of Qin ordered her to play to cheer him up. Lady Hu Ji strummed her *qin* and sang:

> "A fine silk jacket is good to tear,
> A palace screen is good to hide behind,
> The *Ripple* sword is good to wear,
> A wicked man is good to kill!"

The king of Qin was very pleased by her composition and rewarded her with a box of silk. That night he enjoyed himself to the utmost, spending the night in Lady Hu Ji's chamber. Later on, Lady Hu Ji gave birth to a son: Prince Huhai, who eventually became the Second Emperor of Qin. During his reign, the government was even more violent and cruel than under his father. Thus, rebels were able to gather vast numbers of supporters and launch the revolt that finally brought down the dynasty.

An old man, having read *Kingdoms in Peril,* wrote the following poem:

The Zhou dynasty lasted for nearly eight hundred years:
Half their history was created by their own hands, the other half was
    the will of Heaven.

In the long march of history, we can see the records of the noble and
    the brave;
Countries rise and states fall in an endless cycle through time.
The other six kingdoms willingly surrendered to powerful Qin,
The Zhou dynasty owed its collapse to the decision to move to the
    east.
What we learn from the fates endured by these ancient kingdoms in
    peril
Is that everything rests in the quality of those serving at court!